LOST SOULS

Also by Seth Patrick

The Reviver

The Returned

SETH PATRICK

LOST SOULS

Thomas Dunne Books
St. Martin's Press
New York

This is a work of fiction. All of the characters, organizations, and events portrayed in this novel are either products of the author's imagination or are used fictitiously.

THOMAS DUNNE BOOKS.
An imprint of St. Martin's Press.

www.thomasdunnebooks.com
www.stmartins.com

Library of Congress Cataloging-in-Publication Data

Patrick, Seth.
Lost souls : a Reviver novel / Seth Patrick. — First edition.
   p. cm.
ISBN 978-1-250-02171-7 (hardcover)
ISBN 978-1-250-02172-4 (e-book)
I. Title.
PR6116.A8455L67 2015
823'.92—dc23

2015017373

Our books may be purchased in bulk for promotional, educational, or business use. Please contact your local bookseller or the Macmillan Corporate and Premium Sales Department at (800) 221-7945, extension 5442, or by e-mail at MacmillanSpecialMarkets@macmillan.com.

First published in Great Britain by Pan Books, an imprint of Pan Macmillan

First U.S. Edition: November 2015

10 9 8 7 6 5 4 3 2 1

To Dorothy Johnstone Lloyd

For never doubting it would happen

1

Someone was following her.

The alley was a short cut she'd used many times before. Now, late on a moonless night, Mary hesitated. The alley was poorly lit, but she wanted to get home as fast as she could. Once through it she would have a three-minute walk to the door of her apartment, three minutes before she could shake off the feeling she'd had since leaving the party. A feeling of cold eyes watching her.

She stepped into the alley. After a dozen paces it occurred to her that it was different somehow. Darker than she remembered. It made her falter for a moment, seeing how shadows seemed to like the place.

The solitary light was midway along, high up on the wall. She looked at it, wincing at the glare. Yet, bright as it was, it didn't seem to reach far: a small island of illumination on the ground underneath, its edges strangely well defined. The rest of the alley seemed to shrug the light off.

She shook her head and tried to dismiss her anxiety. One more baseless fear to join the others she'd been keeping a lid on for the last half-hour.

You're just scaring yourself, Mary, she thought. *One idiot tries to ruin your night, and you let him.* She was being stubborn, though, and she knew it. It was why she'd walked home instead of getting a cab – angry at being made to feel vulnerable and refusing to give in to it.

Still, something felt different here. It was quieter than normal, the streets empty at both ends of the alley. She told herself it was just the natural unease of a dark and lonely place that she was feeling.

She slowed, keeping her footfalls as silent as she could. Almost at the island of light that marked the halfway point, she paused in the dark. There were sounds behind her, from the end of the alley she'd just come from. Footsteps: a steady walk. She looked back, hoping the darkness around her was as complete as it felt, that she was cloaked from whatever eyes belonged to those feet.

She saw the man, then. His step didn't change as he walked into sight at the alley entrance. She stopped breathing, just watched.

He went on past.

She let out her breath. It hadn't even been *him*. Just a random guy, walking the same way she'd been walking.

Then she froze. Someone was with her, right *beside* her. She knew this, because they had just taken hold of her hand.

Instinctively, she jerked it free. She turned around, quickly stepping into the island of light beside her.

'Who's there?'

But there was nobody. She must have imagined it. *If I thought it was real,* she told herself, *I'd already be running. Right?*

'Who's there?' she said again. A large garbage container thirty feet back the way she'd come was the only place she could see where anyone could have hidden. She kept her eye on it and backed towards the far end of the alley. Towards home.

Three steps took her to the edge of the light. With her eyes still fixed on the garbage container, she paused. She shaded her eyes with her right hand, careful to avoid catching the light above full-on so that she would keep some level of dark-adapted vision. There was no movement where she watched.

Mary took another step and was in darkness once more.

She froze again, still staring ahead.

Something was holding her left hand, holding it tightly. She tried to pull away, looking at her hand as she pulled. In the gloom, all she could see was a shadowy outline against her own skin.

But there was nothing else there.

'Please let me go,' she said. 'Please.'

The shadow around her hand vanished. As it did she felt a sharp pain. Bringing her right hand to her left she could feel wet warmth on her skin that she knew was blood. Wherever she'd felt the touch now seemed to be on fire. Instinct made her stride back into the island of light, her eyes darting around her in panic. She glanced at the wound; countless small scratches had opened the skin and made the blood flow.

She reached into her bag for her cell phone, but it wasn't there. She had a moment of confusion – wondering how and when she'd misplaced it – but then the phone clattered across the ground to her feet, thrown from the darkness. Bewildered and scared, she picked it up and looked at it. The screen was shattered, the phone dead.

Her peripheral vision caught movement. A small, dark shape against the brighter end of the alley, brief and fast-moving. Then the light above her began to grow brighter, the island widening. She felt hope grow for a moment as she sensed the dark retreating, the light pushing it back. But her hope collapsed: the light above her failed, the bulb burning out.

Darkness closed in on her.

Something took her right hand this time. She could see someone walking past the end of the alley, and opened her mouth to call out to them, to *shout*, but the grip on her hand became intense. The pain stole her breath, reducing her cry to little more than a whimper.

She fell silent and the grip relaxed. The pain stopped. The lesson was clear: *be quiet*. She tore her eyes from the end of the alley and looked at her hand again.

Still she could see nothing but a dark outline on the hand itself.

Then the grip released and she felt fingers, long and thin, close over on her shoulder. She glanced. This time she could see something there, glistening in the darkness.

The fingers pushed her towards the wall. She resisted briefly, feeling sharp pain from the skin on her shoulder where the fingers gripped, compelling her onward.

At the wall the fingers let go.

It was behind her.

She began to tremble, knowing that she was about to turn and face it, knowing that she would cry out, whatever pain it would bring down on her. Knowing that she wouldn't be able to stop while there was breath in her lungs.

She turned. Seeing what was with her in the dark, Mary started to scream.

2

It was 9 a.m. on Monday morning. Jonah Miller was sitting at his desk in the Central East Coast office of the Forensic Revival Service.

He'd joined the FRS at nineteen, the youngest forensic reviver they'd ever taken on. This was his ninth year. Nine years of getting testimony from the dead, and it felt harder than it had ever felt before.

Revivals seemed to take more out of him than they used to, but it wasn't just the revivals. *Everything* felt harder. Dealing with relatives had become exhausting, especially when managing their expectations if they wanted to take the opportunity to talk to their loved one, expectations that were frequently thwarted by lack of time.

And with the testimony itself, he was increasingly reluctant to be aggressive with a subject. More than once, an investigating officer had expressed frustration with him. He wondered if he was getting a bad reputation.

Even the paperwork had become a problem.

When a speaking corpse identified someone as their murderer, the defence team usually had little option but to call into question the judgement and professionalism of the reviver, and dig deep for procedural irregularities. As a result, the paperwork for each case felt like a minefield.

On Jonah's monitor was footage from his most recent revival, the paperwork for which he'd yet to complete. The screen showed the image of a dead man lying in a pool of his own blood, a fifty-year-old Polish immigrant called Piotr Zales, whose packaging firm had taken only six years to grow from nothing to a ten-million-dollar business. He had been found dead in his home, his wife out of town; he'd been shot once in the torso and twice in the head. It was the kind of injury that often made revival impractical. With Zales, however, the damage to the brain – although fatal – had been relatively slight. The estimated revival chance had been low, but sufficient to warrant the attempt. If the killer had used a larger-calibre gun, or hollow-point ammunition, the chances would have been non-existent.

Jonah played the footage, speeding past the initial stages: Jonah entering frame, taking the man's hand; a forty-three-minute period of apparent inactivity; the man's chest finally moving as revival was achieved and the lungs filled with air.

To those outside the field, that forty-three-minute period seemed like the easy part. To the reviver, of course, it was where most of the work happened. It had been a tough one, but that was the problem with Jonah Miller. He could bring the tough ones back, better than almost anyone.

So inevitably he had to keep on doing it.

He let the footage play.

The eyes of the corpse had been open, but the eyes played no role in revival. The dead couldn't see, couldn't even move beyond the basic mechanisms of speech – lungs, jaw, tongue. The eyes, staring blankly out past the camera, gave the dead man the appearance of deep despair.

'Piotr,' said Jonah in the recording. 'My name is Jonah Miller. Can you hear me?'

'Yes,' said Piotr Zales.

'Do you know what happened to you?' asked Jonah, treading with care. The majority of revived subjects took a few moments to adjust, to realize that they were dead, but Zales knew exactly what was happening.

And he knew who had killed him.

'My fucking idiot brother-in-law shot me,' said the corpse. His speech was typical of revived subjects; a slow, throaty whisper punctuated by deep inhalations every dozen or so words. His voice was gently accented and underpinned with obvious anger. 'He shot me in the back then mocked me as he came to finish it. I was face down but he *wanted* me to know it was him, so he turned me over. *Idiot*. I saw him. I watched the greed in his eyes as he pulled the trigger. I'd like to see how he looks when he hears *this*.'

Jonah paused the footage. Piotr Zales had stayed lucid for a further eight minutes of unambiguous testimony, far longer than expected. Yet even with such an open-and-shut case, the amount of paperwork was ridiculous. It had always been bad, but recently things had started to get much worse.

*

Revival had first emerged almost fourteen years earlier: the ability to talk to the recently deceased, the audible responses coming from the dead's own lips.

Why it had emerged – and what it really *was* – were mysteries that had resisted years of intensive research. Yet while the research had failed to explain the origin of revival, it had instead provided a foundation for its use as a forensic tool. It was established that a reviver had a close emotional link to the dead subject during revival, one that made it clear when the subject was telling the truth. You didn't just get testimony from the dead – you knew when they lied or were evasive, and the questioning could establish the facts with absolute certainty.

But you had to be quick. Once you'd brought a subject back, the revival might only last a couple of minutes, and once it was over, that was all you got. It was impossible to revive the same subject twice.

Its use in courtrooms around the world had rapidly become a cornerstone of the justice system; public opinion – initially uneasy with the process – was mostly won over by the sheer weight of success.

Mostly.

Resistance to the technique had been led by the Afterlifers, an uneasy affiliation of disparate religious groups that had one shared mantra: that revival was a kind of sacrilege, a blasphemy. In the early days of revival, this belief had been extreme and focused, leading to violent protests and threats to the fledging Forensic Revival Service, but the protests had been small-scale and relatively short-lived. Public opinion placed pragmatism above dogma and stayed on the side of the revivers.

Then, twelve months ago, the Afterlifers had found anonymous backers with deep pockets. With the help of the extra funding they managed to make a dent in the public support of revival. Those in charge of the FRS had grown nervous, and responded with endless tinkering to guidelines and procedures.

In the end, that meant one thing: more paperwork.

'Morning, Jonah. How's life?'

The Northern Irish accent was unmistakeable. Jonah looked around and smiled at his friend. 'Morning, Never,' he said. 'Right now, life's not so great.'

'Paperwork, eh?' said Never Geary, looking at the forms on Jonah's screen. 'Lucky you.' As a technician, Never's role was to set up and monitor the recording equipment required for a revival – three cameras to capture every moment of the session. Unlike revivers, technicians had very little paperwork to fill in, and weren't needed in court. The only testimony they had to worry about came in a variety of audio and video formats.

'Give the Afterlifers a few more months,' said Jonah. 'I'm sure they can make your life awkward too.'

'I don't doubt that,' said Never. 'Meantime, focus on the good stuff. Annabel's back in a week or two, right?'

Jonah nodded. She was coming back the week before Valentine's Day.

'So look forward to that and don't worry about the Afterlifers.' Someone across the office called Never's name. 'Gotta dash. See you later, right?'

'Right.' *Damn*, Jonah thought. Annabel was back soon, and he really wasn't looking forward to it. Compared to thinking about the mess their relationship had become, paperwork didn't seem nearly so bad.

3

After another hour of reviewing the Piotr Zales case, the paper-work was complete. Jonah went to the canteen and made himself a coffee. When he sat, the pain in his chest flared a little, the way it did now and again. It was January, and the cold weather wasn't suiting him.

He gave his ribs a gentle rub until the pain eased, then swigged his drink. There was one thing about serious injuries that you didn't appreciate until they happened to you, he thought – they keep on making their presence felt long after everyone else has forgotten about them.

And how long had it been? Seventeen months? Seventeen months since he'd been shot in the chest, the bullet shattering a rib and almost killing him. Seventeen months since he'd escaped a biotech research facility as it burned to the ground, then watched as bodies on fire fell from the roof.

The nightmares still came regularly. Not just of the fire, of course. It hadn't only been *people* who had died that night.

Among the dead was Michael Andreas, the biotech entrepre-neur whose company owned the facility. Andreas had unwittingly freed something from an ancient prison, a prison constructed from *souls*, and the creature had possessed him. But Andreas had fought back; knowing that the creature was vulnerable in a mortal body, Andreas consigned them both to a terrible death in the inferno that the building had become. He had saved humanity from a creature that had destroyed countless worlds, but hardly anyone would ever know it.

Jonah, Never and Annabel had been among the few to make it out alive, and the truth of what had happened wasn't something they could ever speak about openly.

Ah, Annabel. Of all the things that had happened in the aftermath, Annabel Harker was the one that most vexed him.

He'd made a full recovery, or so his doctors told him – it didn't feel like it. Every morning, he felt the same deep exhaustion that made getting out of bed a challenge and getting through the day a chore. Things had improved as his relationship with Annabel had blossomed, but in the time since, she had devoted herself to finding out all she could about Andreas, to the point of obsession. She spent so much time away, now, and he was convinced that his dark moods were partly to blame.

He loved her, but he knew that he was losing her. He could feel another pain in his chest and it had nothing to do with a bullet.

*

As Jonah returned to his desk, he was intercepted.

'Hugo wants a word with us,' said Never. Hugo Adler was the head of the Central East Coast FRS – their boss.

'What about?' said Jonah, but all he got was a shrug.

Most of the FRS was open plan, but Hugo had an office in the corner. As Jonah raised his hand to knock, Never just opened the door and went in, smiling back at Jonah.

'You wanted to see us?' said Never.

'Ah, yes,' said Hugo. 'Close that, would you?' He nodded to the open door and Jonah obliged. 'I wanted to have a little talk with you both about the Afterlifer situation, and the recent procedural changes. I know there's been some . . . dissatisfaction.'

'Well,' said Jonah, 'the paperwork is a bit more than we'd like, I guess.' He glanced at Never, who gave him raised eyebrows: *Is that all?* 'OK, yes, it's crazy. It feels like you have to answer the same question in a hundred different ways, and that one mistake could be picked up in court and used to beat you over the head.' Jonah didn't like being in court, not one bit. Having his reputation assaulted head-on by arrogant overpaid assholes wasn't his idea of time well spent.

'I know,' said Hugo. 'I'm pushing for it to be streamlined, but these things take time. Part of the problem with the current procedures is that they were largely drawn up by Robert and his legal team.' He was referring to Robert Thorne, the FRS Director. 'They rushed it and didn't consult the rest of us. Inevitably, there are weaknesses.'

'Weaknesses?' said Jonah. 'They're damn near crippling.'

Hugo nodded. 'It was a panic measure, but I can understand why they panicked. It was a shock to all of us how easily the Afterlifers got their consent initiative as federal law, and our procedures had to be bolstered quickly.'

Jonah and Never both nodded. It *had* been a shock. Revival's legal status mirrored that of autopsy; only serious religious objection could typically overrule its use, and the burden of proof was on those seeking denial. Two months ago the Afterlifers had managed to get laws passed to shift that burden. Previously, revival was entirely at the discretion of the police and FRS staff. Now, either an immediate relative had to give permission, or a warrant was required. It meant that delays were more frequent, and for revival delays were a serious problem – the ideal scenario was to revive a subject in the location they'd been found, as soon as possible. Delays could necessitate moving a body from a crime scene and storing it, which made revival much harder.

This, of course, had been the intention. What sounded to the public like a reasonable piece of law was really aimed at making revival more difficult, more expensive, and hence less common.

'Anyway,' said Hugo, 'I hope they'll not make the mistake of rushing things in future, which is why I've put your names forward.'

'You put my name forward?' said Never, alarmed. 'What for?'

'To consult on procedural improvements,' said Hugo. 'Help fix the paperwork problems.'

'Techs don't have any paperwork problems . . .' said Never, then he frowned. 'Uh oh.'

'We need to assume the worst-case scenario about some of the other Afterlifer initiatives being proposed, Never. So yes, Robert and his team are suggesting further changes, and it'll affect everyone. You'll be able to guide that process, and make sure the changes are the *right* ones.'

'Sounds terrible,' said Never. 'I'll end up filling in reams of paperwork and knowing it's *my fault*.'

'It's frustrating, I know,' said Hugo, 'but if we push hard I think we can make sure the end result is positive. There'll be a preliminary meeting in three weeks with representatives from all the FRS offices. They'll also be considering any ideas to counter Afterlifer efforts.'

'Will any private firms be consulted?' asked Jonah. 'They're surely feeling threatened by the Afterlifers, too, and we need all the allies we can get.' Revival wasn't solely used for criminal investigation; companies offered the services of private revivers to the grieving, allowing relatives to make peace and say their goodbyes. Those revivers were paid far more than their FRS counterparts, which sometimes made it hard for the FRS to hold on to staff. And it wasn't just the money, to be fair. Private revivers were there purely to help the family and the deceased. With forensic revival, once questioning was completed there was often no time left for the relatives. Jonah could certainly see the appeal.

'No,' said Hugo. 'Private revival is already based around the prior consent of the deceased so it isn't affected by current Afterlifer initiatives. The companies are certainly anxious about a negative portrayal of revival, but they're just hoping that the impact on them will be limited. They're no different from Robert

Thorne, really. Crossing their fingers, too scared to take the fight to the Afterlifers.'

'Agreed,' said Never. 'Everyone's just kissing their asses and hoping it'll all be fine.'

Jonah nodded.

'I'm glad you both agree,' said Hugo. 'Because there was something else. A case has come up this morning. A sensitive one.'

'Sensitive?' said Jonah. 'In what way?'

Hugo smiled. 'How would you feel about pissing off some Afterlifers?'

4

Jonah drove the marked FRS car, wondering what he was getting himself into.

'This sounds like a fucking terrible idea,' said Never, in the passenger seat.

'So why did you say yes?'

'Hugo asked nicely,' said Never. He grinned. '"We need our best people there! Rock-solid dependable!" I respond well to flattery. It still sounds like an almighty cluster-fuck.'

'It'll be fine,' Jonah said, with no real conviction. Successfully reviving the subject wasn't expected to be difficult, but there was no way Hugo was going to send out their less experienced people. Given the *complications*.

They were on their way to Chesapeake Regional Medical Center to revive a fifteen-year-old boy who had been stabbed in the abdomen in a mugging late the night before. There had only been one eyewitness, who reported seeing someone run from the scene as the victim fell, but they hadn't been able to provide the police with much to go on.

The boy had been brought to the Emergency Department in Chesapeake Regional, unconscious and critical, where the medical team had managed to stabilize his condition. His mother stayed by his bedside all night but a sudden deterioration led to further emergency surgery. He had died shortly after ten that morning.

The police had asked the mother for revival permission, and

that was when the complication came out. The mother's permission wasn't an issue; she and her son had no problem with revival, and she even wished to attend, to speak to her son one last time. However, her ex-husband – the boy's father – did have a problem. Or he would have, when he found out.

The father's name was Clayton Fray, and he was a senior Afterlifer spokesman.

It was a grey area, Jonah knew. The current legislation meant that the permission of a parent or guardian was required, but it was unclear about what should be done in the case of a conflicting opinion. Nor was there anything in the law that compelled the police to *seek* that other opinion. The mother's permission was sufficient, and the Afterlifers could raise all the hell they wanted after the fact.

They arrived at the hospital, following the signs to the side entrance where they'd been told to bring in their equipment. Both Jonah and Never had been here before for revivals, but on those occasions they'd just used the main entrance. Jonah hoped the request to keep a low profile was purely for this sensitive case, and not an indication of a broader change of policy at the hospital.

As they approached in the car, a woman came out and waved, her detective's badge held up. Jonah stopped the car and wound down his window.

'Detective Flores,' she said. She was in her mid-thirties and looked dog-tired. 'My partner is Detective West, he's inside with the mother. He'll be supervising the questioning.'

'I'm Jonah Miller. This is the tech for the case, Never Geary.'

'Glad you came so fast,' said Flores. 'Park up and get your things inside. We'll talk there.' She headed through a doorway that had been wedged open.

Jonah parked, turned off the ignition, and looked at Never. 'Ready?'

'We're risking bringing down some serious fuckery on our heads here, Jonah. Exactly *why* are we doing this?'

'First,' said Jonah, 'a boy was murdered for pocket change. The police want to find out what he saw. And second . . .' He paused. The crime was one thing. He would always feel a powerful drive to help bring justice, whatever the situation, but it had only been when Hugo had told him the rest of the background that his mind had been made up.

'Second?' asked Never.

'A mother wants to say goodbye to her son.'

*

Like most hospitals with a busy ER, there was an area reserved for on-site revivals of patients who had died during transit or treatment. Such facilities were often barely adequate, but the FRS teams were used to making do.

'Ah,' said Never when he saw it, grimacing. It was about twenty feet square, with a separate narrow strip partitioned off to form a small room within the larger. This allowed the technician to sit with the overseeing detective and avoid being a distraction to the reviver as they worked, watching through a large window. The boy's body was already there, on a gurney in the far corner.

The problem was that the room had become an ad hoc storage area, with boxes of medical supplies piled three high everywhere.

Detective Flores apologized. 'We tried to get as much moved as we could, but . . .'

'I know,' said Never. 'Often happens. These places end up being used as dumping grounds. We'll manage.'

'How long before you're ready?' Flores asked.

'Maybe ten minutes to clear a sufficient working area, then thirty for me to set up. Jonah?'

Jonah was in the corner, examining the subject. The boy looked much younger than his fifteen years. He was still intubated, with tape over his eyes that had been left after the failed surgery, his upper body naked. A six-inch incision was gaping in his abdomen, pads packed inside it to soak up the blood.

The location of the stab wound was in their favour, he thought, an abdominal injury not adding to the complications the way an injury to a lung often could.

He looked up at Never. 'I'll be ready by then,' he said. 'Detective, is the mother still sure she wants to speak to her son once we have his statement?'

'She is.'

'I'll need to talk to her first. And we'll need a blanket or something, to put on him before we start. To hide that wound.'

'Understood,' said Flores. 'You want to talk to her right away?'

Jonah took a deep breath. *Want* didn't exactly cover it, but it had to be done. 'The sooner the better.'

*

Flores led Jonah out of the revival room, down a long corridor. She stopped where another detective stood: a man in his late forties, stout, grey-haired. Looking just as tired as Flores. The detective raised his hand as they approached.

'You must be our reviver. Jonah Miller, right? Detective West.'

No handshakes had been offered by either detective, something that made it clear to Jonah that they'd either worked with revivers before or remembered their training well. Direct contact between a reviver and most non-revivers led to a sensation known as *chill*. It varied in strength, depending both on the reviver and on the other person. Some non-revivers didn't get chill at all, Annabel and Never among them. But for those who did, it ranged from a sense of cold – people often described it as someone walking over their graves – to a feeling of extreme fear and a taint of death. With Jonah, it was always at the more severe end of the scale.

'Good to meet you, Detective.'

'The boy's mother is in there,' said West, indicating the office they were standing outside. The door was closed but Jonah could see her through the small window, sitting, staring. Lost. Her expression was one he'd seen many times before. 'Her name is

Katherine Leith. Maiden name. Changed it back when her husband left. You know the ex-husband is Clayton Fray, the—'

Jonah interrupted. 'I know.'

'Just checking,' said West. 'Kid's name is Clayton David Fray Junior, but he uses the name David Leith. Says it all. The boy had been to the movies with some friends. Movie finished nine-forty-eight, the kid left his friends and was heading to a burrito place he loved, a five-minute walk, planned to get a cab home from there. Less than a minute from his destination, he was seen falling, while someone ran. There weren't many people around, all at distance, and only one who actually saw anything. We assume it was a mugging.'

Jonah nodded. 'Any chance it was because of who his father is? Someone that high up in the Afterlifers is bound to have made enemies along the way.'

West shook his head. 'There's nothing to suggest that. Besides, his mother says hardly anyone knows about his father. She managed to boot Fray out a long time ago, back when the Afterlifers were getting their hands dirty. The kid was six years old. Fray has treated her like dirt since, from what I hear – tried to wrestle the kid from her on any number of bullshit premises. The guy must have spent half his income on legal fees, just to make life hard for her. It's calmed down in the last few years. Kid's got older; I'm guessing Fray wondered why the hell would he want a teenager on his hands.'

A thought struck Jonah. He paused before voicing it. 'And what if Fray wanted a new way to get back at his ex?'

West's eyes widened. He looked at Flores. 'And I thought *I* was cynical.'

'You are,' said Flores. 'Comes with the job.' She turned to Jonah. 'We've considered it. Fray sounds like the kind who wants to punish his ex-wife without significant risk. He's twisted, but gutless. We think this was just random.'

West stepped to the office door. 'Shall we?'

Jonah nodded. West opened the door and entered, Jonah behind. Flores stayed outside, closing the door once Jonah was in.

'Katherine,' said West, 'this is Jonah Miller. He's the reviver.'

Katherine Leith said nothing; her eyes were vague and distant. Jonah pulled a chair over and sat beside her. 'Katherine,' he started. Then, too fast for Jonah to react, Katherine's hands shot out and took his. He flinched, but with relief he realized there was no chill.

'I have to speak to my boy,' she said, urgency in her voice, the lost look in her eyes changing to acute desperation.

'I know. We need to talk some things over, first. To explain how we do it, that we—'

'*No,*' she said. 'I mean we have to do it *now*. Before his father hears. Because once he does, he'll find a way to stop it.'

Jonah threw a look towards West. There was unease on the detective's face that was immediately infectious. Jonah nodded, slowly. 'I understand,' he said. 'We're going to start as soon as we can. You'll wait outside the revival room with Detective Flores while we proceed with the revival and find out what your son saw. When that's done, hopefully there'll be time to talk to him. The detective will bring you in. David will only hear me, so I'll have to repeat all that you say. You understand, Katherine? It'll take at least fifteen minutes to revive your son, but it could be much longer. A revival will only last a few minutes, and much of that will be taken up with the questioning. If it doesn't look like there'll be time, what would you like me to say?'

Katherine Leith squeezed Jonah's hand until it hurt, looking straight into his eyes. 'There'll be time,' she said.

Jonah nodded, and stood. 'I'll do what I can.'

As he and West emerged from the office, the county sheriff was standing with Flores. He didn't look happy.

'This is Sheriff Garter,' said West to Jonah.

'The Sheriff has bad news,' said Flores.

'One of my deputies has gone, Detectives,' said Garter. 'I think he has sympathies.'

West looked at him. 'Afterlifer sympathies?'

'Yes. He heard what was going on. Took himself off soon after. It's safe to assume he's passed the information on by now. If I was a betting man, I'd say we'll have company within an hour. Hopefully it'll take them longer than that to get a warrant, but if they come armed with one, there'll be nothing I can do.'

West gave Jonah a questioning look. 'How does that sit with you, Jonah?'

'It'll be tight. Depends on how long it takes to get the kid back, but – look, I have medication to take before I start. That needs five to ten minutes, so it's the set-up we'll be rushing. Let me get back there and see what Never has to say.'

*

On the way back Jonah paused at a water cooler. He took out his pack of meds, a variety of drugs that helped limit the after-effects of a revival. Jonah had more experience than most with how bad those effects could be. He washed down the cocktail of pills as he walked.

When they reached the revival area, Never was red-faced and out of breath. The boxes had been rearranged, piled five high in a few places, and some relocated to the corridor. Now there was enough space to let them get on with it; Never had already started to unpack and set up the recording equipment.

'There's a problem,' Jonah told him.

'Oh joy,' said Never. 'What is it?'

'We think the bad guys are on their way.'

'They caught wind of it, then.'

'Yep,' said Jonah. 'So we need to hurry. How long?'

'Normally another twenty minutes. You sure we have time?'

'We have an hour to turn it around. If we start in twenty, it might be enough.'

He and Never shared an uneasy look, then Jonah stood back and let Never get on with the set-up, knowing he'd slow things down if he tried to help. Three cameras: close-up, mid- and wide-shot. Two laptops hooked up to them. It was only eight minutes later that Never went into the smaller room, where he'd set up the laptops, and started testing the signals. Two minutes more, and he came out with his thumb raised. 'I have a bunch of other tests I'm happy to waive,' he said. 'Just this once. We're not normally so *rushed*. Your meds kicked in?'

They had; Jonah felt a little light-headed. 'All good. I'll get the audience.'

Flores stood waiting outside the door. 'We're ready,' Jonah told her. She hurried off, bringing back West and Katherine Leith.

Jonah met them in the corridor. 'I'll tell Detective West when you can be brought in, Katherine,' Jonah said. 'Be careful stepping over the cabling on the floor inside. We'll not have long. Think about what you want to say. Keep it short and simple. Do you understand?' Katherine nodded. 'This will be difficult, so if you change your mind, tell us at once, and don't be ashamed to say it.'

'I won't change my mind,' said Katherine.

Jonah and West entered the room, Katherine and Flores staying in the corridor.

West shut the door. 'Let's get on with it,' he said, walking into the monitoring room.

'Here,' said Never, handing Jonah his earpiece. 'Good luck.' He followed West and closed the door of the partitioned area behind him.

Jonah moved to where David Leith's body lay and looked at it for a moment. He thought of himself at fifteen years old, probably the worst time in his life – the year after his mother died.

He snapped out of it, hearing a buzzing. The sound was coming from the earpiece in his hand. He looked up at the observation window and could see that Never was speaking. He put the earpiece in place.

'How's the soundproofing?' Never asked.

'I couldn't hear a thing.'

'The mics are picking you up well, so everything's good. That's the only seat I could find, take a minute to adjust it.'

Jonah looked at the ancient swivel chair beside the gurney, then back to the observation room. 'What about you two?'

'We have boxes.' Standing up, Never had a look at what he'd been sitting on. 'I have disposable gloves. Detective West has scrubs. It'll do. Give the word when you're ready.'

Jonah sat in the chair Never had put out for him, pulling it closer to the gurney and adjusting the height. He took David Leith's hand, getting a feel for how it would be to sit like this for up to an hour, immediately realizing that they just didn't have the time.

The seat would suffice. He stood and leaned over the body. As requested, a blanket covered the abdomen and legs. He adjusted it a little, assessing the chance that movement of the chest could make it slip off. He decided it would stay in place, then checked the throat for signs of rigor, just in case.

He looked up at the mid-shot camera, the one Never would be watching.

'I'm good,' Jonah said, sitting down again. The red light on the camera went green. Recording had started. 'Revival of subject Clayton David Fray Junior, known as David Leith. J. P. Miller duty reviver.'

5

Jonah took the corpse's hand in his, fully aware of the time pressure. With such a fresh death, achieving revival could be very quick indeed, but surgical cases sometimes proved more tricky. The reasons were unclear; some laid the blame on the anaesthetic, but no-one really knew.

He closed his eyes. This was the first stage of revival, the part known as the *reversal*: finding the subject, somehow, in a way all revivers intuitively understood but which seemed impossible to quantify, a process that had not even begun to be understood in spite of all the research. He reached out, holding the subject, becoming submerged in the *death* that surrounded him and allowing the cold lifelessness to invade every part of his being. Then he waited for it to dissipate, the subject's injuries gradually reversing in his mind. The worse the state of the body, the longer the process took.

He sensed something and grasped, holding on to what he knew was the essence of David Leith. He felt himself pulled hard and he became disoriented, feeling as if it was his own body lying dead on the gurney now, aware of every part of it, right down to the smallest amount of damage; the initial stab wound, the surgical incisions, even the bruising David had suffered on his legs as he'd fallen after the attack.

Jonah waited, focusing. He pictured the damage retreating, the dead blood purged and invigorated as the body became – in

Jonah's mind – what it once had been. Only when this was done could the essence return.

He wondered how long it was taking. It was difficult to keep track of time during this stage.

Almost there. Almost.

The second stage would come soon. Known as the *surge*, it was often frightening. Whereas the reversal could be anticipated reasonably well from the state of the subject, the surge was impossible to predict. It could be gentle, at its best; gentle and rapid, almost unnoticed, as it had been in Jonah's first, the accidental revival of his own mother. Or it could be a nightmare, a sudden overwhelming flood of experience, like drowning in the screams of the dead – image, sound and emotion swamping him, coming in waves, again and again, leaving him beaten and panicking and wanting to stop.

But if he ever *did* stop, he would have to start again – or find another reviver able to do it – within two hours, or else the chance would have gone forever. And here, now, that simply wasn't an option.

The surge hit him. He braced and tried to ride it, to go with it as the pulses battered his mind. Not an easy one. Not easy at all. But he held his nerve and got the reward.

Jonah opened his eyes. 'He's here,' he said. A moment later the corpse of David Leith took a long, slow breath, the dead lungs filling with the air that would let it speak. Jonah turned towards the observation window, looking at Never. 'How long was I?' How much had he used up of their precious time?

'Seven minutes,' said Never, with a tentative smile.

Jonah nodded. Much faster than he'd thought, and a good start. He turned back to his subject.

'My name is Jonah Miller. Can you tell me who you are?'

'David,' said the corpse, in a whisper so quiet that Jonah wondered if it was enough for Never's hasty set-up to record. He looked at Never again and got a nod. All fine. Jonah could hear everything clearly, of course – for the reviver, the dead voices were *always* loud, as if spoken directly into the ear, but Jonah's experience allowed him to know the true volume.

'Do you know what's happened to you, David?'

A pause. 'I was attacked.'

'Yes,' said Jonah. 'Think, David. Think about what happened to you.' He wanted to give the boy a few moments to remember, to try and work it out. The shock of their own death was typically reduced if the subject could come to realize it for themselves, rather than having to be told.

The sound of a cell phone ringing made him look to the observation room, exasperation on his face. Detective West raised his hand, answering the call; it had happened before, that a detective without the experience in revival cases had simply neglected to switch their phone off, and Jonah shot a look to Never, expecting him to intervene.

But Never was watching West with wary eyes. Jonah suddenly realized what it meant. There was only one call West would have taken.

Detective West's face was solemn as he lowered his hand. 'That was Sheriff Garter at the hospital entrance. His missing deputy just showed up with a lawyer and two other men.' He shook his head. 'They have their warrant. Nothing Garter can do about it.'

Jonah felt suddenly cold. West looked at Never, and Never looked at Jonah. What the hell could they do? He could feel that David was about to speak again. The body had taken another breath, long and slow, while the call had come through.

'Am I . . . ?' David said. 'Oh God. No.'

Jonah's mind was racing. They only had seconds before the law would come down against him, and against David. He made a decision.

'Bring his mother in right now,' he said, looking at Never. 'And buy me some time.'

6

'I died,' said the body of David Leith.

'Yes,' said Jonah. He could feel the emotions David was experiencing. It often took a minute or two of careful handling at this point in a revival, to reassure and console the subject, prevent them from becoming caught up in their own fate and unwilling to talk about what had led to their death. David, though, was accepting. There was anger, yes; regret, too. But it was more annoyance than rage, and it would allow things to proceed more quickly.

Detective West was at the door, bringing in David's mother. 'Stay outside,' he told Flores. 'Go and intercept them. Stall, if you can, but don't overstep the mark. One of us may as well keep their job.'

'I see them,' said Flores. She started walking up the corridor. West looked after her briefly before coming back inside and closing the door.

'Shit,' said West. 'They're coming, all right.'

'Can we barricade it?' asked Never, sounding desperate.

West took a key from his pocket, a key with a huge fob attached. 'They gave me this to let us in here. With luck it's their only one.' He put it in the lock. 'If anyone has cold feet, this is your last chance.'

'Do it,' said Never, and West turned the key.

Katherine Leith walked over to her son's body. She stood by

David's feet, staring at his corpse with despair. She looked at Jonah, and Jonah nodded.

'We do this now,' he told her. 'We don't have long.' He sensed David's confusion at what he was saying. 'David, your mother's here.'

There were knocks at the door. A voice called for it to be opened. Garter's deputy, Jonah presumed.

'Mom's here?' said David. 'Is . . . is my father here too?'

Jonah looked at West, suddenly wondering if Clayton Fray had been in the area, close enough to come himself, but West shook his head. 'No,' said Jonah.

'Good,' said David. He started another long, slow breath.

The knocking at the door became more forceful. 'Say goodbye to your careers, gentlemen,' a second voice said. 'Officer, get this door open.'

'Unlock the door, Detective,' called the deputy.

David was ready again. 'I want to tell you what I saw, isn't that why I'm here now?'

'If there's time, David,' said Jonah. 'I'll be honest, we're under a little pressure. We only have a few moments, and I think you and your mom should use it.' Jonah looked at Katherine and nodded.

There was the rattle of a key. Jonah and Katherine both turned their heads.

'Take your key out of the lock, sir,' ordered the deputy. They must have obtained a spare, Jonah thought; West was holding tight to the end of his, keeping it in to obstruct the lock.

Jonah and Never shared a look, Never's expression a mix of frustration and anger. Jonah looked back to Katherine and signalled for her to begin.

'I love you, David,' she said. Jonah repeated it for David; just as he could hear the words of the dead no matter how quietly they were spoken, the dead could hear what he said even when it was barely audible. He could repeat the words even while Katherine spoke, not an easy skill but one he'd had plenty of practice at. It helped create the illusion that the relative was speaking directly to the subject, and Jonah knew that the illusion was important.

Katherine continued. 'And I'm sorry, sorry that I stayed with your dad as long as I did, that I let him bully us for so damn long. You've always been such a good son, such a sweet boy, and you deserved better.' Her head dropped, tears falling from reddened eyes.

'Don't say that, Mom,' said David. 'You know him. He's an arrogant son of a bitch and you're worth a million of him. You deserve better too. Always. You fought for me because you love me. Dad fought for me because he wanted to hurt you. And I know you won't take him back, whatever he says, but you have to promise me you won't settle for a guy like him again. I want you to be happy, Mom. Not just for you, for me, too. If you're happy, we win. I love you, Mom.'

A sudden thump drew Jonah's attention. The door was shaking with repeated blows. The deputy must have fetched a door ram from his vehicle, and it didn't look like it would stand up to much more.

Jonah looked at Katherine, and she nodded. She knew it was time. 'I love you, David,' she whispered. 'I love you. Now, you have to sleep.'

Another loud thump came from the door, and it started to splinter.

Jonah inclined his head to the far corner of the room. Better for Katherine to stay out of the way. She understood and stepped over to the side.

'David, I'm going to let you go now,' said Jonah.

'Don't I get to tell you what happened?'

The door crashed open.

Jonah looked up as the deputy entered, followed by a shorter man with a thin face that still managed to pack in plenty of hatred. The lawyer, Jonah presumed, and almost certainly a devout After-lifer. Two larger men came next, casually dressed: the lawyer had brought his own backup. Sheriff Garter and Detective Flores followed behind.

'Let's keep this calm, Harry,' Garter said.

'Just doing my duty, Sheriff,' said the deputy. 'Someone around here needs to.'

Jonah looked back to David. 'I'm sorry. We're being made to stop.' David started to take another breath.

Shouts came from both the deputy and the lawyer, with responses from Flores and Never. The exchanges rapidly grew more heated until one of the lawyer's goons grabbed Never's shoulder, throwing him hard into the door of the observation room. His hands went up to his face and came away bloody. As Never moved angrily towards the goon once more, West and Flores stepped in to calm things.

'*Settle down!*' shouted Garter. His voice cut through the uproar, leaving sudden silence in its wake. 'Harry, I said keep this *calm.*'

The deputy nodded. 'Yes, sir.' He held up a sheet of paper. 'We have the authority to halt this revival, and I insist that—'

'Was it my father?' said David Leith. His voice was far louder this time; the anger in it was unmistakeable. The deputy trailed off, staring at the moving corpse.

Maybe he hadn't been present at a revival before, Jonah thought. Natural, if he had Afterlifer sympathies, but the first experience of a corpse speaking was always going to unnerve.

'Did he want to stop this?' said David. 'Because I want to have my say, Jonah. Doesn't that count?'

Jonah looked the deputy in the eye. 'Well, officer? Doesn't that count for anything? I stop now, and it's too late. David can't ever have his say. We have his mother's permission, and the boy *himself* is pleading with you.'

The deputy looked back. Ten long seconds.

'Please,' said David.

The deputy looked at the floor, stunned, torn. At last he looked back at Jonah. 'You have two minutes,' he said, his voice small.

'*No!*' yelled the lawyer. He tore the sheet of paper from the deputy's hand and held it high. 'We don't just have the *authority* to stop this. We are *compelled* to. By the laws of what is *right*, by our duty to this boy's very *soul*. I command you to stop this.' He looked at the deputy. 'Immediately.'

The deputy wouldn't meet his eye. 'He has two minutes.'

The lawyer gave a nod to his men, but Garter stepped forward. 'I wouldn't do that, friends. There are three officers present who would happily see your asses in jail.'

The men looked at their boss. The lawyer's face was reddening with anger but he waved them back. 'Very well,' he said, bitter. 'Two minutes. Not a second more.'

'David,' said Jonah. 'They're giving us a little time. Not long. Tell me what you can about the person who attacked you.'

'It was a young kid, eleven maybe. He pulled a knife, but all I had was sixteen dollars. He looked even more terrified than me. I gave it up. He wanted more, said he'd seen a phone. I was angry. I'd been thinking about my dad earlier, how much he'd done to hurt us all this time, how little he cared about me. How much he'd hurt my mom. She'd struggled for money all these years, but she'd got me that phone. For a moment I thought, fuck him, he can't just *take* it, like my dad tries to take *everything* from us. But I knew that kind of anger was dangerous, it wasn't worth the risk. So I reached to my back pocket and brought it round, ready to throw it at this stupid kid, but I moved too quickly. I saw panic in his eyes. He thought I'd gone for a weapon, and he'd reacted fast. I knew the knife had gone in deep. Then he saw the phone in my hand, and we both understood. He looked at me like he was lost. He ran. Just a scared kid.' David stopped.

From the moment he had started everyone else had been completely silent. The lawyer broke the spell. 'Enough,' he said. 'You've had your time and more. Now stop this. Right this moment. *Stop this.*' Impatient, he shook his head. 'Very well.'

The lawyer reached into a pocket and produced a pair of latex gloves. He put them on, Jonah watching with growing wariness. The man moved towards him and took hold of Jonah's right wrist. Despite the gloves, chill flooded them both; then he took hold of David's wrist, the distaste of touching a corpse clear on the man's face. He pulled, hard, trying to break the physical contact between reviver and subject. Trying to end the revival. Jonah held fast and the man pulled again.

Jonah stood, keeping a tight hold of David's hand, absolute rage in his eyes. *'Take your hands off me!'* Jonah yelled, aware that he was using every ounce of strength he had to maintain contact with his subject. But the anger in Jonah's voice had been enough to make the lawyer let go and step back, looking genuinely frightened.

The man gathered himself and looked at the deputy. 'He's had his time, officer,' he muttered. 'Do your duty.'

The deputy stepped forwards, looking almost ashamed. 'He's right, sir,' he said to Jonah. 'I have to ask you to stop.'

Jonah took a breath. He nodded, sitting back down. 'David,' he said, his voice shaky. 'It's time to go now. Are you ready?'

'Jonah, tell my mom again. I love her. I'm sorry. It was my fault, you see? Moving like I did. It was an accident, really. The kid was terrified, but I caused it.'

'It wasn't your fault, David.' He glanced at the lawyer's glaring face, then back to David's. 'It's time.'

There was a pause as David drew breath again. The lawyer was restless, but the rage in Jonah's eyes must still have been plain to see. The man stayed where he was.

'OK,' said David. 'Jonah, tell my mom again. Tell her I love her. Tell her to be happy.'

Jonah smiled, and could see Katherine Leith smile too, her tears falling. He nodded. 'She heard you, David. She loves you. Good luck.' Jonah let go of David Leith's hand and watched as the breath left the body, the chest sinking back down and becoming still. The corpse was just a corpse once more. He heard a sudden sob from Katherine, then he stood and turned to face the others in the room. The deputy was watching David's body but the lawyer met Jonah's eye with contempt. Jonah started to walk to the door. He needed air.

'I hope you're proud,' said the lawyer.

Jonah slowed momentarily, but kept walking. He looked at Never, seeing the swelling coming up around his eye, the blood still flowing from a split lip. The two men the lawyer had brought with him were standing at the door, not meeting Jonah's gaze.

The lawyer spoke again from behind him. 'You hear me?'

Jonah stopped.

'Jonah . . .' said Never, shaking his head, as Jonah slowly turned.

The lawyer sneered. 'I said I hope you're proud of yourself, you *desecrator.*'

Jonah looked at David Leith's body. He looked at David's mother, watching them, stunned. He looked at the lawyer, the man's face full of self-righteous anger and disgust.

Then Jonah lunged at him.

7

'You comfortable?'

Jonah looked up to see Sheriff Garter's weary face. They'd been in the holding cells in the Chesapeake Sheriff's Office building for eight hours. 'How much longer will we be here, Sheriff?'

Garter sighed. 'Galls me to say it, but the lawyer and his friends were released two hours ago. Judge Forest's decision, same judge that issued the order to forbid the revival. You two will be here for some time yet, I'd guess.'

'How come?' It was Never, from the cell to Jonah's right, a solid wall between the cells meaning that Jonah couldn't even see his friend. 'If we're actually going to be charged with anything, can't we at least get processed? It'd relieve the tedium.'

'Right now you're not being charged for the affray,' said Garter, 'and I suspect you're not going to be. Forest is an Afterlifer sympathizer, but their people were the initial aggressors.'

'Damn right,' said Never. 'My face *hurts*.'

'Even so,' said Garter, 'it was your assault on the lawyer, Jonah, that triggered the second round of fighting. They were trying to make a distinction in law. Forest said he wanted more time to consider. He was happy to order that the others be released but wanted you held pending a final decision.'

Jonah rubbed his side. It hurt like hell; there were little pockets of pain all over him, but his side was the worst. After he'd jumped at the lawyer he'd managed to land two swift punches before the deputy and the lawyer's men had stepped in. The lawyer, back on his feet, had put in a kick to Jonah's side before Never took him to the floor again. He counted his lucky stars that the kick hadn't been at the site of his old gunshot wound. The rest of it was a blur of confused scuffles until the officers present managed to bring it all to an end. 'That's bullshit,' said Jonah. 'They get off scot-free because the judge *likes* them?' He rubbed his tender knuckles, remembering the satisfying burst of chill that had accompanied his punches – something he suspected the lawyer wouldn't forget in a hurry.

Garter smiled. 'Welcome to my world. But I don't think it'll be long before the judge orders your release, given the crowd they've shipped in.'

Jonah stared. 'Crowd?'

'Hell, yes. A dozen folk so far, placards and lots of hot coffee. I expect plenty more will show up. The Afterlifers want some air-time on this.'

'On what?' said Jonah. 'Them starting a fight next to a boy's corpse?'

Garter shook his head. 'They had a warrant to prevent the revival taking place and it went ahead anyway. Whatever the rights and wrongs, whatever the timings, they'll spin it to get their sup-porters' blood boiling. And it'll be much more likely to hit the TV news if you two are released into the middle of a braying mob. The crowd's only just warming up. Once they're ready, I'm guessing I'll get a call from Judge Forest telling me you're free to go.'

'Ha,' said Never, without an ounce of humour. 'I get it. They had their man stall for time so that they could arrange a photo opportunity.'

'Looks like it,' said Garter. 'I've been in touch with your boss, by the way. He's already sent people to collect your equipment from the hospital. We left it locked up once David Leith's body was removed, but I advised your boss to get it dealt with before that lawyer decided to try and grab it.'

Jonah nodded. The footage of the callous attempt to stop David Leith having his final say wouldn't be favourable to the Afterlifers. 'Good call.'

'It was better than good,' said Garter. 'When your people arrived, someone had just scammed the key off a member of staff and was having a good poke around.'

'*Fuckers*,' came the shout from the next cell. 'Nobody touches my fucking kit,' said Never. '*Nobody*. What happened?'

'They gave a vaguely plausible bullshit excuse and left,' said Garter. 'Empty-handed.'

'And the revival footage?' asked Never. Jonah found himself tense.

'All fine,' said Garter. Jonah relaxed, and sensed Never doing the same. 'Anyway, I have no intention of kicking you out into the middle of a mob, so we'll keep you here until the early hours. Your boss will send someone when the crowd's lost interest for the night. Assuming the judge does what I think he'll do. Which he will. You boys try and get some sleep.'

*

Within the hour they could hear the crowd outside. Muffled, the only thing that came through was the occasional chant of 'FRS hands off our kids.'

'I can't believe they're drawing attention to this,' said Jonah. 'We have the footage that shows them being total assholes. On the offensive, I guess.'

'It's more than that,' said Never, sounding grim. 'They'll say we flouted the law and didn't give the relatives their rights.'

'The law was on our side, and what about the mother's rights?'

'I hear you, but all they want is headlines and sound bites that fit their message. Even if the footage got out there, I doubt it'd convert any of their supporters to agreeing with what we did.'

'*Even if* the footage got out? Christ, surely we can make sure it—'

'No!' said Never, sounding appalled. 'That footage is confidential, whatever the situation. It's not getting out into the public domain, not on my watch.'

Jonah stayed quiet. Of course Never was right, but Jonah couldn't help feeling he'd been reprimanded like a child.

*

They were woken at five the next morning to find that their boss Hugo had come to get them himself. They'd both managed to catch some sleep, which was more than could be said for Hugo, from the look of him. Sheriff Garter was there too and looked similarly exhausted. Out of their cells, Jonah and Never appraised each other's injuries, Never with a swollen lip and a black eye coming up, Jonah with an impressive bruise developing on the side of his face.

'Sorry for the early start,' Garter said. 'As I'd been expecting, the call came through from the judge last night at ten, at the same time the crowd was reaching its peak. I gave a statement that you'd be staying in the cells until exactly eight thirty-five in the morning. A degree of precision in a lie is important, I find. They believed me, so the mob drifted home. They'll be back here in a couple of hours, but you'll be long gone by then. They have a handful of people in a car out front keeping watch, so we'll use the back way.'

Garter led them outside. Hugo had brought his own car, unmarked, and nodded to them as they got in, but he was unwilling to give much by way of answers to their questions. Most of those centred on just how much trouble they were in.

'We'll talk about it back at the office,' was all Hugo would say.

When they arrived in Richmond ninety minutes later, it wasn't even seven o'clock. Jonah was expecting the office empty, save for the handful of staff finishing the night shift, but as they came in the door all three of them stopped in their tracks.

'Oh shit,' muttered Never. 'You could've warned us.' He and

Jonah looked at Hugo, but Hugo seemed as taken aback as they were.

The door to Hugo's office lay wide open. Inside, they could see a group of suits waiting, in the middle of whom stood Robert Thorne, the FRS Director.

'I thought this would happen later on,' mumbled Hugo, his hand balling up, knuckles tense. 'By phone.'

The moment Thorne became aware of their presence the dark cloud of disdain on his face vanished and became a salesman's welcome. It gave Jonah the creeps.

Thorne beckoned to them. 'Hugo,' he said. 'Jonah, Never. Come in.'

Jonah saw Hugo's eyebrow rise – no wonder, being *invited* into his own office. They entered and were directed to three chairs that had been set in a line in front of Hugo's desk. Thorne sat down in Hugo's chair, still smiling, and indicated to the four people standing at the side of the room. One woman, three men, their clothes as humourless as their eyes.

'These good folk are from Legal,' Thorne said, giving their names, each of them smiling briefly in turn.

'What is this, Robert?' said Hugo. 'I thought we would be discussing this at ten. That was what you told me.'

Thorne's smile was still there, but toned down now; matter-of-fact, ready for business. 'I decided we need our response nailed down much sooner. Our friends here agreed. I hope you understand.'

Hugo said nothing, and looked from Thorne to each of the legal team. He took his time. 'I can't say I do understand, Robert,' he said at last.

Thorne gave a slow nod. 'Yesterday's events are likely to come under close scrutiny, Hugo. And it's with you that the ultimate responsibility lies. As the regional FRS head.'

'And you're the FRS *Director*,' said Hugo. That made Jonah take in a sharp breath.

Thorne's smile became wary. 'Your team ignored a specific and valid legal warrant to halt proceedings. Then, allegedly, they instigated a physical assault on—'

'That is *not* what happened,' said Never.

Thorne's gaze swung round to him. Jonah could see Never quail slightly under it. 'That's why we're here, Never. To establish what *did* happen. To establish our response. Do you deny you ignored a law enforcement officer's legally backed request that the revival be stopped? And Jonah, you punched a man to the ground.'

Just as Never opened his mouth to answer, Hugo spoke. 'Robert, you know damn well what happened. The revival had already succeeded. It was appropriate to continue. The warrant was to stop the revival taking *place*, not to stop it in progress.'

'That's a subtle distinction,' said Thorne.

'Like *hell* it's subtle, Robert. Considering how *irreversible* that decision would have been. The Afterlifer lawyer pushing this through overstepped the mark by some margin. He attempted to forcibly separate reviver from subject. Besides the fact that Never received notable injuries as soon as the Afterlifer group gained entry to the room – by force, I note – it was clearly an act of assault for that man to put one *hand* on Jonah.'

Thorne nodded, then looked at the legal team. He looked at the desk for a moment, then up at Hugo. 'You don't like me,' he said. 'I know that. You think I'm an officious prick who whittles away at your budget each year because I enjoy it.'

Hugo was uneasy, Never and Jonah likewise. Thorne hesitated and took a slow breath, looking genuinely unhappy. Jonah wondered where the hell this was going.

'I don't enjoy it,' Thorne went on. 'Just like you, I don't enjoy the hard decisions. Just like you, I don't enjoy having to say no to things my staff need. But it has to be done. The same way revivals can't be given to everyone. We have only so many staff. We have only so much money. I try my damnedest to keep worries about higher-level financial concerns to myself. And I absolutely don't enjoy what I have to do now.'

For a moment, Hugo just watched Thorne. Then, slowly, something dawned on his face, and he looked around to Jonah and Never. Something about that look made Jonah extremely nervous.

'No,' said Hugo. 'Absolutely not. You can't just throw your staff to the wolves.'

'Please,' said Thorne. 'I understand what happened. I don't blame you. You saw the opening, and you took it. But no attempt to seek the opinion of the father was made, in spite of – *or because of* – the knowledge that he would have been firmly against it. In the end, Hugo, it doesn't matter what happened. It only matters how the Afterlifers make it *look*. The problem is, they now have the money to buy the media expertise to make us look like the bad guys. Worse, they can push legal action that we simply can't afford to fight. We're in a bad situation and we have to pre-empt them. There'll be an internal investigation, with those involved suspended while that happens. All three of you.'

'For how long?' said Hugo.

Thorne looked at the lawyer to his immediate left. Jonah braced himself.

The lawyer nodded. 'Six weeks minimum,' she said. 'At most twelve.'

'Please,' said Thorne, 'rest assured you'll be on full pay. We'll get through this. You have all our support.'

Nobody said anything. Thorne shifted in his seat.

'Suspension is a hell of a way to show your support,' said Hugo.

'We've underestimated the Afterlifers,' said Thorne. 'All of us. If you don't agree with what I've decided, I'm sorry. But we can't just brave-face this and pretend they'll go away. We simply can't risk taking borderline decisions, not now. There are rumours going around of a concerted effort, behind the scenes, to limit the FRS budget significantly. There are powerful people who aren't quite ready to come out in support of the Afterlifer cause, but who *are* ready to give them what help they can. They're pushing. Everything we say and do from here on in has to be managed with great care.'

'So next time we just lie down?' said Jonah, visibly angry. 'Let them get away with what they tried to do to that boy and his mother? It was the father's spite, that's all, to stop them saying goodbye; a final piece of revenge. If we'd waited, they would've found a way to drag it out until a revival was deemed unnecessary for the investigation, or too unlikely to succeed. Katherine Leith didn't have private revival insurance, and she sure as hell couldn't afford to pay outright for it. That's what you want us to do from now on? We didn't *know* that a judge was going to order a halt, but we knew they'd try to pull something. And we weren't going to wait around to see what.'

Thorne frowned. 'That's an opinion I don't want to hear repeated outside this room. Pressure from the Afterlifers is growing every day, and the last thing we need is to be caught conspiring to deny the rights of a grieving parent.'

'His mother doesn't count?'

'You know what I mean. We're not a charity. Operational decisions can't hinge on whether we would *like* to offer revival to victims and their relatives. Don't make me the bad guy, Jonah. I'm on your side.'

'No, sir. You may not be on the Afterlifer's side, but you're sure as hell not on mine.'

'Jonah, your actions have consequences. The fallout from this will cost the FRS tens of thousands of dollars, maybe hundreds of thousands. All because you wanted a boy to say goodbye to his mother.'

'You're out of line, Robert,' said Hugo. 'That's going too far.'

'Is it?' said Thorne, agitated. 'We have to make shitty decisions every day, Hugo. You know that. We shield our staff as best we can, but every *day* we make decisions that could stop ordinary people getting their last chance at a revival. We make those decisions because it's the best we can do. Compromise. It's not easy, but we have no choice.'

'Uh,' said Never, putting up his hand, 'surely there has to be *some* choice?' He looked at the contingent of lawyers. 'You lot must have come up with other alternatives, right?'

The legal team said nothing but Jonah spotted the youngest-looking, a man furthest from Thorne, glance down fast enough to seem evasive. Hugo had seen it too.

'What was it?' said Hugo, addressing the man directly.

The man looked at Thorne. 'Perhaps if—' he started, but Thorne wasn't having any of it.

'*No*,' said Thorne. 'I made my decision clear.'

Hugo turned his gaze to Thorne. 'Robert, I insist. What was the alternative?'

Thorne and Hugo locked eyes, and the seconds passed. Finally, Thorne shook his head. He turned to Jonah, and spoke reluctantly. 'They want your head. Before any investigation, they want you gone. Then they would back off, or so they claim.'

'Just me?' said Jonah.

'You're one of our best revivers, one of the longest-serving. That's why they want you. They're playing games. They know we won't fire you.'

Jonah thought of the lawyer he'd punched, imagined him putting the proposal together, doubtless gleeful and vindictive. Then he thought of the many court cases where he'd been called as witness, the lawyers coming for him personally. Now the Afterlifers were joining in, painting a target on him, making him the focus of their attack.

He suddenly realized how tired he was.

He thought of how difficult his life had felt lately, and knew it was time to face up to a truth he'd been avoiding for over a year: that there was a reason why everything about his job felt so much harder now.

He knew what he had to do.

'You won't need to fire me,' he said, standing up. 'Not if I resign.' Ignoring the open-mouthed looks, Jonah walked out of Hugo's office.

Hugo and Never followed a moment later, closing the office door behind them. Hugo hung back a little.

'What the fuck?' said Never. 'You can't just jack it in.'

'I've been in this office since it opened, Never. The first of its kind, worldwide, and I was here on day one. I've watched it all the way, watched it grow. It's almost killed me, more than once. Then came Andreas. The fire at Reese-Farthing Medical. Getting *shot*. And ever since I came back to work not one day has gone by without me thinking about shifting to private revivals before it's too late, but my sense of duty was stopping me. The FRS isn't good for me, Never. I've always known that. But I hadn't been able to admit that *I* was bad for the FRS.'

'So take a holiday! If we're all suspended, just take a break and—'

'Suspension still means fighting, Never. I don't have any fight left in me. Thorne's right about the Afterlifers. They're strong, and if we behave like we don't give a damn for their concerns, it'll just fuel that strength. But right now, all I can think of is David Leith and his mother. I can't be in that position again. I *can't*. Because if I am, I'll do exactly what I did this time, and the FRS will take the hit. I can't trust myself to do what needs to be done to protect the FRS. I can't watch that happen and know it was my fault.'

'You'll change your mind,' said Never, stunned. 'By tomorrow morning, I guarantee it.'

Jonah put his hand on his friend's shoulder and looked him in the eye. 'I won't,' he said. 'I mean it.'

They looked at each other for a few seconds. Eventually Never looked away, and nodded. 'I guess you do,' he said.

'But if you do change your mind, Jonah,' said Hugo, walking over to them, '*if* you do, your desk will stay right where it is. However long that takes.'

Jonah nodded. He spent a moment gathering his few belongings in a plastic bag, while Hugo and Never stayed silent. When he had finished collecting his things, he turned to find his way blocked by Never.

'Can't I talk you out of this?' said Never. Jonah shook his head. 'Do you want a hand taking your stuff back to your apartment?'

'I'd rather just go home alone.'

'OK,' said Never, reluctantly. He stepped forward and hugged Jonah.

'It's not like I'm leaving the country.' Jonah could feel his eyes starting to water, and he could see Never's doing the same.

'You've, ah, got something in your eye,' said Never, and Jonah just nodded.

Then, Jonah Miller walked out of the FRS. Going down the stairs, it seemed like he was in free-fall; that he'd jumped from the roof and was taking a long time to hit the ground.

8

When Jonah got back to his apartment he tried to call Annabel. She didn't answer, so he sent her an email to tell her what had happened. By noon he'd still not heard back, but the events of the previous twenty-four hours were catching up with him. Numb and exhausted, he crashed on the couch.

He was woken by his cat Marmite, licking his nose and purring. Feeding the cat had been the only thing he'd had any success with when he'd got home that morning, and it was already time to do it again. The clock on his wall showed just past 5 p.m.

'Come on,' Jonah told the cat, his own stomach grumbling. He fed Marmite and put two slices of bread into the toaster. When they popped, he looked blankly at them for a moment, wondering when the toaster had started making a *buzzing* sound. Then his brain kicked in enough for him to realize someone was ringing at his door.

He shuffled over to the intercom.

'Hi, Never,' he said. Who else would it be?

'Can I come up?'

'Sure. I warn you, I just woke. Might be a little vague.'

'No problem. I brought a surprise.'

'OK,' said Jonah, too foggy to give it any thought. He buzzed Never in at the front entrance, then checked his cell phone for anything from Annabel. There was nothing. Whatever his feelings for her, they were fighting with a general irritation over how hard she was to get hold of – or more specifically, how often she seemed to be avoiding him. It was bad enough at the best of times, but right now it drove him crazy. His finger hovered over her number, ready to give her another try, but then he shook his head. He switched his phone off and threw it over to the couch, ignoring it as it bounced onto the floor. For a moment he felt curiously better for it. He wondered just what that meant for the health of their relationship.

Three loud knocks announced Never's arrival. Jonah opened the door, his sleepy face brightening when he saw who else was there.

'Sam!' he said.

Sam Deering, the man who, until his retirement the year before, had run the Central East Coast FRS, was one of the few people besides Never and Annabel that Jonah was close to. Sam had been in Jonah's life since he was fourteen, when the death of Jonah's mother had simultaneously orphaned him and revealed his revival ability. He was the nearest thing to a father Jonah had.

'When I heard what happened I thought you could do with some company,' said Sam. 'Whether you want it or not.'

Jonah mock-frowned at Never.

'What?' said Never. 'I just happened to be on the phone to Sam, so of course I mentioned it.'

'And what did you just happen to be on the phone to Sam *about*?'

'Ah,' said Never. He shrugged. 'Give me a minute, I'll think of something.'

'Get your ass inside, Geary,' Jonah said, shutting the apartment door.

'It's been a while, Jonah,' said Sam. 'You should call by more often. Helen and I like to see you.'

Jonah did a quick mental calculation. The last time he'd caught up with Sam had been three months before, when Sam had come back from a revival conference in France and had invited Jonah and Annabel over to his house for a meal. 'I'll try.'

'Maybe next time Annabel's here,' said Sam. 'How's that going?'

'Fine, I guess,' lied Jonah. 'She spends most of her time travelling. She's been out on the West Coast for a few months tracking down leads for the story she's building about Andreas.'

'Still on that, huh?' said Sam. As far as Sam was aware, the events of the previous year had been exactly as Jonah, Never and Annabel had told the police: that Michael Andreas had invited Annabel to attend a fundraising event; the event was then targeted by Afterlifer-supporting terrorists.

There was an element of truth to it, although it hadn't exactly been a fundraising event, and the 'invitation' had involved the three of them being rounded up by Andreas's security staff and brought to the Reese-Farthing Medical building under duress.

'Yeah, she's still on that,' said Jonah. 'I don't get to see as much of her as I'd like.'

'Well, she's good for you,' said Sam. 'Helen's keen to have her over for dinner again.'

'She's supposed to be here in a couple of weeks,' said Jonah. 'We'll take you up on it. So, you guys want a coffee or something?'

'No,' said Sam, smiling. 'I'm here to treat you to a meal and get you drunk.'

*

When Sam asked Jonah where he wanted to eat, he opted for Mexican and knew exactly why. After any revival, there were fragments of the revived subject left behind, the smallest traces of them; pieces of second-hand memories, quickly fading.

David Leith had loved burritos and it was the first thing Jonah had thought of.

So they headed out to a Mexican restaurant, Jonah outwardly in good spirits. Sam and Never took that as a sign that he was bearing up well; Jonah didn't tell them that it was mainly due to the sensation of free-fall which hadn't left him since he'd walked out of the office. *For what might be the last time*, his mind yelled at him. He was simply too dazed to be worrying much about his future.

Inevitably, talk turned to nostalgia for the early days of the FRS itself, something that Sam Deering had largely been responsible for creating. It had been Sam's foresight that had led to the research that put forensic revival on a firm foundation. When revival had first appeared, an international research effort had been set up at an old US military site. Known as the Revival Baseline Research Group, the intent – and the expectation – had been to find out how revival worked, and what it meant for humanity. Everyone had thought it heralded something profound, some new, deeper understanding of the human condition.

Instead, there had been nothing but frustration.

As the senior researcher, Sam Deering had chosen to sidestep the theology that so preoccupied others, and instead look to the empirical considerations, the areas that research genuinely could examine. After all, he'd reasoned, physical phenomena like gravity and magnetism are thought of as 'understood', even when their underlying nature is a mystery. Empirical science is precisely *about* quantifying the properties of something that is, at first, mysterious. Thus tamed, the mystery is forgotten, even though it's still there, underneath. That, Sam believed, could happen with revival, too.

The research effort became known just as 'Baseline'; by the time public funding dried up and it was brought to a premature conclusion, people no longer looked at revival as an inevitable pathway to ultimate truths, or to the meaning of life.

It was a tool, the same as any other. And it had its uses.

*

In the middle of the meal Sam went to the restroom, leaving Jonah and Never alone for the first time that evening.

'Have you told Annabel what's happened?' asked Never.

Jonah shrugged. 'I left her some messages, but couldn't get hold of her.'

'Right,' said Never.

Jonah didn't like his tone. 'Out with it.'

'I . . .' started Never, but then he stopped. 'This isn't the right time.'

'*Out* with it.'

'I don't like seeing you this way. Every mention of Annabel, you wince. You need a serious chat with her. If she's so distracted by this fucking *quest* she's taken on, then, well . . . she needs to take a break from it. All I'm saying is the girl has issues, and unless she sorts them, every time she's here she'll just look like she's counting the hours before she can go again. And I see it in your eyes, you know she is.'

Jonah took a deep breath and nodded. 'When she relaxes, it all feels *right*. And I know we could make a go of it, if that was how she always was.' He looked up at Never, miserable. 'But that happens less, every time I see her. Since the last time she came I've been waiting for the break-up phone call. Whenever she rang, I was bracing myself for it.'

'Christ, Jonah,' sighed Never. 'There's nothing I can say, except *good luck*.' He paused, both of them taking a long, wallowing swig of their beer. Then he looked up and grinned. 'But I *can* get you massively drunk. And if ever a night called for it, it's this one.'

Jonah frowned, then laughed. 'I think that'd be a good idea.'

Meal finished, Never cajoled Sam into joining them in their self-destruction. 'One or two, maybe,' said Sam, 'but no more.' Jonah saw the glint in Never's eye.

Two hours later, in a bar three doors down from the restaurant, Jonah was at the sweet spot, feeling disconnected enough to have stopped worrying much about either his job or Annabel, but not so drunk that he couldn't appreciate the feeling. He wanted to keep it going as long as he could, and decided to make the next

beer his last and fend off Never's undisguised goal of total obliter-
ation.

Sam brought the conversation around to Never's love-life.

'Nothing doing,' said Never. 'And to be honest, I've stopped
looking. For a while, anyway. I'm hoping that will somehow *make
it happen*. But I think that might be like stopping buying food and
expecting things to just grow in your fridge.'

'I've seen your fridge,' said Jonah. 'Things *do* grow there.'

'Well, I've quit looking,' said Never. 'We'll see how it goes.'

'You did hit on the new woman in Admin at the Christmas
party.'

'Yeah,' said Never. 'She liked the Belfast accent. Didn't like the
actual *words*, though.'

Sam smiled. 'I suppose you do need someone with a well-
developed sense of humour.'

Sam and Jonah's laughter took a while to settle down, fuelled
by the stern look on Never's face.

'Guys, I'm going once I've finished this beer,' said Sam. 'If I go
now, Helen will be amused when I stumble in. Any more, and
she'd not take long to be *unamused*.'

'Understood,' said Jonah, although Never grumbled.

Sam fidgeted a little, and Jonah had an idea that he was going
to raise an awkward subject. He wondered which it would be –
Annabel, or work.

'You'll be fine,' said Sam. 'I know you will. Wait until the dust
settles, then go back to what you do best.'

Jonah smiled, realizing that the great thing about being a little
drunk was how easily he could convince Sam that there was nothing to worry about. 'Thanks. But with the way the Afterlifer things
are going, private work would be far less of a headache.'

'All this Afterlifer nonsense will settle down,' said Sam. 'It'll
blow over in a matter of months.'

Raising an eyebrow, Never leaned forward. 'You confident

about that? From the FRS perspective things are getting hairy very fast, and no end in sight.'

'I'm confident,' said Sam. He tapped a confidential finger to his nose. 'I've heard things, in the last few weeks. A few rumours.'

'What kind?' asked Never.

'That there's something on the horizon.'

'Yes,' said Never. 'They're going to cripple the FRS with legislation.'

Sam nodded. 'They want to, sure, but I don't think the FRS has much to fear from what's coming.'

Jonah sat forward now. 'You know what's on the way, Sam?'

'I hear things. I can't say much, but I think the FRS will be in a better position in the long run.'

'So if it doesn't kill us,' said Never, 'it'll make us stronger?'

Sam shrugged. 'I'm confident this country will make the right decisions.'

'Well,' said Never, 'the Afterlifers want to make the public wary of revival all over again, and they're suddenly doing a fine job of it. You remember what it was like in the early days of revival? The public supported it in the end, but they easily could've gone the other way. What if the Afterlifers keep the momentum going, if they manage to bring all that fear roaring back? You really think this country will make the right decisions in a climate of fear?'

'What are you saying?' said Sam.

'Put it this way: witch-hunts don't make for good laws.'

Sam shook his head. He smiled, even though Never was scowling. 'The Afterlifer bubble is about to be comprehensively burst, Never. Trust me.' The scowl didn't shift from Never's face. 'Really. When I said things would blow over, it wasn't just the new legislation I was talking about.'

Now the scowl shifted. Never and Jonah were both listening eagerly. Sam just sat there, his smile enigmatic.

'Oh for fuck's sake, Sam,' said Never. 'Either spill the beans or buy another round.'

'OK, OK. I heard something from Stephanie,' said Sam. 'Stephanie Graves.' He looked at Jonah, and Jonah nodded.

Stephanie Graves had been a researcher at Baseline, and had also been responsible for the wellbeing of the revivers there. She'd been the one to understand much of the psychological trauma that revivers could suffer, and had developed widely used treatment methods.

'I didn't think you were on speaking terms,' said Jonah.

Sam shrugged. 'She left Baseline because she didn't like some of the . . . *companies* I'd allowed into the project.'

He didn't need to be more explicit: CIA, NSA, and other less *official* agencies had all had their hand in the revival research at Baseline. Indeed, the work that had led to Michael Andreas's death had originated in secret military research, attempting to exploit revivers as a kind of infallible lie detector. Jonah's greatest fear in the past seventeen months had been that those agencies would come knocking, eager to learn just what Andreas had been up to. He didn't imagine they'd be fobbed off as easily as the police had been.

Pain sparked in Jonah's chest at the thought; it had been an employee of one of those agencies who had put the bullet there.

'Stephanie was right, of course,' said Sam. 'My decisions had undermined what Baseline stood for. I refused to talk to her for years, because I refused to accept I'd been wrong.' He shook his head. 'But that's old news. The point is, two weeks ago Stephanie got in touch and told me something as a professional courtesy.'

'She told you what?' said Jonah.

Sam lowered his voice. 'This goes no further, OK?'

Jonah and Never both nodded, wide-eyed.

'The Government is reopening Baseline,' said Sam. 'In part, it's a way to mollify the Afterlifers, because they've been harping on about how little we really understand revival. They've been blaming the absence of research over the eight years since Baseline finally shut down, but really it was a cheap hook to hang their arguments from – they thought the money wasn't there, and they didn't expect their bluff to be called. But it has been. That's why the legislation will be good, because it'll be ongoing and evidence-led.'

Jonah shook his head, thinking about how all the previous research had hit dead-ends. 'They really think it'll get anywhere?' he said.

'Stephanie does,' said Sam. 'She told me the funding is considerable, and the technology needed to study revival has developed well beyond the level it was at before. She's been making progress herself ever since she left the original Baseline. That's why they brought her in. Nobody else in the world knows more about where the most promising areas of research are.'

Jonah had been treated by Stephanie not long before the Andreas situation came up. He remembered her bemoaning how little money and equipment she had, yet still managing to get serious research done. 'And you think this bursts the Afterlifer bubble?'

'Absolutely. It takes away all their momentum. And there's something else, Jonah. They'll want all the best revivers in the world to take part in the new research.'

For a moment, Jonah was stunned. It wasn't something that had occurred to him, but maybe this was it. Maybe this was what he needed. Then he remembered: 'Except that I'm now officially disgraced.'

Sam shrugged. 'Don't worry. They might not come to you directly, but if you want to take part, I hear they'll move mountains to get the best people.'

Going back to Baseline, he thought, and the feeling that hit him was so unfamiliar it took him a second to place it.

Optimism.

*

Jonah and Never only stayed on for a few more after Sam left. Jonah had another three beers, knowing he'd regret it, while

Never downed four and a chaser, clearly determined that at least one of them would end up insensible. They took a taxi back to Jonah's.

'Can I crash at your place?' slurred Never as the cab pulled up.

'Of course. As long as you promise not to let me drink anything else.'

'Deal,' said Never, grinning. The grin fell away, his eyes looking past Jonah. 'Ah,' he said. 'Actually, best if I just take the cab on home.'

Jonah turned his head. There, by the entrance to his apartment block, was Annabel. She smiled and waved. Jonah returned the wave and looked back at Never.

'Shit,' Jonah said.

'Probably better if you don't say that to her. And in hindsight, let me apologize for getting you quite so drunk. Also, don't get talking about, you know, your relationship. While drunk.'

'I hear you.'

'Good, because that's the only time I *ever* talk about that shit, and you'll note that I'm conspicuously single. Good luck.'

Jonah got out and braced himself, wondering if the smile he was trying to force would look real enough to be convincing. But as he walked towards her and saw her up close, he realized his smile wasn't fake. He was scared of losing her, but by God it felt good to see her again.

'Where the hell were you?' she said, smiling. 'I've been calling you since I landed.'

He thought of his phone, switched off and left in his apartment. 'I was waylaid. Drowning my sorrows.' A sudden thought hit him. 'Besides, I was trying to call *you* all day.'

Annabel smiled. 'Yeah, sorry about that.' She hugged him. 'When I got your message I thought you might need company so I grabbed the first flight I could. Probably would have given it away if I spoke to you from an airport, and I wanted to surprise you.'

'You did,' Jonah said, holding her. Part of him knew damn well that sooner or later they'd have to have that talk and sort things out.

But right now things felt good.

9

The next morning Jonah woke on the couch with a full-tilt hangover. It took him a few seconds to get his bearings and recall what had happened the night before.

Once he and Annabel had got into his apartment they'd shared a long kiss, but he was dead on his feet. Annabel had made some coffee and he'd told her all about the David Leith revival, but the coffee wasn't nearly enough to keep him awake. She'd laid him down, his head on her lap, stroking his hair as he talked about what had happened. And that was the last thing he could remember.

The room was bright enough to make him wince; Annabel must have pulled back the curtains to wake him. He sat up, a blanket around him, feeling guilty. He thought of all the ill-feeling towards Annabel's absence that had been brewing within him, yet the moment she was actually *here*, he'd conked out for the night.

It was still early, just after 9 a.m. He went to the kitchen and poured himself a glass of water, then sat at the table.

'Morning,' said Annabel, appearing at the kitchen door. She'd already dressed, and was watching Jonah with distinct amusement. 'I left you on the couch and took your bed for myself.'

'Sorry about last night,' he said. He lifted his glass up. 'Five more of these and I'll be human again, I promise.'

'You want some coffee and toast?' she said. He nodded, watching her as she moved about the kitchen.

He knew it was unfair of him to be so jealous of her time.

Annabel's investigations focused on the workings of Michael Andreas's various companies, and into the backgrounds of the group of Afterlifer-inspired terrorists who had caused the fire at Reese-Farthing. Her work was an attempt to come to terms with everything that had happened, and with one thing in particular: Annabel's father had been an early victim of those Afterlifers.

So while Jonah wanted to try and forget about it all, Annabel travelled to wherever the leads took her, and she kept herself as busy as possible. She'd inherited a considerable amount of money from her father, meaning that not even the distraction of a job interrupted her goal.

Jonah understood, or at least he tried to. She thought she owed it to her dad, to be the best journalist she could be. She needed time, she needed space.

But it was over now, the danger passed. Eventually Annabel would come to terms with that. Eventually she would exhaust her leads. Hopefully before she exhausted *herself*.

She served up the coffee and toast. Jonah took a wary bite but it seemed to sit well in his stomach.

'So what have you been up to?' Jonah asked her. 'How's the, uh, investigation? You closer to knowing who's in charge?'

One of Annabel's key interests was understanding the structure Andreas's companies had been left with since his death. Some of her earliest enquiries had revealed unnecessarily opaque arrangements and suspicious levels of security in some areas; a hacker she'd used successfully in the past had found plenty of unexpected barriers. Annabel's concern had been *why* such barriers would have appeared, now that Andreas was dead. Why would those high up in the company want to disguise their intentions?

The benign explanation was a simple one, the result of power struggles within a multi-billion dollar business empire, and of senior people covertly jockeying for position.

Annabel, though, wasn't looking for benign explanations, however much Jonah tried to convince her.

'Slow progress,' she said. 'I had some information that Andreas Biotech is investing heavily in areas related to revival at the moment, but none of the feelers I've put out have got me any more details. I'm also trying to nurture some Afterlifer contacts, to see if I can get anything about where all their extra funds have been coming from.'

Jonah groaned inside. It sounded like she was expanding the scope of her enquiries, and if that was true, then the prospect of her stopping was receding fast. 'Well,' he said, 'at least then I'd know who to throw things at.'

'Something interesting came up yesterday,' she said, 'when I was in Fort Worth.'

Jonah looked at her, bewildered. 'I thought you were in San Diego. Hard to keep track of you.'

'Got there the night before last. I had a long talk with someone who used to be involved in Afterlifer fundraising, but they didn't know the source of the extra money. Internally, they're saying it's a huge growth in grassroots donations, but my contact didn't believe that.'

He gave her a serious look. 'You're being careful, right?'

'*Yes*, I'm being careful,' she said. 'Quit nagging me.'

He shrugged. He *did* keep nagging her to be discreet and cautious. The Afterlifers had a violent past, and Andreas Biotech was a wealthy company with dark secrets. It seemed to Jonah that neither organization would need much provocation before resorting to extremes.

And not just them: there were also the military connections, the intelligence organizations who had been keeping their eyes on Andreas and on the Afterlifers. Jonah thought of Kendrick, the man responsible for Baseline research which sought to use revival as a method of interrogation – killing someone, then torturing information from their corpse. Kendrick had been at

Reese-Farthing that day, trying to find out what Andreas was up to. It had been one of Kendrick's men who had shot Jonah. It had always been Kendrick's face that Jonah's fears made him see in crowds, not the face of Andreas.

Because Kendrick was still out there.

It was important that Annabel kept off everybody's radar.

'So how about I make you take a break from all this?' said Jonah, smiling. *Be upbeat,* he thought. *Get her to relax. Maybe she'll lose momentum, lose interest.* 'I'll take you out for a meal this evening. I'll avoid alcohol, you'll get pampered, and we can catch up properly.'

Annabel's smile fell. 'Jonah, I –' She paused, and looked down. 'I can't stay.'

Stunned, all Jonah could do was stare.

'I have to get a flight in two hours,' she said, looking up again.

Jonah said nothing; he walked through to his bedroom. Annabel's suitcase was on the bed, packed and ready to go. He marched back to the kitchen. 'Two *hours*?' he said.

'I'd planned to stay for a few days, but I got a message this morning from someone with information about the new Andreas revival investments. I have to go meet them back west.'

'Jesus, Annabel . . . I haven't seen you in so long, and this is all I get?'

'I can't just turn down information, and this was the only time they—'

He interrupted her. 'Are you even coming back for Valentine's next month? Like you *promised*?'

She wouldn't make eye contact. 'It'll depend on what's happening,' she said. 'You know how important this is to me.'

'I know what's *not* important.'

Her mouth opened a little but she said nothing. He could tell she was taken aback by his tone, but he couldn't quite read her expression: upset, certainly, and uncomfortable. But he didn't know whether she was unable to find the right words to ease his fears, or was stopping herself from saying something more painful.

When things had first become serious between them she'd told him about previous boyfriends, the ones who had outstayed their welcome and had been unable to take her hints. It had been funny, at the time, because she'd been so clear about how relaxed she felt around Jonah, how *different* it all was. Now, Jonah was starting to think that what she'd told him had been a warning: *Take the hints. Don't outstay your welcome.*

'What am I to you, Annabel?' he said. He could feel the despair swirling within him, coming out as reckless words. 'Tell me what I am, because right now you're looking at me like I'm a fucking burden.'

Still she said nothing, but Jonah thought he could read it now. She wanted to reassure him, wanted to please him. But none of it would be true, so she was silent.

He made it easier for her. 'Go,' he said. 'Just go.'

Annabel got her case and walked to the door in silence. She opened it, stepped through, and was about to shut it behind her when Jonah spoke.

'I love you,' he said.

She paused, just long enough for him to be sure she was about to say something, say *anything*. Bring it to an end, he thought, or let him know she felt something in return.

Anything would be better than nothing, surely.

'I'm sorry,' she said.

Then Annabel Harker closed the door.

10

Annabel walked for ten minutes before she called a cab, pulling her rumbling luggage behind her. She was muttering to herself, swearing under her breath loud enough for people she passed to give her a crazy-person look and a wide berth.

The journey back to her apartment in San Diego went pretty much the same way, a constant urge to yell at herself for handling things so badly. By the time she got in a taxi outside San Diego International she'd stopped muttering, but the same thoughts were going round and round in her head.

She'd gone to Jonah's because when she'd heard his message about quitting his job, that had been her first and only instinct. Drop everything and go. Maybe that said it all, but it was also the real problem. Commitment had crept up on her, and commitment wasn't something she did.

Her father Daniel had died twenty months ago, but she knew a truth she found hard to acknowledge: part of him had been dead long before that. Annabel was sixteen when her mother died, and Daniel Harker had been destroyed by her death. He'd breathed, he'd eaten; rarely, he'd even smiled. But it always felt like a show he put on for the sake of his only child. Annabel knew that if it hadn't been for her, he would have ended his own life as soon as he'd been able to.

That was what her parents had taught her of love: it was a wonderful thing, but had a terrible price. The stronger it was, the more dangerous it became. It was a vulnerability she'd been terrified of since her first crush. Now that the real thing had found her, she was horribly aware of it.

In short, Annabel Harker had allowed herself to fall in love. She'd been regretting it ever since.

She'd run with it to begin with. The trauma of the fire at Reese-Farthing Medical, the shock of Jonah's near-fatal shooting, then his long, slow recovery. She felt comfortable around Jonah in a way she hadn't experienced before, and found herself missing him after ever-shorter times apart. She had hidden her fears deep down. She had dared to be happy.

The doubts had returned suddenly one night. In bed, they were kissing; she'd moved to get on top of him and he'd winced, pain growing on his face, hand on the still-angry scars on his chest. The horror must have been clear on her face. Jonah smiled, raised a hand to calm her. After a few seconds he managed to speak.

'Just a muscle spasm,' he said. 'I get them from time to time. It'll pass.'

He looked so grey.

They walked along the beach later that night, and she could see the bliss in Jonah's face that she too had felt earlier that day, but now she understood that the thing she'd always dreaded had found her: Love, and all that came with it. It terrified her.

Since then she'd spent relatively little time in her home in Virginia, focusing instead on her investigation. She knew that this left Jonah confused but she didn't know what else to do. It was the only cure she knew: physical distance, keeping herself busy. Falling for him had been a mistake; unpicking that mistake would hurt both of them, but it was unavoidable. As her dad had always told her, it was better to pull a Band-Aid off quickly. Less painful that way.

'Fucking hell,' said Annabel aloud.

The taxi driver looked up. 'Excuse me?'

'Nothing,' said Annabel.

*

Her apartment was small and sparse. She paid everything in cash and had rented it under a false name – Jonah's repeated reminders for her to be careful were unnecessary, as she always *was* careful. She had another similar place in Sacramento, the benefit of independent means. Since she'd started to spend more and more time in these West Coast boltholes she'd been tempted to make them a little more homely, but part of her wanted to keep things Spartan. She felt she didn't deserve comforts.

She dumped her bag by the couch and checked her watch. She wouldn't have to leave for her meeting for another forty minutes and she wanted to use that time to get her head into the right place.

In the corner of the room was a whiteboard. She rubbed the board clean whenever she was gone from her apartment for any significant time, but while she was there she used it to get her thoughts in order, trying out new ways to link the things she knew. She stepped over to it and picked up the pen, wanting to get her focus back, and to push Jonah out of her mind.

She began by writing the word *Unity* in the top middle of the board. Unity was the group that Michael Andreas, the wealthy biotech entrepreneur, had formed after a research team working on possible military uses of revival stumbled into contact with something they believed was not human. The military had assumed the research was nonsense and abandoned it, but Andreas and his team had continued. These entities were benign, they thought; lost in some unimaginable void that revival had given access to. They termed these beings *Elders*; ancient and alien, wise beyond measure, yet trapped in the darkness for countless millennia and stripped of everything they knew, even how they had been lost in the void in the first place.

The members of Unity believed these Elders could give humankind invaluable knowledge, if only they could be taken from the void and allowed to recover from their ordeal. To do this, they sought a way to join with them – with thirteen volunteers acting as hosts for the thirteen Elders. Not a kind of possession, they claimed, but a true physical unity, hence the name they had chosen for their group. One by one, they'd undergone a process of their own devising; one by one, the Elders had been plucked from darkness, still ignorant of their own pasts.

Unity had been the beginning of it all.

Next, Annabel wrote *Afterlifer*, and below that, *Extremists*: the small group of Afterlifers who had learned of Andreas's plan and believed he was seeking to incarnate some kind of demonic force. They had set out to stop it at all costs, and had caused the inferno that had destroyed the Reese-Farthing building where the Unity group had gathered.

She drew a single letter D and added lines joining it to both *Unity* and *Extremists*. The 'D' stood for *Daniel*; it also stood for *Dad*. Her father, kidnapped and left to die, all because they feared he knew what they were doing and planned to expose them. They had been wrong; Daniel Harker had known almost nothing about it.

She stood for a moment and looked at the solitary letter. It represented so much loss. Also, her father's death was how she had got involved with this whole situation; it was how she had met Jonah.

On the left of the board, she wrote the name *Kendrick*. He was the military intelligence representative in the original research that had caught Andreas's eye. Kendrick had been observing the Reese-Farthing building on the night of the fire; one of his men had been responsible for shooting Jonah. What Kendrick's game was, Annabel didn't know, but she didn't believe the man or his employers had simply lost interest. She'd assured Jonah she wouldn't go digging around in that minefield, but perhaps the time was coming when she would have to.

Next, she wrote *Tess*. Tess Neil, the only Unity volunteer who had survived the fire, and an old friend of Jonah's from his days as a young reviver working in Baseline. Annabel knew all about the crush the teenage Jonah had had on Tess, six years older than him. She'd reappeared in his life for a one-night stand before vanishing again, just before all the trouble started. Finding her at the heart of Andreas's group had been a shock; it had been while Jonah helped her escape from Kendrick's men on the night of the fire that he'd been shot. The bullet intended to wound her had almost killed him.

Locating Tess had always been Annabel's main goal, although she'd not mentioned this to Jonah. Or to Never, come to that, as Never seemed to gets his hackles up whenever he heard the name mentioned. But Tess was crucial. She had been close to Michael Andreas, and would be able to tell Annabel much of what she wanted to know. More than that, she was the only survivor who carried within her one of the Elders. If she recovered those memories, she would know the full story of the dark creature that had come so close to destroying everything.

And that brought her to the last of the key players: *Andreas*, she wrote in large letters at the bottom of the board. His faith in the benevolence of the Elders had been unshakeable, and he had been dismissive about the fears of the Afterlifer extremists. In the end, though, they had both been right. For although the Elders were benign, they had forgotten their purpose: they were jailers, their very souls used in the construction of a prison to trap an ancient evil, a creature that went by many names. It called itself the Great Shadow, but whatever name it used, it fit any reasonable definition of Satan.

And as each Elder left the void, they unwittingly abandoned their position. Once all were gone, the creature they'd imprisoned was free. It had taken Michael Andreas's body for its own. The real Andreas and the newly freed Elder were both trapped within, as the creature rejoiced and planned the annihilation of every life on Earth; a plan brought to an end when Andreas was consumed by the inferno that the Afterlifers had started.

Annabel stepped back and looked at what she'd drawn. She

circled three of the words in red: Tess, Andreas and Kendrick, the areas she felt still had the most promise. She drew more connecting lines, writing notes and speculations beside the links.

After ten more minutes, the board was a thick tangle of fact and guesswork: a jungle that looked much the same as it usually did. There were only so many ways to rearrange the same things, but she was always hopeful that the jungle would spawn something new. A tiger to leap out at her.

She wrote the word *funding* and linked it to *Afterlifers*, then added a tentative line to Kendrick, who she suspected had known about the Afterlifer extremists well before the fire. Perhaps that had extended to funding them, but surely it had nothing to do with the mystery source of income the mainstream Afterlifers now had.

She studied the board, adding a few more notes here and there, but as she did, part of her mind crept back to her disastrous goodbye to Jonah. Before she knew it, she'd added his name to the jungle in front of her. Worse: she'd placed it next to Tess.

She set down the pen and rubbed the board clean again.

*

Annabel's meeting had been arranged in Carlsbad, an hour's drive up the coast. She took her own car and parked outside the coffee shop where her only contact instruction had been to look for a goth called Takeo. She sat and waited, tempted by the smell of coffee but wanting to stay in her car until the guy showed up.

At 6 p.m., Takeo appeared. He looked young, early twenties, comparatively understated but unmistakeable. Black jeans, long black top and black lipstick; a mean set of piercings in his right eyebrow, but that was it. He was looking around warily, so she got out of her car and approached.

'You're Takeo?' she asked, holding out her hand. They shook. 'I'm Penny.' Penny was the alias she'd been using when she'd made an online approach to someone claiming to be able to get sensitive industrial information to order, someone who just went by the handle *kt44*.

Takeo smiled. 'Good to meet you. Come with me.' He turned and walked past the entrance to the coffee shop, Annabel following with a vague disappointment that they weren't going inside.

Takeo walked ahead, looking around uneasily. Two streets along he went inside a small bar and led her to a table where a petite young black woman sat, about the same age as Takeo, wearing blue jeans and a simple white top; she gave Annabel a smile.

'OK, here we are,' said Takeo. 'Can I get you a drink?'

'Cola, I guess,' said Annabel, and Takeo headed off to fetch it.

'I'm Kaylee,' said the woman, offering her hand. 'I'm the one you were talking to online. Takeo's a friend. He's always worried the people I meet with might turn out to be some kind of lunatic. His heart's in the right place, though.'

'So how does this work, Kaylee?' said Annabel. 'Your message said you had something for me. It mentioned the fee but it was short on details. What did you find out that you think I'd be interested in?'

'You wanted information on Andreas Biotech investments,' said Kaylee. 'Specifically revival, but instead I've got something else the company is spending money on. Something you might not have known about.' She smiled. 'Cryogenics.'

Annabel couldn't help but raise an eyebrow. Michael Andreas had been interested in cryogenic techniques years before revival first appeared, part of a long-standing fascination with death. Once revival came on the scene, though, the cryogenics subsidiaries had done little but tick over, and she'd not heard anything to the contrary.

Takeo returned with Annabel's Coke and put a beer in front of Kaylee, who smiled at him. 'Takeo here has known me since we were thirteen. He's well trained.'

Takeo gave Annabel a grin. 'She makes me sound so useful,' he said.

Annabel looked at Kaylee. 'Cryogenics. You're sure?'

'Yes,' said Kaylee, visibly pleased that Annabel sounded so intrigued.

'And where does this information come from?'

Kaylee took a drink of her beer. 'No specifics, but a guy I know, he . . . does some stuff, you know? Hacks around.'

'You asked him to look into Andreas Biotech?'

She laughed. 'He doesn't do this shit for free. He has clients. But he lets me know what he's been doing, and I keep my ear to the ground in case somebody else might want it too. My friend's always happy to sell the same thing twice, if I can find buyers. Then I get a little commission.'

'So somebody else was investigating Andreas Biotech, and paid your friend?'

Kaylee nodded. 'There are a few competitors around in cryogenics, they caught wind of Andreas Biotech moving back into the field and wanted whatever my friend could get. Then you wanted information on Andreas Biotech's revival investments, so—'

'OK, what do you have?'

'This.' Kaylee delved into a bag beside her and pulled out a large envelope, fat with paper. She waved it, then put it away again. 'You pay, you can see.'

'How do I know it's worth it?'

'Come on, *Penny*,' said Kaylee. 'You want it or not?'

Annabel didn't like the way Kaylee had emphasized her alias, but hell. It wouldn't surprise her if 'Kaylee' wasn't really *her* name, either. 'What's in it? I'm not handing you a cent unless I have some idea why I should give a damn.'

Kaylee shrugged. 'Fine. I'll give you the summary, you decide if you want the evidence.'

Annabel nodded.

'Andreas Biotech have a facility in Nevada,' said Kaylee, 'place called Winnerden Flats, out in the middle of nowhere, staff living on site. Andreas wanted it to become his flagship cryogenic storage location, something he could present as self-contained and remote. A bunker, kinda. The market didn't grow the way he'd expected, then revival came along and he got distracted. The Winnerden Flats site made a sizable loss each year but Andreas kept it going. It was a reputation thing, apparently – he made a big deal of trust. He had a very expensive way of running his cryo places, and wouldn't cut corners the way everyone else did, so his competitors weren't worried about him expanding.'

Annabel nodded. 'And then Andreas died.'

'Precisely. Someone in the company presumably decided they could cut corners, be competitive, and grow the business.' Kaylee pulled a sheet of paper from the envelope and laid it down on the table: a site plan. 'This was phase one of the rebuild. The old facility has been massively extended. Their competitors think they're going to try and corner the market.' Annabel reached out to take the paper, but Kaylee snatched it away and put it into the envelope. 'You want?'

Annabel pretended to give it some thought before nodding. 'It wasn't quite what I was looking for, but I'll take it.' She wasn't going to say so aloud, but there was a chance that Andreas Bio-tech's supposed revival investment was merely creative accounting to cover this cryogenic push. When she'd told Jonah about the revival funding, she'd underplayed her own fears that the company was up to something new – something related to the creature Michael Andreas had mistakenly summoned. It was oddly reassuring that her fears might simply come back to good old-fashioned greed: that the board wanted cryogenics to turn a profit, in a way that Michael Andreas had always blocked.

She took a roll of cash out and offered it to Kaylee. Takeo snatched it and peeled off the rubber band, then riffled through.

'Are we good?' said Kaylee.

Takeo nodded. 'We're good.'

Kaylee handed the document envelope to Annabel. The weight of it was encouraging. 'That's all at the moment,' said Kaylee. 'But there might be more coming. We'll contact you if there is.' She and Takeo stood.

Annabel stayed seated, looking up at them. 'Any chance you could arrange for me to meet your friend face to face?'

Kaylee and Takeo looked at each other, then Kaylee smiled. 'Not a chance, *Penny*. Not a chance.'

The pair walked out, leaving Annabel smarting. Part of her wondered if Kaylee and Takeo knew *exactly* who she was. She could almost hear Jonah's voice, chastising her. *Being cautious, huh?*

'Shut up, Jonah,' she said. 'Shut up.'

11

Eleven days later, Never was making the ninety-minute drive to a case in Roanoke Rapids. Stacy Oakdale, one of the top three revivers in the office, was in the passenger seat.

The deceased was a drowned man, pulled from the lake early that morning after a lakeside fisherman spotted the body floating on the surface. An initial examination suggested he'd been dead for four or five days, and had probably been submerged for most of that time. The large stones in his pockets and a significant wound on the back of his head were more than enough justification for revival.

As Never drove, he wondered how Jonah was, but he tried to put his worries to the back of his mind. He was rationing himself to a single call a day to check up on his friend.

Jonah had told him the unpleasant details of Annabel's visit the day after it had happened, but since then the topic had been avoided by both of them. The last time Never had seen Jonah was two nights earlier. Jonah had been far more upbeat than Never had expected, keen to hear about the daily happenings at the FRS. Jonah wanted it almost case-by-case, albeit necessarily vague. After all, Jonah was no longer an FRS employee, so confidentiality rules applied. Even so, Never found it hard to self-censor while talking to him. It just didn't feel right.

Part of Jonah's upbeat mood was down to the fact that his resignation had indeed taken the wind from the sails of the Afterlifers.

Even though they had not pursued Jonah for his supposed assault, they had still been trying to stoke a public furore about the David Leith case. With the FRS looking like it had taken decisive action, that furore wasn't materializing.

The irony, Never thought: Robert Thorne, a man Never had always pegged as someone who would cut people free the moment they became a liability, had shown no intention of sacrificing his staff to the gods of public opinion. Yet the sacrifice was exactly what had been required. Part of him wondered if Thorne was less brutal than he'd assumed, or if the man had instinctively known that Jonah would offer to fall on that particular sword. The thought made him shiver.

As for the situation with Annabel, Never was almost tempted to call her and find out what the hell was going on. Jonah had left him with a stern warning not to get involved, though, so it was out of the question. When it came to Jonah's love-life Never had always been over-protective, but the way Annabel and Jonah had acted around each other in the early months had made even the cynical side of Never smile. Success in relationships had evaded Never for so long that he didn't tend to get optimistic about those of others, but he'd actually started to think they had a good chance of making a go of things, as good a chance as anyone he knew.

That was what made it all so galling, now that it looked like it was going belly up.

Fuck it, he thought, and concentrated on the road.

When they arrived at the crime scene, two forensic tents had been set up close to the shore of the lake. One contained the corpse and would be where the revival took place. The other, a few metres away, was for him, his monitoring equipment and the police representatives.

'You OK?' he said to Stacy as they got out. She'd been quiet for the whole drive from Richmond, but he'd left her to it. Different revivers coped with the build-up to a case in their own ways. Some became talkative and a little hyper, but Stacy tended to be more on the silent-anxiety side.

'Yeah,' she said. 'I'm fine.'

He gave her a smile and returned a wave from the detectives at the scene.

It took five minutes to talk through the case, then Stacy and Never put on their forensic coveralls. It was going to be a non-vocal revival, given the waterlogged lungs and swollen vocal chords. The cops had been a little deflated by the news – in a non-vocal case the corpse remained silent to all but the reviver, and the resulting footage lost that compelling immediacy that played so well with juries. It also made the reviver's court appearance more likely as their own interpretation of the exchanges made an easier target for a defence challenge.

Before she could proceed Stacy had to drain as much fluid from the lungs as possible. Even with a non-vocal procedure, movement of the torso was expected and spasms were a possibility; fluid present would leak from the mouth. At the very least this was an unpleasant distraction mid-revival, but more crucially an analysis of the fluid in the lungs could prove useful for the coroner. Hence, the pre-revival prep involved pulmonary suction to drain the fluid; beside Stacy, the water-thinned clotted froth poured into a storage container.

As the container filled with the dark, rank liquid, Never looked on with revulsion. 'That is disgusting,' he said.

Stacy smiled, flicking off the suction and pulling the hose out of the dead man's mouth. She swore as some liquid spilled from the hose over her gloved hands, getting under the cuff of her protective suit. 'That's gone through to my shirt sleeve,' she said, grimacing. 'I can feel it.'

When she was finished preparing the corpse Stacy took her medication while Never got on with setting up the cameras. Ten minutes later Stacy glumly entered the tent and sat cross-legged on a simple mat by the corpse, Never watching her on his monitor, already recording. His equipment was set out on two small folding tables and he was sitting in a camping chair. There was a spare seat for the detectives, but neither of them had chosen to sit. Their loss.

'I'm ready when you are,' said Stacy to camera.

'OK,' said Never. He turned to the detectives watching. 'OK by you?' He got the nod. 'We're on, Stacy.'

Stacy took the corpse's right hand with her left; in her other hand, she held one of the portable stenography machines most revivers favoured for non-vocal cases. 'Revival of Devin Turner,' she said. 'Stacy Oakdale duty reviver.'

They waited in silence.

The younger of the two detectives was fidgeting within the first three minutes, the rustle of clothing enough to irritate Never to the point of a well-timed glare. 'This may take a while, Detective,' he said, once he'd made sure the audio feed from them to Stacy wasn't active. 'This your first time?'

A nervous nod.

'Take a seat,' said Never, and the detective did. The older detective, a woman Never hadn't worked with before, didn't even look away from the monitor. She was focused and patient.

After almost half an hour he could see that Stacy was making progress. As revival grew close he noted some of the tell-tale vibrational motion that was often observable in the corpse as success approached. It was usually eyelids, jaw, cheek; simple twitching, rapid pulses of movement. He glimpsed the young detective beside him, the man's face getting paler and paler as the movement became obvious even to the untrained eye.

'Is that . . . is that *normal*?' said the detective.

'Pretty common,' said Never.

Stacy looked at the camera. 'He's here,' she said, and Never turned to the young detective in time to see his eyes roll back in a dead faint.

The questioning proved straightforward enough, a few leads

and no drama. The senior detective was happy with the result, although the first-timer looked like he'd prefer a hole to open up in the ground and swallow him.

After the drive back to Richmond, Stacy looked shattered. 'I'm heading off early,' she told him. 'I'll do my paperwork tomorrow. I want to get home and change.' She held up the stained shirt-sleeve.

'Yeah, you'll want to get that washed as soon as you can. Not sure if anyone does stain removers specifically for corpse effluent.'

'White wine will do the trick,' said Stacy. 'Believe me.'

He furrowed his brow. 'Isn't that just for red wine stains?'

She levelled her gaze at him. 'I mean to *drink*. So if anyone's heading out later, let me know, OK? You should ask Jonah. It'd be good to catch up.'

'I'll try,' said Never. 'He's nursing his wounds. He'll probably still be doing that in six months' time.'

'Well, if he's working privately in six months, he'll be earning twice what we earn.'

'Twice what *you* earn, Rockefeller,' said Never. 'We lowly techs can barely scrape by.' He grinned. Stacy flipped him an amiable finger as she left.

He grabbed lunch at his desk and got through what little paperwork there was, eager to be left clear for the afternoon. Having been on one call today he was at the bottom of the call list, and it would give him some time to try out some new cameras they were considering upgrading to. A few on-sites this winter had been marred by occasional image glitching, and condensation problems when the cameras got back to the office. Hopefully, the ones he was trialling would have better tolerance of large shifts in temperature.

As he broke one of the cameras from its packaging, his phone rang.

'Hi, Never. Been a while.'

It took him a moment to place the voice. Then he had it:

Detective Bob Crenner, the Washington DC cop who'd handled the investigation into the murder of Annabel's father, Daniel Harker.

'Bob! Good to hear from you. How's tricks?'

'Word got to me about Jonah leaving. I wanted to see how he's doing. Ray sends his regards, by the way.' He was referring to Detective Ray Johnson, his partner. 'So is it true that Jonah's left the FRS?'

'It's true. Jonah's a little shaken, but he'll be OK.'

'Look, Never,' he said. 'Is Jonah available to do any private work?'

'You need a private reviver?' said Never, suddenly wary. The last time he'd heard from Bob Crenner was a few months after the fire in Reese-Farthing, and that had been by email. Phoning him out of the blue like this wasn't just a courtesy call . . . the detective clearly wanted something he felt awkward asking for. There was enough of a silence on the line to confirm it. It occurred to him that maybe there'd been a family loss. He knew Bob had a wife, and also a son in his early twenties. It didn't seem like the man's style, but sometimes people just asked. 'Bob, are you OK? Has something . . . happened?'

'This is a little delicate,' said Bob. 'The thing is, yes, I'm looking for a private reviver, but it's not for anything personal. Jonah's a licensed reviver still, right? I mean, does he need to be working for a company to do a private case, or can he just take on any job he chooses?' Bob paused and took a long breath. 'Me and Ray will be in Richmond tomorrow, on police business. Any chance we could meet up? We have a favour to ask Jonah, a *big* favour. But I think we'll need to explain in person.'

*

'And you have no idea what this is about?' asked Jonah.

It was lunchtime the next day, Never having met with Jonah around the corner from the cafe where they'd arranged to meet the detectives. 'I just know they want a reviver,' Never said, shrugging.

'Bob approached me first to see if it was even possible, and to make sure you'd not be offended.' A thought struck him and he smiled. 'It's like I'm your pimp.'

Bob Crenner and Ray Johnson were already there when they entered; in a secluded corner, burger and fries in front of Bob, a salad in front of Ray. 'What'll it be, gentlemen?' asked Bob. 'Lunch is on me.'

They both went for the burger option. Bob caught the eye of the waitress and ordered himself a triple espresso as well. 'I live on coffee,' said Bob. 'Keeps me going. Three years back, my wife started to worry I was drinking too much caffeine so she got decaf for home. Didn't tell me. I spent a week falling asleep in the office every morning before she confessed.'

Jonah turned to Ray Johnson. It was a year and a half since Jonah had first met him, on what had only been Ray's second revival as a detective. 'Good to see you, Ray,' said Jonah. 'So how many revivals have you attended now?'

'Not that many. I'd say maybe an even dozen.'

'Eighteen,' said Bob, with a certainty that put a wry smile on Ray's face.

'Eighteen,' said Ray. 'Time flies, huh? How about you?'

Jonah smiled. 'I don't keep count.' Even so, he wondered how many it had been. Daniel Harker had been his last official revival before the Reese-Farthing fire, when his injuries had put him out of action for four months. He guessed at forty or so revivals since then. If he'd still been going at the rate he'd averaged before Reese-Farthing, it would have been well over a hundred by now.

Bob looked at him. 'So how's your health?' Both Bob and Ray had sent messages of support to Jonah while he was in hospital.

'As good as it could be, I think. Still hurts sometimes.'

'I hear getting shot does that,' said Bob. 'I don't ever intend to find out myself.'

'Anybody ever shot *at* you, Bob?' said Never. 'Ray, maybe?'

Ray laughed. 'I've been tempted.'

They caught up a little and swapped tales, Never grossing Bob out with Stacy's lung effluent experience from the previous day. When they finally got to the story of David Leith's revival, the mood darkened.

'Yes,' said Bob. 'It's not just you that's been having trouble with the Afterlifers.' He avoided eye contact and shifted his position in his seat. 'I'm sorry. I've been stalling. You know how it is. I feel bad putting you in this position, but I have to ask. And don't think you have to say yes. I'll understand.'

Here it comes, thought Jonah. Because whatever Bob wanted from him, it surely boiled down to a very simple question.

Jonah caught Never's eye, then asked it: 'Who, Bob?' he said. 'Who do you want me to revive?'

12

'Two weeks ago,' said Bob, 'the body of a woman called Mary Connart was discovered in an alley in the north east of DC. Me and Ray were on the scene within fifteen minutes. Her injuries were . . .' He shared a look with Ray, who shook his head grimly. 'Unusual. We requested a revival, but we had some trouble. The same trouble you had with the teenage boy.'

'Afterlifers?' said Jonah.

Bob nodded. 'Mary's only living relative gave us revival permission, so we didn't seek a warrant. Just as we were gearing up for the revival, we were stopped.'

'The Afterlifers must have ears everywhere,' said Ray. 'Turned out, Mary's name was in their membership database. They went to a sympathetic judge and came back with a denial.'

'Hold on,' said Never. 'Revival is pretty much automatic for murder. Why did the judge grant the denial?'

'It's complicated,' said Bob. He shared another look with Ray and sighed. 'The whole damn thing is complicated. Maybe you should see the victim before we get into the details.' Bob rubbed his eyes and took out his phone. He looked around to make sure they had privacy, then held it so that Jonah and Never could see. The first few pictures were of a young woman, some of her on her own, some with friends. Always of her smiling. 'That's Mary Connart. Twenty-seven years old. Born in Green Bay, Wisconsin. Father left when she was three and her sister was nine. He died five years later in Florida. Their mother died three years ago. Her sister is her only living relative. Mary worked for a PR company in DC. On the night of her death she'd attended a party thrown by her employer for clients. She left early, saying she was tired, wanted some fresh air. Forty-eight minutes after she walked into the night she was found dead.' Bob paused and gave Jonah and Never a long, sober look. 'Before I go on, I have to warn you. I've been a detective for twenty-two years. This . . . this is one of the worst things I've ever laid eyes on.' He waited until he had a nod of assent from each of them, then swiped through to the next image.

Jonah and Never stared at it.

'As you can see, Mary's left arm is gone,' said Bob. 'Abrasive wounds penetrated four inches into the shoulder. Likewise, deep wounds to the back of the head and left side of the face, removing flesh and bone. A large portion of that side of the face is missing. Most of the left part of the jaw is intact but exposed.'

'Jesus,' said Never. 'What the hell did that? An industrial accident?'

'We don't know how the injuries were caused,' said Ray. 'But we don't believe this was any kind of accident.'

Jonah shook his head. 'You said she was found forty-eight minutes after leaving the party. How the hell does that give someone time to . . . do this?'

'Next image,' said Bob. He advanced the picture. Jonah winced, as Bob continued his commentary. 'The injuries higher on the face reach the lateral wall of the orbit, the, ah, the eye socket. A third of the socket gone. The eyeball is damaged, but it just adds to the confusion. Any industrial injury, dragging injury, any kind of mechanical abrasion, would almost certainly have devastated the eyeball. Instead the injury seems to follow the same line as on the bone. For the soft tissue that just doesn't make sense. The eye tissue along the wound is almost cauterized, creating that apparent shrinkage. Cauterization is a feature common to all these wounds, yet the flesh itself doesn't seem to be heat damaged and there's no sign of chemical burns. Cause of death is thought to have been blood loss. When she was found there was very little blood at the scene, but two thirds of her blood volume was gone.'

'Christ,' said Never. 'What the hell happened to her?'

'Getting back to the question you asked first,' said Bob, 'yes, revival is damn near automatic for murder, but we can't even demonstrate that this *was* murder. The initial coroner's report was clutching at straws. It speculated the injuries were road drag, that maybe she fell under a truck and was pulled along unnoticed.'

'What?' said Never, dismissive. 'Then the truck drove up the alley and she was left behind?'

Bob frowned. 'Like I said, clutching at straws. Road drag just doesn't do that. You get an uneven result, flesh stripped raggedly, irregular wear on the bone. There was no CCTV covering the alley, though. We just don't know what happened down there. There was one witness, the man who found the body, and his statement – let's just say it didn't clarify things for the judge.'

'The upshot of all this,' said Ray, 'is that the coroner wouldn't classify Mary's death as homicide. It was put down as "unexplained". Wouldn't even rule out accidental and go to "suspicious". The Afterlifers considered this as an unnecessary revival of one of their own, and they saw a chance to make legal precedent.'

Jonah shook his head. 'Surely there's a clear public interest here? That should take priority, so you have good grounds to appeal the decision.'

'We did appeal,' said Bob. He took out a piece of paper and handed it to Jonah. 'Here's the judgement. It didn't go our way. The decision was considered borderline. A judge needs a damn good reason to overrule a fellow judge.'

Jonah scanned the judgement and looked up. 'The ruling of accidental death and the victim's Afterlifer membership were the two primary reasons given by the judge, but he also said he wasn't willing to put the victim through the trauma of a revival given the severity of the injuries. That traditional investigative methods should be sufficient to explain her death.' Mary Connart's horrific wounds were still visible on Bob's phone. 'Maybe the judge had a point,' said Jonah. Everyone turned to look at him, surprised. He could understand. Even he was surprised to hear it from his own lips; surprised to feel distaste at the thought of forcing a revival subject to confront the terror that had led to their death, considering how many times he'd done exactly that.

'Come on, Jonah,' said Ray. 'Imagine if she'd somehow survived. Do you really think we'd even *consider* not getting her side of things, just because it might distress her? The question wouldn't be whether we talk to her or not. The question would be how we go about it. We'd do it with people who are trained for that. People who could help her through the process. People like you.'

Jonah said nothing at first, and the silence was an uneasy one. 'Tell me why I'm here.'

'My apologies, Jonah,' said Bob. 'I know I'm taking the long route, but I just want you to know how we got to this position. You see, if we challenge again it'll go to the Court of Appeal, then maybe to the Supreme Court. We might not get a final decision for six weeks. What do you honestly think the chances of a successful revival would be?'

Jonah thought for a moment. 'Injuries that extensive? If you did it now, you'd be very lucky to get thirty per cent. Every additional week the chances will drop by a third or more. In another six weeks . . . even being generous, it'd be one per cent or less.' An ominously low figure, for a specific reason: 'That's below the FRS threshold.'

'See?' said Bob. 'The Supreme Court probably wouldn't overturn the decision because even if they did, FRS guidelines would force it to decline the revival.'

'So there's no point challenging,' said Ray. 'And the Afterlifers know it. They've won.'

Jonah frowned, confused. 'I don't understand. Are you asking me to be ready, just in case the court overturns the decision? You want me to attempt it if the FRS declines?'

Bob gave a sly smile and shook his head. 'We'd run out of options, Jonah, but when I heard you'd left the FRS, I realized we have one last throw of the dice. You see, all of this legal argument is related to the new laws the Afterlifers pushed through, and those are explicitly directed at forensic revival. Private revival is covered under separate legislation, which wasn't changed.'

'Yeah,' Never nodded. 'It was part of the deal between the insurance people and the Afterlifers: don't touch our stuff and we won't fight you.'

'So . . .' said Ray. He paused, looking like he was waiting for the penny to drop. It didn't happen. 'Guys, private revivals only need a relative's permission. The denial that was issued just covers a forensic revival. It doesn't prevent a private one from taking place.'

'Think about it,' said Bob. 'The moment we accept defeat and withdraw the request for a forensic revival, the autopsy can go ahead within twenty-four hours. And as the only close relative, the sister has the right to have the body released for a private revival in advance of an autopsy, at the discretion of the senior investigating officer.' He raised his coffee. 'That'd be me.'

'Christ,' said Never. 'A private revival for a murder investigation.' He scowled. 'You should either be very proud or deeply ashamed of yourselves.'

'We're not proud,' said Ray. 'It's unfair to get you here and ask you like this, Jonah, but that's how desperate we are.'

Jonah shook his head again. 'I'm not going to do a private revival on an Afterlifer, Bob. I want to keep my head down.' And not run roughshod over the victim's wishes, he thought, certain now that he'd been suppressing that kind of concern for far longer than he was willing to admit.

'I understand,' said Bob, 'but it's not as simple as that. Mary's sister said they both joined the Afterlifers as teenagers, over a decade ago. They only paid for one year and didn't even update their addresses, but the Afterlifers keep you on the system unless you explicitly request to be removed. Calling her an Afterlifer is stretching the truth somewhat. If they'd not gone to a sympathetic judge, we would already have had our revival.'

Jonah was still uneasy. 'But is there any reason to think she changed her mind?'

'Yes,' said Ray. 'The sister took out revival insurance for herself a few years ago and said that Mary had expressed interest, but that wasn't enough for the judge. Turns out the sisters weren't *that* close, so he didn't put too much stock by it. Also, none of the victim's friends thought she was an Afterlifer supporter, and a few were adamant that she wasn't. But again, it's not hard evidence.'

Jonah said nothing.

'Please, Jonah,' said Bob. 'Trust me. You're the only person I can ask for this. We don't have the money to hire someone, and the victim wasn't insured. Even then, I doubt any private reviver would have the guts to take it on. But this is our only chance to hear what she has to say. You understand what that means. You can talk to her, you can help her through it. I believe she was murdered, but the investigation has stalled. You're the only one who can make sure that what was done to her doesn't go unanswered. Promise me you'll think about it.'

'Look at her, Bob,' said Jonah, pointing to the image of her injuries. 'Look at what she went through.'

Bob nodded. 'I know. But too much about this case doesn't make sense, Jonah. The guy who found the body said things that gave me the creeps, and I'm convinced this was murder. It'll happen again unless we stop it. I'm certain of that.'

'The coroner called it *accidental*,' said Jonah. 'Why are you so sure it was murder?'

Bob looked him in the eye. 'Because I don't think Mary was the first.'

13

'The day after Mary's body was found I spoke to a friend,' said Bob. 'A homicide detective in Denver. I told her the nature of the injuries Mary had, just to see if she'd ever come across anything similar. Turned out she'd heard of one locally, a young woman in an apparent suicide. Fell from a highway overpass around three a.m. and was run over by a truck. The only CCTV was too far away to record why she fell. The fall and the vehicle meant that she'd died immediately, but she had injuries to her hands they couldn't quite explain. Flesh stripped from the palm, bones damaged. She was missing several fingertips on both hands. Those injuries weren't made with a blade. They were described as abrasive wounds. Not cut, not sawn. Like she'd grasped a coarse sanding belt. They were also described as cauterized, just like Mary's wounds.'

'Nothing else implied foul play,' said Ray. 'At first the injuries were put down to road drag, even though the vehicle that hit her stopped immediately.'

'This was thirteen weeks ago,' said Bob. 'Three weeks after that, the body of another young woman was found in a park in Minneapolis. Strangled. This time the fingertips of the right hand were gone, but the whole left hand was missing. Again, no CCTV, but a definite homicide this time. The damage to the hands was put down to an abandoned attempt to hide the identity of the victim, but again the injuries resembled severe abrasive wounds.

Again, they seemed cauterized. They arrested an ex-boyfriend, but the case against him is weak.'

'Were there revival attempts?' asked Never.

'Not with the apparent suicide,' said Bob. 'The fact that the wounds to the hands were inconsistent with the vehicle having stopped quickly was only noted after the autopsy, so it was too late for revival. With the strangling, there was an attempt at revival but no success. It was considered a fifty per cent chance, so they were unlucky.'

'Have you told those involved about your suspicions?' asked Never.

Bob shook his head. 'It'd be dismissed out of hand. There's nothing else to link them. This is pure gut, but I *know* it's connected to Mary somehow. Please, Jonah. I need your help.'

Jonah looked at Bob. He was about to turn him down when the detective spoke again. 'Look, you know I mentioned the man who found the body?'

'You mentioned he'd given you the creeps,' said Jonah.

'I think you should hear what he told me. Directly from him.'

'Can't you just tell me now?'

Bob shook his head. 'I can see it in your eyes, Jonah. You're on the verge of saying no. We're heading back to DC. Come with us and hear the guy out. If you still don't want to do it, then I'll understand.'

'I'll think about it,' said Jonah. 'If I decide to come, I'll drive up there myself. That's all I can promise.'

'OK,' said Bob. He stood, and so did Ray. 'Third District Police Station. We'll be there all day.'

The detectives left, and Jonah turned to Never. 'Do you think they really had any police business in Richmond, or were they here just for me?'

'Oh, you *were* the police business, Jonah. Did you notice how vague they kept some things, just to pique your interest? *Wait till you hear what the eyewitness said* . . . Asking you to go to DC is an old trick, too. If you want people to do something big, get them to agree to smaller stuff first. In for a penny, you know? Uh, are you OK?'

Jonah was staring at the exit, only half paying attention. He turned to Never. 'What about what Mary wants? Bringing her back, asking her to go through it again. What will that cost her?'

'Justice always comes at a price,' said Never. 'You of all people should know that.'

*

Jonah sent Never home and got himself another coffee so that he could sit quietly and fret.

Bob Crenner had played things well, he thought. For a moment he wondered if the other cases Bob had mentioned could have been entirely invented, just to give him that extra push. *No*, he thought. There was a simple reason he wanted to think that way: the possibility of a killer out there, poised to do it again, left him with no real choice.

He didn't know if he was starting to agree with the Afterlifers about Mary's right to be left undisturbed, but even if he was, it was a right that had limits. Justice did carry costs, as Never had pointed out. The cost to Mary was far lower than the cost of there being another victim.

He finished his coffee and took the ten-minute walk home from the cafe. Marmite, as ever, pestered him for food and a fuss. Jonah did it quickly, wanting to set off for DC as soon as he could. He wouldn't call ahead to the detectives, though. In case he changed his mind on the way.

As he was about to leave, an email came through from Annabel.

I'm sorry, she'd written. *Things are busy and my head is a mess.*

That was it, as far as anything personal went. The rest was a summary of bits and pieces of information she'd gathered, a clear attempt to demonstrate that she was making some progress.

Encouragingly, her fears that Andreas Biotech was ramping up revival work seemed to have been misplaced, the money being spent instead on cryogenics. Attached to the email were scans of some documents she'd managed to get hold of relating to an Andreas Biotech site in Nevada.

Hearing from her at all was positive, he hoped. Still. It had been almost two weeks without a word, and all she could say was *Things are busy and my head is a mess.*

Join the club, thought Jonah.

*

The drive to Washington DC gave him plenty of time to think, but when he parked in the Third District lot he wasn't much closer to knowing how he felt.

Bob and Ray were pleased to see him, though. 'Can't tell you how much this means to me,' said Bob, rising from his seat as Jonah walked over. His desk was overloaded with junk, his monitor half hidden in Post-its; Ray was sitting behind the adjacent desk, which was pristine.

'OK, but don't get your hopes up,' said Jonah. 'I'm here to listen to your eyewitness, that's all.'

'I've already set up a meeting,' said Bob. 'Well, I know his delivery schedule for the rest of the day. Same thing. We can go now, if you like. You want to tag along, Ray?'

'You go ahead,' said Ray. 'I'm processing paperwork for some witnesses from the party.'

'OK. Jonah, follow me.' Bob grabbed a coat and led the way to his own car. Once they were both in, he checked his watch. 'The guy in question is called Eugene Harding,' he said. 'Forty-eight. Works at a food wholesaler's, delivers to restaurants and takeaways across the city. With luck he'll be at the wholesaler's now.' Bob started the engine and talked as he drove. 'Eugene found Mary's body. When I spoke to him, the first thing he said made my blood go cold, but he immediately retracted it. Said I'd misheard him, became a little evasive. We had two things to rule out: first, that Mary had been dragged by *his* vehicle and second, that he had potentially dumped the body and pretended to find it. Eugene's delivery truck was impounded for examination and nothing came up, and CCTV within the restaurant he was delivering to gave him a solid alibi. After completing the delivery he ate a meal there. He was inside for forty minutes.'

'What was it he said, Bob? What was it that gave you the creeps?'

Bob looked like he was considering it, but he shook his head. 'Let me try and get him to tell you. He's not exactly the brightest guy in the world, but he comes across as observant and honest. And very wary. In his version of events he heard a scream and went up the alley, where he found Mary's body.'

'He heard her scream?'

'Swears to it. And I guarantee there's something he wasn't telling us.'

*

'That's him.'

Jonah looked. Bob had parked up at the rear of a wholesale food warehouse in the east of the city. A battered pickup was parked by the open shutters, and a large man was hauling plastic sacks and putting them in the back of the vehicle.

Jonah looked at Eugene Harding. He seemed older than his years, overweight and wearing a constant expression of earnest effort. Bob got out of the car and Jonah followed.

'Afternoon, Eugene,' called Bob.

Eugene glanced up, his face sweaty in the cold air. His expression became instantly nervy the moment he laid eyes on Bob. 'Detective,' he replied, then went for another sack.

'What's that you have there?' asked Bob.

'Oh, deliveries. Rice. Stuff.' He put the sack in place and stood by the vehicle, wheezing a little, with his work-gloved hands on his hips. 'How can I help you?' He tried to smile. It made him look even less comfortable.

'I wanted to talk to you again about the night you found Mary Connart's body.'

'Oh,' said Eugene, sweating even more now.

'This man is a reviver,' said Bob, nodding to Jonah. Jonah saw Eugene's wary expression intensify the instant his eyes reached Jonah's face. The man was full-blown scared now. 'With luck, he'll be talking to Mary soon. He can ask her what happened.'

Eugene's eyes darted back and forth between Bob and Jonah. He said nothing.

'So,' said Bob, 'was there anything else you wanted to tell us? About what you saw?'

'I . . . I only saw what I told you I saw.'

'So tell us again. Make sure we got it right.'

'OK, OK.' Eugene looked down at the ground and took a moment before he started. 'Well, I'd been making a late delivery.'

'Wasn't it unusually late, Eugene? This was almost ten in the evening.'

'No. See, we close later some evenings, and I always get something at Chu's place when we do. Sometimes I drop stuff off for him on the way, if it saves the trip in the morning.'

'So you were getting some late dinner.'

'Sure.'

'You remember what?'

Eugene looked a little confused. 'Why? Look, we've been over all this.'

'Like I said, I just want to make sure we got it right. What'd you eat?'

'Yellow bean chicken, like always.'

'Then you were about to head home,' said Bob. 'Is the pickup yours?'

'No, but they let me use it sometimes. They were none too happy about losing it for a week.'

'Yeah, sorry about that, Eugene. We had to do that, just to rule it out.' Bob smiled. 'So you were parked at the rear of the restaurant.'

'Yes.'

'And you offloaded your goods, got your food, got back in. This was at ten-thirty. The pickup was facing out into the alley across the street.'

'Yes.' Eugene looked scared again.

'You notice the darkness? That the light in the alley had burned out?'

'Not until I heard the scream and turned my headlights on. And . . .' Eugene looked at the ground, kept his eyes there. 'Everything was dark.'

'Eugene, what aren't you telling me?' The man didn't look up. 'Eugene?'

'I told you everything.' Eugene's voice was shaky, eyes still on the ground.

'See,' Bob said to Jonah. 'When we spoke to Eugene before, this is how he was. He told us how he heard a scream, went to see what had happened, called for help. You were crying a little, Eugene. Remember? I thought you were scared because someone might think you were involved. But you're smarter than that. I guess I didn't really appreciate it then. I was happy to think you were just scared of getting the blame for something you didn't do. And you let me think it.'

Eugene Harding looked up, fear in his face, mixed with a little shame, and maybe a little pride. He nodded.

'There's more, isn't there?' said Bob. 'You started to tell me. Why did you stop?'

'Nobody would believe me,' said Eugene. 'They'd wonder why I was making up a crazy story, and they'd only think one thing. That I was hiding something. That I did it.'

'So tell me the truth,' said Bob. 'This is your last chance to tell us, you understand? We need to know.'

At last, Eugene gave a nod. 'But I ain't saying anything on the record. If anyone asks me I'll deny it.'

'So tell *him*,' said Bob, nodding to Jonah. 'Off the record. Start with the first thing you said to me, the thing you claimed I'd misheard. Or have you forgotten what it was?'

Eugene shook his head and slowly turned to Jonah. 'It looked at me,' he said, his eyes wide and desperate. '*It looked at me.*'

14

'I saw her fall,' said Eugene. 'When the light from my pickup hit her, I saw her fall.'

Bob looked at Jonah, then back at Eugene. 'There was someone else in the alley?'

Eugene shook his head. 'Not some *one*. Some *thing*.'

'What?' said Jonah. 'What did you see?'

'The dark,' said Eugene. 'The dark was holding her. Standing there. A shape. Just *dark*. Huge, and hunched over. It seemed to look up as the light hit it, look up at *me*. I couldn't see its eyes, but I could feel the gaze burning deep into me. And then it was gone. Just *gone*, like it had never been there. And she fell to the ground. I got out of the pickup and ran to help, then I stopped.' He looked at Jonah, eyes round with fear. 'I stopped because I could still feel it. I couldn't see it, but it was still there. Every part of me was colder than I'd ever felt in my life. A few seconds later, I could feel it go.'

Jonah suddenly realized how cold he felt himself, right now. 'How did you know it had gone?' His own voice had the sound of desperation in it.

Eugene shook his head. 'I don't know how, but if I hadn't been sure, believe me, I wouldn't have been able to go down that alley. And then when I did, and I saw what it had done to her . . . I don't ever want to stand there again. Not even in daylight.' He stopped, folded his arms around himself and rubbed. 'I need to warm up and get back to work. Are we done?'

'You swear that's everything you saw?' said Bob.

Eugene nodded.

'Then we're done. You can go.'

As Eugene started to turn away, Jonah spoke. 'You're a brave man, Eugene. Walking down that alley after seeing what you saw. I don't think I'd have the guts.'

Eugene said nothing for a moment, looking at Jonah with something close to bitterness. 'And what good did it do me? I can't stop seeing her. It'll be with me my whole goddamn life. If I'd known better, I would've stayed where the hell I was.' He paused, then met Jonah's gaze with sudden intensity. 'Not a word I should say, not now. *Hell*. Was that what it was? Was that where it came from?'

Jonah couldn't answer.

*

The winter sun was already setting by the time they reached the alley where Mary Connart had died. The air was cold, and the alley seemed desolate.

'That's the light,' said Bob, pointing high up on one wall.

'What had happened to it?' said Jonah.

Bob shrugged. 'The bulb had just blown, Jonah, nothing more.'

They walked down slowly until Bob showed him where Mary's body had been found. There were no marks, no dark stains.

They stood there, silent, Jonah trying to make the decision that Bob needed from him. He closed his eyes, picturing a dark, hulking shape behind him, as Eugene had described. A cold breeze blew through the alley. He suddenly wanted to get home, wanted nothing more to do with it.

Bob drove them back to the station. 'Well?' he said.

'What do you want me to say?'

Bob shook his head. 'Damned if I know. Devils are a little outside my jurisdiction. You really think Eugene could have seen what he said he did?'

'I hope not,' said Jonah.

'Let me know your decision by tomorrow,' said Bob. 'If you agree, we'd be able to go ahead within forty-eight hours.'

'If I do it, you understand it'll be non-vocal, given how long she's been dead?'

'I understand,' said Bob.

'I'll let you know in the morning,' said Jonah. 'Say goodbye to Ray for me.' He went to his car and was home by eight, Marmite keen for attention. To distract himself, he looked through the documents Annabel had sent him, about Winnerden Flats and the cryogenics push Andreas Biotech was going to make.

While he read, he felt a sense of dread creep up on him. He'd clung to the hope that Andreas's death had been the end of it, that the darkness within him had perished utterly, but as he'd stood listening to Eugene Harding he'd found himself questioning that hope.

It all seemed so *unfair*. Annabel had been the one to worry about the things they'd experienced with Andreas being somehow unfinished, and now that her fears had subsided his own had grown.

When he went to bed, sleep didn't come easily. Every time he closed his eyes he could see the pictures Bob had shown them, Mary Connart with her arm gone and the side of her head devastated. He thought of Eugene's insistence that he'd heard her scream, and knew the implication: that she'd been conscious as it had happened.

And when he did finally sleep, it was shattered by a dream that brought back an image he'd seen at Reese-Farthing. The image had filled his mind when he confronted Michael Andreas – or the creature *within* Andreas – in the burning building. Andreas had put his hands around Jonah's throat, and as Jonah felt his consciousness failing he'd experienced a vision he instinctively knew was from the creature's past.

A huge beast, dark and winged, striding towards a vast city, destroying all before it. Its great black claws reached down, charring everything they touched.

And then the dream changed, and he was in the alley with Mary, watching as the same claws burned through the woman's flesh.

Jonah woke with a cry; sweating, pulse racing. He sat up and knew the decision had been made.

If he wanted to know what had happened to Mary Connart, there was only one way.

He would have to ask her.

15

Jonah called Bob in the morning to tell him his decision. Within an hour Bob had called back to let him know things were under-way, and that if all went well, the revival would happen in two days' time. Then he rang Never to tell him the news.

'I've kept my plate pretty clear,' Never said. 'I can take it as vacation.'

'You're not coming,' said Jonah. 'There's no point you getting into hot water. OK?'

'OK,' said Never, giving up far more easily than Jonah had expected.

*

On the morning of the revival, Jonah's phone rang. 'We're good to go,' said Bob. 'We expect the body to be released within two hours.'

'I'm on my way.'

As a post mortem was still going to be performed, the revival had to take place under more controlled conditions than a typical private revival would require; that meant a low-temperature room similar to the revival suites back at the FRS. Bob had given Jonah the address of a private revival firm in Sterling, north of Dulles Airport, which was fully equipped to handle it.

When he got there, Bob and Ray hadn't arrived, but there was one car outside that Jonah recognized. He walked over and the driver wound down his window and grinned. 'Morning,' said Never.

It explained why it had been so easy to get him to agree not to come. 'You don't need to be here,' said Jonah. 'I have my own camera and a tripod, it'll be enough.'

'Sure,' said Never. 'And maybe Bob can film it on his *phone*, too. I'm here now. And if a world of shit descends afterwards, I can just say I recorded everything to make sure you bastards didn't get away with it.'

Jonah looked in the back and noted the boxes of equipment in the car. 'Hang on,' he said. 'There's no way we can use FRS kit for this.'

'It's not FRS stuff. Not quite. The cameras are being trialled, the laptop's my own. I nicked a keypad and some cables, I'll give you that.' Never grinned again. 'Now hop in.'

They waited in the car, unable to raise Bob or Ray on their cell phones. Forty minutes later they started to assume the worst: that the Afterlifers had managed to block it, somehow. The sky darkened, threatening rain and matching Jonah's mood.

Then a car and van pulled into the revival firm's lot. On his own in the car was Ray Johnson. Bob was sitting in the passenger seat of the van, which Jonah recognized as a body-transportation vehicle, fitted with refrigerated units in the rear and able to carry up to six bodies at once, although there would only be one body in there today. He waved to Jonah and Never, then got out.

'Any problems?' asked Jonah.

'No,' said Bob. 'A little stalling, which is why we're late, but their hands were tied.'

'So no chance of interruptions?' If there was anything Jonah wanted to be sure of, it was to avoid a repeat of the catastrophe with David Leith.

Bob grinned. 'We *may* have inadvertently given an incorrect location for the revival. And we made damn sure we weren't followed. So I think the chances are slim to none.'

Jonah nodded, relieved. Then he realized there was one person still missing. 'Is the sister on her way?'

'She's not attending,' said Bob.

Jonah's eyes widened. Not having any relatives present under-
lined just how unorthodox a private revival this was.

'At my suggestion,' said Bob. 'They weren't very close, and
given the nature of the case – well, I got the impression she felt
obliged but, frankly, she looked ill at the thought. She was glad to
be given the opportunity to duck out. She's given me a message for
you to pass on.' He held out an envelope.

Jonah took it and pulled out the single sheet within, a short
word-processed printout. It was vaguely impersonal, the writing
formal, stilted. The sister had written of a few childhood memories, expressed regret that they'd not been in touch more, and
wished Mary well. For all its inadequacy, it was probably the
hardest thing the sister had ever had to do.

He put the sheet in his back pocket. If the time came, he had
easy access to it.

So, no family were here for Mary, and no friends. Jonah
wondered again if he was doing the right thing.

'OK, then,' said Never, clapping his hands together and looking
up to the sky. Spots of rain had started to fall. 'Let's get inside
before it starts to piss down, shall we?'

*

Jonah had brought his FRS medication with him. He swallowed
the pills while out of Never's sight, feeling strangely hypocritical
after telling Never off for using what he'd thought was FRS equipment. Skipping his medication wasn't an option, though.

By the time the meds took effect, Never had completed setting
up in the cold room they would use for the revival. Space was tight,
and there was no separate area for Never, Ray and Bob to sit,
so Never had set up his laptop in the far corner to give Jonah as
much room as possible.

The only other people present were the driver of the body
transport vehicle and an older woman Bob introduced as the

revival firm's owner. Once Mary's body had been wheeled into the building, the driver returned to wait it out in the van; the owner watched the preparation for a few minutes, looking on warily without a word. Then she left them to it.

'Old acquaintance,' said Bob as the woman left the room. 'Not happy about this, but, well, she owes me.'

In the centre of the room was the gurney from the transport van; beside it was the chair Jonah would sit in. The body was still bagged, no-one keen to open it until it was absolutely necessary. Bob stepped forward and looked at Jonah, waiting until Jonah gave him a nod. The noise of the bag's zip seemed unnaturally loud. Bob pulled the side of the bag down, and Jonah felt his face slacken.

He thought he'd been prepared, having seen the pictures and having so much experience with bodies that had been twisted and torn every way you could imagine. But there was something different here.

Something plain *wrong*.

'Shit,' said Never. He approached the body, standing closer than Jonah would have felt comfortable being. *Yet*, of course – in a few minutes he'd be taking the dead hand against his bare skin, watching the corpse twitch back into activity that would, with luck, shed some light on what had happened to her.

'My God,' Jonah said at last. He stepped forward to Never's side. 'My God.' The injuries followed an unnervingly straight line through the left side of her body: the arm missing, the shoulder gone, deep into the joint, the line continuing through that and a good part of the head. He spent a moment peering at the surfaces of naked bone, seeing the fine irregularities. He looked at the exposed section of brain, only a few inches across, above what remained of the left eye. He turned to Bob Crenner. 'What the hell can have done this?'

'Rogue Jedi,' said Never, shutting his mouth the moment Jonah's sharp look hit him.

Jonah reached out to the woman's right hand, which he would be holding for the revival, and turned it palm up. The flesh around the base of the little finger was gone, exposing bone. The rest of the palm was covered in miniscule scratches.

'First thing I want is an account of that evening,' said Bob. 'Get some facts straight before we tackle how she died. In case it proves too much for her.'

Jonah nodded. The reliving of something so obviously trau-matic could easily end the revival. Better to get something concrete first. 'I'll try.'

Bob cleared his throat. 'Jonah . . . there's something else.' Bob wasn't meeting his eye.

'What is it?' said Jonah.

'I was hoping . . . Look, tell me if it won't be possible, but you remember the case of a guy called Howard Reeder?'

Jonah nodded. Of course he did. Howard Reeder had been shot resisting arrest in Los Angeles five years back, following a robbery that had seen two young cops killed. Word on the street had put Reeder at the scene, and when police went to bring him in, the man came out shooting. He'd been hit, but had escaped.

Reeder had died alone, hiding in a disused warehouse. The body wasn't found for twelve hot days. Revival was a necessity, and would normally have been non-vocal given the state of the fly-blown body.

But there were complications, loud claims of a set-up, sugges-tions that the true culprit was being protected by the police with Reeder a fall-guy. The taint of conspiracy fell on the revival itself. If it had been non-vocal, the reviver would be reporting what was said. Normally this would be above suspicion, but not this time. Instead it had been done as a vocal, with the reviver also docu-menting the subject's words – perfectly audible to them, just as in a non-vocal case – via the usual keypad.

The corpse was almost impossible to understand without the help of the words being typed, but the critical thing was this:

knowing what was said made the sounds undeniable. The half-formed words, the slurred and guttural attempts at speech, had carried more weight than the reviver's testimony alone. Together, there was enough proof to quash the accusations of cover-up.

Jonah had watched the footage of that revival. It was grim, something that even he found hard to view. And now, with Mary Connart, Bob and Ray wanted to do the same. 'Are you serious? This is a clear-cut case for non-vocal, Bob. If you want it vocal, it won't be pretty, and it'll almost certainly mean we have less time.'

'I know. But if we get something difficult to believe, hell, I've brought you in, and you're a friend. They'll call foul and ignore whatever we get. It's a private revival, Jonah; in theory, you can say whatever you want without fear of prosecution, make up every word. They can just claim you lied, and ignore whatever Mary tells us. But not if they can hear it for themselves.'

Jonah looked at the body of Mary Connart. He thought back to the footage of Howard Reeder, the body twisting, spasming even. The corpse almost *choking* out the words. 'I'll need to examine the body.'

He walked over to Never, who was making final preparations on his laptop and pretending not to be listening.

'You hear that?' said Jonah.

'Of course I fucking did. You trying it? Tell me you're not.'

'I trust their judgement. It might be the only way to make sure Mary is believed. I'll have to check the vocal chords first, though. It might not even be possible. I just need the— Damn.' He'd realized that they didn't have the kit he needed to do the necessary examination. Then he saw a sheepish look on Never's face, and Never bent around to the equipment box behind him, coming back with a bag in his hand.

'Confession,' said Never. 'I, uh, brought a fair bit of FRS kit after all. Just in case.' He handed it over. 'You sure about this?'

Jonah nodded and unzipped the bag. He dug around and pulled out a rigid laryngoscope, essentially an eyepiece and a thin metal tube with a small prism at one end. Another search produced an endoscope with a longer flexible tube, ready to check the lungs and make sure they could provide enough air for the process.

He fished out some latex gloves and put them on. The examination took a few minutes. Bob stood nearby while he worked; Ray took a seat beside Never in the corner.

Jonah opened the mouth of the corpse, then closed and opened it several times. The body was not in as bad a condition as he'd feared. He reached in with his fingers and palpated the tongue. There would be some mobility there but it was too swollen for fine control. The laryngoscope showed the vocal cords to be viable, barely. The tone of the voice in such a revival was more dependable than the shaping of words, but in such a condition the body would deteriorate rapidly, the harsh forces involved liable to create microtears in the muscle. If the revival lasted more than a couple of minutes, the voice emerging would be little more than a deep growl.

The lungs were clear enough to proceed; as the revival went on, some fluid would probably seep from the surrounding tissue, but it wouldn't be significant.

On the damaged side of Mary's face the flesh of much of her cheek had gone, allowing air to escape. He reached into the kit pack for a flexible patch and some sealant, hoping it would be effective on such a large wound, especially with the skin so degraded, but it went on easily. He waited the required three minutes to allow the work to set, then examined the repair. It seemed to be holding well without restricting the movement of the jaw.

'Ready here,' said Jonah.

'And here,' said Never.

'How do you rate our chances?' said Bob.

Jonah thought for a moment. 'The body's not in too bad a condition, so it comes down to how the injuries will play out. The damage is severe but localized. The arm won't matter, or the shoulder. It'd be the head wound that might cause trouble, I think. It's maybe half an inch into the brain, over an area three inches wide, but it's not core damage. Frontal lobe.' The thing that really played havoc with revival success was *devastation*, the deep destruction of a gunshot to the brain, or the widespread penetrating torso injuries of a car crash.

Bob nodded and went to sit by Never and Ray. 'Then let's get started,' he said.

16

Jonah sat by Mary Connart's body and adjusted his chair until he was comfortable. The keypad he would be using to transcribe the conversation had been taped to one arm of the chair. He tested it out then took a deep breath.

He removed his gloves and took Mary's hand in his, flinching inside a little as he felt the rough damage to the flesh of her palm. He let the feeling settle, getting used to the sensation of the dry exposed bones of the hand. He was reluctant to begin, and hesitated long enough for Never to prompt him: 'I'm recording, Jonah.'

'I know.' He took another few seconds, and began. 'Revival of subject Mary Connart. J. P. Miller duty—'

He stopped. He'd been reciting the standard FRS revival opening: *J. P. Miller, duty reviver.* But this was not the FRS, not now. 'I'll start again,' he said. 'Revival of Mary Connart. Jonah Miller reviving.'

He looked at the wounds to her face. Her right eye was closed. The damage to the left eye socket had stopped it *being* an eye, instead it was just dead tissue. He looked at the shoulder and thought back over the years, trying to recall a revival with injuries analogous to this. Bob Crenner had mentioned dragging wounds; Jonah remembered a revival four years before of a cyclist who had been hit by an eighteen-wheeler. The driver hadn't even noticed. Tangled between the drive axles the victim had been dragged for fifteen miles, his right leg and hip in contact with the road. The man had been conscious and had bled to death, but the resulting injury had been very different from what Jonah was looking at now. Then, the flesh had been stripped unevenly from bone that sat proud of the remaining muscle. Here, bone and muscle were level, and the edge of the wound was well defined.

His reluctance was getting in the way now. He had no choice but to go ahead and see what happened.

Reversal, the first stage. Losing himself, exploring the damage to the corpse in his mind. Reaching out. The injury to the head proved to be less of an impediment than he'd feared. The missing arm and the shoulder, largely peripheral. The overall level of decay was better than expected; navigating it took experience and determination but held no surprises. It all added time to the process, taking much longer than David Leith, but it wasn't the tortuous challenge he'd feared.

Just hold on. Hold on for the surge.

And what form would it take here? Had Eugene Harding really heard her scream? If the injuries had been inflicted while she was conscious . . . a bad death often showed itself as a difficult surge.

It took time to arrive. When it came, though, it was surprisingly brief. Not easy, but hardly what he'd been tensing against. A sense of plummeting through random moments in the woman's life, no more remarkable than many revivals he'd experienced.

Maybe it was a sign of how the revival would go. Maybe it would all be easier than he'd been fearing. Jonah felt himself relax slightly, suddenly hopeful.

There was a flicker of movement on Mary's face. First, her upper lip twitched briefly; then her right cheek did the same.

'She's almost here,' Jonah said.

'Well done,' said Never, the surprise clear in his voice.

'How long?' asked Jonah.

'Fast, all things considered,' Never told him. 'Twenty-nine minutes.'

Then they all fell silent, as the corpse of Mary Connart began to take a very slow breath, the chest straining, the lungs filling with air. At last it stopped. Revival had been achieved.

'Mary,' said Jonah. 'Mary, my name is Jonah Miller. I'm a reviver. Can you hear me?'

The body of Mary Connart lay still for a moment, the lungs holding. Then Jonah felt a vibration in the hand, a rapid trembling that spread up the corpse's right arm to the shoulder. The wheels of the gurney the corpse lay on began to rattle in unison, the sound growing as the vibration grew increasingly violent.

The trembling reached the head. The jaw slackened wide then continued to push open, Jonah's eye on the patch he'd applied as it was stretched to its limit, the bottom of the jaw reaching the chest. He could see the tongue, quivering, pulsating, and all the while the movement grew.

He heard Bob whisper in horror to Never: *'What is this?'*

Fear, thought Jonah. An initial response of uncontrolled movement was a rare manifestation of fear in the subject. An ongoing tremble in the muscles of the face, say. A regular twitch of the hand. The greater the fear, the more movement could be observed.

For it to be so extreme . . .

Dear God, he thought, *Mary, what happened to you?*

He turned his head to Bob, about to try and reassure him, but then he felt her, and the terror in her; it swamped him, greater by far than the emotional turmoil of the surge. The air from her lungs at last began to leave, her vocal cords working well enough to produce a low, rasping cry.

Then Mary Connart screamed.

17

The moment she stopped, the lungs began to fill with air again, the vibrational movement continuing. Another scream would follow if Jonah didn't get her attention.

'Mary,' he said. 'Talk to me. I want to help you. Please.'

He felt her become aware of him. There was a fractional decrease in the shaking.

'*Mary!*' he shouted.

Abruptly the trembling stopped. Then in the silence – slowly – the jaw closed. It was a few seconds before she spoke.

'Where am I?'

The sound was harsh. He knew the words would be indistinct to the others listening, but they were clear in Jonah's mind. He typed them, and would easily be able to keep pace, however fast she went.

'You're safe now,' he said. The first task: ensure she was aware of her own situation, of her own *death*. If possible, give her the space, and hope she already knew.

Silence, but he could tell it was a thoughtful silence. She was trying to remember.

'I died. In the . . . in the *dark*.'

The last word had an edge to it, an edge of terror.

'I'm a reviver, Mary. My name is Jonah Miller. I want to ask about what happened at the party. Do you remember the client party?'

A few seconds passed. Mary's jaw began to move slowly up and down, then it began to tremble again – but the vibration didn't spread, lasting only for a moment. Jonah didn't feel confident about how long this revival could last.

'I left,' she said.

It was too early to risk her becoming lost in the actual attack, however much Jonah needed to know the truth. 'Did anything happen at the party? Anything you want to tell us?'

'It . . . I was tired. It was too hot, too loud. I'd spoken to the people I needed to, shown my face long enough. And a man . . .'

Jonah shifted in his seat, recognizing the level of importance Mary herself felt, and knowing this was critical. Mary's lungs were empty. He tensed as they filled, wary in case another bout of trembling set in. It didn't. He prompted: 'A man, Mary. What man?'

'I didn't know him. He didn't say who he was. I went to the restroom and when I came back he took my arm, half pulled me to somewhere quiet.' Her breaths came regularly, and with each one Jonah tensed. 'He was drunk. Told me he needed to ask me something. But he was smiling, then. I thought he might be flirting. Then his smile left his face, just left it as if it hadn't existed. He started to ramble, wanted to know if I'd *told* anyone. He said I must have seen it.'

'Seen what, Mary?'

'I don't know what he meant. I told him so. He didn't believe me. He said someone's name. Winterton. Had I told anyone about Winterton? I didn't answer. Winterton's a firm in New York that was trying to headhunt me. I'd been talking about it earlier with a friend and this guy must have overheard. I said it was none of his business. He leaned close and snarled that it was *exactly* his business, that if I couldn't keep my mouth shut he'd shut it for me. I told him to go to hell. His eyes were so damn cold. I saw my friend, hurried to her. I was about to tell her about the creep but he'd already gone. She could see something was up and asked if I was OK but I brushed her off, told her that I was just tired, that I was going. I crept out a back exit, didn't want him to see me go. I walked fast. I was stupid to walk home, but you do that. You try and act normal to show yourself it was nothing. I kept thinking he was following, but I couldn't see him. And then I—'

She stopped. Twenty seconds ticked by before Jonah spoke. 'Mary?'

'Ask her what route she took home,' said Bob. 'See if we can establish that before we ask about the alley.'

'Mary,' said Jonah, but he was cut off as Mary's emotions went crazy, a sudden rush of impossible terror. It filled Jonah, too, and he shot a panicked look to Never. He could see that Never understood something was wrong.

Mary's hand began to tremble again, more forcefully than before, the gurney wheels rattling hard as the vibration spread, the jaw of the corpse extending unnaturally wide, the tongue quivering. The whole upper torso shook, risking the body shifting in position, possibly falling.

Jonah stood from his chair and held Mary's shoulder with his left hand, trying to keep the body secure. The others hurried over, keeping a wary distance.

'Can we do anything?' asked Never.

'I don't know. Brace the body, maybe it'll pass again.' Stepping forward, Never leaned across the body's waist and held on, the look on his face one of bewilderment: after years of experience, he suddenly found himself uncertain how to proceed. Jonah felt exactly the same way. Bob and Ray held down her legs.

The lungs filled with air as the rapid shivering increased. Mary Connart screamed again, the vocal chords deteriorating audibly, the tone of her cry deepening, turning it into a guttural howl.

Jonah looked at Bob; the detective's face was grey, eyes horror-struck. 'If this doesn't stop,' said Jonah, 'I'm going to have to let her go.'

The detective looked at him, then back to the body, but said nothing.

The lungs had emptied but the vibration didn't let up. Without a pause the lungs refilled and the screaming continued.

The terror within Mary Connart was absolute, flooding Jonah and leaving him barely able to think. He didn't understand what was happening but he couldn't see how he could do anything useful now. '*I have to, Bob,*' he called over the screaming. '*I have to let her go.*' He wanted Bob's permission; years of training, years of routine, always needing the official in charge to give the go-ahead to end it. Bob was just staring at the body, lost.

'*Please, Bob. I have to let her go.*'

Abruptly the screaming stopped. The body sagged.

Jonah held on to her as the others stood back. Mary was still present, but only just. The amount of effort expended in that fit of screaming had left her with almost nothing in reserve. She had only moments left.

'Mary?' he said.

Her mouth moved, fractionally. With no air left in her lungs there was no sound, but Jonah could hear it in his mind. Hear what she told him, just before she faded completely.

'*The shadow,*' said Mary Connart. '*The shadow has teeth.*'

18

Jonah stood still, breathless and lost, staring at Mary Connart's face.

He let go of her hand and stepped back, bumping into the chair, pushing it away from himself with a shout of frustration and fear. The chair tipped on its castors and fell into one of the camera tripods, knocking it down.

He heard Never approach and right the tripod, then felt Never's hand on his shoulder. Nothing was said.

Teeth, Jonah thought, looking at the rough surfaces of exposed bone on Mary's body. Her own fear, her own confusion, had been so extreme. Her words meant nothing, surely.

He shuddered.

He turned to Bob. 'I'm sorry,' said Jonah. He felt desolate and realized he was close to tears. 'I don't know what happened. She was terrified and confused. After everything you'd been hoping for . . . I'm sorry.'

Bob shook his head. He looked as stunned as Jonah felt. 'Don't be. It's something. We have to trace the man she spoke about. What was it he said to her? Somebody's name?'

'Winterton,' said Jonah. 'A company that was trying to head-hunt her.'

'He clearly thought she knew something she shouldn't,' said Ray. 'There was explicit threat in what he said to her.'

'The encounter Mary had with the man didn't come up when

we spoke to any of her friends,' said Bob, looking to Ray for confirmation.

'No,' said Ray. 'One told us she'd seemed upset, but didn't know why. Somebody must have seen it, though. It was a big party. The client companies invited had been allowed to bring up to seven people each. The organizers don't know exactly who was present, and there could have been over two hundred guests in all. We've spoken to thirty at most. Our focus has been on those who were outside at the time, trying to find someone who witnessed her leave.'

'Well,' said Bob, 'this guy's our best lead so we've got a reason to look harder. Jonah, you said Mary was confused. Are you sure we can trust that part of her testimony?'

Jonah nodded. 'Her memory of that was clear. She only became confused later.' *When she started to remember what had happened to her in that alley.*

He stood to the side as Never took down the equipment. He remembered the envelope Bob had given him, the note from Mary's sister. Inadequate as the words were, he'd not even been able to offer Mary that comfort. There was a wastepaper bin in the corner of the room. He pulled the note from his pocket, crumpled it and dropped it in. Guilt was coursing through him. He couldn't pretend that what he'd done had been to Mary's benefit.

He looked at her, thinking about the rough screams that had poured from that corpse, now silent and motionless in the centre of the room.

Thinking about the words she'd whispered at the end, and one word in particular.

Shadow.

*

Jonah and Never made the drive back to Richmond in silence, Never only speaking as they pulled up outside Jonah's apartment building. 'What the hell *was* that?'

Jonah shook his head. 'She had a bad death. More than that I don't know.'

'I've seen footage of shit like that, but you kind of hope you won't witness it. Are you going to be OK? I'm off for the rest of the day, if you want the company?'

'I'm fine.'

'Well you *look* terrible.'

'It was a tough revival, that's all.'

'There's something you're not telling me,' said Never, his eyes narrowing.

'There's nothing,' said Jonah. 'Really. I just wish we'd got more for them to work with. I'd hoped we'd find out what happened to her.'

Jonah went up to his apartment, knowing that Never didn't believe him. But it was the truth, wasn't it? He simply wanted to know what had happened, there was nothing else worth mentioning.

Shadow.

Well, he thought, *there was that.*

It wasn't just a desire not to worry Never with unjustified paranoia. It was a desire not to even think about it, to *fuel* it.

His head started to pound. It was probably a combination of the stress of the revival and a side effect of his medication. He knew he'd better eat something, but he was far from hungry. Marmite crawled out of a pile of unwashed laundry in the corner and sat by his dish, expectant. The fishy stench from the pouch Jonah opened almost made him gag, chasing away any thought of food.

'How the hell you eat that shit is beyond me,' he said, ruffling the cat's fur as Marmite chowed down.

He remembered the email from Annabel and decided to have a closer look at what she'd sent.

The first attachment was a site plan for Winnerden Flats, the Nevada research facility that Andreas Biotech was renovating. Also attached was a document detailing some of the widely varying investments that the company was engaging in. The sums were eye-watering, and the investment areas appeared almost random. Cryogenics was the only one that seemed to fit Andreas's old passions; the rest included specialists in communication infrastructure and processor fabrication, about as far from the company's biotech roots as it was possible to get. Annabel had commented to the same effect, saying that it reflected two things: first, that Andreas's business had huge sums of money to invest; second, that the company seemed to be diversifying so much that it smacked of flailing around – panicking almost, now that they lacked any real vision. Andreas Biotech had no grand plan. Not any more.

Exactly the kind of reassurance he needed right now.

There was also a schematic of equipment he couldn't quite work out at first. Then he realized there was a place within it for someone to lie down, and the rest began to make sense. It was tapered, almost wedge-shaped, narrowing from the end with the head to that with the feet, with an array of small windows by the head. He looked at Annabel's notes to see what the hell it was: their latest whole-body cryogenic unit. An image came to him of row upon row of these things, all filled with the paying dead, their faces staring out of cold glass. It made him shiver, and he laughed at himself. *Christ,* he thought, *if anyone should be immune to finding that kind of thing creepy, it's me.*

All the scanned documents were marked with prominent 'confidential' declarations, of course. Sensitive company information, all of it. He wondered if they were aware that it had been stolen. He wondered how the hell Annabel had managed to get hold of it.

Jonah sat staring blankly at the screen and wondered what Annabel was doing right at that moment. He closed the email and spent the next few hours watching random junk on television, but the day had taken it out of him. He was in bed asleep by nine.

*

The night brought its own terrors. The face of Mary Connart, twisting in fear, screams deepening until they became the growling of dogs. The dream shifted, and again he saw the vast shadow, striding across a city that, this time, looked very much like Richmond, burning all that it touched.

And in his dream, Jonah looked at the ground at the creature's feet and saw it stirring, boiling with movement, as uncountable shadows ran over the terrain underneath their master.

The disciples of the beast. Its servants. Its *acolytes*.

And their touch was just as corrosive.

He woke from the dream, shaking.

*

In the morning he was restless enough to contact Bob Crenner.

'Nothing to report yet, Jonah,' said Bob. 'Me and Ray are going over witnesses from the party to see if we can identify the man. We've also got a few feelers out for the name Mary mentioned. She assumed he meant Winterton, the New York firm that wanted to hire her, but it might be coincidence. It might have meant something very different to him, especially given the strength of his reaction.'

Winterton. Jonah swore aloud. When he'd heard it from Mary before, her voice had been so clear in his head that it was absolutely precise. *Winterton*. Hearing it from Bob Crenner now, the word was less distinct, allowing him to make a connection he'd missed. A crazy thought, just fuelling the paranoia already inflamed by the word *shadow*, and by his dreams.

'Jonah?' said Bob.

'The PR company that arranged the party,' he said. 'Mary's employers. How many client companies did they have at the event?'

'We've not gotten around to checking with them all, if that's what you mean. Why do you ask?'

'See if there are any Andreas Biotech affiliates, Bob.' *Please, don't find anything*, he thought.

'Andreas?'

'Just check. It's probably nothing.'

'OK,' said Bob, after a pause. 'We've secured an extra four detectives for the investigation. I'll get one of them to look into it.'

Jonah was about to hang up, but he came to a sudden decision. 'Bob,' he said, 'I want a favour. In return for the revival.'

'Anything.'

'Once you find this guy . . . I want to be there when you talk to him.'

After he hung up, Jonah realized he was shaking a little. He opened Annabel's email again, and looked at the attached site plan for the Andreas Biotech research facility in Nevada.

He looked at the name of the site, and told himself it was just coincidence.

'Winterton,' he said aloud.

It was nothing like it, really.

Nothing like Winnerden. Nothing like Winnerden Flats.

19

Jonah got another call from Bob in the early afternoon. By 4 p.m., he was back inside the Third District Police Station.

'We got the lead just before midday,' said Bob. 'We have a team of fourteen now, talking to as many party attendees as possible. Finally got a witness who saw Mary talk with a man, then tell him to go to hell. They could only give a vague description, though.'

'Meantime,' said Ray, 'I was checking out your suggestion. The only company at the party that had an Andreas Biotech connection is listed as ARI. That's Andreas Research Investment, a DC-based daughter company. We got a list of attendees from them, only two of whom were male. I culled pictures from their Facebook pages and we showed them to our witness.' He held up a printout of an image. 'Positive ID. Blake Torrance, thirty-seven years old. He's been with the company for eight years.'

Bob turned to Jonah and asked the question that had probably been on his mind all day. 'Why *did* you think there was a link to Andreas?'

'The name she gave,' said Jonah. 'Winterton. There's a facility Andreas Biotech is upgrading in Winnerden Flats, Nevada.' Bob waited for more, his eyebrow raised. 'It was just a shot in the dark. Given what happened at Reese-Farthing, Annabel takes an interest in things like that.'

Bob didn't look satisfied with the answer but he let it go.

'I'd heard you and Annabel Harker had hooked up,' said Ray. 'Going well, I hope?'

Jonah nodded with all the enthusiasm he could muster, which was very little. 'When are you going to talk to Torrance?'

'Soon,' said Ray. 'I've already been to his office. I asked him to come in to answer some questions. He obliged, so he's sitting at the far end of the building as we speak. If he'd refused, I would probably have arrested him, and I think he knew that. Now, we just have to wait for his lawyer to get here.'

*

It was another fifty minutes before the lawyer showed. In the meantime, Jonah sat by Bob's desk watching him put away more coffee than was surely safe for human consumption, Bob and Ray discussing what approach they would take in questioning.

When the time came they showed Jonah to a one-way observation window looking into the cramped interview room. Two minutes later the detectives entered, followed by the lawyer, a dishevelled older man with bags under his eyes that looked like they were filled with overwork. Then came the man himself.

Jonah looked him over. He was a young thirty-seven, handsome, cocky. And there was something else. Something *wrong* with him. Jonah couldn't tell what, but he'd felt the hairs standing on his arms from the moment Torrance entered the room.

Torrance sat, and as he did so, he placed his left hand on his right shoulder and scratched. He did it again a moment later, and Jonah found himself staring at where Torrance was scratching. He felt suddenly cold, his heart rate quickening. He had an urge to run but he didn't understand why.

Then he saw it. Just for a moment. He rubbed his eyes and looked again, seeing nothing now. But he was sure he'd not imagined it.

There had been something there.

Something dark, crouching on Torrance's shoulder.

*

Bob nodded to Ray, who was standing by a small control panel on the wall. A red light went green and Ray sat down. Recording had started.

Bob made the introductions for the benefit of the cameras. Torrance acknowledged his name with a single 'yes' and a bored sigh.

'Do you understand why you're here?' asked Bob.

Torrance looked at his lawyer, who nodded for him to answer. 'You believe I was one of the last people to speak to a woman who was murdered,' Torrance said. 'I agreed to come so we can handle this quickly and I can get back to my job.'

'Well, Blake, if you give us full answers to our questions, this shouldn't take long.'

'So get started,' said Torrance, not holding back on the disdain.

'You work for Andreas Research Investment, is that correct?'

'Yes.'

'And what does your job entail?'

'Our remit is wide. Mainly, we have a team of analysts who look for promising companies or projects that might benefit Andreas Biotech. Start-ups, parts of larger companies. Recruitment of academics and graduates, too, sometimes.'

'You're one of these analysts?'

Torrance laughed. 'No. I'm one of the senior staff. I oversee funding and project coordination, among other duties. I practically run the place. That's why I'm so *busy*, Officer.'

'*Detective*,' corrected Bob. 'Not too busy to party, though?'

'Not at all. It's an important aspect of what I do. I like to be hands-on with prospective purchases or research funding. We have a great relationship with universities too. If you want the best people, you have to make them feel welcome. Keep them happy.'

Bob looked at Ray, who took over. 'You don't always make people feel welcome, though. Do you, Blake?'

'I have no idea what you mean,' said Torrance.

'Take your mind back three weeks,' said Ray. 'On the night of the sixteenth. Friday. The victim's employer, a public relations firm called Manor Williams, threw a party for clients. You were present, yes?'

Another look to the lawyer; another nod. 'I was.'

Ray looked at Bob, who took a picture from a folder in front of him and slid it across the table. It showed Mary Connart, smiling. 'Do you recognize her?'

Torrance shook his head. 'No.'

'This is the victim, Blake,' said Bob. 'Mary Connart. We have a witness who states you were speaking with her on the night in question.'

'If I was, I don't recall it.' Torrance rubbed at his shoulder. Jonah found his eye creeping back there again and again, seeing nothing; he was beginning to think the dark, formless shape had only been in his imagination.

'The witness states that Mary Connart told you to go to hell,' said Bob. 'I'm surprised you don't remember.'

The lawyer spoke up. 'And your witness could identify my client?'

'She already has,' said Ray. 'She would identify him in court if necessary.'

Torrance was starting to look less comfortable. He rubbed at his shoulder again. 'OK, OK. Now I remember who she was. I made an advance. She declined. That was it.'

'Did the witness overhear the conversation, Detective?' asked the lawyer.

Bob smiled at him. 'As I understand it, your client kept his voice low enough that being overheard was unlikely.'

The lawyer sat back, looking satisfied.

'However,' said Bob. 'Mary Connart heard every word.'

The lawyer leaned forward again. Blake Torrance glared at Bob then looked at his lawyer, whose face had soured. 'Revival,' said Torrance. His lawyer put a fast hand on Torrance's arm and squeezed to stop him saying more.

'Am I to understand, Detectives,' said the lawyer, 'that a revival of Mary Connart has taken place?'

'Oh, I think you know damn well it has,' said Ray. 'I'll bet you're itching to know what she said.'

The lawyer smiled. 'And am I to understand that what was purportedly a private revival was also used to pose questions to the victim relating to the evening of her death?'

Bob paused before he answered. 'I'm impressed with how much you already know about a case your client had no involvement with, sir.'

'It's incumbent on me to ascertain as many facts as possible, *sir*, when my client's freedom is at stake. Please don't confuse competence with guilt.'

'Guilt?' said Bob. 'Right now all your client is being accused of is talking to someone.'

The lawyer took a deep, unhappy breath. 'This is nonsense. We don't have to answer any more questions, Blake. Let's go.' He stood. Blake Torrance stayed where he was, watching Bob with wary eyes, his hand straying to his shoulder. 'Blake?'

Torrance began to stand.

'I'd advise you not to leave,' said Bob. 'Unless you want us to arrest you. Right now, you're just assisting the inquiry. You want to avoid arrest, I suggest you keep assisting.'

Torrance and his lawyer shared a look and reluctantly took their seats. Torrance muttered: 'What's keeping her?'

'Calm, Blake, please,' said the lawyer. 'She'll be here soon.'

Bob looked at Ray, then back to Torrance, uneasy. 'Who'll be here soon?'

'Oh, just moral support,' said the lawyer. 'Now believe me, Detective, we have no desire for an arrest. We'll assist you, within reason. For now. I'm sure my client would appreciate it if you lessened your hostile attitude, perhaps?'

Bob nodded. 'Then maybe you could tell us, Blake, exactly what you and Mary spoke of?'

'I don't remember *exactly*.'

'Do you have any memory at all of the content of that conversation?'

'It was small talk.'

'Small talk that she took offence at? Enough for her to tell you to go to hell?'

'Sure. It was a party, I'd had a drink. You know what women are like.'

Bob took his time to share a look with Ray. 'Oh, I know what this woman was like, Blake. At least, I know what she was like shortly after you spoke to her.' He reached into his folder and took out a series of photographs, turning them around. Mary Connart's brutalized corpse, lying in the alley.

The lawyer visibly flinched, turning away. 'Dear God, there's no need for that.'

Jonah was watching Torrance, watching his eyes. They hadn't left Bob's. He hadn't even *glanced* down. Bob raised the photograph into Torrance's line of sight. Torrance looked at it briefly, then his eyes went to the table. 'I didn't have anything to do with it,' he said.

Bob put the pictures to one side and took a sheet of text from his folder. The transcript of Mary's revival.

'*He said someone's name,*' Bob read. '*Winterton. Had I told anyone about Winterton? I didn't answer. Winterton's a firm in New York that was trying to headhunt me. I'd been talking about it earlier with a friend and this guy must have overheard. I said it was none of his business. He leaned close and snarled that it was* exactly *his business, that if I couldn't keep my mouth shut he'd shut it for me. I told him to go to hell. His eyes were so damn cold.*' Bob looked up. 'Have you any comment to make?'

'I don't remember the conversation.'

But Jonah had seen, and he was sure Bob and Ray had noted it too: Mary's explanation of why she knew the name, and why she'd been talking about it, had made Torrance's eyes widen for a moment.

'This is from Connart's revival?' asked the lawyer. 'A *private* revival?'

'Yes.'

'Then it has no place in court, Detective. You know that. Don't try and bully my client with invention.'

'Invention? These are Mary's own words.'

The lawyer shook his head. 'The standards for court use of non-vocal revival testimony are long established, and—'

'This was recorded,' said Bob. 'The standards are high. I have enough experience here, sir, to know that this evidence is entirely valid. And compelling: the revival was vocal.'

The lawyer opened his mouth to speak, then shut it again.

'And the name?' said Bob, turning to Torrance once more. 'Winterton? Surely that means something to you?'

Torrance shook his head. 'Nothing.'

'You were the one who said it to her, so it has to mean *something*. Maybe she misheard you. Maybe it wasn't Winterton. Have you heard of Winnerden Flats, Blake?'

Torrance didn't reply but Jonah could see his eyes widen once more; clearly the man was uneasy. Torrance's hand went to his shoulder and Jonah felt a sudden cold as he saw it again, the darkness skulking there, *roosting* almost, but gone in an instant.

A shadow, thought Jonah.

Torrance looked at his lawyer, agitated, but the lawyer shook his head.

'That's an Andreas Biotech site, isn't it?' said Bob. 'Have you had any involvement with that site? Recruitment, maybe?'

'I can't discuss internal company matters,' said Torrance, furious.

'We'll see,' said Bob. He let Torrance sit in uncomfortable silence.

There was a brief jingle from the lawyer's pocket. He produced his phone and glanced at it. His smile returned, broad and gloating. 'It seems our time with you is over, Detectives.'

'I very much doubt that,' said Bob.

'Oh, I mean it. My client has an alibi. A good one.'

Bob frowned, saying nothing.

'Your *moral support*?' said Ray. 'You're going to try and wriggle off like *that*? I'm disappointed. So you left the party with someone who'll say whatever you pay them to say?'

Torrance's face was relaxing, Jonah could see. It didn't bode well. There was almost a smile there, creeping in at the corners of his mouth.

'Don't be so uncouth, Detective,' said the lawyer. 'My client's alibi is much simpler than that. You see, he didn't leave the party at all.'

20

Bob and Ray left Torrance with his lawyer in the interrogation room. Jonah stayed by the observation window on his own, watching the pair sit in silence. The lawyer glanced up from time to time at the window, and whenever Torrance started to speak, he told him to keep calm and wait.

Say nothing, thought Jonah. That was the implication. *Say nothing. They may be watching.*

At last, Ray returned.

'What's happening?' Jonah asked.

'His alibi checks out,' said Ray. 'The woman they were waiting for is a work colleague, present at the same party. She has footage. Stills and video from the night. Enough to force us to let Torrance leave, for now at any rate.'

'She on the level?'

'I think so,' said Ray. 'Doesn't much *like* Torrance, that's for sure. Said he was exactly the kind of man who could piss any woman off at short notice. But she has enough footage of him being a dick in public throughout the night to seal it, I think. She says he didn't leave the party until at least eleven. Crucially, though, between nine-fifty and ten-twenty Torrance was asleep in a chair with a fucking *clock* on the wall behind him, and she made sure she caught it on camera. She thought it was hilarious, thought it would get him *into* trouble rather than out of it. Given that

Mary's body was found at ten-thirty, it's about as good an alibi as he could want.'

'Can we trust the footage?' said Jonah.

'Pretty sure we can,' said Ray. 'I don't think she's lying. Doesn't sound like they're the best of friends. I think we just have to accept it. Torrance isn't our man.'

'There's something about him,' said Jonah, watching Torrance's shoulder.

'I know, I would've put money on him too, the way he was behaving. He was our big lead, and the only Andreas Biotech link I found. Your hunch just didn't play out.'

Through the window they saw Bob enter the interrogation room and break the news to Torrance.

'Thank you, Detective,' said Torrance. 'Now maybe I can get back to the office and catch up with the *work* I was trying to do before the interruption.'

'Detective,' said the lawyer in farewell. Bob nodded, then looked up to the window and shook his head.

Ray and Jonah followed Torrance at a distance, seeing a brief exchange between him and a woman: he thanked her, his expression gleeful, hers tolerant, before Torrance and the lawyer left. The woman stayed where she was, and when Bob arrived she stepped towards him.

'Can I have my phone back, Detective?' she asked. She was in her mid-twenties, and pretty. Jonah could understand why she would have developed a strong dislike for Torrance.

'We have the footage copied off it, I believe,' said Bob. 'Maybe a few minutes longer. I'll send my partner to fetch it. Ray?'

'On it.'

'In the meantime,' said Bob, 'we'd like to talk to you before you leave. A few questions about that night. We've been contacting as many people as we can for statements.'

The woman looked annoyed. 'Detective, I have a date this

evening. Bad enough I have to come here and get Blake's sorry ass out of trouble, but it's going on for six o'clock.'

'Five minutes. Promise.' Bob showed her to his desk, and indicated for Jonah to take a seat as well. 'So, it's Miss Norwald, right? Can I call you Mia?' She nodded. 'You have, shall I say, no love for Mr Torrance?'

'He's a prick, Detective.'

'What exactly is your relationship?'

'I have to work in the same office as him. My primary role is to do the half of his job he's incapable of and smooth over the friction he causes from time to time.'

'Your work involves acquisitions, I understand. For Andreas Biotech.'

'Not just that. Our office also deals with interactions between the various Andreas research subsidiaries, and handles some building development. We coordinate a little PR as well. We tend to use the Manor Williams people for most of it, but sometimes we do it ourselves. Well, mainly me.'

'And what exactly does that entail?'

'Not much, maybe a few words with a journalist when an acquisition goes ahead or we want to get interest in something. Showing our faces at conferences, sometimes, especially at universities. We'll go to give our researchers support. Blake likes to attend as much as possible. He gets a kick out of having his ass licked.'

'Did you see this woman on the night of the party, Mia?' Bob held up the smiling picture of Mary Connart.

Mia looked at it and shook her head. 'Not that I remember. Sorry.'

'And when did you leave the party?'

'Eleven o'clock. Me and another woman from the office. It was starting to wind down by then. Blake was still there when I left, he'd got a second wind.'

'But you'll stand by what you said, that Blake Torrance was

asleep between nine-fifty and ten-twenty, the time of the last footage you recorded?'

'He was. He woke up with a start a little later, but I didn't catch that on camera.'

'What do you mean?' Jonah asked. Mia Norwald looked a little alarmed, as if she'd forgotten he was there. 'He woke up with a start?'

'Ah, you know, he was disoriented. Stood up, glanced around him like he wasn't sure where he was. He looked like a fucking idiot so I wish I'd caught it on camera, but it was quick and I was laughing too hard. He gave me a hell of a glare when he saw me. Man, he was embarrassed.'

'Do you know what time he woke?' said Jonah.

'He was sitting under a clock,' she said with a shrug. 'It was ten-thirty.'

Ray came back with Mia Norwald's phone and they let her go, Ray seeing her out of the station.

'Why did you ask that?' Bob said to Jonah. 'About him waking with a start?'

Jonah shook his head. 'I don't know.' He really wasn't sure why he'd asked, but there was something nagging him.

After a minute, Ray returned. 'All done.'

'I'll order in some pizza,' Bob said. 'Jonah, we're back to square one here. You should get home. The only thing happening now is paperwork.'

'Don't worry,' said Jonah. 'I'm used to that. You mind if I grab some of that pizza? I'd be better eating before I drive home, and there's something bothering me I can't put my finger on.'

'Like?' said Ray.

'Torrance woke up at ten-thirty. The same time Mary Connart was found. The *exact* same time.'

'I know,' said Ray. 'The moment his alibi wasn't needed. The story's a little too neat, right?'

Jonah nodded, but that hadn't really been his point. Although what his point actually was, he didn't know.

He picked up a newspaper that was on Bob's desk and read it while the detectives got on with the endless form-filling the day had incurred. He found himself skipping over anything unpleasant, only reading the run-of-the-mill and the vacuous stories, entertainment sections, events. He started on the crossword, and gave up on it when the pizzas arrived.

As he ate, the only thing in the paper he'd not read was the business section. He started to read it all the same. He stopped suddenly, one paragraph into an article on the challenge of wine-growing in the area. There were interviews with several local producers, but it was one specific word that made him stop, a single word that was also in the headline: Local Wine Producers Hold Conference.

Conference.

'Uh, Ray, can I use a computer? I want to check something.'

Ray wheeled his chair over to the next desk, which was empty, and logged in for him. 'Be my guest. Just don't gamble or watch porn. Our IT guys keep track of that kind of shit and it's my account you're using.' He smiled. 'What are you after?'

Jonah shrugged. 'Just killing time.' He took position, grabbing a pen from a desk tidy, and starting to write on a blank pad by the keyboard.

Conferences, too, sometimes, Mia Norwald had said. *Especially universities. We'll attend to give our researchers support.*

It didn't take long to find. He felt cold as the results came up, and the timings matched.

'Bob,' he said. 'Ray.' They both looked up from their pizzas, the tone in his voice enough for them to know this was serious. 'You remember what Mia Norwald said about them attending conferences when Andreas Biotech teams were involved?'

They both nodded, and shared a look.

'There are two specific ones you should hear about. Thirteen weeks ago, a conference on bacteriophages at the University of Colorado, in Denver. Three weeks later, a gene therapy conference at the University of Minnesota in Minneapolis.' He let the locations and timing sink in.

Denver, thirteen weeks ago.

Minneapolis, three weeks later.

The two previous cases Bob had told him about.

Bob was staring at him. 'Jesus Christ. You think he was there?'

'He knows, Bob. There's not a doubt in my mind, he *knows* what happened. And maybe more than that. He woke up when Mary Connart was found. The *exact same time.*'

'His alibi is bullet proof, Jonah. Unless he can be in two places at—' Bob stopped, looking spooked; Jonah was nodding at him. 'Shit like that may be hard to get past a judge,' he said.

'Shit like what?' said Ray. 'Are either of you going to come out and say what the fuck you mean?'

'There was something about Torrance,' said Jonah. 'There was something *with* him in the interview room. Something dark. Some kind of shadow.'

Bob looked at him for a moment, then grabbed his coffee cup and downed the cold remains. 'Fuck it. Ray, call Mia Norwald. If she can confirm Torrance was at those conferences, we move. Whatever his alibi, if he was in the neighbourhood of two other killings, we have more than enough to justify arresting him.' He turned to Jonah. 'We'll bring him back in, and worry about what the hell we can charge him with later. You coming?'

Jonah thought of the shadow clinging to Torrance's shoulder in the interrogation room. He didn't relish the thought of laying eyes on it again, but he had to see Torrance's face when he found out he'd been linked to the previous cases. He had to.

'Wouldn't miss it for the world,' he said.

21

Andreas Research Investment had thirty staff and took up the sixth floor of an office building near Dupont Circle. It was seven forty-five by the time they got confirmation from Mia Norwald that Torrance had attended both the conferences Jonah had identified. She herself had only been present at the Minneapolis one, but she was familiar enough with Torrance's schedule to know about Denver.

It was dark and cold as they parked in front of the building. Most of the windows above them were unlit but the sixth floor had a bright cluster at the far end, and a solitary light at the other, which hopefully meant people were still there.

'We can't be certain he's here,' said Bob. 'Hopefully, he's true to his word and came back to get some work done. If not, he lives out in Beltsville, so we'll go there next.'

The building entrance was locked, but a cleaner was running a floor polisher over the tiled entryway on the other side of the glass door. Bob held his badge to the glass and knocked hard until the cleaner noticed. He pointed at the door and the cleaner obliged.

'Detective Crenner,' said Bob. 'You know if anyone's still working on the sixth floor?'

'I just finished up there ten minutes ago,' said the cleaner, eyeing Bob cautiously. 'There were a handful left.'

Bob nodded and went to the elevator, Ray and Jonah following.

They walked out into the sixth-floor vestibule just as a young man and an older woman came out of the floor entrance, which closed behind them. Bob held up his badge again. 'Detective Crenner. Is Blake Torrance inside?'

Both the man and the woman gave Bob a look Jonah recognized; the expression of wary interest people had if they weren't used to encountering the police. 'Yes, Detective,' said the woman. 'He's the last one in the office now, so he'll be locking up when he leaves. Is there a problem?'

'We just need to talk to him. If you wouldn't mind letting us inside.'

The woman nodded. She had a security card on a chain around her neck and reached for it.

The man beside her frowned. 'Now hold on a minute,' he said. 'We can't just—'

'See this?' said Bob, waving his police badge. 'This says you can.'

The woman swiped them inside and the pair hurried on to the elevator, not looking back. Bob had just been pushing his luck, Jonah knew, but it had worked, the pair washing their hands of the situation.

Ray smiled, holding the office door open. 'Guess they have somewhere better to be. Grab that for me, Jonah.' He pointed to a fire extinguisher by the wall, which Jonah brought over and set against the open door to stop it locking again.

Bob led the way. The offices by the entrance were brightly lit but empty; most of the rest of the floor was dark, the motion-triggered lights having timed out. The only other lit office was at the far end, and it had to be Torrance's. As they walked, the motion-sensors triggered the ceiling lights along their path, flickering noisily into life one by one. They reached the office at the end. Blake Torrance sat at his desk.

For an instant Jonah could see the darkness on the man's shoulder again. The same ill-defined shapeless form, but this time there was something he could see more clearly. Under the shape, four long dark lines extended down over Torrance's collarbone, like thin fingers.

'You forget something, Jim?' said Torrance, only looking up once he'd finished speaking. His relaxed expression dropped away. 'Detectives,' he said. 'Can't say I'm pleased to see you.'

'We have more questions, Mr Torrance,' said Bob, smiling. 'If you wouldn't mind coming with us.'

Torrance stood. 'God *damn* you people, I have too much to do. Can't it wait until tomorrow?' He hurried past them out of his office, still complaining, leaving Bob and Ray wide-eyed and sharing a cautious look. They followed. Torrance headed a few doors down and turned left into a small canteen area. He went straight for a coffee vending machine and was punching buttons as they entered. A paper cup dropped down and started to fill.

'No, it can't wait,' said Bob, slow and serious.

'Then ask me what you want to ask,' said Torrance. 'Here and now. Everyone else has left, so we have total privacy.' Torrance looked at Jonah, then back to Bob. 'Who's this?'

'Mr Miller is a consultant on the case,' said Bob. Torrance raised an eyebrow and said nothing. 'You want to talk to us now, then that's your decision. But it's on record.'

'Go ahead. The faster we clear this up, the better.'

Bob shared a look with Ray, who nodded, taking his cell phone out of his pocket ready to record whatever Torrance said. Jonah understood the surprise he could see in the eyes of both detectives: Torrance was arrogant enough to think he didn't need his lawyer.

'Fine,' said Bob. He nodded to the vending machine. 'Dial up something black and strong for me and we'll do it right here.'

Torrance obliged and handed Bob a cup. They all sat, Ray placing his phone on the table in front of them, recording.

Bob took a sip of the vended coffee and winced, setting down the cup. 'Now, Blake. If I were to say Minnesota and Denver, what would you say to me?'

Torrance's cocky expression fell away in an instant. He rubbed at his shoulder, staring at Bob. 'What did you say?'

Bob smiled. 'See, the look on your face right now, Blake – that tells me everything. Tells me you're guilty as hell. Whatever your alibi for Mary Connart's death, all I need is that look on your face and I know you're in it up to your neck.'

'I didn't . . . I—'

'Something else I can see in those eyes of yours, Blake. You really didn't think we'd link them to you. Not even for a second. Now that we have, you have no idea what to do. Maybe there are other deaths, huh?'

Torrance looked down, silent. Jonah could see he was trembling a little, his hand still rubbing his shoulder.

'I'll take that as a yes,' said Bob. 'We'll get you to the station again, Blake, and you'd better start telling us the *how* and the *why*. That, and who else is involved. Because whatever part you played, you sure as hell didn't kill Mary Connart. Not in person.'

Torrance stopped rubbing his shoulder. He took a deep breath and let it out slowly. He looked up, smiling. 'Didn't I, Detective?' he said, dropping his hand to his side, his voice deep, slow and angry. 'Oh, I killed her. I'd tell you how but you wouldn't believe me.'

It was an admission, but Jonah didn't like the look Torrance was giving them. He didn't seem hunted, suddenly. Quite the reverse.

'Try us,' said Bob. 'Get it off your chest.'

Torrance seemed to find that funny. He rubbed at his shoulder again. 'It's part of me now,' he said. 'Or am I part of *it*? I'm not sure. It's not what I expected. I didn't think I would find it so freeing.' He smiled at the puzzlement on Bob Crenner's face. 'Nobody ever found the first three. It doesn't take long for there to be almost nothing left. The ones that were found were the ones that were rushed or interrupted. I was lucky with them, though.' He looked pointedly at the phone in front of him. 'Sorry, you are getting all this, aren't you?'

Bob looked at Ray, concern on his face. Jonah wondered what was going through the detectives' minds. 'Tell me about Mary Connart,' said Bob, steering Torrance while avoiding interrupting the flow of the man's confession, however little sense it seemed to be making.

'I was drunk and careless,' said Torrance. 'I thought I heard the woman talk about things she shouldn't have known about, and I overreacted.'

'Winnerden Flats,' said Jonah.

Torrance looked at him with narrowed eyes but said nothing. He just looked back to Bob and continued. 'I thought I should silence her, and do it quickly. I was cocky. Before, I'd been so much more careful. It was just an overreaction. All this fuss, for an overreaction.' He shook his head. 'I think some of the others must have suspected after Minneapolis, but they couldn't know it was *me*. Until now. I wonder what they'll do? They'll be angry, I know that.'

'The others?' said Bob.

Torrance ignored him. 'I can look through its eyes if I want to,' he said, his expression almost wistful. 'It's not easy, but it's worth it. I wasn't sleeping at the party, you see. I was watching. I closed my eyes and saw what it saw as it left me, as it followed her. I enjoyed doing that. I liked seeing the fear. It can be fun to watch it with your own eyes, too, let it run free and see what it does.'

Jonah stared at Torrance's shoulder. The shadow was beginning to form again, darkening with every second, its outline becoming more defined. The long downward tendrils he had seen earlier reappeared beneath, thickening. Jonah realized that it was his *vision* that was changing here, his ability to see something that had always been present. That wasn't all: he could feel a terrible sensation of foreboding. 'Bob,' he said, 'something's happening . . .'

'Well, Detectives,' said Torrance. 'Pleasant as this was, I think I'll be getting along.'

'You're coming with us,' said Bob.

'Oh, you're not leaving,' said Torrance, standing up. 'I have plans, and they involve me being very far from here, very soon.'

Bob stood and stepped back from Torrance, drawing his gun. Ray did the same. 'Stay right where you are,' said Bob.

'You don't believe me?' said Torrance. 'We'll see.' The black tendrils were growing clearer and clearer, like dead, ancient fingers embedded deep within the man's flesh.

'Blake Torrance,' said Bob. 'You are under arrest for—'

The fingers started to move, pulling out, ever longer, coming free now, coming *free* . . .

'*Bob*,' said Jonah.

The lights went out.

22

The darkness was total.

'*Don't move,*' said Bob, but Jonah heard Torrance rush for the canteen door. They heard the door shut; the sound of a lock turning. Then footsteps hurrying away.

There was a click; Ray was holding a flashlight, minuscule but bright. He stood and went to the closed door and tested it. 'Locked,' he said. 'It's sturdy, but I think I could break it down.'

'Hold on,' said Bob, sounding shaken. He fumbled in his pockets until he produced his own small flashlight. 'Call this in, Ray. He might be running, but he could easily have gone for a weapon. Let's keep back from the door, keep our voices down. Jonah, you knew something was going on. What did you see?'

'I don't think he was alone. I think whatever killed Mary Connart was right here with us.'

'Come *on*, Jonah,' said Ray, swinging the flashlight towards him. 'What the hell does that mean? The guy was rambling.'

'I think he sent out whatever killed Mary,' said Jonah. 'Something dark, something that was always with him. Like a *familiar*. The moment Eugene Harding interrupted what was happening, Torrance sat up because it was *him* that Eugene had interrupted. Him, and the thing he was controlling.'

'That's crazy,' said Ray, without much conviction.

'Maybe,' said Jonah. 'But I saw it, just now. On his shoulder. I saw it wake.' *Wake*, he thought, *and start to detach.*

'Call it in,' said Bob.

Ray took his cell phone from the table. He scowled and held it up higher. 'Nothing,' he said. 'No signal. You?'

Bob and Jonah both tried their phones. Nothing. They didn't comment on it, but they were in the middle of the city and had no signal. It didn't make sense.

'What do you think?' asked Ray. 'You think he's running?'

'No,' said Bob. 'He wasn't confessing. He was boasting. Now, he's waiting for something. He told us he wasn't going to let us leave. He must have gone for a weapon. Jonah, take a position at the back wall. Stay down. Ray, I'll cover you as you get the door open. Then we wait a little before I go out there. Got it?'

'Got it,' said Ray. He passed Jonah his flashlight.

Jonah felt sick at the thought of the door opening into the absolute darkness of the corridor. 'What if something's out there? Some kind of *guard*?'

'Jonah,' said Bob, 'if something's out there, it can come in and get us any time. Positions.'

Jonah switched off the flashlight and crouched behind some chairs near the coffee machine. Bob stood in the centre of the room, holding his flashlight to give Ray just enough light to see by.

Then Jonah heard it. Something scuttled past him on the floor. He jumped to his feet and backed away.

Bob had heard it too, and swung the light around. 'What was that?' he said.

Jonah kept backing off. 'It's still in here,' he said. He switched his flashlight back on and shone it around the floor, thinking of what Bob had said about Torrance: *he must have gone for a weapon.*

He hadn't needed to. The weapon was already in the room.

They heard it again, a scuttling across hard floor, and this time Bob got the light over quickly enough to catch a glimpse of a small dark shape, long thin legs trailing as it fled under a table in the corner of the room.

'Did you see it?' said Jonah.

Bob nodded. 'Ray,' he said, flashlight and gun aimed at the corner, 'get the door open.'

Ray took a kick at the door. Then another. At the third, it started to give. One or two more, and—

'Jesus Christ,' said Bob. Jonah looked back to the corner of the room to see the table Bob's light was trained on tilt, then fall, as, underneath, there rose a dark shape that seemed to just swallow up the beam of the flashlight. The darkness unfolded rapidly, growing tall, thickening, a hulking mass the height of the room, visible in outline, arms outstretched.

And now Jonah could see glints across the whole of the shadow mass, glints that moved, glistening shards that brought back Mary Connart's last words.

The shadow has teeth.

The creature stood motionless as all three of them looked on in horror. Ray was the first to snap out of it, giving the door another desperate kick, but it still managed to hold.

'Come *on!*' cried Ray in frustration. The creature stepped towards him as he kicked again. The door finally swung open.

Bob raised his gun and fired at the shadow: three times, without effect. The creature took slow strides in Ray's direction and swept its arm out towards the man, seizing him, then throwing. Ray landed on the other side of the room, gripping his bloodied arm, face in agony and terror as the shadow turned and closed in on him.

'No!' shouted Jonah. It turned towards him and took a step in his direction. For a moment it stood still, and Jonah sensed that it was wary of him. Guns didn't seem to concern it, but there was something about Jonah it didn't like.

He felt panic rising but he pushed back the fear; the terror that could bleed into him from revival subjects was something he had become used to suppressing. Pointing the flashlight at it, he moved towards the shape in the darkness, testing what his instinct was telling him.

And the shape stepped away.

'I'll hold it back if I can,' said Jonah, his voice trembling. 'You two get out of here.'

Bob moved to Ray and helped him up. 'Then what?' said Ray, eyes wide.

'Find Torrance,' said Jonah. 'I hope to God he's still here. Find him and make him stop this.' *If he* can *stop it*, Jonah thought.

Jonah stepped to his side, coming between the creature and the door as Bob and Ray rushed out. He could feel its gaze on him, and could sense its uncertainty. It came forward a little, then backed off again.

His nerve was starting to fail, though. The shape stepped forward and paused. Too close for comfort, Jonah stepped away from it. And it came forward again.

'Bob!' he called. 'Hurry!'

He was the one backing off now. The creature was still wary but it was advancing. Jonah moved out into the corridor and retreated towards Ray, who was propped against the wall thirty feet further on, blood pouring from the wound on his arm.

Past Ray, Jonah could see the movement of flashlights at the far end of the building. He heard Bob shout Torrance's name.

Jonah shone his flashlight back along to the canteen door as the dark mass emerged and turned, seeing him. It waited for a moment. Jonah found enough courage to move towards it again, but this time the creature seemed to know the threat was an empty one.

It came for him. Jonah held his ground. He raised his arms as behind him the shouting grew. He heard gunfire, but still the shadow drew closer, picking up speed. Three more strides at most, he thought. He braced and closed his eyes, dropping the flashlight, not wanting to see death bear down on him.

But nothing happened.

For a moment he thought it was standing over him, waiting, wanting its victim to see it before it struck; then he opened his eyes, grabbed the flashlight from the floor and swung it across the corridor.

Nothing was there. He turned and saw Bob walk up from the far end of the office. They both converged on Ray.

'Torrance?' said Jonah.

'Alive, for now,' said Bob, holstering his gun. 'He pulled a gun on me. I shot him twice. He's unconscious.' He looked around. 'Where is it?'

Jonah shook his head. 'I think it's gone.'

'Fucking thing bit me,' whispered Ray. 'Threw me, but it felt like a *bite*.'

With a thunk that startled all three of them, the lighting directly overhead flickered on. The rest of the corridor was still dark.

'Shit,' said Ray, shocked by the sudden brightness. He looked terrible, blood soaked through his jacket from shoulder to elbow, his shirt scarlet. Jonah suspected that if he looked closer at his wounds, they would look like abrasions. Scratches of varying depth and ferocity. He thought of those obsidian teeth, glinting in the dark as the creature had approached him. He thought of Mary Connart.

Jonah took out his phone. 'Signal's back,' he said. Somehow he wasn't surprised. He walked to the end of the corridor, lights flickering on overhead as he triggered the motion sensors.

Torrance was lying on the floor bleeding profusely from two wounds that looked serious, one in the stomach and one on the left side of his upper torso. Beside him was a flashlight and a travel bag. He had no doubt now that Torrance had intended to kill all three of them before making an escape. Locking the door had been Torrance's way of buying enough time to set it all in motion.

The man's breathing was strained and uneven. On his shoulder Jonah could see a faint trace of the shadow, returned now. Home.

He went back to Bob and Ray.

'I've called it in,' said Bob.

Ray looked at Jonah, urgently. 'What the hell was it? Where did it come from?'

'You both saw it, then?' said Jonah. They nodded. Jonah shook his head. 'I saw things like this in dreams. Visions.'

'Jesus,' said Bob. 'Nobody's going to believe a word of this.'

'Torrance mentioned that there were others,' said Ray. 'Did he just mean others who knew about it, or others who were like him?'

'Or maybe others who—' started Bob, but then he stopped, staring at Jonah. 'Others who might want to keep this quiet. Others who might be in a *position* to keep it quiet.'

Jonah felt his stomach drop at the thought. 'We have to act like we saw nothing.'

Ray looked at Bob. 'So what the hell do we say just happened?'

'We say that Torrance was rambling and then resisted arrest,' said Bob. 'Backup's five minutes away. We need to have our story straight by the time they get here.' He turned to Jonah. 'And you should leave.'

Jonah shook his head. 'I don't understand.'

'Until we know more about what's going on here, we have to be cautious. If there are others, whatever the hell these things are, none of us wants to look like a threat. And I saw it back off from you, Jonah. It might be simpler if you weren't here when backup arrives. We took you to your car before we came to this office, understand?'

Jonah looked at Ray, who nodded. 'Get going,' said Ray. 'Prop the front door open on your way out, huh? I'm not quite up to moving just yet, and I'd rather Bob didn't have to go down and let backup in. I don't want to be left alone up here.'

*

Jonah wedged the doors open as requested and started to walk fast. He was shivering, and not from the cold. Sirens were close; he ducked into the dark entrance of a shop a hundred yards down the street as half a dozen police vehicles converged on the building he'd just left. A minute later an unmarked car came from another direction, driven with urgency. A suited man got out and was intercepted by one of the uniformed officers setting up a cordon, the cop raising a palm to block his way.

The suited man held up ID; the cop took a look and nodded. They spoke briefly before the cop waved him through, but Jonah was finding it hard to concentrate on what was said.

Because Jonah's eyes were on the suited man's shoulder. At the shadow perched there, clearly visible.

Glistening in the streetlight.

23

Annabel was sitting in the same bar where she'd met Takeo and Kaylee two weeks before, finding out just how bad their coffee was.

Her thief hadn't shown yet. The day before, Kaylee had sent her a message: their friend was willing to meet her with new information, for a price. She'd not had to give it much thought, and she'd been waiting over an hour for the man to show up. Instead, she'd had two cups of murky water and thirty minutes of glances from a guy on the far side of the room, who'd been there when she'd come in.

Shit, she thought, as he finally decided to venture over and try his luck.

'You mind if I join you?' he said.

'I'm waiting for someone.'

He sat anyway. 'I'll keep you company until they get here. Want a drink?'

Annabel nodded at the coffee. 'I'm OK,' she said, with a flat voice. 'And, like I said, I'm waiting for someone, so . . .' She looked at him, expecting him to get the hint.

The man smiled. It was an appealing smile, the kind that begged to be returned, but she resisted. 'I understand,' he said, then he lowered his voice. 'I'm Yan, by the way.' He held out his hand.

Annabel smiled now. Yan was the thief. She shook his hand. 'You let me sit here and drink this terrible coffee?'

'Just being careful.' He looked at her, appraising. 'I'll get you a decent drink, then we'll talk.'

She let him get her a beer, and when he came back she handed him his payment, up front as agreed. 'So why meet me in person?' she asked. 'Why not send the other two?'

Yan passed her a USB stick. 'Means they don't take a cut,' he said. 'Besides, Takeo said you were pretty, and I'm *very* shallow. I wanted to see for myself.' He smiled again, but Annabel wasn't about to let him distract her.

'So what did I buy?' she asked.

'You bought a puzzle,' said Yan. 'Two sets of documents. One is a detailed five-year plan for the expansion of the Winnerden Flats site, aimed at crushing the competition in the cryogenics business. Significant increase in capacity, and a huge new research wing that's already nearing completion. This was what my original clients were most interested in, and it was pretty easy to get hold of. The other is a *different* building plan for the works at Winnerden Flats, completely at odds with the rest.'

'Couldn't it just be an outdated plan?'

'No. It was more recent. And hidden.'

'How and when did you get hold of this information? If you're happy telling me.'

He shrugged. 'Allow me to keep it vague. It was over four weeks ago. I lifted the first set of documents from a system that was relatively insecure. The other came from data I managed to get from a much harder target before I got cut off. Everything was encrypted, and this was the only thing I managed to dig out. I couldn't do anything with the rest but pass it on. I doubt my clients managed to decrypt it either.'

'You were cut off? So they knew someone had been there?'

'Yes, but they had no way to trace it back to source. Anyway, I told my clients what I thought had happened.'

'Which was?'

'They were being played. They heard the rumour about

Andreas Biotech expanding their cryogenics business, and these convenient documents showed up, confirming the rumour, stored in the first place anyone from outside would have looked. Too easy to find, meaning the company had *wanted* them to be found. Which was why I kept looking. The second set of documents, these are the real plans.'

'So Andreas Biotech were trying to mislead them?'

'The first documents show an expansion over five years. My clients think the intent was to lull them into complacency. They feared a rapid expansion into their markets, so a long-term plan was less of a threat. Me, though—' He shook his head, reluctant to continue.

'Go on.'

'I think my clients are wrong, but I don't understand *what* the intent was. The whole thing is a puzzle, and I don't *like* unanswered puzzles. One of the reasons I wanted to meet you is to ask you, face to face: if you work it out, tell me. Please. Before it drives me crazy.'

'I don't follow. Why do you think your clients got it wrong?'

'It's not about lulling them into complacency, because I don't think the real plans are anything to do with expanding their cryogenics business.'

'How come?' said Annabel.

He shrugged. 'Look at the alternative site plan and ask yourself a question: if they're expanding, where do they put all the extra customers?'

*

Annabel left Yan after getting him to promise to send anything new, should he manage to decrypt the other files; Yan had been keen to meet up again, either way. She'd declined as politely as she could and headed home.

When she got back to her apartment and looked at what was

on the memory stick he'd given her, the first thing she did was bring up both site plans for Winnerden Flats and compare them.

In each, the facility had improved residential quarters for a significant number of staff, and a gym area including a pool. In the first plan – the dummy if Yan's instinct was correct – the entirely new wing consisted of storage areas for the bodies of future clientele, to complement the existing storage area marked within the older part of the building.

In the alternative plan, this area was designated as research labs, with a large circular region annotated 'MCH'. There was no additional storage.

'I see what he means,' said Annabel out loud. 'Where do they put all the extra bodies?'

She closed the document with a sigh. She'd have another look tomorrow, she thought, although she was aware that it was all just detail, an excess of information that didn't really tell her anything useful about Andreas Biotech. Just distraction.

She poured herself a drink and threw a sandwich together, and thought about Yan's enthusiasm to meet up again. Flattering, yes; Yan had been easy on the eye. The depressing part had been that, for the briefest of moments, she had considered saying yes.

'You're an idiot, Annabel Harker,' she muttered. It was an old habit, she knew. Yan was blatantly the kind of guy for whom any relationship would have a built-in self-destruct mechanism. Even *considering* seeing him again was the first step on the path to using him as an emergency parachute. Something to allow her to flee a relationship that had grown beyond the confines of her comfort zone, and to enter one that could only be a disaster.

In the past, it wouldn't have been nearly so long before her self-preservation had kicked in and made her unconsciously look around for an escape route. It was high praise in a very twisted way, although she couldn't imagine Jonah taking it as a compliment. 'You're so important to me, Jonah,' she said to her kitchen, 'that I've put off consideration of infidelity for over a year.' She shook her head. 'Classy.'

With impeccable timing, her phone chimed; a text had come through from Jonah. *Call me*, it said. *Need to talk. Now.*

She set her phone down. She wasn't ready for a heart-to-heart, not by a long way.

She sat and ate, marvelling at how the intense love her parents had shared had left her with an allergy to commitment. Witnessing the loneliness of her father after her mother's death had inoculated her against it. She couldn't bear the dread of finding herself, somewhere down the line, so alone and so unhappy.

Annabel looked around at the empty kitchen in her empty apartment and let out a cold laugh at the irony.

Then she got another text from Jonah. There were only three words this time, but it was enough to make her freeze.

Three words that changed everything.

24

That same morning, Never Geary had come to the FRS office earlier than normal. He'd woken at a crazy hour and been unable to get back to sleep, and he knew exactly what the problem was. It had been three days since the Mary Connart revival and he'd not heard anything from Jonah since the drive back to Richmond.

'You worry too much,' he told himself, and it was true. But there had been a time, not so long ago, when Jonah had made all of Never's fears come to pass: when Never had found his friend in a mess on his bathroom floor, surrounded by pill-laden vomit.

Something like that tended to sharpen your instinct for worrying.

This time he'd left Jonah alone for a full twenty-four hours before he'd even called and left a message. A difficult revival could hit hard – and Mary Connart had been difficult – so he'd not been surprised that Jonah would retreat for a while, but today was the day that he would move up from tentative messages on his voicemail and knock on Jonah's door.

The office filled up. After Hugo's regular update meeting Never got back to his desk and went through his schedule for the day. He planned to get downstairs and finalize the new equipment tests, avoiding any on-site duties so that he could devote himself to proper, full-scale worrying.

Then Hugo called him into his office.

Hugo's door was open a crack, so he walked in after a token knock in case anyone else was with him. 'Hey, boss,' he said.

Hugo looked up from his desk, hands folded, biting at the nail of one thumb. He sighed and held up a thick wad of stapled pages. 'My eyes only,' he said. 'So shut the door.'

'Right,' said Never. He shut it and came over to Hugo's desk, glancing back to make sure the window slats were closed. He looked at the top page of the documents Hugo was holding. *FRS Director and Office Managers Only*, it said. 'On pain of death,' mused Never aloud. 'You sure I can look?'

'Officially we're telling staff about all of this tomorrow – well, about most of it. This is to give me a little time to prepare. And I know you can keep a secret.'

'Ha,' said Never, grinning, but then he caught the look on Hugo's face and put his grin away. 'Right, yes, I can keep a secret.'

'I'd appreciate it,' said Hugo. 'You've been here longer than I have, Never – longer than anyone in the office. I want to hear what you think: they're starting up Baseline again.'

'I'd heard the rumour,' said Never.

'Really?' said Hugo. 'This was news to me. There's going to be an announcement this afternoon, I'm told. A televised press conference. But . . . well.' He flipped through the document and passed it to Never, his finger pointing at a specific paragraph. 'There.'

'Shit,' said Never once he'd read it. He looked up. 'Do they really . . . ?'

Hugo nodded. 'An open offer to high-rated revivers to join the research team on a full-time basis. Well paid. At least as good as the salary private insurance firms offer. And a damn sight higher than the FRS scales.'

'Ouch,' said Never. The figures the document listed were almost painful, and Never suddenly understood why Hugo had wanted to confide in someone. 'How many will we lose?'

'There are limited spaces, so it depends on the uptake. I mean, for the best private revivers it might not be tempting enough, at least financially. The location hasn't been announced, so relocating will be a disincentive, but . . .'

'Is there a chance they'll use the old site?' The original Baseline location had been taken back by the US Army when Baseline had closed, but it was just over an hour's drive away. 'If they do, we're fucked, surely . . .' Theirs was the nearest FRS office. It could prove to be a rout.

Hugo nodded. 'They have a minimum rating as a guideline, but a third of our revivers are eligible.'

'Have you talked to Thorne? Maybe he'd be willing to consider raising pay to keep them?' He knew it was a forlorn hope, even as he said it.

'I've talked to Robert, yes,' said Hugo. 'There's no chance the FRS can match this. The biggest problem he sees is that once people have tasted the higher salary they won't come back, even once the research project finishes.'

'How long until it does?'

'It's funded for at least a year, but it could be longer.'

'What about the Afterlifers? Surely some of them will be uneasy about this?'

Hugo shook his head. 'Page twelve,' he said, and Never hunted through the document until he found it. 'The Afterlifers are part of the picture. The research has their full support, and after that it'll be pending . . . what did they call it?'

'"Pending a full review of the judicial use of Forensic Revival in the United States",' read Never. 'Fuck. A full review.'

'And the Afterlifers have something else, something they couldn't have dreamed of,' said Hugo. 'The review board will include several senior pro-Afterlifer members, and the review will have the power to halt revival completely. I would hope that's unlikely, but it's not impossible.' He reached out his hand and Never passed back the document. 'Of course if we lose the revivers, inevitably some technicians will go too. We'll have to wait and see, but just be aware of the possibility.'

'Ah,' said Never, realizing that he would be the one who gave out any bad news.

'There's one other thing,' said Hugo. 'How's Jonah doing?'

'He's fine,' said Never, a little too quickly. 'Why?'

Hugo rummaged among the papers on his desk and produced several envelopes. 'I have these to hand out. Personal offers to selected revivers to assist with the Baseline research. The people they're approaching directly get first refusal. Our top-rated people, of course. Jason and Stacy. Jonah's offer has been sent here too, I guess his resignation hasn't quite trickled through the system yet. Still a valid offer, though, I think. I was wondering if you'd give it to him once it's all public, after the press conference?'

'Sure,' said Never. He took the envelope, knowing what it meant. He'd been holding out hope that Jonah would be back at the FRS within months, but the offer in his hand was a guarantee that he'd be gone for at least a year. Worse, he'd be gone to whatever part of the country played host to the research. He knew Jonah would want to be involved; he'd have wanted to be even if they'd been paying peanuts. To be part of finding out what revival was, and what it *meant* . . . It seemed a foregone conclusion that Stacy would sign up, too, for the same reasons. As for Jason, even if the guy wasn't exactly burdened with *principle*, the money would sway it.

He wondered again where the new Baseline site would be; suddenly the idea of it being local had some appeal, since Jonah wouldn't have to move away.

The envelope felt far heavier than its physical weight.

When he'd first heard the rumour about Baseline starting again, the one thing that hadn't occurred to him was saying goodbye to friends.

*

It was 2 p.m. when Never showed up unannounced at Jonah's apartment. Jonah was slumped on his couch in T-shirt and pants when the intercom sounded. He lifted his purring cat from his lap and got a look of feline disapproval, then walked to the door.

'Just checking you're not dead,' said Never on the intercom.

'Subtle,' said Jonah.

'As always.'

Jonah buzzed him up. He threw some jeans on in the interim. Since getting home from the confrontation with Blake Torrance – and with whatever had been on Torrance's shoulder – Jonah had stayed indoors, curtains drawn. The image of the suited man arriving at the scene had stayed with him. The man, and the darkness he carried, making Jonah certain of one thing: the *others* Torrance had spoken of were very real. How many of them could there be? There was no way to know.

Worse, this second shadow had looked far clearer than Torrance's. *Stronger*, Jonah thought.

He'd ignored Never's calls even though he knew he would eventually have to tell him and Annabel what had happened. It looked like the time had come.

'Afternoon,' said Never, peering into Jonah's gloomy flat like a disappointed parent. 'Thought I'd come by and kick you out of your bed.'

'I was already up,' said Jonah.

'Arguably,' said Never. He held out an envelope. 'I have news.' Jonah went to take it, but Never snatched it back. 'Not so fast. You remember what Sam said about them reopening Baseline?'

'Really?' said Jonah, smiling when Never gave a nod.

'Really,' said Never, looking uneasy. 'There's a press conference in an hour or so to announce it. And this is your invite to join the team.' Jonah lunged forward and grabbed the envelope, then tore it open. 'I'm supposed to wait until . . .' said Never, then he shrugged.

It was light on detail, promising more in the days to come, but it was confirmation. The letter was signed by Doctor Stephanie Graves, Head of the Revival Baseline Research Group. He read it again, only then noticing that the offer came with a salary that was more than double his FRS pay. 'They want a response by tomorrow,' he said. He looked at Never, confused by the anxious expression on his friend's face. 'Why so worried?' he said. 'This is better than I could've imagined.'

'Does it say anything about where it'll be?'

Jonah checked again and shook his head. 'Nothing. There's a number to call for queries, but only after the press conference.'

'I take it by the look on your face you plan to accept?'

'Of course I do,' said Jonah. 'Especially now. There's something I need to tell you. You and Annabel. Something I've been putting off for the last few days. But I think *this* –' he brandished the letter – 'this gives us a way to fight back.'

'Fight?' said Never. He scowled. 'What's been going on, Jonah?'

Ten minutes later, Jonah's account of what had gone on in DC had left Never looking ill. 'Fuck off,' said Never. 'Fuck *off*. You told Annabel any of this?'

'Not yet,' said Jonah. 'How long before you head back to work?'

'After what you just told me I'm not sure I plan on going back *outside*.'

'That was my reaction, too,' said Jonah.

'You think these . . . creatures . . . you think they're something to do with what Andreas brought through?'

'I think so. What's been left behind, maybe. In the vision I had when Andreas tried to strangle me, I think I saw something like them. Servants, perhaps. Or disciples. Acolytes.'

'And there are definitely others?'

'I only saw one but the way Torrance spoke, there have to be at least a few more of them. It could be dozens.' *Or hundreds*, he thought to himself. 'If that's true, then I'd guess they would be keen to get into influential positions. Jockeying for power. Baseline reopening is crucial, though. It means we can find out what's going on.'

'You think anyone will believe you?'

'I'm sure Stephanie Graves will listen,' said Jonah. 'She'll have the power to do something about it. These things are physical, at least in part. Somehow I can see them when they're attached to their host, but they seem to be visible to everyone when they detach. With her help, we can do the research; we'll be able to learn what they are and defend against them.'

They hunted around the news channels until they found one that was readying broadcast of the press conference. Jonah took his phone and sent Annabel a text. *Call me. Need to talk. Now.* Given that she usually knew about everything before he did, he expected her to already be watching. He didn't think she would get back to him right away. If at all. Even so, he held his phone in his hand, hoping.

The picture cut from the wide shot of the conference room and the waiting audience, back to the newscaster. She explained that the press conference was revival related ('although at this time we have no further details'), and that they would be rejoining it as soon as it started.

After twenty minutes the channel returned to the press conference, starting with the wide shot, then moving in to show only the conference panel. Stephanie Graves was sitting in the centre seat. The seat to her left was empty and in the remaining three sat people Jonah didn't recognize. Doctor Graves waited for a minute or so; at last she nodded, smiled, and began.

'Good afternoon,' she said. 'My name is Doctor Stephanie Graves. It's my privilege to announce today the launch of a new research project, to extend the work of the Revival Baseline Research Group. With the support of every side in the revival debate, it will further our knowledge of what revival is, and what it means for us.' She paused and took a sip of water from the glass in front of her. 'The research will be carried out on a site generously provided by the project's key benefactor. The site is self-sufficient and will act as home to the estimated two hundred staff involved, which will include one hundred of the best revivers we can attract to the project.' The camera pulled back to include the screen behind her, which was now displaying a photograph of a large building in a desert plain. 'Located in Winnerden Flats, Nevada, the facility features state-of-the-art laboratories, with access to bespoke technologies that will allow us to explore the nature of the most baffling phenomenon known to science.'

'That's the place, right?' said Never, looking uneasy. 'The Andreas Biotech site you mentioned?'

Jonah nodded, suddenly very nervous, wondering what it meant. He'd thought that the work at Winnerden Flats must have been deeply sensitive for Blake Torrance to be so desperate to protect it, yet this was very, very public.

'And now,' said Stephanie Graves, 'I would like to allow our key benefactor a chance to take us through some of the additional details of the project and its aims.'

She nodded ahead of her, clearly to a person sitting off screen. The picture cut to a shot that encompassed the whole room, viewed from a camera right at the back. Someone in the audience stood at the left side of the front row and made their way around to the empty seat beside Stephanie. The room was suddenly filled with an excited murmur, and as the man took his seat, the picture cut back to a close shot of him.

Jonah stared at the face that appeared on screen. A face that belonged to someone who should be dead, a face he'd watched *burn*, hair on fire and skin blackening in the flame. Yet there it was, the face now pristine, uninjured.

Smiling.

'That's impossible,' said Never. He looked at Jonah, his expression a mixture of outrage and fear. 'That's *impossible*.'

Feeling numb, Jonah listened to what the impossible face said, not wanting to miss a single word. And as he listened, he sent another text to Annabel.

Three words.

Andreas is alive.

25

Andreas held up a hand and waited for the murmur of the audience to settle. 'Rumours of my demise –' he said, then paused as a ripple of laughter spread through the room. He smiled, then his expression grew serious. 'A year and a half ago, one of my research facilities was targeted by a group of terrorists claiming to be affiliated to the Afterlifers. In the resulting fire many good people died. It has been the official position that I was among the dead. As you can see, that was not true. Luckily, I was not at the facility that night. This good fortune saved my life. However, the security forces that keep our country safe – those who protect us each day without fanfare or glory – advised me that the danger was not gone.' He paused, and smiled in a reassuring way, a paternal way.

'But the terrorists behind the attack did not truly represent the beliefs of Afterlifers. Far from it. The Afterlifer cause is an expression of reasonable concern for the use of a power we do not yet understand. It simply counsels caution. I have always taken the position that this caution is unwarranted, but in this great country we are free to disagree. The original Revival Baseline Research Group was brought to a premature end, before the truth about revival could be found. Now it is time for us to put aside our differences and to give full backing to this new venture in understanding. We seek nothing less than the truth about death, and what lies beyond. I believe that the truth is within our grasp. And when we find that truth –' Andreas paused, held the moment. He knew how to play to an audience. 'When we find that truth, we will share it with the world. And it will be the most important day in human history.'

The room broke into applause. Andreas smiled, ignoring the shouted questions from gathered journalists.

Looking vaguely shell-shocked, Never turned to Jonah. 'So,' he said. 'Are you still planning on signing up?'

*

After the press conference ended, Jonah went to his PC with Never close behind. He found the attachment to Annabel's previous mail. 'This is what Annabel sent me before.'

Shooing Jonah out of the way, Never took the seat and looked through what was there, bringing up the unofficial floor plan showing the original buildings and the rough layout of the extensions.

'Up until now it's been a cryogenic storage facility,' said Jonah. 'Annabel's notes have plenty on it. Top of the range, all their, um, clients are kept at most two degrees above absolute zero.'

'Cosy,' said Never. He opened Google Maps and hunted for Winnerden Flats. It wasn't marked, but eventually he found the location in a scan of an older map of Nevada, and zoomed down into the satellite imagery. 'Looks like it's on the fucking moon,' he said. It was isolated, surrounded by vast desolation. There were buildings around a central courtyard, a few roads, and a clear perimeter fence much further out. 'I'm guessing this is before they started any of the new work.' He brought up the extension plans they had, the outline of the original buildings matching perfectly. 'This place has been there for a while, right?'

'Originally built nineteen years ago,' said Jonah. 'Seven years before revival emerged.'

'Did her notes say how many clients they currently have?'

'There was something from the original brochure . . . hang on . . . there. The storage capacity is four hundred full-body and one thousand partial. I guess that means just the head. Neither option was cheap.'

An annoying jingle started to come from Never's pocket. He took out his phone and looked. 'Annabel,' he said.

Jonah immediately felt like a poor relation. 'Why's she calling *you?*'

'She's using a secure calling app she told us about. I'm guessing you didn't bother installing it?'

Jonah felt his face redden. No, he hadn't. In the first months following the fire at Reese-Farthing, Annabel had put together a suite of secure communication apps, something Jonah had resisted, desperate to believe that there was no reason to worry. Any talk of covert communication flew in the face of that and made him very uncomfortable.

The phone was still ringing, Never looking at the screen as if it was something contagious. Jonah could see in Never's face the same reluctance he felt himself. In the space of a few minutes, things had changed completely. Answering the call felt like another step away from their old lives.

Finally, Never answered. 'Hi, Annabel,' he said. He put the phone on speaker. 'I assume you saw the press conference.'

'I saw. Is Jonah with you?'

'Right here,' said Jonah. 'Are you OK?'

She paused. 'No,' she said, and Jonah knew exactly what she meant.

*

They shared their news in detail. Jonah told her about Mary Connart and Blake Torrance; about the shadows lurking, and his previous assumption that they were left-overs, stragglers abandoned by their defeated master. Not now, with Andreas alive.

And, of course, he told her about his invitation to join the research.

In turn, Annabel told them what had happened at her latest

meeting, and the new information about Winnerden Flats. 'Given the timings with your Torrance case,' she said, 'it might have been the theft of these documents that had Torrance on edge about the name Winnerden. I think we have to assume the alternative site plan is the real one. The question is, what are they hiding?'

'I don't know how they could expect to hide anything,' said Jonah. 'Stephanie Graves is in the process of assembling her team of researchers, and they're taking revivers from around the country and beyond. There's no way they can keep something big from all those people, surely?'

There was silence.

'Jonah,' said Annabel, 'your invitation to join the project: does it say how soon people will be going?'

'It'll be ready to take people within the next few days. They want the facility fully up and running in two to four weeks.'

'Maybe you should consider it,' she said. 'Being inside the facility would be a great place to find out what was going on.'

'Come on, Annabel,' said Jonah. 'The only reason I got invited is because it would be conspicuous if I wasn't. There's no way Andreas would want me there. I'd guess he would rather we weren't *anywhere*. Right now all I want to do is get as much cash as I can lay my hands on and vanish before he decides to do something about that.'

'Jonah,' she said, 'if Andreas cared what we thought, he would have done something about us long before now. He's had plenty of opportunity. If we don't seem like a threat to him, he mustn't care. You think we have to run to be safe, but running would do exactly the opposite. It would make us look dangerous.'

'Please, Annabel,' said Jonah. 'We can just go somewhere. Vanish. Together.'

'We don't know what's going on,' she said. 'Maybe Andreas is trying to get people with these shadows into useful positions, political and civil. Maybe it's a long-term goal, and he's just rounding up the best revivers to keep them from seeing the shadows the way you can, and revealing their existence. Winnerden Flats could be a decoy. If we run, we're not in a position to find out what's going on. And then we're defeated.'

'I still say we should run,' said Jonah. 'We're sitting ducks. Last time we were caught up in this we nearly died, but if we'd been safe at home that night? Nothing in our lives would have changed. We would've been blissfully unaware of it all. I want to go somewhere and forget about everything.'

'Nothing would have been different?' said Annabel. 'Tess would be dead, for a start.'

Jonah said nothing.

'What about you, Never?' said Annabel. 'If we run, we all have to do it at the same time. We need to agree, and the votes are one for, one against.'

'Oh great, deciding vote,' said Never. 'Well, I agree about the risk of drawing attention to ourselves if we panic. And I suppose I can keep my ear to the ground at work. The FRS will be a way to hear what's happening in Baseline, and there's something else: Stacy and Jason were invited to Winnerden Flats too. I need to warn them off before I'd even consider running.'

'They could prove useful as contacts,' said Annabel.

'Fuck that,' said Never. 'I'd rather my friends weren't stranded out in the middle of nowhere with Andreas for company.'

Jonah nodded. 'Agreed,' he said. 'But you can't tell them outright. You'd sound crazy. Play to their loyalty to the FRS, maybe.'

'That I can do,' said Never. 'As for my vote . . . I don't know. Not yet.'

'OK,' said Annabel. 'Let's say we take forty-eight hours to think about it. Pack a bag in case anything happens. If it does, we alert each other securely and vanish. We can survive, Jonah. Maybe long enough to find Andreas's weakness.'

'If you're right about Andreas not caring what we do,' said Jonah, 'then maybe he has no weaknesses.'

26

Once they'd ended the call, Jonah gave Never his phone so he could install the suite of secure communication apps.

'Seriously?' said Never, looking at Jonah's cell phone as if it was a slice of cold sick. 'You really use this? I thought you upgraded.'

'I didn't see the point. I only use it for voice calls and browsing.'

'Well,' said Never, with what could only be pity in his eyes, 'you need to go out and buy yourself a decent no-contract phone. If we do end up running, we'd have to ditch our old phones anyway. Even if they couldn't decrypt the calls themselves, they'd still be able to track us on them. I'll give you a list to pick from and the link you need for the app suite. Pay cash for the phone, too. And don't just buy it down the street, OK?'

He agreed, and Never headed back to work.

*

Jonah spent some of that night and most of the following morning getting a small backpack ready. He kept it light, making sure the damn thing didn't look like it was ready to burst. It had to appear casual, day-to-day. He had a few hundred dollars in there, some spare clothes. Hardly anything else would be coming with him.

If they ran.

It felt unreal, like some kind of training exercise. The events of the days before already had the quality of a bad dream, and he kept catching himself doubting the sense of Annabel's plan either way. Running seemed crazy. Waiting seemed equally insane.

He heard from Never mid-morning, a matter-of-fact phone call about the gradual flow of information reaching the FRS about Baseline. Stacy and Jason both had rest days, so Never hadn't been able to talk to them yet, something he wanted to do in person. Jonah felt his gut twist at the thought of Stacy, and even at the thought of Jason, being co-opted for Andreas's research plans. He hoped that it was all part of some kind of front or distraction; or even, as Annabel had suggested, an effort from Andreas to tie up the best revivers around. To simply keep them out of the way, in case they could see the shadows just as Jonah could.

Yet even if Never could talk Stacy and Jason out of joining the research, there would be many others who would go eagerly. *Hell, Jonah thought, I would have been one of them, if I didn't know any better.*

Late afternoon, Jonah took his backpack, got into his car, and headed out to get that new cell phone. Before he went, he spoke with his neighbour, making sure she still had a spare key and would check in on his cat if . . .

If something came up.

He took the fifteen-minute drive from his apartment to the mall near Huguenot Park. He'd been there with Annabel when she'd visited the previous spring – she'd dragged him there and made him buy more clothes in one day than he'd bought in the last five years. With the shopping done they'd settled down for a long, leisurely coffee upstairs in a small cafe that Jonah had appreciated, because even though they were beside a large window, he'd felt himself able to people-watch without feeling visible. It had been one of those simple, perfect afternoons, Annabel feeling so close to him and a whole new world opening up.

He'd been back on his own a few times since then, taking comfort from the memory as things between the two of them changed and drifted. It was something to warm himself by.

After buying his new phone, he went to the same cafe and found that the table by the window was empty. He sat and began to configure the phone with all the bells and whistles Annabel and Never insisted on.

He looked down to the mall below, finding himself tensing.

Because, apart from the memory of that afternoon, there was another reason he'd come here: to people-watch again, this time with a very specific purpose in mind.

The thought had come to him the night before. The darkness he had seen on Blake Torrance's shoulder had been invisible at first; by the end, it was irrefutable. Being able to see it had felt like a new skill, a new ability forged.

Since the appearance of Andreas at the press conference, his mind had gone back again and again to the words the creature within Andreas had used at Reese-Farthing: *we are Legion. We are all we have ever consumed.*

How many shadows were out there?

He had come here to watch the crowds, in the hope that he would see nothing.

He watched the people walk past down below. His stomach clenched any time a hand reached up to a shoulder; to rub it, or scratch it. Jonah watched, his eyes moving from person to person, seeing every motion as a sign, every gesture as a clear *tell*. There: a tall man, holding the hand of a child, reaching with the other to itch at his neck. There: a woman, suddenly clutching at her shoulder. He wondered how it was done. *Recruitment*, he thought. How did it happen? Was it something Andreas had to do in person, or was it like a virus, like a plague?

A plague, he thought. *Dear God, how many might there be?*

Jonah closed his eyes. In his mind he saw darkness on the shoulders of every man and woman down there. Dense glistening shadows, nuzzling to their hosts, pulsating in a terrible synchronicity, their dead fingers loosening, gradually freeing, pulling clear just so that they could lift up towards where Jonah sat, lift up and *point*.

He opened his eyes again, feeling cold. It had been a mistake coming here, tainting a treasured memory with this fear, this paranoia.

The shoulders of the people below him carried no shadows he could see. All he could do was hope that it meant nothing was *there*.

His old cell phone rang, making him jump. He laughed uneasily at his own state of mind then took his phone out, answering it before he'd even checked who the call was from.

'Hello?' he said.

'Jonah Miller?' said a voice. A man's voice. Familiar somehow, but he couldn't place it.

'Who is this?'

'This is the FBI, Jonah. My name is Special Agent Heggarty.'

Jonah paused, feeling his heart rate shoot up. 'How can I help you, Agent?'

'I'd like to talk to you. Today, if possible. I'm in the area.'

'What about?'

'The current whereabouts of Tess Neil.'

The last thing he needed right now was to be on the radar of the FBI, not if he hoped to quietly disappear. 'Tess?'

'It's important, Jonah.'

He felt himself smart at the informality. 'I haven't seen Tess Neil. Not since the fire at Reese-Farthing Medical. Anything you need to know is covered by the statements I gave then. So please, don't waste your time. Or mine.'

'I was under the impression that you had plenty of time on your hands, Jonah.'

There was a tone of sarcasm, of *arrogance*, in the man's voice. The lack of professionalism took Jonah by surprise, and for a moment he didn't know how to respond. '*Excuse* me?' he managed.

The man laughed. 'I've been asking after you today, I heard you were taking, uh, a sabbatical.'

'So you thought you'd call and mock me? Special Agent Heggarty, was it? What office do you work out of, *sir*?'

'Forgive me, Mr Miller. I only wanted to discuss the Tess Neil situation with you. Entirely at your discretion. If it would be convenient, just say where you'd like to meet.'

'Nowhere. You can read whatever statements I've already made. I have nothing to add.'

'So you haven't seen her recently?'

Jonah felt his cool slipping. 'I *told* you. I haven't seen her since the fire.'

'And you haven't had any form of communication from her? No emails? Letters? Phone calls?'

'Are you even listening to what I'm saying? No.' Jonah was about to hang up on the man, but there was something he wanted to ask. 'Why now? It's been a year and a half, why the sudden interest?'

There was no reply for a few seconds. 'You want to know why?'

'Yes.'

Again, there was a delay. When Heggarty spoke at last, his voice was dismissive. 'I think we're done here, sir. Sorry to have bothered you.'

There was a click as Heggarty hung up on him. Jonah stared at the phone, bemused and angry. Dredging up Tess, and then acting as if it had been Jonah wasting *his* time? He shook his head. Then he wondered again why the voice had sounded familiar.

He took his new phone and composed a message for Never and Annabel, telling them that the FBI were asking questions about Tess. He finished his coffee, deciding it was time to set off home and call a halt to his experiment. An experiment in just how paranoid he could make himself.

Idiot, he thought. Seeing shadows everywhere he looked, then reading nothing but peril into the call he'd just received. Hell, the reappearance of Andreas would have been enough of a prompt for the authorities to look again into the circumstances of Reese-Farthing, and that naturally led to curiosity about Tess Neil. That was all the timing meant.

Nothing more.

*

He returned to his car and started to drive home. A little way along he spotted a police cruiser behind him and remembered a faulty brake light he'd not got around to getting fixed. He'd already been given a warning about it, three months back. He cringed inside as the cruiser put on its lights, the driver signalling for him to pull over.

Jonah cursed quietly as he stopped at the roadside. He was supposed to be all about low-key behaviour, silent and unnoticed, ready to vanish if Annabel gave the word. He smiled grimly and shook his head.

There were two officers in the cruiser. They got out and approached, taking position at both driver and passenger windows. Jonah opened his, ready to apologize about the brake light.

The cop leaned down. 'Little erratic there, sir,' he said.

Something made Jonah grip the steering wheel just that bit tighter. What the hell was he talking about? 'Officer?'

'I observed you veering some, out of your lane. Licence and registration, please.'

Jonah reached over to his glove compartment and hunted around, his face pricking with heat when he couldn't immediately see it. Then he had it and passed it over. 'I don't know what you mean. I didn't think I was—'

'Get out of the car please, sir.' The officer's voice was suddenly hostile.

'What?' Jonah could feel the heat on his face return, but now it was accompanied by a sick feeling deep in his gut. *What the hell is this?*

'You heard me. Out. Put your hands on the roof.'

Jonah complied. The cop frisked him, removing his wallet and his old cell phone from his back pocket. The other officer opened the passenger door and dipped down out of sight. It was a matter of a few seconds before he emerged waving a small sealed plastic bag, a white powder within. 'Look what I found,' he said.

Jonah felt reality drain away, replaced by cold dread. 'That's not mine.' It was all he could say and it sounded like bullshit. Then Jonah noticed something, and it made him think about Heggarty's phone call, and the way it had seemed like the agent had been stalling him, keeping him on the line just long enough and no more.

He thought of what Never had said the day before: *we'd have to ditch our old phones anyway, they'd be able to track us on them.*

Both officers were wearing gloves. Unusual, perhaps; but not if they knew they were going to meet a reviver.

The first cop got him to turn and hold out his hands, wrists up. The officer put a pair of handcuffs on him and bundled him into their vehicle, while the other locked up Jonah's car and returned with the keys.

At that moment Jonah placed the voice of the FBI agent and felt the blood drain from his face. It was the man who had shown up outside the building on the night Blake Torrance attacked them. The man who had carried a strong shadow.

The back of the cruiser smelled a little of vomit. The cops said things to him, but whenever Jonah replied he kept his eyes to the floor, not wanting to look at them.

Not wanting to see their shoulders, in case anything was there.

They drove, the police radio barking unintelligible noise every dozen seconds or so. Jonah stole glimpses of their shoulders as they went, flashing his eyes up then back to the floor. Each time his gazed stayed a little longer. Each time there was nothing.

The officers had taken his old phone, but he was keenly aware that they'd missed the new one in the front pocket of his jeans. He used the motion of the car to cover his movement, getting the phone out, holding it as low as he could. He opened the messaging app.

Arrested, he wrote. *Planted drugs. Never, get me out of here.* His thumb hovered, ready to send it. He wasn't in any doubt that he was in trouble, but sending the message meant admitting to himself just how serious this was.

'You got a problem there, son?' said the officer in the passenger seat, looking in a secondary rear-view mirror.

Jonah's blood froze. He let the phone slide to the floor and brought his cuffed hands to his face, then rubbed at his eyes. 'Travel sick, officer,' he said.

The cop's eyes narrowed. Jonah couldn't see the smile on the man's face, but he could tell how cold it was. 'Wouldn't be the first.'

Jonah leaned forward as far as he could and let out enough of a moan to sell it. The vehicle slowed for some lights and as they halted he grabbed the phone. He moaned again.

'Don't you throw up back there,' said the cop. 'You hear me, fucker?'

'I won't,' said Jonah.

He sent the message.

As they crossed the James River he wondered which police station they were headed for. Plenty of people *knew* him, for Christ's sake. All he needed was a friendly face, and then, surely . . .

The car turned left when he'd been expecting a right. They weren't heading for the city.

'Where are you taking me, officer?' he asked, trying to make it sound neutral. But it had come out cold and scared.

The officer in the passenger seat gave him another predatory smile. 'You just hold tight, son. We'll get there.'

Jonah knew where they were headed soon enough. It made a kind of sense, he guessed. They entered the car lot of the Richmond FBI building, passing the artificial lake. It was still a beautiful day, thought Jonah. Strange how it seemed that nothing bad could happen with the sun in the sky.

He leaned forward again, feigning illness to cover another message on his phone. He needed to let Never and Annabel know this was it: they had to vanish, and they had to do it now. *At FBI office*, he wrote. *It's them. Run.*

The car went around the rear of the building and parked. The two officers guided him in silence to a closed door. It opened. A man in a suit took Jonah by the arm with a grip that felt like it would leave one hell of a bruise. The man dismissed the cops with a nod and led Jonah inside.

'Where's Heggarty?' asked Jonah. The man smiled but said nothing. He took Jonah down an empty corridor, around a corner and through a second door, handling him too roughly for Jonah to be able to get a good look at him. Another man in a suit was sitting behind a table in what looked like a meeting room. Jonah heard the door click shut behind him.

'Let's get those cuffs off him,' said the seated man. 'No need to be uncivilized.'

'Heggarty?' said Jonah. The man nodded. Jonah looked at Heggarty's shoulder. There was a vague darkness there, as there had been at first with Torrance, nothing like as clear as it had been when he'd seen Heggarty before. His skill at seeing the shadows was an inconsistent one, it seemed.

'Indeed. This is my colleague, Special Agent Piras. Say hello, Jake.'

'Hello,' said the first man without a hint of sincerity, as he removed Jonah's cuffs.

'I had hoped,' said Heggarty, 'that we could maybe talk a little more. Our previous discussion seemed rather *curt*.'

'Look,' said Jonah. 'I don't know what you think you—'

He stopped. Suddenly, he *saw*.

It had felt like something clicking into place in his mind; Jonah tried to pull his eyes away, but it was impossible. The shape on Heggarty's shoulder was dark, with long fingers burrowed deep into its host. It was tangible, undeniably real, with a hint of moisture to it that made it glisten in the overhead lighting. For a moment, Jonah could smell rotten meat.

He managed to tear his gaze away, but only as far as Heggarty's face. There was a knowing smile on the man's lips, and an expression that, strangely, didn't seem at all hostile. Just amused.

'I see we understand each other, Jonah,' said Heggarty.

27

Piras drew up a chair and directed Jonah to sit, then moved near the door and stood guard.

In case I tried to make a run for it, Jonah thought. As if there would be any point. He was starting to understand that it was all far too late. Too late to run. Too late to hope: for Piras had a shadow crouching on his shoulder, too – not as clear as the one Heggarty carried, but impossible to miss now, the ebb and flow of Jonah's ability to see these creatures still beyond his control.

He wondered how far this had spread. If he'd not abandoned his attempt at people-watching, would he have started to see them after all?

'We'll let you go,' said Heggarty, 'if you cooperate. If you tell us where Tess Neil is.'

'You think I would trust you to keep your word?' said Jonah. 'You're the one with a fucking *leech* watching your every move.'

'Don't be disrespectful,' said Heggarty. 'What you see is not a parasite. It takes some sustenance and provides a service – symbiotic; I think that's the word.'

'It comes from Andreas?' said Jonah, and Heggarty smiled. Confirmation, if he really needed it, that Andreas was at the root of this. 'I saw what it did, Heggarty. I saw a vision of what the creature in Andreas did to other worlds. How can you want that? How can you want everything to be destroyed?'

Heggarty frowned, shaking his head. 'You think you know what

Andreas is? You think you know what's to come? You don't know anything. I was one of the first, approached by Andreas himself. He can look at someone and know what's in their hearts. People who know what their country needs. People who know how to make it great again. And when we stop bickering amongst ourselves, think of what we can achieve. Working together. As one.'

'Working to bring everything to an end,' said Jonah. 'Nice plan.'

'Andreas is the vessel of the Lord,' said Heggarty. 'And the Lord doesn't want to destroy. Unless His people are defiant enough to incur His wrath. But we'll make sure it won't come to that. You see, Jonah, the only thing wrong with our world is that freedom is wasted on the weak.'

'Were the cops who brought me here infected too?'

'Please.' Heggarty scowled. 'Calling it *infection* is just bigotry. And no, the officers who brought you are not so blessed. Money is still a perfectly good incentive for corruption. There's no need for everyone to be granted the gift. Every shepherd needs sheep, yes? We are here to usher in a new era.' Heggarty's expression was one of utter sincerity.

'The only thing Andreas wants to do is *devour*,' said Jonah. 'To wipe out everyone, whether they join you or not. Whatever bullshit he's spinning you.'

'It must be so frustrating for you, Jonah. To not be believed. Nobody out there in the *real* world would take one bit of interest in your ramblings. You think we're devils, when really we're here to help.' Heggarty smiled inanely, as though he was serving fast food. 'Now, Tess Neil. If you please.'

'Why are you interested in Tess? Why now, but not before?'

'We were always interested, Jonah. Tess was the reason you lived a normal life since Reese-Farthing. If she emerged from hiding convinced that Andreas was dead, she would have contacted you. If you had no reason to fear, then she would have felt free to return into the open. That was the hope. Really, you and your friends were harmless, nothing but a useful lure. And you could be harmless again if you cooperate. He won't hurt her, I promise. There's no need for *anyone* to get hurt.'

Jonah looked at the glistening shadow on Heggarty's shoulder. 'Tell that to Mary Connart. Tell that to the people Torrance killed.'

Heggarty shook his head. 'Torrance was a murderer, simple as that. This *bond* is a blessing. Torrance accepted the gift and he abused it. Don't be in any doubt: the impulse he acted on came from within the man, nowhere else.' Heggarty looked at his own shoulder; the darkness there seemed to preen for a moment. 'Of course, we suspected that someone was . . . misbehaving. There were other cases your friends Crenner and Johnson hadn't dug up yet. Only a matter of time. Had we known it was Torrance, he would have been dealt with much sooner. We were closing in on him. His days as a killer were already numbered.'

'I wouldn't have thought being in a prison cell would be much of a hindrance.'

Heggarty laughed. 'You hadn't heard? Torrance died from his wounds. Tragic. Isn't that right, Jake?'

'Well,' said Agent Piras from behind Jonah, 'that's the official story.'

'We may have made certain of it, I admit,' said Heggarty. 'Much easier that way. The only other option would have been to break the bond of sacrament, which would have left him a husk of a man. The Lord is *merciful*.' He looked at Jonah, darkly. 'Your presence was noted, by the way. Your detective friends covered for you, but Torrance told us you were there. Before he . . . died. I'll ask one last time, Jonah. Where is Tess?'

'I told you I haven't heard from her.'

Heggarty nodded. 'I believe you. I do. But we have to be sure. I'd like you to meet someone who can help you *convince* us.'

Jonah didn't like the way Heggarty put an emphasis on *convince*. 'And if I decline?'

'Once we're satisfied you've told us the truth about Tess, you'll be taken to the new Baseline facility. To help with research. If you come quietly, your friends will be left alone.'

Jonah noted that Heggarty had simply ignored his question; declining wasn't an option, of course. 'To help with research? What kind of help can I be to a man like Andreas?'

Heggarty shook his head. 'Not for me to say.' He smiled, malice in his eyes. 'Perhaps you can make the coffee. Whatever role you have, I'm assured you'll be treated well. Eventually you'll be released. *If* you cooperate.'

The thing on Heggarty's shoulder pulsated slowly, shifting position a little. Heggarty reached across and stroked it.

Jonah looked away, suddenly queasy. Play along, he thought. Look like you're willing to listen, like you believe what he's telling you. Hope that their guard goes down long enough for you to be able to run, because running is the only option left.

A phone started to ring, a jaunty piece of terrible elevator music. Heggarty raised his eyes to the ceiling.

'Default fucking ring tones,' he muttered. 'Piras, remind me to change the damn thing sometime, OK?'

'Always do, sir,' said Piras.

Heggarty raised the phone and frowned. 'Yes?' he said. 'What? *Now*?' His frown deepened. 'We'd agreed that while in the area we could use this room unimpeded. This is a sensitive investigation, requiring total independence.' He listened, and the frown became a scowl. 'Very well,' he said, then hung up. 'Piras, stay here. I have to see Ferrara. I have some appeasement to make.' He looked at Jonah. 'Ferrara is the Special Agent in Charge here. She doesn't trust us out-of-towners, especially since we won't tell her exactly what we're up to. You sit tight, and give your options some consideration.'

Options, Jonah thought, seeing the mockery on Heggarty's face. *Sure.*

The creature on Heggarty's shoulder was pulsating again, more rapidly than before, like it was breathless. He left the room.

Piras stayed by the door.

Jonah stood slowly and turned, looking Piras over again. The agent's shadow was a squat, limp thing in comparison to Heggarty's. 'I need the toilet,' Jonah lied.

'Sit in your fucking seat or I'll tie a knot in your fucking prick,' said Piras.

Jonah sat back down. Well, at least he knew how things were.

*

The clock on the wall had ticked through an hour of slow minutes by the time the door opened again. By then Jonah had gone over every scenario he could think of for getting away. Trying to get help from others in the building was risky, without having a good idea who Heggarty's confederates were. They would have to transport him, though, taking him out into public areas. Making a break from whatever vehicle they would use seemed like his best chance. Whatever he did, success depended on an element of surprise, on them believing he was going without resistance.

And on them not handcuffing him.

And on them not being armed.

He wished he could go back a few days to when the worst of his problems had been heartbreak. He hoped by now Annabel and Never had at least seen his message and realized that the balloon had gone up. He prayed that they would have the good sense to run.

But as the door opened, he heard a voice that meant his prayer hadn't been answered.

28

'That's the lad,' said Never Geary.

Jonah turned to see Never enter the room; Bob Crenner came in behind him with a middle-aged woman Jonah hadn't seen before. Heggarty followed, the scowl on his face a permanent feature now.

Seeing Never, Jonah smiled, but said nothing.

'Jonah,' said Bob. 'I hope you've not been mistreated. This is Special Agent in Charge Kim Ferrara. The moment Never called me, I called her.'

Special Agent Ferrara nodded. 'Detective Crenner explained the situation. Special Agent Heggarty, I have to say I'm disappointed. Such petty reprisal is beneath this organization. You can be damn sure I'll be reporting this.'

'Petty reprisal?' said Jonah, puzzled. He could see the same puzzlement on the face of Agent Piras.

'Yes,' said Ferrara. 'Because you assisted these detectives, Special Agent Heggarty lost out on taking credit for an important case. He was close to tracking down a murderer called Blake Torrance, apparently. That's what this harassment is about.'

'I can assure you,' said Heggarty, teeth gritted, 'this is not a trivial matter. As I explained to you, we believe that Mr Miller's life is at risk. He is simply in our protective custody, and—'

'Enough, Heggarty,' said Ferrara.

'I have my orders, ma'am,' Heggarty growled.

Ferrara glared at him. 'Orders you won't clarify. Details you won't provide. One telephone call from your Section Chief doesn't give you carte blanche, Agent. I outrank you, and right now my opinion is all that matters. Go sit outside my office. Both of you. We'll see what your people back west have to say.'

Heggarty stood his ground, his eyes not leaving Ferrara's. Jonah could see the shadow on his shoulder squirm, the deep-rooted fingers shifting, as if they were yearning to leave Heggarty's flesh and wrap themselves around Ferrara's throat.

But Heggarty wasn't Torrance, of course. He had more control than that. 'Yes, ma'am. We'll see what they have to say.' He walked out of the door, Piras in tow. There were other agents waiting in the corridor, clearly there to escort them to Ferrara's office.

Jonah breathed out, long and loud, then caught the expressions on the three faces around him. None were smiling.

'I'll hold them here for as long as I can,' said Ferrara. 'But Bob, if there's any chance they'll get whatever sanction they need, you should go. Now.'

Bob nodded. 'Thanks, Kim,' he said. 'I owe you.'

She shook her head. 'My pleasure. I didn't like Heggarty the moment I met him. It felt good to catch him out. He thinks he can do what he likes, but something about him . . . something doesn't feel right.' She looked at Jonah.

Jonah said nothing.

*

Bob, Jonah and Never hurried to Bob's car and got on the road as fast as they could.

'Thank you,' said Jonah. 'Both of you.'

'I should've seen your message sooner,' said Never, apology in his voice. 'I called around to see who had leverage here. Bob was the one who came through. He told me to sit tight.'

'I got in my car and drove,' said Bob. 'As soon as Never called me to say you'd been taken to the FBI field office, I knew it had to be linked to Torrance. I've known Kim Ferrara for thirty years. She's one of my wife's best friends, field agent in Washington until she got promoted.'

'Did you tell her about Torrance?' said Jonah. 'About the shadow I'd seen on his shoulder? About it attacking us?'

'I rang Kim to see if she knew anything about you being detained,' said Bob. 'I told her a little about Torrance, yes, but all I said was it was creepy, and had FBI involvement. Heggarty was her first thought. Said he'd shown up two weeks ago wanting to use their facilities for a time, not giving much detail. But, as she just told you, there'd been something about him she'd not liked right away.' Bob pulled over suddenly and looked at Jonah. 'Was he like Torrance? Was he one of the others Torrance mentioned?'

Jonah nodded.

'Jesus,' said Bob. 'I told Kim something dubious was happening and she said she'd do whatever she could. Thank God someone had noticed you being brought in. Kim's impression was that Heggarty had taken a dislike to you after the Torrance case, blaming you for treading on their toes, stealing their thunder, so they wanted to harass you.' He started to drive again. 'She knew damn well something else was going on, though, but hell, even I don't know what that really is, and he –' Bob nodded to Never – 'he wouldn't tell me anything else, just that you need to get away.'

'Damn right,' said Never. 'The less you know, the better. Really. You need deniability. You're just a friend, helping out some pals. Who've, uh, gone mad.'

'I wish you'd let me do more,' said Bob. 'You need money?'

'No,' said Never. 'We just need to get off the map. A friend's lending me his car, he left it for me over in Wyndham. If you could drop us off there, Bob, that'd be great. If anyone asks you where we went, don't worry about telling them where you left us. We'll be long gone. Then . . . forget about all this.'

'Easier said than done,' said Bob. 'I saw what was with Torrance, remember? I heard him say there were others, and now one of them shows up in the FBI. They could be everywhere, planning Christ knows what. Exactly what the hell do I do with that knowledge?'

'Nothing,' said Jonah. 'Absolutely nothing. Don't call attention to yourself any more than you already have, Bob. What's the status of Mary Connart's case? Torrance's alibi means her murder can't be officially pinned to him.'

'The FBI furnished us with details of an accomplice,' said Bob. 'Conveniently enough, the accomplice committed suicide soon after Torrance's death. Case closed, as long as you're willing to overlook all the inconsistencies.'

'So overlook them,' said Jonah.

'How can I?' said Bob. 'If those *things* are commonplace . . .'

'They're not,' lied Jonah. 'Trust me.'

Bob's phone rang. He pulled over to the side just before the I-295 junction to take the call. Everything he said was brief: How. Where. When. Even so, Jonah could hear the tone in his voice change as he spoke, see his face go grey. From the front seat, Never turned his head to Jonah, wary. Bob ended the call.

'What?' asked Never.

'Ray,' said Bob, keying a number on the phone. 'It was about Ray. That was a local cop, they said. Seems . . . some kind of incident out near Lake Anna. I don't know what the hell he was doing out there. He was supposed to be home letting his wounds heal, decorating his fucking house.' He put the phone to his ear and listened for a moment. 'His phone's going to voicemail,' he said.

Jonah and Never shared a look. Bob Crenner's voice was shaky.

'What's happened, Bob?' asked Never.

'They said he'd been shot.' Bob started to drive again, and fast. 'They said he'd been killed.'

29

Bob drove, his face dark and focused. 'When we get there,' he said, 'take my car and go on. Understand? If you need to run, then run.'

There was no need for discussion, Jonah knew; Ray was the priority. They would do as Bob said, take his car and go on alone. But only when they knew what had happened to Ray.

By now they were driving along a country road, forest either side. Jonah thought they must be five or ten minutes from the location Bob had been given.

At the sound of a ringtone, Never pulled out his phone and looked at the screen. 'Shit,' he said, passing his phone to Jonah. 'I was supposed to call Annabel the moment we got you out of there. I'd already told her what was happening.'

Jonah took the phone, feeling an unwelcome sense of nerves that, given everything else that was going on, had no damn right being there.

'Never?' she said as he answered.

'It's me,' said Jonah.

There was a pause. He heard Annabel breath out. There was such intense relief in the sound that Jonah felt suddenly dizzy. It was the thought of how scared she'd been, making him realize again how deep a hole he'd just been dug out of. And how much she still cared for him.

'Jonah,' she said. It was all she seemed able to manage for a moment.

'Bob and Never got me out. I'm OK.'

'Did the people who took you say anything?' Her voice was uneven, shaky. He supposed his own must sound the same.

He kept his voice low, not wanting Bob to overhear. 'They claimed Andreas is looking to carve out some kind of Utopia rather than blow it all to hell. That he wants to get his disciples positioned and take over. It was plainly bullshit, but I think his followers believe it. And I know why they left us alone all this time.'

'Why?'

'They want Tess. We were a trap. If anything had happened to us, she would've been scared off, losing them their only lead.'

'Why do they want her?'

'He didn't give anything away.'

'Jonah,' she said, 'you need to get as far as possible from there as fast as you can. You understand me? You and Never need to split up. I'm leaving too, right now.' She paused. 'We'll be safer on our own.'

He heard the phrase and closed his eyes. He knew it summed up the way she'd already been thinking about their relationship, and it hurt. It hurt, because that was exactly how he'd felt since the age of fourteen, since his mother had died. The pain of loss, making you curl up, hide from people. Hide from letting yourself be dependent on them.

It had taken him over a decade to finally let himself fall in love, and the woman he'd fallen for had the same damn problem.

We'll be safer on our own.

But now, the truth of it was undeniable.

'I know,' he said. The admission hurt. 'Look, something else has happened here, Annabel. Something serious, but as soon as we can run we'll be gone. We have to – hang on a second.'

Ahead, a police cruiser was slung across the lane, a solitary cop standing in front of it. On the left side of the forest road, Jonah saw a smaller road at right angles to it, a black van moving slowly down it towards them. The cop raised his hand and Bob stopped the car, lowering his window, but the cop went around to Never's side and waited for Never to lower his. It struck Jonah as odd, but he didn't give it any more thought.

'Crenner?' asked the cop.

'Yes,' said Bob, killing the engine.

'OK. Wait there a moment.' Another car pulled up behind Bob's, a family, rowdy kids laughing in the back. The officer waved it past then looked along the road in both directions. 'Give me a minute, fellas. I just need to check something.'

The cop stood a little back from the car, Bob and Never watching him.

'What's the deal?' asked Never.

Bob shook his head. In the distance, Jonah could see the car that had passed them vanish over the crest of a low hill.

'You still there?' Jonah asked Annabel.

'Of course.'

'I couldn't talk for a moment. I have to – look, we might not see each other for a long time.' *If at all*, he thought.

'I know.'

'I still love you, Annabel Harker.'

She didn't reply for a few seconds. To Jonah it seemed like forever.

'I love you too, Jonah,' she said.

And then he heard the sound of an engine revved high, screaming with power, closing in. No time to think, for any of them: all they could do was turn to their left and see the black van accelerate over the five-car distance it still had to travel. Then the vehicle smashed into them.

30

Jonah came to. He could hear Annabel's voice from somewhere distant: Never's phone, lost in the car. She called his name, halting and scared. Then she hung up. Jonah understood she must have been calling out since the moment she heard the impact. *Run*, he thought. *Run, Annabel, and don't look back.*

He knew he'd blacked out but had no idea how long for. It couldn't have been more than moments: airbag powder filled the air around him. He tried to move, his back and side shrieking at the attempt. Something deep was torn, but he checked himself over quickly. Battered but intact.

He looked around and despaired. Bob was slumped forwards and to his right. He wasn't moving at all. Jonah couldn't see much of him, but anything he could see was wet with blood.

In the front passenger seat Never was leaning against his own door. He was moaning, his hand coming up to his head.

The van had hit the front-left side of the car; the driver-side door had been impacted hard enough to be pushed in deep, the metal touching the steering wheel. Jonah tried to look outside but the glass next to him was opaque, a shattered web barely held together.

There was enough light coming through to suggest that the van wasn't there now. For an instant he wondered if help could already have arrived, but he knew that was the thought of a man desperate to hang on to the possibility that this had been some kind of *accident*. That the 'cop' who'd waved the other car through hadn't simply been waiting for potential witnesses to vacate the scene.

Everything about the situation screamed set-up, but the logistics of it seemed impossible. Heggarty would have needed people in place who knew where Bob's car was, and knew where to send them so that they could be intercepted, detained.

Dealt with.

Jonah tried to speak but just ended up coughing. Then he heard footsteps.

Someone pulled Bob's twisted door, managing to force it open, the metal crying out. A hand came in and undid Bob's seat belt, then grabbed him by the shoulder and pulled roughly.

Jonah heard himself protest, his voice little more than a croak. Then his own door opened and hands took hold of him, dragging him onto the cold, damp ground, the pain overwhelming. Twelve feet away he could see Bob lying motionless where he'd been dropped. Someone in a long black coat strode over to Bob and raised a hand. Jonah saw the gun, saw it fire, saw Bob Crenner's head come apart.

'*No!*' he screamed. '*No!*' He kept screaming it, again and again, as the figure turned to him and approached; he tried to scramble backwards, unable to get to his feet, inching away pathetically as the black coat came for him.

He thought of Never. He thought of Annabel. Then the figure leaned down beside him and he felt the sharp pain of a needle; as he lost consciousness, he thought of Annabel's father, Daniel Harker, who had felt a similar stab in his arm before waking up to a long, slow death.

31

After she ended the call, Annabel stared at the phone.

She'd called out Jonah's name repeatedly, getting silence in return, and panic had taken hold.

No coincidence. No way. The thought had made her hang up, an image forming in her mind of people closing in on the other phone, hearing her voice, knowing somehow where she was. And if it *was* just an accident, Jonah would be able to contact her, assuming . . .

She closed her eyes.

She was ready. Bag packed. Ready to leave, to disappear. And to hope that Jonah and Never would be in touch soon.

Then there was a knock on the door of the apartment.

Her blood froze.

Andreas's people couldn't know she was there, surely. She was renting with a fake ID, and she'd been damn careful. They couldn't know.

The knocking grew louder. *Ignore it*, she thought. *Stay calm.* It had to be innocent, and there was no point in her rushing out to the fire escape for something *innocent*.

With her eyes locked on the front door she reached over and grabbed the shoulder strap of her bag. She lifted it, slow and silent, and backed off to her bedroom, pushing the door across but not quite closing it, realizing just how familiar she'd made herself with the sounds her apartment could make: the door swung over without noise, but the handle would squeak if she used it, and shutting it without turning the handle would produce a resounding click as the latch found home.

She opened the bedroom window, knowing it was silent. She stepped out onto the fire escape, something she'd tried twice in the weeks before. Three floors up, she'd not actually attempted the descent, but everything had looked well maintained.

Now it was time to see.

The knocking stopped, and so did she, half out of the window, not knowing if there would be the sound of a splintering door or if whoever it was would appear on the back street below at any moment.

Then the knock came again, and she moved, closing her window, descending with care. Rather than lower the final section of ladder she opted to drop from the lowest point of the fire escape to a garbage container, then to the ground. She followed the route she'd planned, keeping as casual a stride as she could, cutting through a cemetery and heading for the parking lot where she'd been keeping a second car. As she exited the cemetery she knelt down and retied the shoelace on her left foot, giving cover as she reached over to the storm drain beside her and dropped her phone into the darkness. Just in case. As soon as she could, she would source a new phone.

She stood and walked.

Annabel blanked her mind and focused on getting out of there, on losing herself and keeping her head down.

They couldn't have known where she was. Ditching the phone had been an unnecessary precaution. The knock on her door had been innocent.

And Jonah was fine.

She knew, deep down, that at least one of those things wasn't true.

32

Jonah opened his eyes to darkness, uncertain if he'd opened them at all.

Something was covering the lower part of his face, and he couldn't move his arms or legs. There was a smell of antiseptic in the air. *Hospital*, he thought, but he wasn't in a bed; he was seated, lying back, like in a dentist's chair.

He didn't know where he was, or why; he could only remember that something was *wrong*. He felt content, in a way he was immediately wary of. Given how badly injured he'd been when he was shot, he was familiar with the euphoric glow of opiate painkillers.

He blinked, unseeing, as the memory of the car being hit returned, along with the image of Bob Crenner's head fragmenting, and the sound of his own screams as the dark coat approached him.

This was no hospital.

He was aware of the pain lurking underneath the medication, in his side most of all, but every part of him seemed to have some grievance and the effect of the medication was fading fast.

He tried to move again and could feel straps on his arms and legs; whatever it was on his face, it had his jaw clamped shut. His head was restrained. He listened: the echo of his own breathing suggested the room he was in was small.

He thought of Never, moaning in the front seat of the car. Still alive. Back then, at least.

The lights in the room stuttered on, chasing away the last of the euphoria.

The white room was tiled and bare. *Easily cleaned*, he thought. Up high in one corner, a camera watched over him. Unable to turn his head, he could just see a table on his right but couldn't tell what was there. Glints of steel, though.

He closed his eyes again.

A sound made him look to the far wall. A door opened; as pure white as the wall, it seemed to appear from nothing. Through it came a short man with a genuine smile. He wore a white coverall, the kind Jonah wore at revivals to keep from contaminating the scene. The kind that kept your clothes clean, too. When there was too much blood.

The man's face was ruddy, his hair short and failing. There seemed to be nothing crouched on his shoulder but Jonah knew he needed to be wary of his new-found ability.

The man closed the door and approached, the smile growing. 'Welcome,' he said.

Jonah tried to talk, but it was muffled by whatever was covering his face.

'Wait, wait,' said the man. 'Allow me.' He leaned across and gently removed it; a leather mask. Before Jonah could speak the man brought over a container with a plastic straw, placing the straw in Jonah's mouth.

'Drink,' said the man. Thirsty, Jonah took a short sip before he thought he should be suspicious of what was offered. It seemed to be just water. 'Now,' said the man. 'What do you wish to say?'

'The others . . .'

'Ah. Well, now. I'm afraid the grab team let us down. We were supposed to have all three of you here, but the impact had been misjudged. The injuries of your detective friend were such that the decision was taken to leave him. Naturally, he had to be finished in a way that rendered him impossible to revive. You understand, Jonah?' The man paused, seeming to expect an answer.

'Fuck you,' said Jonah, the sound of his voice appallingly small.

The man frowned. His hand shot out, slapping Jonah across the cheek hard enough to daze him for a moment. 'No,' said the man. 'Respect me.' He watched Jonah, their eyes locking, Jonah confused and scared. 'Your other friend is here,' said the man. 'In the room next door, with my colleague. Listen.'

He reached somewhere out of Jonah's sight. There was a click, an intercom. 'Can you hear me?' said the man.

'I can,' said another man's voice.

'Jonah wants to hear his friend. If you would oblige.'

'Of course.'

A few seconds passed. Then there was the sound of a dull impact and a muffled yell, followed by a string of angry cursing. Unmistakeably, it was Never.

The intercom was flicked off.

'There. You see? He's perfectly well.'

'Why am I—' started Jonah. He was cut short by another expertly delivered slap.

'Speak only if I tell you to,' said the man in a calm voice, raising again the mask he had removed from Jonah, fitting it back with practised ease. 'There. Better.' He smiled in his genuine way.

A man who enjoys his work, thought Jonah, rage building within him alongside the fear.

'Now,' said the man. 'You want to know what this is. I understand. And luckily, I plan to tell you. You're here to answer one question. Your friend is here to *help* you answer. Are you ready?'

Jonah stared. The man raised an eyebrow, prompting a response. With his head restrained, Jonah was only barely able to nod.

'Good,' said the man. 'My question is this: do you know the whereabouts of Tess Neil?'

Jonah shook his restrained head as best he could.

'Have you had any encounter or communication with Tess Neil since the Reese-Farthing incident?'

Again, Jonah shook his head.

'Good, good,' said the man. 'I believe you, Jonah. I believe you.' Then the man's smile faded, his face growing theatrically sad. 'Unfortunately, that's not how this works. You see, I'm a compassionate man. I'm far too trusting. As such, procedure demands that my own feelings are left out of this. Instead, I have to make sure. Make sure that anyone interested in the answer will also believe you, when they watch the footage.' He nodded to the camera in the corner of the ceiling. 'It's really very similar to your own line of work, in that respect. You understand. As one professional to another.'

Again, the man looked at Jonah and waited for a response. Jonah nodded. Tears were starting to creep out of his eyes now, as if they were deserting him. Trying to escape.

'You can call me Hopkins,' said the man. 'Not my real name, of course, but our subjects perform better if they have a name for their . . . advisor.' Hopkins allowed himself a chuckle. 'It's good that I can be open with you, Jonah – a fellow inquisitor. Of course, with you, your subjects are dead *before* they enter your care. But you see how our terminology is similar, yes? Subjects? And "advisor" is *so* like "reviver", isn't it? They take equal liberties with meaning, I think. We "advise" our subjects just as meaningfully as you "revive" yours. I doubt that our subjects feel that much useful advice has been imparted by the process, and your subjects, I think I can safely say, don't exactly feel *recovered*, mmm?' The hostility in the man's eyes contrasted horribly with the smile on his lips. 'So, yes, Hopkins is how you should think of me. I almost always use that name in a session. It's a joke, of sorts. My colleagues believe it's a movie reference, which is true in a way, but not the one they think. Do you have any inklings, Jonah?'

Jonah shook his head, but part of him thought he knew.

The man's face fell. 'Shame, shame. No matter. But we have

business to attend to, yes? So we'll begin, in earnest. Let me explain. My employers wish to know the whereabouts of Tess Neil. You have already claimed not to know. So, too, has your friend, Mr Geary. I believe you, but you are faced with a problem, because my beliefs are irrelevant. You must convince everyone who would ever conceivably wish to know.' He paused and gave another pointed look to the camera. 'That task can be difficult. Achieving it requires some considerable skill, if I say so myself. In recent times, another route to certainty has opened up, given – ironically – the services of a reviver. When it has been deemed important that the subject remains alive, of course, that option is unavailable. And if the questioning – shall we call it *pre-mortem* questioning – fails to be conclusive, a revival is a useful thing to fall back on.'

At this, Hopkins began to put latex gloves on his hands. 'Now, you're not to worry,' he said. 'I pride myself, I really do. I promise you, today there will be no need to fall back on anything. It is down to me to help you be as . . . *convincing* as possible.'

Reaching out with a gloved hand, Hopkins wiped away the tears that were falling freely from Jonah's eyes. 'There, now,' he said, that horribly genuine smile back on his face. 'We have work to do.'

33

Hopkins turned to the table just out of Jonah's sight. Jonah closed his eyes, hearing the clink and rattle as Hopkins examined the tools of his trade.

The room was warm but Jonah started to shiver; whatever had torn in his back in the collision was becoming more and more painful as a result, but he couldn't stop shaking. The pain relief he'd woken to was entirely gone, now.

'Jonah,' said Hopkins. 'Open your eyes.'

He did as he was told.

'When I started my career,' said Hopkins, 'I had a fondness for brutality. Getting the truth was the goal and brutality certainly seemed to achieve it. People like to think that such terrible pain makes the subject lose consciousness. Sometimes, yes, but rarely in the face of an active threat. After all, pain focuses the mind. That's why it *exists*.' As he spoke he lifted a scalpel from the table and held it in front of Jonah, turning it over in his hand. 'But listen to this: "It has always been recognized that this method of interrogation, by putting men to the torture, is useless. The wretches say whatever comes into their heads and whatever they think one wants to believe." You know who said that? Napoleon. And the problems were known even before *his* time. But each generation thinks they know better. I was young. I thought a skilled practitioner had the experience to know what to trust, what to discard . . .' He returned the scalpel and picked up a small bone saw. 'My revelation was this: the greatest skill is to extract the truth *without any physical harm*. With no *outward* sign that anything has happened at all. I'm a hopeless idealist, I know, but there are practical benefits. It allows a subject to be questioned repeatedly, and lets you keep them as a healthy prisoner for as long as they're useful. The difficulty is *speed*. With things like sleep deprivation and waterboarding it can take so much *time* to break a subject down. The longer it takes, the greater the risk that the subject becomes so traumatized that they cease to know what is truth and what is desperate invention. And if *they* don't even know, how can *we*?' He returned the saw. This time, he chose a long thin metal spike. 'So with time pressing, brutality is often the best option. I came to realize that it was my destiny to refine the art. I wasn't alone in the thought. We have a common acquaintance, you and I, beyond Michael Andreas. You knew Kendrick, yes? Kendrick thought torture outdated, that revival was cleaner and faster. I despised the idea. Perfection is to get the truth without any physical harm, yet Kendrick would have us *kill* a subject as the very first step? That is *defeat*; he thought it was progress. Nowadays, if a subject is considered expendable – and believe me, that is *most* of them – they kill them at once and hand them to the revivers for interrogation. Barbarians . . .' He caressed the metal spike, then shook his head and looked away from Jonah, his eyes unfocused. 'People like me are looked down on now,' he said, sounding melancholic. '*Artists*, spoken of in the same breath as basement electrocutioners, as if we're scab-faced thugs caring little for the quality of information extracted.' He reached to his table of equipment once more, setting down the spike and returning with what looked like a small wire cutter. 'I used to be the most important employee they had, before the revivers came. I could take all the time I wanted. An artist needs to practise their art, and we used to have so many to practise on. Just a trickle now, Jonah. It's enough to make a grown man cry.'

Hopkins fell silent for a moment, then seemed to shake off his distraction. 'These are mostly for show,' he said, using the wire cutter to gesture to his table. 'For a particularly *special* subject we might occasionally peel the flesh, either from them or from a loved one – the sight of your child's blood is *such* an incentive, as you can imagine. Such brutality is typically used to make a *point*, though. To set an example, say. Nothing to do with information retrieval.' He set the wire cutter down, and returned with a glass vial in one hand and a hypodermic syringe in the other. 'So you see, I'm not going to mutilate you. Isn't that good news?' He up-ended the vial and half filled the syringe, bringing it close to Jonah's face for a moment, smiling at the terror visible there. 'Don't worry, I'm not injecting this into you. This is much more interesting.' Hopkins waggled the syringe and nodded. 'I've used it all, you know. Jellyfish, bee, scorpion. All the tricks the animal kingdom has for us. My favourite used to be a little known tropical jellyfish, a tiny thing. A human would hardly notice being stung by it and it escaped our attention for many years. Yet for its size, the sting is particularly effective because it also injects something that amplifies the neural response to pain. Wonderful efficiency. Ten times more painful without having to generate all that extra venom. Then our good folk in the lab came up with something better. You ever hear of the bullet ant, Jonah? They say its sting feels like being shot, hence the name. Trying to figure out its secret, they wondered if the jellyfish's trick couldn't be made to work alongside it. They came up with this. You know what you get? A thousand-fold increase. Don't even have to inject the stuff.' Hopkins reached back to the table. A moment later, he returned holding a long cotton swab stick in one hand and a small glass beaker in the other. In the base of the beaker was some liquid. 'When it soaks into the skin, any sensation at all makes your nerve endings *scream*. I've diluted this, don't worry. It's not full strength.'

Hopkins dipped the cotton into the liquid and dabbed it on Jonah's cheek. For a moment it simply felt cold; then it was like fingernails digging into his skin, pushing harder, the pressure increasing until it felt like the flesh would burst. His hands struggled against the straps holding him down, urgently wanting to get at his offending skin and tear it away. Jonah heard himself start to wail but all his attention was on the small piece of his cheek that was burning now, an intense, white-hot pain that—

It was gone.

Jonah breathed in short, stunned bursts.

Hopkins smiled. 'You see how quickly it stops? The pain is extreme, but precise. The real beauty of it is that there's no damage, not even inflammation. It allows repeated use, even when targeting more sensitive tissue. This is best demonstrated by a single drop of a stronger solution, applied to one eye. Short-lived, but unbearable. Don't take my word for it, though.' Smiling, Hopkins set the cotton swab and glass beaker on the table beside him, and flicked the intercom. 'Take the word of your friend.'

Jonah shook his head, the despair in his soul deepening with his fear for Never. *No*, he tried to say, but it just came out as a moan, again and again, growing in volume while Hopkins turned to the intercom.

'Begin.'

34

Knowing what was coming, Jonah thrashed against his restraints. Hopkins watched with amusement. Suddenly there was a muffled roar over the speaker, a horrifying cry of agony. Jonah struggled harder, his tears uncontrolled as the stifled screaming continued. Five, ten, twenty seconds.

Then it stopped. Drained, Jonah lay still.

Hopkins flicked the intercom off. 'The nearest correlative experience is having your eye burnt out with an oxyacetylene torch. The comparison, I assure you, is not simply guesswork.' He smiled. 'But when the pain stops, it stops entirely. No damage done. Think of a bad tooth, the worst pain you've ever known, pain you believed would scar you for life. Then you visit the dentist, and it's like it didn't happen at all. The mind forgets, soon enough, even with this. But after the fourth or fifth time, there's a moment, a sweet spot, where I can ask any question and get an honest answer. The mind is clear enough to understand, yet desperate enough to tell. No blood. No marking. Better than your *revivals*, Jonah.' He reached out to Jonah's face and undid the straps on the mask again. 'Now tell me one more time. Have you had any communication with Tess Neil since the fire at Reese-Farthing?'

Jonah shook his head. When he spoke, he wasn't even sure if what he said was audible. 'No. Please. No.'

'Good,' said Hopkins. 'I'd say you would convince maybe three people out of four. Seventy-five per cent. We're making progress.'

Jonah looked up to the corner of the room, seeing the camera. He felt like he was already dead, the subject of some hellish revival. 'Tell Kendrick,' he said, stuttering. 'Tell him to go fuck himself.'

Hopkins grinned. 'I already did. Kendrick is no longer with us. He had a disagreement with the management. Thankfully, everything is now in the hands of those with the will to do what's necessary. Now, Jonah. Two drops, this time. One in each eye. But I'll give you the choice. Whose turn is it? Your friend again? Or you?'

Jonah felt numbness spread through him as the words sank in. He opened his mouth but found he couldn't speak.

Hopkins smiled again. 'Choice made,' he said, then leaned to the intercom. 'Begin,' he said.

'*No!*' shouted Jonah. 'Please. I choose me. *I choose me.*' Hopkins loomed over him, forcing the mask back over his face as Jonah continued to plead.

'The choice was made, Jonah,' said Hopkins.

Jonah braced for it, trying to twist his head to block out the sound as Never started screaming. But this time it was even worse, and it felt eternal.

When it finally stopped Jonah could feel himself start to pass out. A sharp odour brought him back, face to face with a contented smile as Hopkins waved something under his nose. 'Don't bail out on me, Jonah. We're making such good progress. Now, here it comes. I'll take your mask off again. You will convince me. Or your friend will die. Do you understand?'

Jonah knew he didn't understand anything any more. He nodded all the same.

Hopkins removed Jonah's mask and flipped the intercom back on, to the immediate sound of Never's muffled pleading. 'My colleague will kill your friend, Jonah. Convince me.'

'I haven't had any contact with Tess,' Jonah said, his shivering enough to make his chair rattle. It brought back thoughts of the gurney Mary Connart had been on as she screamed. 'I haven't seen Tess since the fire.'

'*Convince me.*'

'Please, I haven't seen Tess. I haven't seen her. Please. Let him go. *Let him go.*'

'*Convince me.*'

'She ran, she ran and she got away and I haven't – *PLEASE, PLEASE, BELIEVE ME, LET HIM GO . . .*'

Hopkins held up a hand and nodded. 'I believe you, Jonah.' He reached over and replaced the mask. Jonah didn't struggle. 'We'll call that . . . ninety per cent?' Hopkins turned to the intercom. 'I think we're done with Mr Geary,' he said. 'Finish it.' The gunshot overlapped Jonah's own muffled shout of his best friend's name.

Jonah looked at Hopkins with hatred. 'What would you have me do?' asked Hopkins, his face earnest. Jonah sagged, staring ahead. 'The only option would be to keep hurting him. Is that what you wanted? Of course not. Now it's just you and me.' He leaned to the intercom. 'You can head on home once you've put the body into storage, Jeff,' he said. 'The cleaners will sort everything else out in the morning. I'll lock up when I go.' He flipped the intercom off again and turned to Jonah. 'My employers want you alive, useful leverage for when they finally locate Tess Neil. Your friend, they didn't care about. He'll be revived tomorrow when one of our revivers becomes available. Did you know that research was done into how best to kill, to maximize the chance of a successful revival?' Hopkins smiled, looking wistful. 'The results always fascinated me. The most reliable forms of lethal injection tend to significantly reduce revival chances, which rules them out. The most humane method to kill, for those so inclined, is inert gas asphyxiation; a simple mask supplying only nitrogen, for example. Rapid loss of consciousness, entirely painless. Inexpensive, too! Anyone who tells you that the death penalty isn't about retribution, just ask them how they would feel about giving a murderer such a peaceful death. For revival, however, the method exposes

the revived subject to an increased risk of dissociative fragmenta-
tion; more chance of being vague and unfocused, useless to us.
The best ways are those that are quick, painful and loud. The
subject comes back angry and scared. And best of all, talkative.'
He nodded towards the wall, indicating the neighbouring room.
'Single shot to the heart. Standard practice. Now as I said, we're
almost done. Just that last ten per cent. I have a few more things
I'd love to try out, and I so rarely get the chance these days. Not
since the revivers came.' Hopkins paused, and for a moment he
looked at Jonah with real malice. Then his smile returned. 'We
have such a range. Mechanical, electrical, chemical. Things that
cause exquisite agonies, without damage. It's my life's work. I
think you'll find it interesting.'

Hopkins reached back to his table. 'I want you to see how far
I've come,' he said, rummaging. 'I know you think me the lowest of
the low, Jonah. You think of your own career as if everything
you've done has been for the greater good. Then you think of what
I do, and you want to spit in my face. But you don't know me. You
can't *judge* me. Really, I'm a forward thinker. An innovator. Technology has brought us many wonders, Jonah.' He turned. In his
hand was a bizarre metal implement that Jonah didn't want to see,
or understand. 'Let me share them with you.'

There was a noise from the far wall: a creak of the door.

'I said I'll lock up, Jeff,' said Hopkins, angry at the interruption, starting to turn. 'You know how much I look forward to my
private time—'

Hopkins stopped. Jonah looked. The door had swung open,
but it wasn't Jeff. Standing in the doorway, with face and clothes
covered in blood, was someone else entirely.

'Evening,' said Never Geary, sounding exhausted. 'You weren't
fucking expecting to see *me* again, were you?' He looked like he
could hardly stand, but the grin was broad and angry, the tone as
cocky as ever. Then Never backed away into the corridor, out of
sight.

For a moment Jonah's heart soared, but Hopkins reached over, his face dark and – Jonah struggled to identify the expression – *offended*. Setting his chosen implement back down, Hopkins took a gun from the side and strode to the door.

'I don't know what you think you're going to be able to do, Mr Geary, but you won't get out of this building.'

Gun raised, Hopkins leaned out through the doorway, looking to where Never had gone. An arm appeared from behind the door itself and thrust out towards Hopkins. Jonah could hear the loud crackle of a stun gun. He watched with satisfaction as Hopkins fell, twitching.

The owner of the arm stepped around the door and strode over to where Jonah was strapped in place, looking at him with cold, assessing eyes that Jonah hadn't seen in almost eighteen months.

'Jonah Miller,' said Kendrick. 'It's been a while.'

35

Jonah watched Kendrick come closer. Part of him was certain he was imagining this; that the sight of Never in the doorway had been entirely in his own mind, and that seeing Hopkins drop unconscious to the floor was pure fantasy.

Kendrick was wearing a dark suit and black gloves, and was holding the gun Hopkins had taken when he'd gone after Never. He set the gun down on the table beside Jonah and undid the mask straps.

Jonah's eyes did not leave the man's face. There was – dear God – real concern there, Jonah thought.

Kendrick. This was the man who had pushed through the illicit experiments that Hopkins had referred to: researching how revival could be used as an interrogation technique, how best to kill a subject in preparation, how to force information out of them. How to train your own operatives to be able to resist, even after death.

In turn, those experiments had led to an attempt to revive a living subject – to use cryogenic techniques to take the living to a state between life and death, and see if revival could be achieved. Instead, the experiments had opened doors that had revealed the Elders. They had paved the way for Andreas's plans; they had spawned Unity and all that came after.

Kendrick was, in a very real sense, to blame for it all.

And the last time Jonah had seen him, it had been moments

before one of Kendrick's own men had shot Jonah as he gave Tess Neil her chance to escape.

This *had* to all be in his mind.

'You're not real,' said Jonah. 'None of this is real.'

From the doorway came a dragging sound, a hunched figure moving backwards into the room.

'Mr Geary,' Kendrick called, turning his head. 'Your friend needs reassurance that we're real.' Kendrick turned back and set about untying the restraints that held Jonah to the chair.

The hunched figure stood and turned, leaving the unconscious Hopkins on the floor. 'Hey,' said Never. 'It's me.' He smiled, but it was a broken one. He looked exhausted; blood covered his face and chest. Jonah gaped at it.

'The blood's not his,' said Kendrick. 'It belongs to his *advisor*.' He looked at Never. 'If I'd had the opportunity to act earlier, I would have, but I had to be cautious. This building has a lockdown system that even I can't override. If it had been triggered we would have been stuck here. I apologize.' Staying silent, Never nodded once.

Kendrick unfastened the last restraint. Startled by the sudden freedom, Jonah sat upright, then attempted to stand. Kendrick lent him an arm for support, either not noticing or ignoring Jonah's look of mistrust.

Everything hurt. His back was the worst, but the competition was fierce.

'What do we do with him?' said Never, nodding to Hopkins on the floor.

Kendrick guided Jonah away from the seat. Still weak, Jonah leaned against the wall while Kendrick bent down to lift Hopkins under the arms. 'Grab his feet,' Kendrick said, and Never obliged. Together they placed him in the chair. Kendrick fastened the straps around his arms and legs, Jonah observing just how proficient he seemed at the task. A little too familiar.

The table was still in arm's reach. Instinctively, Jonah stepped forwards and took the gun that Kendrick had left there. He backed away with the gun raised.

Kendrick turned slowly. 'No need for that, Jonah,' he said.

Behind him, Never quietly sidled out of the line of fire, frowning. 'What's the problem?' he said.

'You haven't actually laid eyes on Kendrick before,' said Jonah. 'Allow me to introduce you.'

'Oh,' said Never, eyes wide, looking Kendrick up and down. 'Shit. Right. Your reputation precedes you.' He turned to Jonah. 'When he killed the other fucker, he just said he was here to get us out. I was assuming it was a cavalry moment. Turns out it's more of a frying-pan/fire thing.'

'Right now,' said Jonah, 'I have no idea *what* this is.'

'Well, you'd better decide fast,' said Kendrick. 'We don't have the luxury of time.'

'You think I'm going to trust you after everything you've done?' said Jonah.

'If you think this is an elaborate ploy, then I'm flattered. But even I would draw the line at killing my own staff.'

Jonah looked over at Never, who nodded. 'The man in the next room *is* thoroughly dead.'

Jonah kept pointing the gun at Kendrick. 'So why are you here?'

'It was my team that pulled Andreas from the fire,' Kendrick said. 'I helped him recover. By the time I found out what he really was, his influence was too strong for me to do much about. I'd been used, Jonah, used to undermine the security infrastructure I'd devoted my life to. Now I want to stop him.'

'But why are you *here*?'

'I promised someone I'd keep you safe.'

Jonah looked into the man's eyes, the eyes of a professional liar. He lowered the gun, all the same.

'Do you think we can believe him?' asked Never.

'I think we have no choice,' said Jonah. He turned the gun and offered it grip-first to Kendrick.

Kendrick took it, smiling. Again, the nature of the smile took Jonah by surprise. There was nothing triumphant about it. 'Good decision,' said Kendrick. 'Now, there's something I need to know.' He looked Jonah in the eye, his expression serious. 'Is it true that you can see them? The shadows some of them carry?'

Jonah nodded. 'I don't know how to control the ability, but yes. I can see them.'

Kendrick pointed to Hopkins, still out cold and strapped to the seat. 'And does he carry one? Look at him, Jonah. *Does he have one?*'

Jonah looked. He hadn't seen a shadow there before, and couldn't see one now – but then, he'd had other concerns, other distractions. He kept looking, with Kendrick's eager eyes watching his face. He tried to bring back the feelings he'd had before, seeing the crouching presence on Torrance, and the squat pulsating creature that Heggarty had been host to.

'*Well?*' said Kendrick.

'Nothing,' said Jonah. 'As far as I can tell. I can't be absolutely certain, but . . .'

Kendrick nodded, looking oddly disappointed. 'You two might want to step out for a while,' he said. 'This may not be pretty.' He looked through the contents of the table by the seat and took an ampule, breaking it open under the man's nose. Hopkins gasped, immediately awake. Seeing Kendrick's face, he looked around at Jonah and Never. Kendrick reached for a syringe, filling it from the vial Hopkins had used earlier. He glanced at Jonah. 'You'd be appalled if you knew how much this costs to produce,' he said. 'At this concentration a few CCs is quite fatal. Not *quick*, but fatal. I'm not sure I can think of a more expensive way to kill someone.' He turned his gaze back to Hopkins. 'Or more painful.'

'You know I won't tell you anything,' said Hopkins, watching the syringe. There was contempt in his voice but fear in his eyes. Jonah found it hard not to take a degree of satisfaction from that.

'Oh, I'm sure you wouldn't. But I doubt you know anything that'd be worth a damn to me anyway. Who wants the honour? How about you, Never?' Kendrick offered the syringe. Staring at it, Never shook his head. 'Or you, Jonah? No? Very well.'

Hopkins started to babble as Kendrick exposed his forearm. 'It wasn't personal, Kendrick. You know it wasn't personal. Dear God, nobody deserves this, nobody—'

The needle entered his arm.

'*You* do,' said Kendrick. 'You always did enjoy these things a little too much.' He plunged the drug into the man's vein.

Hopkins was suddenly silent, staring at Kendrick, in shock that the deed was done.

'It takes a few seconds,' Kendrick said, looking at Jonah and Never. 'It has to reach the nerve endings before anything will happen, you see, and so much of the body is devoid of them. You two will probably want to wait in the corridor.'

Jonah closed the door as soon as they were both out of the room. The scream that came built slowly, underpinned by the sound of thrashing and clattering, but soon it was the forceful scream of an animal, unrecognizable as human.

They moved further and further from the door, the screams hardly diminishing, the echo of the corridor somehow making it worse as they went. All Jonah could think of was the last thing he'd seen Kendrick do as they left the room – unfasten the arm restraints. He thought of the urge he'd felt when Hopkins had daubed his cheek: the urge to bring his fingers to his own face and make the pain stop. The urge to tear out the offending flesh.

After a time the screaming of the man grew hoarse. The sound of a gunshot brought it to an end.

Kendrick emerged from the room. 'There,' he said, his face stone. 'I put him out of his misery. Don't let anyone accuse me of being heartless. Now, come and give me a hand.' He went down the corridor and entered the next door along.

Jonah and Never shared a wary look before following him.

36

The man who had been ordered to shoot Never lay in his own blood by the interrogation chair in the next room. In the middle of his forehead was a ragged hole where Kendrick's bullet had emerged. The three of them wrestled the corpse into a body bag, Kendrick waving away the issue of the blood pooled on the floor. 'Ignore it,' he said. 'We're only cleaning up a little. I'll dispose of the bodies later. I want to leave some mystery behind.'

They returned to the other room and Jonah and Never put Hopkins into a second body bag. Kendrick had already covered the man's face by wrapping a towel around it. The towel had been white; now it was red. Jonah tried to ignore it.

Kendrick left the room again, and when he came back it was with a smile. He nodded to the cameras, holding up a little black USB stick. 'Just wiped their entire system,' he explained, and Jonah saw a look of extreme interest on Never's face.

Emerging into the night, Jonah was so disoriented he had no idea of the time or place until Kendrick told them. The facility they'd been brought to was in an isolated corner of an industrial park in Newington, to the south of DC. From outside, it looked like a run-down heating distributor. Just another derelict business. One among many.

The industrial park was dark and desolate when they left, Kendrick driving the black four-by-four. Jonah was in the passenger seat, glad of its darkened windows, feeling like every pane of glass he saw on the buildings they passed had eyes behind it, looking for him. He was keenly aware of the two extra passengers they carried in the trunk, cold and silent in their body bags.

Once on the road, Kendrick drove with a calm precision that belied the intensity on his face. 'We have a long drive ahead,' he told them. 'I know you want to bombard me with questions, but all you need to know is that you're safe. It's important that you trust me enough to believe that, at least.' He looked at them both; Jonah turned to see Never, his face still caked in blood, staring at Kendrick like he was speaking in tongues.

Jonah felt the same way. *Trust me.* Two words he wouldn't have expected to hear from Kendrick. Two words he wouldn't have expected to believe.

But somehow, Jonah did. Enough to let the man get them away from danger, at least. He nodded once.

'You should sleep if you can,' said Kendrick. 'Mr Geary, you're a mess. The small bag beside you has some cleaning materials. The larger bag has spare clothes. Clean the blood off your skin and swap everything you're wearing. Put it all back in the bag.' His tone made it clear it was the end of any discussion.

Certain that the idea of sleep was ludicrous, Jonah watched the traffic, unable to put any coherent thoughts together. The next he knew, his shoulder was being shaken.

'Wake up,' said Never, from the back.

They appeared to be in a multi-storey car park. Jonah looked to his left, noting the empty driver's seat. He turned around to Never; his friend's face was clean now, and he was wearing fresh clothes. 'Where are we?'

'Baltimore,' said Never. 'Changing vehicle. Kendrick said he'll be back in minute.'

'Did you sleep?'

'Not a wink,' said Never. 'I hurt all over and my back's spasmed after the fucking impact on the—' He suddenly stopped, and looked at Jonah, horror in his eyes.

'What? Christ, Never, what is it?'

'Jesus. Jesus. I forgot about Bob Crenner. When they took me out of the car they'd already shot him. Christ. I still can't believe it.'

Jonah nodded in silence, seeing again the image of Bob's head, knowing they must have used specialist ammunition to cause such devastation. He thought of Ray Johnson, hoping that the call about Ray had simply been part of the ruse, a lie to lure them onto unpopulated roads for an ambush. The level of organization required to pull something like that off at such short notice was terrifying.

He thought of Annabel, too, but had to push the thought away. Hope seemed like such a pointless thing to harbour now.

A brief honk made him turn to the front to see Kendrick sitting in an aging red Honda, out of his suit and in casuals, wearing a red baseball cap. Jonah was unsettled by how different he looked. The other thing he was wearing made Jonah even more uneasy, though: that smile again.

Kendrick reversed into the bay to their left.

With nobody else around, they swapped the bodies from one vehicle to the other. Jonah and Never both moved with slow, wincing caution, Kendrick looking impatient yet half amused.

They left Baltimore, heading towards Philadelphia. It was midnight; traffic was light.

'Why are you helping us?' asked Jonah. 'You said you made a promise.'

Kendrick looked at him, taking his eyes off the road long enough for Jonah to be relieved when he finally looked back where he was driving. 'I have my reasons.'

'Any chance you might tell us what those are?' asked Never. 'I mean, seemed to me that you knew that guy. That you had unfinished business. Right?'

'My advice, Never, would be for you to stay quiet. We still have some way to go and I've been awake for over twenty hours. Let me concentrate on driving.'

With a grunt, Never complied.

'What about Ray Johnson?' said Jonah. 'Answer that, at least.'

'Who?' said Kendrick.

'Bob Crenner was the detective who was driving when we were attacked. They shot him at the scene. He'd got a call that his partner, Ray Johnson, had been killed.'

'Ah. I knew a cop had died when they snatched you, but no other deaths were reported. That call was probably just to reroute your vehicle.'

Approaching Philadelphia, they turned off before the city and took I476 out past Norristown. The cloud cover had broken up enough for the bright moon to lend some light to their surroundings, woodland and wide grass banks at the sides of the road, houses infrequent. Finally, they pulled into a driveway. The house at the end of it was a large wood-clad relic, white paint clinging on for dear life.

Kendrick killed the engine. 'Now. Your answers. We're at a safe house. You were taken on the orders of Michael Andreas. No surprises there, I'm sure. He's left you alone all this time for one reason.'

'Tess,' said Jonah. 'He wants Tess.'

'Indeed. He didn't want to risk scaring her off.'

'So how the hell did you know where to find us?' said Jonah.

Kendrick smiled again. 'That's what I do. I know things. I get things done. Impressed by how quickly they set up your ambush? I used to *run* things like that. Once they knew you were going, all they needed was a tracker on your car and a ten-minute head start. Wherever you are in the country you can be damn sure there's a team nearby ready to go, with a dozen potential grab locations already identified and analysed. They pick one, they get there, they know how to send you in the right direction.'

'And all these people work for Andreas now?'

Kendrick shook his head. 'They're just part of the security network, Jonah. They do what they're told. Andreas only has people placed here and there, but it's enough. If he wants something done, it gets done because people follow their orders. I didn't really appreciate that, at first. I could see Andreas had a few people in his pocket, but it reached a critical mass before I knew it.'

There was a snort from the back. 'And now you're fighting the good fight,' said Never. 'Sure.'

'I want revenge,' said Kendrick. 'Plain and simple. Andreas is the greatest threat this country ever faced, and he abused my trust to put himself in that position. He betrayed me.'

'And you got us out because you think we can help?'

Kendrick's smile spread across his face. 'No, Jonah.' He pointed up to the doorway on the front of the house. It opened, and a figure stood there silhouetted in the rectangle of light. 'I got you out because *she* insisted.'

Jonah looked at the figure. Backlit, too far for him to see clearly, but he knew who it was.

Tess Neil.

37

They headed for the house, Kendrick leading the way. At the door Tess gave Jonah a long hug that felt damn good until he caught the expression on Never's face, one that said *be careful.*

Kendrick nodded to Tess. 'I have a few things to unload from the car,' he said. 'Get them inside and bring them up to speed. I think it's better coming from you.'

The inside of the house was run-down, sparse and musty, but it was clean; Never looked up as they entered and Jonah followed his eye line to see cabling running along the ceiling, and odd, fat-bulbed light fittings every eight feet or so. They shared a look and Never shrugged.

Tess brought them through to a large kitchen, an old oak table in the middle. They sat as she crossed to the fridge, returning with a pack of beer cans. Jonah could see that Never was torn between the cold beer and his antipathy towards Tess, so he reached for a can and passed it over to him.

'Cheers,' said Never, snapping it open and gulping down half of it without a breath.

Jonah took one for himself. He looked at Tess in the artificial light of the kitchen; it was good to see her, but she didn't look well. Thin. Tired. The smile on her face seemed ready to flee at the slightest noise. He had a hundred questions, but one seemed appropriate to ask first. 'Do you trust him?' he said, tilting his head to the door.

'Larry?' said Tess.

Jonah and Never looked at each other for a moment. 'Larry?' said Never. '*Larry?*' They both burst into laughter; it built until it felt dangerous, but both of them needed the release. Given everything that had happened to them, hysteria seemed the natural response. *Better for it to come out like this*, Jonah thought.

Kendrick walked in a few moments later, visibly bemused by the laughter. 'Something funny?'

'No, Larry,' managed Never, before he and Jonah started laughing again.

'Good,' said Kendrick, walking off.

'Larry's complicated,' said Tess, when they'd finally settled down.

'No shit,' said Never.

'He believes this is largely his fault,' she said. 'Somehow Andreas managed to escape from the fire, horribly burned. It was Kendrick who found him, who kept him alive, who brought him to his superiors and convinced them to take him seriously. Then Andreas started to improve, to recover. You've seen how he looks now.'

'As if nothing had happened to him,' said Jonah. 'That didn't ring any alarm bells?'

'They thought they *knew* what had happened,' she said. 'They'd known what Andreas *believed* he was doing, and they took his word that he'd succeeded. Making contact. Bringing something ancient and wise into the world, ready to reveal the secrets of an advanced race. They wanted a piece of it. They shielded him, gave him access and support. To them, his physical recovery was just proof that he had power. By the time Larry realized something was wrong, that Andreas wasn't what he claimed, Andreas was already keeping him at arm's length. So, yes, Larry Kendrick can be trusted. At least as far as wanting to bring Andreas down. He blames himself for the greatest threat facing the country he's spent his life protecting. And whatever you think of him, he's a patriot.'

'Right,' said Never. 'Patriotism: the last refuge of psychopaths.'

'He *did* save our lives,' said Jonah. 'I think he's earned some leeway.'

'Maybe,' said Never. 'But I doubt he saved us just because Tess asked him to.'

'Larry thinks the best way to get Andreas is with my help,' said Tess. 'But when he tracked me down, I told him keeping an eye on you was part of the deal.'

From the doorway came Kendrick's voice, making Jonah start. 'That's not to say you can't earn your *keep*,' he said. He opened a cupboard and pulled out a bottle of bourbon, filling a glass as he spoke. 'Andreas underestimated me, Jonah. I'd worked out something was *off* with him, long before he knew I had. Long enough to put things in place, things that would let me watch what they were up to. I knew they were coming for you forty-eight hours before they came. From the moment the shit with Torrance hit the fan they got the jitters. Andreas decided he was going to get you off the street one way or another as soon as possible. It's my business to know these things. But there's one thing I don't know enough about. The *shadows*. The ones that you can see.'

Jonah shook his head. 'I don't know what they are. I think I saw them in a vision I had, Andreas laying waste to a city as the smaller shadows flowed on the ground at his feet. I could only guess, though.'

'And what was your guess?' said Kendrick.

'That they're pieces of what's inside Andreas,' said Jonah. 'His disciples. His acolytes.'

Kendrick looked at Tess. She nodded. 'You're right. They're fragments of the whole. A host accepts them willingly. It gives them strength, but I think it acts like a drug. Gradually the host cedes control until they're just extensions. Puppets.'

Jonah quailed. 'If they're parts of it, does that mean when Torrance or Heggarty saw me, Andreas saw me too?'

'No,' said Kendrick. 'Andreas uses normal channels to communicate with his people. If they shared some kind of direct link, they'd not need to risk anyone eavesdropping. I've known about these creatures for a while. I was already aware that the shadows can be seen when they separate, but until you, I didn't realize we could tell who was infected by sight alone.'

'I can't be the only one who sees them,' said Jonah.

Tess nodded. 'So far, it's just you.'

'The FBI agent who brought me in had one,' said Jonah. 'Him, and his partner. He claimed that Andreas wanted to rule, not destroy.'

'And what do you think?' said Kendrick.

Jonah shook his head. 'The only thing it wants to rule over is ash.'

Kendrick nodded, and a sombre silence fell. 'Enough,' he said, waving it away. 'We all need sleep. Tess, you go on ahead. I'd like to make sure our guests know the house rules.'

'OK,' she said. 'Jonah, Never. I'll see you in the morning.' She smiled, or tried to.

Once she'd gone, Kendrick sipped his whiskey and frowned. 'There's something ancient and brave inside her,' he said. 'Ancient, brave and lost. And it might be our only hope.'

'But the Elder she's host to, it's part of her now,' said Jonah. 'Isn't it? That was the whole point of Unity.'

Kendrick shook his head. 'That was the goal, yes, but it didn't seem to work out. She was broken when I tracked her down. Traumatized. Before it all went wrong, Andreas and the others had hoped their Unity with these creatures would be effortless, a perfect union of minds. At the time of the fire, Tess was the only one among them who had been showing any progress. Dreams, visions. Overwhelming but manageable. When she was on the run it turned out to be one long series of nightmares. She was close to madness when I found her, Jonah. The only thing that saved her was the medication you revivers take, to counter post-traumatic stress disorder.'

'BPV,' said Jonah.

'Yes. Large doses of it stopped the nightmares, but it also silenced the Elder. Andreas is desperate to find her. He must be scared she knows too much, and if he's scared, there has to be some vulnerability, some way to defeat him that the Elder knows. But she'd have to come off the medication and face the nightmares again. The prospect terrifies her. Almost as much as the prospect of Andreas finding her.'

'But you got her first,' said Jonah.

'Before I realized he was playing me, he told us she was crucial to revealing all the secrets he promised us. None of our people could track her down. When I saw the light and got out of there, I found Tess by myself within three weeks. I beat him to the punch. That's what happens when you fuck over the best.' He raised his glass and nodded. *The man's taking a bow*, thought Jonah.

Kendrick offered his bourbon. Jonah and Never both declined and took another beer instead, Never wincing as he reached across for it. 'Between being crashed into and being tortured, I think my body broke today,' he said.

Kendrick reached into his pocket and produced a blister pack of pills, sliding them towards Never. 'If you're hurting, take two tablets. You'll sleep better. You can have another two in the morning, if you need it.'

'Oxycodone,' read Never. He looked at the pills with undisguised suspicion, then looked at Kendrick the same way.

'A little trust would be welcome,' said Kendrick.

'Fuck it,' said Never, and took out two, washing them down with beer.

Jonah did the same. He was too tired to try second-guessing Kendrick's real intentions.

'You'll feel worse tomorrow,' said Kendrick, 'but you're both young enough to shrug it off in a few days.'

'Listen to Old Gramps,' said Never, getting a tolerant smile from Kendrick.

Jonah looked at the man, and wondered what age he was. Anywhere between forty and sixty. 'How old *are* you, anyway?'

Kendrick shrugged. 'Lives like mine are measured in dog years.'

For a minute or so they drank in silence, but there was something Jonah wanted to broach. 'Kendrick?' said Jonah. 'Uh, Larry?'

Kendrick raised an eyebrow. '"Kendrick" is fine.'

'I want to get a message to Annabel. Annabel Harker. I was talking to her when we were attacked. She must have gone on the run by now, but I want to let her know we're OK. We'd agreed on ways to get in touch if something happened. Safe ways.'

Kendrick frowned. 'Safe ways, hmm? I'll consider it. Your disappearance has hit the headlines, by the way. The story they put out has you – a *top reviver*, no less – kidnapped by extremists, and in the current climate it's a firecracker. They released phoney descriptions of two of the attackers. One looked very like Tess, apparently. The other could have been my twin.' He raised a sarcastic eyebrow. 'What are the odds?'

There was another concern Jonah had, one he wasn't eager to raise. 'The medication Tess is using,' he said. 'It's dangerous at high doses. You must know that. She looks sick.'

'I know,' said Kendrick. 'But the medication alone doesn't explain how quickly she's been getting worse. She thinks she'll lose her mind if she stops taking it, but I think the lack of contact with the being inside her is the main problem.' Kendrick drained his glass. 'I think it's killing her.'

38

Jonah woke in pain the next morning. His hand went to his cheek for an instant, to the spot where Hopkins had daubed his favourite drug, but it was the complaints from the rest of his body that were the source of it: every muscle in his back, every sinew in his neck.

The pain spread to his mind, then, as the pieces came back. The impact. Bob Crenner's death. The screams of Never across the intercom as the drug was put in both eyes . . .

He got up with care. He'd kept the blister pack of pills Never had handed him, and now he took two right off as he pulled on his clothes. He'd slept solidly – Kendrick was right about that at least. He lay down on the bed again, waiting for the medication to grant its respite. Only then did he take time to glance around the room he'd slept in. The night before, he'd not paid the room any attention, oblivion sneaking up on him before he knew it. The room was bare bones just like the rest of the house, with another of the odd lamps on the ceiling by the door. 'Sunlamps,' Kendrick had explained when they'd asked. 'Tess insisted. To ward off the shadows. Whether they're worth a damn or not, well, let's hope we don't have to find out.'

As the pills kicked in, Jonah heard snoring from the room next to his. He got up and entered, to see Never fast asleep and looking peaceful. He left the pills by Never's bed and went downstairs.

Tess was sitting at the table, blank-faced and staring ahead.

He said nothing, thinking of sleepwalkers, of the notion that waking them was a terrible thing to do. Her expression scared him, the sheer weariness it carried. He crossed to the kettle and switched it on, hunting for the makings of coffee, being noisier than was really necessary.

In gradual steps her awareness surfaced from somewhere deep inside. 'Jonah,' she said, his presence a surprise to her.

'You want coffee?' He hoped his question sounded casual enough to hide the anxiety he felt for her.

'No . . .' she said, still vague. Then she looked around herself, and shook her head. 'Jesus. This must look terrible, but please don't worry. I'm just a little *dazed* now and again. It's the medication I'm taking.'

'Kendrick told me.'

She nodded. 'Did he explain why?'

'He did. You can't keep doing it. Not indefinitely.'

She changed the subject. 'Larry's gone out for supplies,' she said.

'Kendrick thinks there must be a way to stop Andreas. He thinks you're the only hope for finding out how. All this time, I hadn't doubted for a second that Andreas died that night. I saw what it was inside him. I saw it destroy other civilizations, and I knew that if Andreas was alive, then it would already have happened here, too. So why hasn't it?'

'The power it had was vast, Jonah,' said Tess. 'This is a creature that gains its strength from the souls it consumes, and it had eaten the souls of a thousand worlds. It escaped its prison with only a fraction of its power. The rest would have taken weeks to come through the conduit that had been forged. Then it almost died, and the conduit collapsed. The flow virtually stopped. If it hadn't, the world would have been lost to the Shadow long ago. The Beast would have won. The evil that's in Andreas is nothing compared to what it would be if it could find that power again, and unlock it. Andreas believes he's close to knowing how to do that.'

'Is that what Winnerden Flats is for?' said Jonah. 'Finding out how to open the door?'

'The lead researcher at Baseline is someone you know, right?'

'Stephanie Graves, yes.'

'She's not one of Andreas's people,' said Tess. 'Neither are the researchers she's gathered, as far as we can tell.'

'I thought it might be some kind of misdirection. To keep the strongest revivers out of the way, and reduce the chance of them stumbling into something the way I did.'

'That's probably an important part of it. But half of the facility is hush-hush, supposedly where the cryogenics research continues. As far as we know it's really where the work to open that doorway is going on. Baseline's acting as a smokescreen to let them funnel money into the project.'

He reached out and took her hands in his. They felt cold. 'Do you think we can stop Andreas?'

'I don't think he's invulnerable, but beyond that I don't know. I'm scared to learn anything new now. Knowledge could be dangerous. I could learn exactly what would allow Andreas to rise. That's the word he uses for regaining his power: his *rise*. And then – well, you know what happens then.'

Jonah nodded his head, the sound and sight of the Great Shadow filling his mind: the Beast strident, destruction at the tips of its claws. He remembered feeling the certainty within the creature's mind, the utter lack of doubt, lack of *weakness*. He thought of Andreas, on fire and smiling, the ceiling crashing down. Somehow he'd got out of the building. Somehow he'd made his recovery, with no visible sign of injury.

Rise. 'Yes,' he said.

*

When his coffee was finished, Jonah left Tess in the kitchen and took the opportunity to look around the safe house, using the time to get familiar with the layout. Every room had the same level of faded décor, the same sparse furnishings, the same cabling and sunlamp fittings along the ceiling. The entire building was devoid of identity, almost as if the house itself was in hiding.

Upstairs, he checked in again on the still-sleeping Never, the snoring even louder than before. Thoughts of what they'd experienced the previous day loomed in his mind; he shoved them away, hard. He closed his eyes as tears started flowing. He left Never's room and wiped them away, angry and confused. He leaned against the wall in the corridor, breathing slowly, the tears not stopping.

He punched the wall and swore at himself, a whispered hiss of frustration.

'Don't,' said Kendrick's voice from beside him. Jonah snapped open his eyes, stunned that the man could have got so close without making a sound.

'Don't what?' he said.

'Fall apart. We don't have time.' Kendrick nodded towards Never's room. 'And your friend needs you to be as normal as possible.'

'He's coping better than I am,' said Jonah. 'I don't know how, but he is. Listen to him.'

'At five a.m. he woke up screaming. You didn't stir. What your friend went through will take a while to work itself out, if it ever does. It's a kind of mental shrapnel. What they gave him was far stronger than the solution they gave you, and in the eyes . . . a terrible, consuming pain, but one that cuts off suddenly with no lasting physical effects. Like you imagined it all, like it meant nothing, but the memory is so *strong*. The incongruity is difficult to process.' Kendrick's eyes went to the floor. 'It won't be easy for him.'

Jonah made the connection. 'You went through the same thing.'

Kendrick nodded. 'With the same man who tormented you; Never was right about that. It was after I'd realized the truth about

Andreas, while I was still faking my loyalty. But I'd been careless about a small matter. They doubted me. I convinced them.' He fell silent for a moment. Jonah thought about the pain he himself had gone through. He couldn't imagine the strength it would take to be able to keep up a deception under that kind of torment, let alone under what Never had experienced. He looked at Kendrick with a new level of respect – and a new level of wariness.

'I'd regained their trust,' Kendrick said, 'but only enough for them to let me live. That was when I knew the moment had come for me to vanish. Now, though, it's time your friend was awake. Once we've had breakfast, I'll explain the job I have for you.'

*

Jonah shook Never from his sleep. They took turns to shower, the water tepid and insubstantial but a godsend, nonetheless. Part of Kendrick's supply run had included toothbrushes; Jonah marvelled at the way a clean mouth made him feel better armed against whatever was coming. He voiced this to Never.

'I know what you mean,' Never said. 'And if fluoride *is* fatal to the terrifying shadow demons, we're sorted.'

By the time they went downstairs a smell had filled the house, one that was calling to Never like piper to rat.

Kendrick was standing by the sink, plunging a frying pan into the water. On the table three places were set, the plates loaded with scrambled eggs, bacon and pancakes, toast on the side.

'Wow,' said Never. 'He also cooks. I'm not hallucinating, am I? I can eat that, right?'

Kendrick nodded.

'Larry, my man,' said Never, taking a seat. 'You are full of surprises. And not just the lethal national-interest kind.'

'I'm also hopeful,' said Kendrick, 'that a full mouth is a quiet one.'

'A funny man,' said Never, starting to shovel food into his eager maw. 'Optimistic, too,' he said around it.

'Where's Tess?' asked Jonah, taking the seat next to Never.

'She's sleeping,' said Kendrick. 'She needs it.' He sat and started to eat. 'You asked me last night about Annabel. You mentioned ways to contact her. I need to know the details of what you'd agreed.'

'What for?' said Jonah.

'To bring her here. For her own safety. My sources tell me Andreas is very keen to locate her. It's possible he wants her as a bargaining chip, but there may be more to it than that. Whatever the reason, if I can frustrate their efforts, it'll make me a happy man. For that, I need to know what "safe" ways you've arranged to get in touch.'

'Oh, do you, indeed?' said Never, eyebrow raised.

'I do,' said Kendrick. 'Or maybe you think this has all been an elaborate ruse just to find *her*?'

Grudgingly, Never shook his head. 'OK, OK,' he said. 'I'll tell you. We'd planned for this. Well, not *this*, exactly, because that would have been some fucking *spectacular* planning, but we'd planned how we could get in contact securely, so even if any of us was caught, their phone couldn't link back to us. I mean, if a specific phone is ever linked to you, it can be tracked, but we have a bespoke proxy server making all communication anonymous. As long as your server isn't compromised, it's impossible to trace. Ours is state-of-the-art, Annabel had a guy, a—'

'A hacker in London?' said Kendrick.

Saying nothing, Never closed his mouth. His eyes narrowed.

'A hacker,' continued Kendrick, 'who had helped with Annabel's initial investigations into the death of her father, and who was again helping with her work investigating Andreas Biotech. A man distinguished by being exceptionally good at breaking the law, yet one Annabel has placed her full trust in.'

'Yeah,' said Never, wary. 'That's the one. Somehow I don't think I'll like what you're about to say.'

Kendrick reached into his pocket and pulled out a sheet of

paper. He unfolded it and held it up. A printout, small-font text filling the lower half, the image of a man's face above. An overweight, unhappy, and notably *bruised* face.

'Terry Weald,' said Kendrick. 'Based in London. Married with four kids. Annabel Harker was first put in contact with him a few years ago while researching a piece on hacker activists. Only ever knew him by the online alias Yaffle. Terry was arrested four days ago. I say arrested, but really it was much less formal than that. He's been *helping with inquiries*, shall we say, into a recent spate of hacking offences in this country. We have such a *close* relationship with the British. From the look of the bruising, they must have used rather basic methods of ensuring the suspect's cooperation. But it clearly did the job.'

'Fuck,' said Jonah. He looked at Never.

'Yes,' said Never. 'Fuck.'

'Indeed,' said Kendrick. 'What was it you said, Never? Everything is fine as long as your server isn't compromised? I think you'd better tell me all you can about the server you were supposed to use. Then you'd better hope Annabel Harker doesn't use it. Because if she does . . .' Kendrick put the sheet of paper on the table, Terry Weald's bruised and defeated face looking up at them all. 'Then they can locate her phone. And they'll know exactly where she is.'

39

Annabel was asleep before she hit the bed.

The hotel was just outside Billings, Montana. Her eyes had taken in so much asphalt that when she closed them all she saw was road.

She'd driven almost solidly for twenty-four hours. Besides refuelling she'd had only one other roadside stop – what she'd intended as a brief sleep, necessary the moment she recognized the onset of a dangerous fatigue. That had been close to dawn; as she'd long-since dumped her cell phone, she had no alarm clock, but she'd thought the light of day would wake her within an hour or so. Instead, she woke over three hours later in a haze of terror, the sensation of being hunted all that she remembered from her nightmare.

Since taking her car and leaving Sacramento she'd headed north, thinking only to put as much distance between herself and her apartment as she could. It was only when she got as far as Portland that her thoughts turned to any kind of planning, rather than just the simple urge to run. Run, and blank out what she'd heard on her phone before she'd left. Jonah, crying out in fear. An impact.

Then silence.

Of all the things she was frightened of it was her own tears that had scared her the most, streaming out of her even though she felt numb, tears that seemed entirely divorced from emotion. A purge that her damn *tear ducts* seemed to understand better than her mind did.

She'd kept the radio on. News was still coming in about Andreas and his research effort. Any uneasiness about the repercussions of soaking up the best revivers in the country was muted. There was a palpable feel of expectation. Andreas himself was interviewed at the Winnerden Flats facility, and Annabel had to restrain the urge to switch off. It occurred to her that instinctively she'd chosen to drive north because it took her further away from the site, away from Andreas.

And then it had come: breaking news. Extremists, trying to derail Andreas's grand project. A murdered detective. A kidnapped reviver, identified as Jonah. No mention of Never, either way.

Kidnapped.

The tears began again, but this time there were emotions behind them, a confused bag of fear and hope and pain.

A plan formed, for what it was worth. Head east, back towards Richmond. She could keep her head down but at least be nearer to where the kidnapping had happened, where the investigation into it would take place. And she would be a few thousand miles away from Andreas.

Caffeine and purpose fuelled her body; gas fuelled the car. She drove, half-hypnotized by the road, barely aware of the miles as she left Oregon, then Washington, then Idaho.

By the time she'd hit Billings she could feel herself close to collapse and had known she had no choice but to stop and rest properly. She'd swung into a hotel car park, taken a room, and had aimed herself at the bed.

She woke ravenous, showering fast and getting directions to the nearest grocery store, loading up with an assortment of canned food, bottles of water and cola to keep her on the road as long as her body could stand it.

She sat in the car in the store's parking lot and ate a can of corn with one of the plastic spoons she'd bought, so damn hungry it didn't really feel like it counted as eating. It was just something she had to do, and she might as well get it done quickly.

Then she hit town, getting just one thing: a prepay phone. She needed to get online in case she got word from Jonah or Never.

Back in the hotel she set the phone up, configuring it to her London contact's proxy server. She hunted around online for what little additional information she could find about Jonah. Still exhausted, she planned to get another few hours of sleep before she continued on the road.

And before she let herself sleep, she went to the Richmond FRS website. There, not yet removed from the staff profiles, was Jonah's picture. She looked at the smiling face for long minutes, finding herself unable to close the browser, feeling a curious superstition that if she did so, the picture would vanish from the site forever.

At last, she set the phone beside her and went to sleep.

40

Kendrick ventured out after breakfast with stern warnings to the others about keeping inside the safe house. With little to distract him, Jonah found himself obsessing over Annabel: where she was, whether she was safe, what she'd heard about his own disappearance.

When Tess emerged from her room at noon, she looked just as tired as she had before her sleep. She and Never stayed out of each other's way, and it was almost a relief when Kendrick returned to the house late that afternoon and told them all to sit.

'I'm taking Jonah out to earn his keep,' Kendrick told them. 'To understand what you're going to do, Jonah, you need to know more about Winnerden Flats. Tess has already told you there's more than meets the eye to what's happening there.' He laid out a plan on the table. Jonah recognized it as the alternative site plan Annabel had uncovered. He shared a look with Never, but said nothing.

Kendrick continued. 'This is the restricted part of the facility – supposedly where their cryogenics work continues, but really it's the core of Andreas's plans. Now, here in this circular area: MCH. That stands for 'machine'. They're building something, but 'the machine' is the only way they refer to it. They're cautious in related communications, so a lot of this is reading between the lines. We assume the machine is how Andreas intends to locate and open the doorway that will let him regain his power, and we know that it's not yet functional. We've also learned that two key components had been proving problematic, but that one of them has now been sourced.' He laid out another sheet – again, it was something Annabel had already found, the schematic of a whole-body cryogenic unit. 'This might be it. From what we've managed to intercept, we believe Andreas will be at the heart of the machine during the process. We think this is the design for the chamber he'll be in. It might be similar to the live revival methodology, the one needed for Unity. Cool the body to the point of death, then use revival to open some kind of door. That only leaves one key component that's not ready yet.'

'That's what we're trying to find out,' said Tess. 'What the last component is, and where it's being developed.'

'We've identified a company affiliated to Andreas Biotech as a likely candidate,' said Kendrick. 'It specializes in communications technology, but a new research group was started there eight months ago. Big funding, small team. Secretive.' He took out his phone and pulled up an image of a burly, smiling man. 'This is Lucas Silva. Key player in the research team, he's someone I've managed to get some surveillance on.'

'Surveillance?' said Never. 'When are you managing to fit *that* in?'

'We're not alone in this,' said Kendrick. 'We have people helping us. Now, if Silva carries a shadow, we'll know we're on the right track. If not him, we've got a higher-ranking target to consider next, but Silva is the first to try as he's more open in his movements and easier to monitor. He cycles to work, so we'll follow him as he leaves for home at the end of the day. Jonah, you'll be in the car with me. All you need to do is take a good look as we pass him in the road, and tell me if you see one of those things on his shoulder. OK?'

'I don't know,' said Jonah. 'I mean, whatever this ability is, I'm not sure if I can bring it on at will yet.'

'Understood,' said Kendrick. 'Do your best. The company in question is at a site outside a city north of us: Bethlehem.'

'Hell of a location,' said Never.

Kendrick nodded. 'From my experience of Andreas, he probably finds it amusing. Maybe he knows his Yeats. "*And what rough beast, its hour come round at last, slouches towards Bethlehem to be born?*"' Kendrick's smile was almost mischievous.

Jonah glared at him. 'Thanks for that. Makes it all seem *far* less ominous.'

*

They left Never and Tess at the house and drove out towards Bethlehem. The sun was bright. Both of them wore baseball caps and sunglasses, enough to hide their faces. Kendrick parked up across the street from the main entrance to a large car lot; Jonah could see three buildings in the complex, the nearest called Cooper Communications.

At 5 p.m., there was a steady stream of workers leaving for the day.

'Damn,' said Kendrick. 'That's Silva. Black jacket getting into the passenger seat of the grey Ford.'

'Not cycling?'

Kendrick shrugged. 'Not today it seems. We'll follow at a distance to begin with. Then I'll try and get alongside him so you can get a look.' He waited for the Ford to exit the site before he started the car, then slotted them into the traffic ten vehicles back. 'He's heading into the city,' Kendrick observed. 'His home's the other way.'

As they followed, Jonah tried to regain the sense that had allowed him to see the shadow on Torrance and Heggarty. He knew he was missing something.

The traffic was growing heavier as they went through the city.

'Hold on,' said Kendrick. Ahead, the grey Ford was pulling over. Jonah saw Lucas Silva get out of the car and wave to the occupants. Kendrick passed the vehicle and pulled over further on.

'You see anything on him?' said Kendrick.

Jonah concentrated. Maybe there was something, but . . . 'I'm not sure. Maybe I'm too far away. I don't think it's working.'

'So get after him until it does. We need to be certain.'

'Get after him?'

'Get close enough to check him over, then come back. I'll stay here.'

'Shit,' said Jonah, getting out. He caught sight of Silva as he vanished around a corner ahead. He followed. The street was dotted with restaurants, cafes and bars. It was getting busy, the sun low in the sky. The air had a chill, but it was warmer than the last few days had been. A relaxed Friday. Jonah rounded the corner in time to see Silva slip into the growing crowd. He hurried on, finding himself moving against the flow of people. He caught a glimpse of the man's head further on, going into a shop. Jonah drew closer, slowly, until he reached the store window. He looked through the glass. The man was at the back of the store browsing through a rack of gift cards. Jonah watched him, looking hard at his shoulder. He thought he saw some kind of dark blur there for a moment, but then there was nothing – he couldn't be sure if he'd not just imagined it. He was trying to understand what let him see the shadows. It didn't matter how close he got if he couldn't manage that.

When Jonah looked up to the man's face, Silva was looking right at him. Jonah met his gaze for an instant before he turned away; long enough to know Silva was wary of the scrutiny.

As Silva left the store Jonah was careful to keep his eyes else-where, but he was sure he could feel the man glance towards him. He waited a few seconds before risking looking.

The man was weaving through the stream of people. Jonah could see nothing on the shoulder now, but he didn't think he'd recaptured his ability. The whole exercise was at risk of being a complete waste of time. He pushed onwards, keeping his distance, desperately trying to think himself into the required state, what-ever that was.

Silva stopped outside a restaurant window at the corner of the street ahead and stood, clearly waiting for someone. Jonah looked at the ground as he walked. He would only have one more chance, he thought, and it all depended on regaining whatever sight it was that let him see the creatures. Then all he would have to do would be to walk past, snatch a glance from close quarters, and it would be done. He could return to the safe house and lock the door again.

He thought back to Torrance in the interview room, Torrance in his office; and Heggarty, too, the pulsating shape crouching there, almost nuzzling the agent's neck.

He could *feel* it happen then, as he recalled Heggarty's smiling face looking at him. He could feel the fear creep in, his skin grow-ing cold, the hairs on his neck bristling, and with it he felt the almost-familiar sensitivity return. Now he just had to get close enough.

But as he looked up, Silva was nowhere in sight. There was nobody standing outside the restaurant as he reached it. He looked around urgently, and peered through the restaurant window, but he couldn't see Silva anywhere.

Then a hand fell on his shoulder, gripping it.

'Are you following me?' said the voice behind him.

Jonah turned, freeing himself from the grip. He saw the wary look on Silva's face as he studied Jonah. Doubtless the man was wondering if he was a threat: a thief perhaps, following him to evaluate a potential target. Jonah was ready with his excuse: *I thought you were someone I knew . . . My mistake.*

But nothing came out.

Instead, Jonah's eyes locked onto the man's shoulder, onto the glistening shape he could now see there. It was far smaller than Torrance's, but Jonah could tell that his sight was sharper than it had ever been. He could see it so clearly, even against the dark material of the jacket Silva wore. The fingers, thin and long, stretched down over the collarbone, black lines buried in the man's flesh. The bulk of it was on his shoulder, the size of a fist, the skin that of a mollusc, dark and moist, mottled with a lighter brown like that of a slug. Barely moving, the shape was without much form, save for slow protuberances pushing out and receding slightly, as if it was tasting the air.

Jonah was suddenly aware of the smell of tainted meat.

'Are you *following* me?' the man said again.

Jonah tore his eyes from the thing on Silva's shoulder, aware of the unease that had to be clear on his face. 'I'm sorry,' he said, his voice uneven. 'I thought you were someone else.' His eyes sought out the shape again, briefly, and he could see the man noting the glance.

Silva's hand went to his shoulder, Jonah's unease growing as the hand seemed to pass through the shape to scratch at the flesh below. The creature's movement increased, pulsing regularly, giving it the look of a rotting heart trying to beat into life. The man's eyes turned back to Jonah. The cold glare made it obvious that he'd realized Jonah was a greater threat to him than a mere thief.

Silva was taller than Jonah and well built. The man's hand came out and grabbed Jonah's upper arm, holding tight. Jonah tried to pull away but the grip was solid. It would take a much greater effort to tug free, he knew; it could trigger a scuffle, enough to draw much more attention from those around him. He wasn't quite ready to force such an escalation, not yet.

The man reached into his pocket and took out a phone. Jonah had a sudden image of reinforcements being summoned, of being surrounded by malevolent faces, every shoulder bearing a large, pulsating shadow, eager to loosen its fingers and pounce. The image made him lash out with his free arm, taking Silva by surprise. The phone clattered to the ground, out of reach. Silva swore and made to step nearer to it, but he wasn't going to let go of

Jonah, and Jonah was holding his ground. For a few seconds, neither moved.

'Lucas?' said a voice. Jonah looked to his right and saw her, a tall Asian woman with a boy of six or seven holding her hand.

'Daddy!' said the child, oblivious to the tension, but the woman's face showed real concern.

She looked between Jonah and Silva, wary. 'Lucas, what's going on?'

'He was following me,' said Silva.

'I thought he was someone I knew,' said Jonah. He knew he had to get as much fearful vulnerability into his voice as possible, but he didn't have to work hard to fake it. 'Please. It was just a misunderstanding.' He looked pointedly at where Silva still had a tight grip on his arm.

The woman clearly didn't approve of what Silva was doing. 'Come on, Lucas,' she said. 'The table's booked, just let the guy go.'

Silva said nothing, but seemed reluctant.

'I just want to have a nice meal, honey,' she said. 'Don't be like this.'

'He was *following* me,' said Silva, anger in his voice, but the woman stayed quiet, not one to take no for an answer. After a moment Silva let go.

'Thank you,' said Jonah. The woman's eyes showed no patience: she was giving him the benefit of the doubt and, in turn, he needed to be out of their sight as soon as physically possible. Jonah wanted to do exactly that, but instead he froze.

On the woman's shoulder was something different, something new. A small thing, flat, thin; little bigger than a quarter. The same slug-like skin of the shadows, and a regular pulse.

It was a bud, he thought; the beginnings, a seed taking slow root.

He looked at the woman. Her face was growing more hostile, but he was certain the hostility was simply because he'd not left yet, not because of what he'd seen. *She doesn't know*, he thought.

She doesn't know it's there. Jonah's mouth opened as if he was about to speak, but he didn't know what to say. He looked back and forth from her eyes to her shoulder, the blood draining from his face. The woman's hostile expression shifted to bewilderment, then to concern.

Beside her, a small voice spoke up. 'Is the man sick, mama?' said the little boy, and Jonah looked down.

He stared, suddenly dizzy. 'I'm sorry,' he managed to say. He strode off, hoping the dizziness wouldn't make him stumble; stumble, then fall and wake to a crowd of unkind faces. He picked up speed, crossing the street, looking ahead desperately for Kendrick's car.

He tried not to think about the woman, or about the second dark bud he'd seen, growing on the child's shoulder.

41

Annabel heard the knock in her dreams. Her unconscious mind incorporated the sound; she woke from an image of an ancient door, set deep in stone, beginning to swing wide open.

She sat up. The knock came again – her hotel room door. 'Coming.'

She'd slept in her clothes. Given the daylight creeping around the edge of the curtains in the hotel room, she realized she'd slept for far longer than she'd intended. She reached for her phone, wondering if it was past check-out time and the knock could be someone from the hotel come to evict her, but it was only nine-forty.

She tugged the curtains back and opened her eyes wide into the bright day, wincing. Then she went to the door and looked through the peephole. Outside stood a slight, young woman in staff uniform. Short, bored, and barely out of school by the look of her, Annabel thought. College job, maybe. She opened the door.

'Hi,' said the woman, with a staff smile. The smile faltered when the door across the corridor opened behind her, and a family of two tired parents and two exuberant children emerged.

Annabel felt the hairs on her arm stand up. Something was wrong here, something about the way the woman's smile had changed as she'd turned to look at the family.

Just being stupid, she thought – the half-remembered dream had left her a little shaken – but even so, she found herself moving back from the door while the woman was distracted, crossing the room in four quick strides before the woman's face turned back to her. There was an element of confusion clear on it, presumably from Annabel's rapid retreat.

'Sorry,' said the woman, the staff smile back in place. 'My name's Lisa. We have a little problem with water coming through the ceiling downstairs, right under here. They sent me up to check if the source might be your bathroom.'

Lisa motioned to the bathroom door, clearly wanting Annabel to approach it. Annabel stayed where she was, watching as Lisa managed to let her smile slip again, just a fraction. Lisa entered the hotel room fully, closing the door behind her, then walked over to the bathroom and put her head inside for a moment.

Annabel still felt dazed from waking so suddenly, but her adrenaline was flowing. Every movement the woman made seemed suspicious to her now.

'Ah,' said Lisa, looking back to Annabel again. 'Yes. Take a look.' Annabel noted that the woman had one hand tightly closed.

'Sure,' said Annabel, her left hand reaching to the wall-table beside her and grabbing hold of something she'd seen the moment her suspicions had started, keeping it close to her side, out of sight; something that was probably the reason she'd crossed the room in the first place.

She walked towards Lisa, who had put her head back inside the bathroom. With every step, Annabel wondered if she was making a terrible error of judgement.

Lisa suddenly began to turn towards Annabel again. Startled, Annabel swung hard. The flat metal of the hotel iron she was holding connected with Lisa's forehead; there was a look of sheer disbelief on the woman's face as her head shot back and thumped against the door frame. She fell.

Annabel dropped the iron. 'Holy fuck,' she said to the quiet room, appalled at what she'd done, suddenly certain that she'd been wrong, that being torn from a bad dream had left her so disoriented that she'd ended up doing something unforgivable.

She knelt and checked the woman, who seemed knocked out, no worse, her pulse and breathing normal.

Shit, she thought. She didn't need trouble, not now. Plan, then: get out of the hotel. Drive. Housekeeping would find the woman soon enough, right? Hell, the people who'd sent her to check on the plumbing would . . .

'Hang on,' Annabel said. She stood, and stepped inside the bathroom. Nothing was wrong – nothing visible anyway. *Take a look*, Lisa had said. What the hell at?

She knelt by the woman again and spread the fingers on Lisa's left hand, the hand that had been kept closed since she'd entered the room. Within was a white plastic aerosol of some kind. She took it from Lisa's hand and examined it. No markings, no label. Just a small canister, maybe three inches long. She wondered what the hell it was. It looked like a breath freshener.

Or mace.

Annabel ran her hand under the small of Lisa's back, only half surprised when she found a gun. Extremely compact, thin, lightweight. No ordinary firearm, not by a long way.

She looked at the woman, reassessing the impression she'd had of a young student making a little extra cash.

Then Lisa's eyes snapped open. Annabel froze, seeing the dazed look in those eyes change in a flash to single-minded focus. The woman lunged. Annabel let out a yelp as she lost balance and went over, the gun falling from her grip, Lisa on top of her now, the unexpected strength in those slight arms threatening to overwhelm her. She tried to wrench free. Lisa's hand was tight around her wrists, but the woman wasn't quite over the blow to her head; for an instant her eyes lost focus again and her grip slackened. Annabel felt it start to tighten up once more but she took the opportunity and slipped her left hand from Lisa's grip, bringing up the white canister.

'Wait!' was all Lisa managed to get out as the fine spray hit her in the face. Annabel didn't dare breath. She watched as Lisa slackened, then slumped.

Annabel worked her way out from underneath the woman's dead weight. She stood, staring at the canister in her hand, then checked Lisa's pulse again. It seemed OK. 'I guess that answers one question,' she said. Whatever the hell was in the canister, it wasn't mace.

She grabbed her bag, threw the gun and the canister into it, and left the hotel.

42

It was dark and cold by the time Jonah and Kendrick got back from Bethlehem to the safe house. The heating in the old house was having trouble keeping the chill out, but as Jonah thought about what he'd seen perhaps nothing would have made him feel warm.

They all sat around the kitchen table as Jonah described what had happened. Tess, Kendrick and Never were nursing mugs of coffee, while the only thing Jonah was nursing was a pounding headache that had been growing ever since he'd laid eyes on Silva's child.

'What the hell *were* they?' said Jonah. 'I'm pretty sure his wife had no idea it was there. And as for the boy . . .'

Tess shook her head, uncertain. 'Maybe it's more like an infection than we thought.' She stood and went to the kitchen window. 'I just don't know,' she said, frustrated.

Kendrick frowned. 'Much of what we know about them is from surveillance I conducted shortly before I was ousted,' he said. 'I know that some were wary of what they'd agreed to host, but they all seemed to think they were a chosen few.'

'But if it just *spreads*,' said Jonah, 'there'd be no limit to how many of these things are out there.'

'It can't spread easily,' said Kendrick. 'If it did, Andreas would just have to wait until it was everywhere. There has to be more to it.'

The room was silent for a few moments. Jonah looked around at them in turn. Kendrick was grim, while Never seemed exhausted, the previous day and his broken night of sleep catching up with him. And Tess . . . well, Jonah didn't want to think about how Tess looked.

'Have you eaten?' he asked her. 'I'm going to fix something.'

'I already ate,' Tess said. Jonah held her gaze long enough to be sure she was lying. She looked away.

'So what's the plan?' said Never, draining his coffee.

Kendrick checked his phone before he said anything. 'We wait.'

'For what?' said Jonah.

'Information. I told you, I'm not alone in this. I have people loyal to me. They can focus surveillance on Silva and we'll learn what we can over the next few days. With luck we can find out enough to disrupt Andreas's goals. Ideally, we prevent him completing his machine. Sabotage is our best strategy.'

'Won't that just slow him down?' said Never. 'He'll keep on trying. We need something that can *stop* him. Permanently. You said he was vulnerable.'

'This is our best chance,' said Kendrick. 'For now. Until we know *how* he's vulnerable.'

And as he spoke, Jonah saw him do as he had done: glance towards Tess, the only person who could answer that question.

*

Jonah offered to take the first watch that night, giving Kendrick a chance to sleep. Tess went to bed early too, but Never stayed up with him until well after midnight.

Kendrick hadn't left them with any means to go online, much to Never's annoyance. They did have a TV, though, and kept the rolling news on in the background with the volume turned down low. The safe house was stocked with a range of old DVDs and books, and they both picked out a novel to read and sat in near silence, with one eye on the news.

When an extended feature about Winnerden Flats came on, they turned the volume up and watched eagerly. The official launch of the new Baseline project had been that afternoon, and the feature included brief interviews with some of the revivers and researchers who had already made their way to the facility, to live and work there.

Stephanie Graves was interviewed at length, clearly enthused by the prospect of proceeding with the well-funded research she'd been dreaming of for so long. Uptake among revivers had exceeded all expectations, with priority given to those willing to join the project quickly. Doctor Graves estimated that all the required revivers would be resident at the site within ten days, and the research effort could begin in earnest.

Jonah found himself tensing during the few short clips that featured wider angles of those present – of the canteen, for example, or shots showing living quarters and recreation areas – to see if he recognized any of the revivers taking part. Jason and Stacy should both have returned to work by now and received their invitations, but the only warning Never had managed to give them had been by email, and was necessarily vague. Yet even if both had declined to go, others he knew may have gone in their place.

He found the interviews depressing. There was a universal display of genuine hope and enthusiasm for the research – research which Jonah thought was, at the very least, a distraction. And that was the best-case scenario – while it was certainly possible that assembling the best revivers in one place was just a means to get them out of wider circulation, Jonah wondered if there was more to it than Kendrick thought.

Once the Baseline story ended, the news channel gave a brief recap on Jonah's own kidnapping. It was surreal to watch, and painful when it included footage of Ray Johnson standing beside Bob Crenner's wife, comforting her as he praised his partner's courage and dedication. At least they finally knew that Ray was safe. They turned the TV off once the story finished, and Never went to his bed.

The requirements of Jonah's shift of keeping watch were limited. Around the outside of the house were three motion-sensing closed-circuit cameras that would alert him if anything needed attention.

Kendrick came downstairs just after 2 a.m., red-eyed and monosyllabic. Jonah took the novel he'd started reading up to bed. After an hour he was still no closer to sleeping; too much was circling in his mind, too many images that he knew would stay with him. Bob Crenner's death; Torrance's shadow coming towards him, preparing for the kill; the pulsating darkness on Heggarty's shoulder. And Silva's wife and child, oblivious to the shadows that had laid claim to them.

Thirsty, he decided to get something to drink. Being as quiet as he could, he made his way downstairs; something hot, he hoped, would let him settle. He reached the kitchen. There was no sign of Kendrick. There was, however, an open laptop on the table.

Jonah stared at the image on the screen.

It was footage of a small bare room. The camera was high up, looking down at a man lying on something flat, possibly a gurney.

The man was strapped to it, restless but barely moving. He was gagged.

Jonah felt cold. He'd come downstairs in T-shirt and underwear, and the house was chilly, but the real cold was deep within himself.

He recognized the man.

It was Lucas Silva.

43

Jonah heard the flush of the toilet down the hall. The other internal door in the kitchen led to a small utility room; he stepped inside, hiding in the shadow but still with a clear view of the laptop.

Kendrick came into the kitchen, careful to close the door to the hall behind him. He sat in front of the laptop and waited.

Jonah kept his breathing as quiet as he could, the cold working its way up through his feet and into his bones. After a few minutes a window opened on the laptop screen, showing a bearded face. A gruff voice came out of the speaker. 'Are you there?'

'Here,' said Kendrick. 'It took an age to come up, but the feed is showing now. Was he as easy to take as you thought?'

'Yeah,' said the bearded man. 'It was a good choice. His house is out of the way, no risk of being seen when we did it. By ten his wife was asleep. He came out with the trash. No problems. He might not even be missed until morning.'

'And he's said nothing yet?'

'Nothing about his work, no. Just clams up when we ask him.'

'What about his wife and kid?' said Kendrick.

'He claimed they weren't involved,' said the man. 'We told him we'd seen the things on them, and he denied it but he didn't look happy at the idea. I got the feeling he doesn't know about them. Hell, I don't think he's that clear on what *he's* carrying. The thing you asked us to try with the lights was interesting, though.'

'You've already done that?' asked Kendrick.

'Yeah, we left him alone, like you said. Didn't take long for something to show up on the sensors. You can see it in the image. I've uploaded the footage for you to take a look. Like you thought, it's visible when it detaches from the host. Physical, too – it couldn't get out of the room. When it got more aggressive we hit it with the sunlamps, full on. The thing vanished.'

'You sure you didn't kill it?'

'Absolutely. We repeated it a dozen times, same thing. It definitely went back to him. Same thing happened when he lost consciousness while it was detached. We remotely pushed Propofol through a cannula in his arm. The moment he was out, the shadow was gone. Also, it can't even detach when those lights are on.'

'Good work,' said Kendrick. 'How much longer will you try getting him to talk?'

'Depends,' said the man. 'Something's stopping him saying *anything*. It's like he can't.'

'Damn,' said Kendrick. 'The shadow?'

'That would be my guess. We'll see how it goes later.'

'If he doesn't talk, there are other questions we need the answers for,' said Kendrick. 'I'll leave the decision to you.'

'Understood.'

Kendrick ended the call. He took a long slow breath and poured a bourbon, waiting for a progress bar to fill; Jonah assumed he was downloading the footage the bearded man had mentioned.

When it completed, he started to play it.

Silva lay there, the light in the room low. After a while it started to become visible – a smudge of darkness, on his shoulder. It became more defined on the screen, the fingers discernible now, clear of the flesh. It fell, sliding from the man, out of sight on the floor.

There was nothing for a minute or so. Then it crept back into shot, and it was growing. Jonah thought of the creature Torrance had unleashed, looking like it had unfolded itself, stretching impossibly. Here it was again, but on a smaller scale. The resulting shadow was the size of a large dog, pacing the room, trying to look for a weakness, a way out.

The lights in the room brightened suddenly, washing out the image. Jonah saw Silva spasm in pain, screaming past the gag covering his mouth, tears in his eyes. The shadow was gone.

'You wanted to capture one of them,' said Jonah, stepping out of his hiding place. Kendrick turned round slowly, looking irritated at being caught in the act. 'That's really why you rescued me, whatever Tess thinks. That's what I was for. You wanted one of their lower ranks identified, to interrogate. To experiment on. To torture.'

'Of course I did,' said Kendrick.

'He's going through what I was going through,' said Jonah, his voice raised.

'Yes, he is. More or less.'

'And will you let him go?' Jonah was trembling now, the cold engulfing him.

'We'll hold him as long as we need to.'

'That's not what I asked!' Jonah shouted. He lowered his voice again. 'Are you going to kill him?'

Kendrick raised an eyebrow. 'He's too valuable to kill.'

There was a folded blanket on a table in the corner of the kitchen. Jonah shook it out and wrapped himself in it, the trembling becoming worse as his anger grew. 'We're supposed to be better than this,' he said, dejected. He sat in the seat across from Kendrick and put his head in his hands. Then he looked up again. 'I was just getting used to thinking of you as the good guy.'

Kendrick drained his glass and poured himself another. 'Good?' he said. 'Hell no. But there are worse things than *me*. You live in a world where the terrors have all been pushed back until most people have forgotten them. Those in the First World, at least. There was a time when pain was the norm, when fear was universal, when justice was the exception. Go right back, Jonah, back to the dawn of humanity. When people gathered around a fire forty thousand years ago, they would look out into the night and they would know what was out there. Hungry creatures, sharp teeth; pain and death. Civilization is a fire that holds back the dark, Jonah. The fire grew so big people forgot there was a fire at all. But the dark didn't really go away. Fires can die, no matter how big they are.' He took another drink, and jabbed an accusing finger in Jonah's direction. 'You're happy for people like me to go off into the night, as long as you don't see what we do. We dig around in the muck and bring back the firewood so all of you *good people* get to sit and warm yourselves. Sit in the glow and congratulate each other about how damn *clean* your hands are. But whenever things go wrong, whenever you're scared that the fire is dying . . . you turn to people like me.'

'This is different,' Jonah said.

'Oh, it's *always* different,' said Kendrick. 'You people are never to blame. I'm just someone who's prepared to do what it takes to get the job done.'

'I'll risk my *life* for this, Kendrick, but I won't sink to what you're doing.'

'Easy to say, Jonah, but the line is not defined by what *you* would risk. The line is defined by what you would have someone *else* risk, to achieve your goals. And whether you'd have the decency to acknowledge it and accept your own guilt.'

'You kidnapped a man so you could torture him for information. What the hell does that say about us?'

'Oh, I know *exactly* how much guilt I bear, and I'll accept the burden rather than ignore the blood on my hands. But what about you? What would *you* get someone else to suffer, when it suits your objectives?'

Kendrick's words caught Jonah off guard. What sacrifices was he prepared to get others to make, in the name of what *he* thought was right? Revivals of unwilling subjects, dragged back to relive traumas in the name of justice whether they wanted it or not. Guilt? His career was one long trail of it.

A trail that had ended with Mary Connart, screaming.

'And what would you get *Tess* to risk?' said Kendrick.

Jonah froze.

'I saw the way you looked at her earlier,' said Kendrick. 'You know she's the only person with the information we really need. Tell me you wouldn't want her to do it. That you wouldn't want her to risk her sanity on the slim chance that she can tell us the way to defeat Andreas. You want her to go through hell, to be *tortured*. Just to get information you can't even be sure she has. Sound familiar?'

Jonah glared at Kendrick, furious that he'd try to make the link between Tess and Silva. 'Tess is ill,' said Jonah. 'Either it's the medication killing her, or the separation from whatever she's host to, but it comes down to the same thing. You said it yourself. There may not be a choice.'

'Even if there *was* a choice,' said Kendrick, looking almost bitter, 'you'd rather she faced something that could destroy her, on the slim chance that it'd help us. You'd risk her sanity on a whim. Tell me you wouldn't. *Tell me.*'

No matter how much he wanted to deny it, Jonah said nothing. He looked away from Kendrick.

And saw her there. At the door, watching.

'Tess . . .' he called, but she was already gone.

44

The atmosphere in the house the next morning was sombre and uneasy. Fresh from a full night of medicinally aided sleep, Never had emerged from his room to find himself in the midst of a cold silence, which became even chillier when Jonah explained what had happened the night before.

The physical chill of the house was more pronounced, too, as the overnight temperature outside had plummeted. Once he'd eaten breakfast, Never excused himself. 'I'm going down to the basement,' he said. 'I'll see if there's something I can do about the boiler. Maybe I can improve the heating before we all die of pneumonia.'

Jonah gave him a sceptical look. 'You're not just going to hit it, are you?'

'Not *just*,' said Never.

Kendrick muttered inaudibly and went upstairs to his room, taking his laptop with him. Jonah watched the man leave, knowing exactly what he was doing: getting an update on Lucas Silva. His mind had been going over it endlessly in the early hours, and he'd slept very little – wondering exactly what Kendrick's team was doing to him.

Tess sat with coffee and toast, looking even more pale and dark-eyed. She'd hardly moved since Jonah had come downstairs, and had avoided making eye contact with him.

'Maybe Never's right,' he said, trying to break the silence. 'This cold can't be good for any of us.'

She looked at him, hurt and wary. 'Maybe,' she said. 'Although I doubt it's me he's doing it for. I don't think Never likes me very much.'

'He's a little overprotective,' said Jonah. He smiled, hoping for one in return. It took a few moments, but he got it, albeit tentative.

'Because every time I show up, it's bad news?' said Tess. 'I'm sorry, Jonah. If I hurt you. Coming to see you after so many years, then leaving the way I did. I'd hoped it would be a kind of closure.'

'It was,' he said. 'You didn't mean for things to turn out the way they did. You hadn't even wanted me to be involved in Unity.' He took a breath. This was old news; they were talking around the real issue, avoiding it. But it had to be faced: 'I'm the one who's sorry, Tess,' he said. 'About last night. You were the first friend I had at Baseline. I was a frightened fourteen-year-old, and you made it OK. You'll always be important to me. I'm ashamed at how I behaved last night. This isn't your fault, and—'

'Don't be so sure,' she said. 'I was the first to achieve Unity. I was the best placed to see the dangers that were coming. If I'd been able to integrate, embrace the Elder I was host to, if I'd *understood* . . . maybe everything could have been avoided.'

'There were eleven others who went through the same process after you, and before Michael Andreas. None of them managed it either.'

'I know,' she said. 'But the others are dead. I'm the last. My failure to bond with the Elder within me is *my* failure, Jonah.' She paused. 'They came through like waking dreams, at first – these memories that weren't my own. Vistas of such beauty, skies with impossible colours. Cities that were inconceivably vast and complex. But most of it seemed like visual noise, things I couldn't hope to understand. We all thought understanding would come eventually – that we would take shelter, and have time to learn how to see the truth in these visions, and help each other. Then I found out the real truth. That by taking the Elders into ourselves, we'd made them abandon their posts, and the evil they'd vowed to guard was free. I could feel the Elder within me flinch, then hide from it. Its fear was what made the visions turn to nightmares. Absolute terror. Absolute despair. I couldn't cope with it. Whatever I learned seemed to be so pitiful in comparison.'

'But you knew some things,' said Jonah.

'I did. I knew about the sunlight, and Larry put these in place to ease my mind, with a generator in the basement.' She gestured to the lights high on the ceiling. 'Buying time, Larry said, but I think he was humouring me.'

'He trusts your judgement,' said Jonah.

'My judgement?' she said, shaking her head. 'It was my judgement that got me into this. I believed in what Michael was doing.'

'Michael Andreas was a good man, Tess. And strong. I can't imagine what it would have taken to suppress the creature possessing him, long enough to try to destroy it.'

'Yes,' said Tess, sadly. 'He's still inside. You realize that, don't you? The darkness that took him, it consumes souls, corrupts them until they're just another part of it, but Michael is still alive. He must see everything it does, powerless to stop it.' She smiled, tears in her eyes, her gaze drifting off. 'People used to read more into our relationship than was there, but it was a simple love. I would have done anything for him. If I could do one last thing, it would be to bring him peace.' She looked at Jonah. 'I have to face it, sooner or later. I have to do whatever I can to grant him that.'

'Maybe when you're better, Tess,' he said. 'When you've got your strength back. But we have options now. We have to see where they lead.' The image came to him of Lucas Silva's terrified face, and the faces of his wife and child. He could see Tess's troubled expression, and suspected she was thinking the same thing.

We have options now.

But at what cost?

*

By the time darkness fell that evening, Never's quest to improve the heating had paid off, Kendrick having given him five minutes of closely supervised time online to hunt down advice on the model of boiler. 'I did also hit some things,' admitted Never, but nobody was complaining. While the house was far from cosy, the chilly bite had gone from the air.

Kendrick remained surly and untalkative all day, and although the others avoided mentioning Silva and the ongoing interrogation, Jonah presumed it was foremost on their minds. He wondered how Never was dealing with it, as the one to have suffered the most. Here they were, complicit in the torture of another man, telling themselves that he was the enemy, knowing that doing anything to stop it would put their own lives at risk and undermine their chances at defeating Andreas.

The unconscionable took so little effort to justify, Jonah thought.

As darkness fell, Kendrick was with them in the kitchen making himself some coffee when his phone rang. He put the phone to his ear. 'Yes?' he said, sounding hopeful. Then his expression changed, and with it the mood in the room: he looked anxious. 'Power's out? How long?'

Kendrick sat quickly and put the phone on speaker, placing it in front of him.

'Two minutes,' said the voice on the other end of the line. It sounded like the bearded man Kendrick had spoken to the night before. 'Ako went to the basement to see what the problem is. Nash is here with me.'

'Have you had any problems with the power before?' asked Kendrick.

'None,' said the man. 'That's why I called you. It doesn't feel right.'

'Get Nash to take a look out an upstairs window,' said Kendrick. 'Check how widespread the power outage is.'

They heard muffled speaking, then a shout. 'She says the streetlights are on.'

Kendrick thought: four long seconds. He came to a decision. 'You need to get out of there,' said Kendrick, tense. 'Now.'

'Yes, sir,' said the man. 'Ako!' he shouted. 'We're leaving.'

Another voice, a woman: 'Something's outside.'

There was a loud thump. 'Front door! Front door!' came a shout, followed by another thump and the sound of splintering wood.

Kendrick closed his eyes as the gunfire started, rapid bursts interspersed with barked commands, shouts. Then a man screaming, desperate and terrified. The screaming went on and on, not stopping, sounding more and more strangled, then *wet*.

Kendrick ended the call. He sat, intense and silent, worrying his thumbnail as he thought hard.

'Do your friends know our location?' asked Tess urgently. Kendrick didn't reply. '*Larry!*'

'Andreas's people will be able to get nothing from them,' he said. 'They can reel off a thousand decoy addresses, useless to Andreas.'

Jonah found it horribly unnerving to see just how shaken Kendrick was. Something else was unnerving him, too. 'But how could they have been tracked down?' he said.

'The shadows must be able to find each other after all,' said Kendrick. 'We'd considered that unlikely, but this isn't something we could risk trying again.' He looked at Jonah. 'Happy now?'

Jonah glared at him. 'You think I'm glad your people are hurt, or dead? Fuck you.'

Long seconds went by before Never broke the impasse. 'This isn't going to help us,' he said. He looked at Kendrick. 'How many people do you have loyal to you? If Andreas does get his machine built, can they destroy it?'

Kendrick shook his head. 'If we use up every advantage we have to destroy the machine, I suspect they'd be able to rebuild it quickly.' Jonah could hear the frustration growing in Kendrick's voice.

'Attack Andreas directly, then,' said Never. 'There has to be a way for—'

'*Stop!*' shouted Kendrick. 'Stop it. I need to think. Yammering in my fucking ear doesn't help. I just need to think.' He went upstairs again, a cloud of agitation around him.

'He'll come up with something,' said Tess, looking exhausted. 'He always has backup plans up his sleeve.'

'Given that his last plan involved kidnap and torture,' said Never, 'I'm not sure I want to know.'

Tess ignored the comment and stood.

'Are you going to talk to him?' said Jonah.

She shook her head. There was something about her that worried him, something *resigned*. 'No,' she said. 'I think I'll try and get some sleep.'

'Is she OK?' said Never once she'd gone. 'She really doesn't look well.'

'She's not,' said Jonah. 'Maybe sleep is what she needs most.'

*

As the night wore on, he tried not to think about any of it. Their future, whether he liked it or not, was in Kendrick's hands, and there was nothing Jonah could do to contribute. While Never flicked between channels on the TV, Jonah attempted to read, struggling through sentence by sentence, not really connecting with the words. He gave up, and instead turned his eye to the television and the bland distractions Never had found.

As midnight approached, he was slipping in and out of a welcome doze when a sound wrenched him into sudden awareness.

Tess was screaming.

45

Jonah ran upstairs with Never on his heels. As he reached Tess's bedroom door Kendrick was just going inside.

Her screams had been heartrending, with the same visceral punch of those wet-sounding cries they'd heard over the phone earlier. Panic, desperation and terror. The screams broke down into gasping sobs. Jonah entered the room and saw Tess clutching Kendrick so tightly her knuckles were white.

'It's OK,' Kendrick was saying. 'You're safe.'

She looked up, trembling. 'It was so frightened,' she said. 'So alone. And then –' She closed her eyes, shaking. When finally she opened them again, she looked at Kendrick, terrified. '*It talked to me*,' she said.

*

She paused for a moment, composing herself, then stood and walked across the room, picking up a bottle of pills from a table. She shook out two capsules and swallowed them dry. 'I didn't take my medication,' she said. 'I had to try. We had so little time, I *had* to. Then, as I dreamed, it came to me. The Elder was frightened, and it was angry. It showed me terrible things . . .' She paused, staring ahead of herself. She looked at Kendrick, drained. 'Terrible things. It was punishing me for abandoning it, I think, but it was so scared. It thought it was being watched, and . . .' She tailed off, closing her eyes, visibly trembling.

Kendrick looked at Jonah, accusation on his face. 'Was this you? Did you tell her to do this?'

Jonah shook his head, raising his voice. 'Don't you *dare* try and duck out of this, Kendrick. You were the one who brought up the idea, the one who kept planting the seed.'

They were face to face, now, both voices growing louder as they bickered back and forth.

From behind them, Tess spoke in an exhausted voice. 'The rise,' she started, but she was ignored by them both.

'Hey,' said Never, 'can you two shut it? Tess is—'

They ignored him, too, until he stood between them and yelled: '*For fuck's sake, shut up!*' He turned and gestured to Tess; Jonah and Kendrick, shamefaced, looked at her.

'The rise,' she said. 'That's when it's vulnerable, the only time it will be. The shadows are part of the whole, but so is what's inside Andreas. Just a *part*. The connection it has with the bulk of its power has to be severed. Destroy the body of the vessel when it attempts its rise, and the connection could be closed forever.'

'The body of the vessel . . .' said Kendrick. 'You mean Andreas?'

Tess nodded.

'How do we even know we can kill him?' said Jonah.

Tess looked at him. 'It nearly died the last time, in the fire. It was frightened. It hates you, I could feel it. I could—' Fear returned to her face; her hands went to her mouth. 'Oh God, I could *feel* it,' she said, still looking at Jonah. 'What if it sensed me? What if it *saw* me? If they found Silva's shadow, what if they can find the Elder I carry? Maybe that's why it's been so afraid. Afraid of being seen.' She turned to Kendrick, panic rising. 'I could feel it! What if they're coming? *What if they're coming for us?*'

Kendrick threw Jonah a look; if the team who'd taken Silva had been found through the presence of the shadow, what did that mean? They couldn't know what was possible. 'Nothing's coming, Tess,' said Kendrick. 'You woke up disoriented, that's all. There's no need to panic. If they could trace the Elder, they'd have found you long ago.'

Tess shook her head. 'I don't know,' she said. 'I don't know. But it felt like something was *close*. Watching me.'

Kendrick stood and went to the hall, Jonah and Never following him. 'OK,' he said. 'We need to keep calm. She's had a scare, so it's natural for her to feel spooked. But she's got me spooked too. Maybe they can find the Elder, maybe they can't, but we've done all we can here and it's time to move on. Agreed?' Jonah and Never nodded. Kendrick stepped back into Tess's room. 'Forty minutes, then we're going,' he said. 'We don't take the chance.' Tess nodded back, relieved.

With little to pack, Jonah and Never threw on sweatshirts and a coat then stood in the kitchen waiting, Never keeping one eye trained on the monitor that showed the feeds from the external CCTV.

'This is just a precaution, right?' Jonah said.

'Of course it is,' said Never, not moving his eyes from the screen.

Soon, Tess came down the stairs with a small backpack. It was another fifteen minutes before Kendrick joined them, with a large black carryall that gave a heavy thump as he put it on the kitchen table. 'Two more bags from the cellar,' said Kendrick. 'Ten minutes, twenty at most. Then we're out of here.'

'There's, uh, a van approaching outside,' said Never, pointing at the CCTV monitor. 'On the road.' He flinched a little under the stare Kendrick aimed at him.

'I told you not to *panic*,' said Kendrick. 'It's a public road. Even at this time of night we get vehicles passing.'

'This one's going *very* slowly,' said Never.

They looked at the screen and watched in silence as the vehicle drew closer to the house, curiously slow, reaching the end of the driveway. Every breath in the room was held.

The van continued past, speeding up. Jonah breathed out, feeling the relief. Kendrick's expression, however, had darkened.

'Get the generator started,' he said to Never, urgency in his voice. With a nod, Never headed to the basement. Kendrick turned to Jonah. 'Check the shutters are secure upstairs,' he said. 'I'll check down. Tess, keep an eye on the cameras.'

Jonah turned to move just as the lights dimmed momentarily. They all shared a look, then Kendrick reached into the carryall on the table. He pulled out a flashlight and a gun and offered them to Jonah.

Jonah took the flashlight but declined the gun. 'Is that even any use?' he said.

'Sure,' said Kendrick. 'Against people.' He handed the gun to Tess.

As Jonah went upstairs he heard the purr from below as the generator started. The sunlamps around the house started to glow, switched at a low setting. In each room he checked that the shutters had already been put in place. Everything seemed fine.

He went back down to the kitchen. 'All secure upstairs,' he said, then got close enough to Kendrick for Tess to be out of earshot. He kept his voice low. 'If it's them, we don't stand a chance, do we?' All he could think of was the sound of Kendrick's team under attack, a group of trained professionals defeated in seconds.

'There's always a chance,' said Kendrick. 'And anything you do that buys you time is worthwhile.'

'Time? For what?'

Kendrick's smile was almost a grimace, and there was more than a hint of crazy to it. 'You'll see,' he said.

The sunlamps suddenly faded, then brightened again.

'It's OK,' said Kendrick. 'It's just a little jittery when it's started up.'

The sunlamps faded completely and the purr of the generator stopped dead. Then the main house light dimmed, almost to nothing. Flashlight beams pierced the gloom.

'Stay with Tess,' said Kendrick. 'I'll help Never.' He ran to the cellar.

A few seconds later they heard the generator splutter, coming back on but sounding uneven. The lights and sunlamps came back, brightening slowly. Relieved, Jonah switched off the flashlight.

There was a thump from upstairs. Jonah and Tess looked at each other. They waited for a few seconds, listening, but there was silence. 'Stay here,' said Jonah. 'I'm going to check. It's probably nothing.'

'If it's nothing,' said Tess, wary, 'then ignore it.'

But Jonah was already bounding up the stairs. He was fired up by the need to prove to himself that something had simply fallen over, maybe something he'd knocked when he was checking the shutters, because whatever Kendrick said about buying time, if they'd really been found, there was no hope for them.

'Jonah,' Tess called, unnerved.

'I'll be two seconds.' He went from room to room, and each shutter was exactly as it had been. The house was still secure.

He was in his own bedroom when the sunlamps darkened again; the main house lights dimmed and flared before going out. His bravura suddenly seemed like a terrible idea, his feet feeling heavy now. He put his flashlight back on and went to the corridor. As he backed towards the stairs, the sound of smashing glass came from behind him: the bathroom, its door wide open.

He swung the flashlight. The bathroom window had no shutter, but it was miniscule, two iron bars running vertically within the frame. There was a hole in the glass, now. Jonah strode over and closed the door, unable to shake off the paranoid sense that he'd felt something *scuttle* past him.

He swung the beam of the flashlight left and right. The filament of the sunlamp above his head glowed a fraction then brightened. He could hear the wheezing splutter of the struggling generator, and the house lights came on again.

He ran downstairs to the kitchen.

'Everything OK?' said Tess, looking anxious. 'I heard something smash. And the lights keep—' The lights dimmed on cue but came up again. Tess raised her eyebrows. '*That*. I wish that'd stop.'

Jonah suddenly felt cold. Dear God, he felt cold. He could feel it. It was in the room with them.

'Tess,' he said. Panic was close to overpowering him. He tried to stay calm, to move slowly. 'I think we should get to the cellar.' His eyes darted around the room, then settled on Tess. She nodded, seeing the fear in his eyes.

As she stood, all the lights went out. In the flashlight beam Jonah saw it scuttle forward from the darkness near his feet, crossing the floor to behind Tess. Then it *unfolded*, opening out into a creature the height of the ceiling, all in the space of a breath.

It was huge, larger than the one Torrance had sent at them. It had just been waiting for the dark to return. For its chance to come.

Jonah stared, frozen. Tess could see the look on his face, see where his eyes were fixed. She turned and saw, and moved to run.

But it had her. One vast dark arm swept her off the ground, held her despite her struggling, the hand of the shadow clamped over her terrified face. Jonah thought of Mary Connart, and of the horrifying wounds these creatures could give by touch, but Tess tore free briefly to call his name and her face was unmarked. The hand seemed only there to silence her cries. The creature didn't want her dead.

'*Kendrick!*' Jonah screamed, his inertia overcome. '*Get the lights back on! Get them on full power!*'

The creature stepped towards him. It paused. For a moment Jonah thought it was wary of him, the way Torrance's shadow had been. And perhaps it was, but only for an instant. It came, striding, Jonah seeing the sheer terror in Tess's eyes; it swept him aside and he felt the pain of its touch the instant before he was slammed against the wall.

He heard the generator roaring to life. Sunlight exploded

around him. Barely able to see in the glare, he stood again. The creature halted momentarily, screeching as the intensity of the light took its toll, the shadow flesh seeming to boil at its surface, tendrils of black, living smoke streaming away from its body. With each instant it seemed diminished, yet it still stepped forward, strong enough to keep its hold on Tess.

Jonah ran to it, seeing it weaken, its frame almost skeletal now. He kicked out at one of its legs, pulling away a moment too late as it spun and lashed out, connecting and sending him sprawling back. Yet as he regained his feet, he felt hope. The creature was being torn apart before his eyes. Ahead he saw the front door, the bolts in place.

He ran at the creature, and had almost reached it, emboldened by its weakened state. All he had to do was slow it down, all he had to do was . . .

Hope died.

The front door crashed open, forced from outside. The devastated shadow stumbled onwards and out, taking Tess along with it.

And through the door came another shadow, even more imposing than the first. Jonah halted, feeling the gaze of this second creature squarely on him, watching the boiling shadow flesh leech from it in the intense light; yet it seemed unfazed.

Jonah stepped back as the creature's arm rose. It held something in its hand: a slat from the fencing at the front of the house.

'Shit,' he said, knowing its intent.

Hissing in triumph, the creature swung out and smashed the first of the sunlamps.

46

It came towards him, taking out the bulbs one by one. Jonah backed away, despairing.

From behind came gunfire: four rapid shots painfully loud in the confined space. Jonah could see where the bullets tore through the creature, pulling a shriek from it but not slowing it down.

He felt a hand on his shoulder.

'Come on!' Kendrick ordered. Jonah turned and followed. Kendrick directed him through the door to the basement, down the steep wooden staircase lined with blazing sunlamps. Jonah stood at the base of the steps and watched Kendrick lock the upper door behind him, as a huge crash came from just outside it.

'I think that was the kitchen door,' Kendrick said. 'Go on, we won't have long.'

There was more smashing; the lamps in the kitchen being taken out.

At the base of the steps was a steel door. Jonah went inside, seeing Never standing by the noisy generator in the far corner, looking agitated.

'This will hold long enough,' Kendrick said, pushing the steel door closed and locking it. 'Kill the power to the upper circuit,' he called to Never. 'Before it occurs to them to overload the whole damn thing.'

'On it,' said Never, hitting a switch. He looked at Jonah. 'Tess?'

'They took her,' said Jonah. 'One of them got inside, it just grabbed her. But it was *working*. The light was *working*. What the hell happened? The power kept fading. What were you *doing*?'

'We put the generator on full as soon as we could,' said Never, visibly stung by Jonah's tone. 'The mains power going wasn't our fault.'

They could hear the continuing impacts on the upper door.

'What do we do?' whispered Never.

'We do the only thing we can,' said Kendrick. 'We die.'

Jonah and Never glanced at each other, then Never shook his head. 'Shit plan.'

'Look around you,' said Kendrick. 'You know how much fuel there is in here?'

They looked. There were jerrycans everywhere. 'Way too much?' said Never.

'You know why?'

It took a few seconds before Never's face fell. 'Now hold on, I can think of better ways to go than burning to death . . .'

Kendrick shook his head and looked at Jonah. 'I told you we just had to buy time. So give me a hand.' The floor was flagstone. Jonah stepped over as Kendrick threw him one of two short metal pry bars. Jonah set his flashlight down and together they lifted a stone near the corner, pushing it to one side.

Underneath was a hole; there was a smell coming from inside it that Jonah found worryingly familiar.

The smell of death.

Kendrick knelt and began to heave up a large black plastic sack, nodding for Jonah to assist. As Jonah took hold, he recognized what kind of bag it was. He dragged it to the centre of the room, while Kendrick called for Never to help with a second body bag.

One by one, they unzipped them, tipping the corpses onto the stone floor: Hopkins and his colleague.

'For what it's worth,' said Kendrick. 'A decoy, when they go through the ashes in the morning. They'll think we're dead, for a few hours, at least. Longer, if we're lucky.'

Jonah knew enough about what a fire could do to a body to know that if the blaze Kendrick planned was intense enough, fragments might be all that remained. Identification could take days.

Kendrick walked to the side and knelt, reaching behind some of the jerrycans. He pressed something that let out a short tone.

'The clock is ticking,' Kendrick said. He picked Jonah's flashlight up from the floor and passed it to Never, then pointed to the hole he'd taken the bodies from.

'Down. Go a few metres into the tunnel. Leave enough space for Jonah and me to follow. Then we'll seal it.'

'Tunnel?' said Never, casting his light into the dark, looking warily at the dank earth below.

'Thank God for Prohibition,' said Kendrick.

They heard the upper door give way, accompanied by the screeching of the shadows.

'We know sunlight hurts them,' said Kendrick. 'Let's see what an inferno can do.'

*

The screeches continued. One by one, they heard the sunlamps smash.

The creatures were just outside now; Never dropped into the hole and vanished from sight. As Jonah lowered himself down, the corpses came directly into his eye line, Hopkins still with the towel covering his mutilated face. He thought of the way that Kendrick had kept hold of the corpses, just in case they were needed, just as a way to *finesse* an escape. It didn't even seem like an extravagance. It was simply what Kendrick did.

He ducked down, lying flat and following Never. The tunnel was tight, perhaps three feet across. Cold, damp earth that felt like clay surrounded him, barely high enough for him to be able to rise onto his knees, frequent wooden supports making the space even more constricted.

With Never in front he felt hemmed in. Buried. He prayed the tunnel was short because more than a few minutes spent here would leave him close to madness.

Behind him he could hear a deep scrape as Kendrick carefully replaced the flagstone in the basement floor. By now the steel door was taking a battering.

After a few metres of suffocating progress, Jonah stopped when he felt Kendrick's hand tug on his foot.

'There's a support back here I need to kick down,' Kendrick said. 'Above us is a mound of earth; I need to seal off the tunnel before the fuel goes up. The rest of the tunnel should hold, but if it starts to give, get moving as fast as you can.'

'How long until . . . ?'

'In about sixty seconds.'

Jonah found himself counting backwards from sixty as he kept going, the downward slope of the tunnel more and more pronounced. He hissed ahead at Never to speed it up, hearing the sound of kicking behind him, then the soft murmur of a steady flow of earth. He stopped, listening, waiting for the sound to grow, to approach along the tunnel and consume them all.

All he heard was Kendrick's breathing.

'Move on,' whispered Kendrick, and Never picked up the pace, Jonah still counting down the seconds in his head. He reached zero.

Suddenly, behind, above, below, came the thump of ignition transmitted through the ground, and the inhuman screams of the shadows caught in the flame. Jonah paused, breath held for a moment, a trickle of debris falling.

The tunnel remained intact.

The screaming was still audible, punctuated by the additional thumps of fuel canisters catching.

'Get moving,' said Kendrick. 'The tunnel dips down even more ahead. It gets a little damp then comes back up.'

'Just how deep are we?' whispered Jonah.

'Maybe fifteen feet,' said Kendrick. 'This goes on under a twenty-foot fence by a disused rail track out at the back of the property. When we're through, a five-minute run along the old railroad will bring us to where I have another car.'

Jonah tried to picture how far they still had to go before they got out. He'd not paid much attention to the layout of the grounds outside the house. He couldn't recall even *seeing* a fence at the rear.

'How far to the end of the tunnel?' he asked.

'Eighty yards, give or take,' said Kendrick.

They kept going, slow progress that seemed interminable. They hadn't heard sirens yet, but surely the fire at the house had been called in.

As they went, the muddy clay underneath started to get increasingly damp and slippery. Jonah began to lose his grip, his legs sliding. When his right foot hit a support strut a little too hard, Kendrick scolded him.

'This tunnel is almost a century old,' Kendrick said. 'It's survived a lack of repairs and plenty of subsidence, so be careful.'

Damp gave way to wet, a thin layer of cold water which deepened as they continued along the tunnel's downslope. Soon it was a foot high. Jonah started to shiver. Claustrophobia was taking him, now. It felt like the air was impossibly sparse.

'Not far,' Kendrick kept saying.

Then Never stopped ahead. 'Uh, problem,' he said. 'It dips right here.'

'Keep going,' said Kendrick.

'You don't get me,' said Never. 'It *dips*. There's hardly any air space above the water. I think the tunnel's completely submerged ahead.'

'So turn onto your back,' said Kendrick. 'We have nowhere to go but forward. It should only be a couple of metres before it rises again. Jonah and I will stay here. Flash your light three times when you're through, and we'll follow.'

There was silence for a few seconds, then Jonah heard the deepest sigh he'd ever heard anyone take.

'Right, then,' said Never Geary. 'Wish me luck.'

It took Never a few moments to turn onto his back, then he started to move forwards slowly, his feet slipping now and again and forcing muddy water into Jonah's face. Soon all Jonah could hear were the gentle ripples hitting the side of the tunnel beside him. He watched the light as it went. It faded for a moment, came bright again, then vanished.

'His flashlight went off,' he said to Kendrick.

Kendrick switched his own off, leaving them in absolute black to give them the best chance of seeing Never's. 'It may have failed in the water,' said Kendrick. 'Or the water itself could just be too opaque. Keep looking for it.'

They waited, Jonah keeping watch, hoping for some sign. 'I can't see anything,' he said.

'The tunnel can't be submerged for very far,' said Kendrick. 'He's had long enough. Get after him.'

'But what if—'

'Get after him,' said Kendrick, putting his own flashlight back on. 'We can't afford to spend more time here, and that's our only way out.'

Jonah twisted until he was facing the tunnel roof. It looked soft, fragile. Given a regular flooding, the supports here must surely be rotten. What if the tunnel was blocked? Slowly, he moved on, Kendrick's light just enough to see by at first, but his ears were in the water now. His neck already ached, holding his head as high up as he could manage, breathing in the limited air.

His hands were numbed by cold, his arms and legs were stiffening.

Buried, he thought.

His foot slipped; he felt the impact of it against the side wall but kept his head above the surface.

The water was higher with each movement.

Buried.

The light was almost gone, just vague glints now on the wet roof an inch above him. He was breathing through his nose, his panic hard to suppress, moving at a slower pace to avoid disturbing the water. He closed his eyes as the water lapped up into them.

The sense of being in his own waterlogged grave was unbearable.

The water was too high now to afford reliable breathing. It was time to go under, to keep pushing forward until his breath failed him or, dear God, he found his shoulders pressing against Never's dead feet.

Now.

He took his final breath, meagre as it was, keeping on going, eyes closed, counting to himself, slipping, feeling complaints from his lungs, wondering how far he had gone, how far there was left.

His hands were sliding, his feet the only propulsion that seemed to be getting him anywhere, then one foot struck another support and he was certain it moved, certain he'd dislodged it. The pain in his lungs was growing, urging him to take a breath that would be his end, as the walls seemed to narrow and the roof pressed down, down, *down* above him.

And then he saw the sparks that preceded unconsciousness, flecks of false light in his eyes; too far to go, his coordination failing, reducing him to a frantic scrabble for any kind of purchase. Too far, and—

A hand on his shoulder, gripping his clothes, dragging him. A voice, muffled by the water, then clear as the water fell away from his ears.

'It's OK,' said Never. 'You're through.'

Taking a sudden breath that set him coughing, Jonah opened his eyes, Never's face right above his own, his flashlight working.

'The tunnel comes out into a brick room, just down here,' said Never. 'I thought I'd come back and see if you needed me. You seemed to be taking forever.'

It took Jonah a long time to answer. Breath was precious. 'Yes,' he said. 'We couldn't see your light. Too muddy.'

'I tried calling out, but couldn't risk being too loud.'

Jonah managed a smile, an edge of desperation to it. 'Come on,' he said, aware that Kendrick would be coming through any moment. 'I don't want to spend all winter in this fucking tunnel.'

'Me neither,' said Never, starting to shuffle backwards, the upward slope quickly taking them above the water. 'Promise me we can have a holiday soon. Somewhere sunny.'

They both started to laugh. Then Kendrick emerged behind, and, like kids caught by a teacher, they stopped.

'Break over,' said Kendrick. 'Let's get to the car.'

47

It was early morning when Annabel reached the outskirts of Chicago. After leaving the hotel in Billings, she'd ditched the unusual gun she'd taken off the woman but had kept the canister that had saved her. Then she'd spent a frantic few hours putting in as much driving distance as she could before it had occurred to her to change the damn car. However they'd tracked her down, the hotel had required her licence plate at check-in, so she had to assume they had it by now. She had parked up in Rapid City, abandoning the vehicle a few minutes' walk from a used car lot where a man who seemed constructed entirely from wrinkles, tan and leer had sold her a battered Toyota worth half what she paid. It left her with only nine hundred in cash, but there was no way she was going to use the one credit card she had left; she'd used the other for the hotel, and while both were – in theory – impossible to trace to her, she must have screwed it up somehow. It had to be how they'd found her.

Cash only from here on in.

She stopped for gas, and to get change for the road tolls she knew were coming. The exhaustion that had hit her in the hotel – and which had meant she'd stayed longer than planned, long enough to be caught out – had only grown worse overnight. Further on, she stopped again and grabbed an hour of rest, but, given her underlying panic, she wasn't certain how much actual sleep she'd managed in that time. She dreamed of that door again,

vast and dark, something hitting the other side – a dream triggered by a basic fear of looming peril, that was all, but after that
she gave up any further attempt at sleep.

Her stash of cola was enough to keep her going through the
early hours, into the overcast morning. The Sunday traffic was
light and the driving monotonous, but her mind was scrambled by
the combination of caffeine and adrenaline. She was on autopilot,
and glad that she couldn't contemplate what was looking for her,
glad that she couldn't think clearly about the fate of Jonah and
Never.

And now, after twenty hours on the road, she was nearing
Chicago. She came up to an automated toll, dug around in her
pocket for the change, and wound the window down. Then she
fumbled it, catching the top of the window as her hand went out.
The coins spilled from her grip, hitting the tarmac.

She threw a look to the heavens, swore, and got out. Sparse as
the traffic was, there was a car in the lane to her left. The lane to
her right was clear, then another car in the furthest of the four.
She gathered up what she'd dropped. As she began to stand, she
saw a black four-by-four stop behind the car in the lane furthest
from her. It was stationary for only a few seconds, the car in front
starting to drive off, but it was just long enough for Annabel to
note the strange choice, with a free lane right beside her.

She stood fully. The driver of the four-by-four had wound
down his window ready to pay. The man's eyes met hers then
looked away fast.

Too fast.

She got back into her car with the same feeling of imminent
danger she'd had in the hotel, the one she'd almost ignored, the
one she'd thought was stupid.

The one that had been the difference between escape and capture.

She sat where she was, money in hand, and waited for the
black car to go. Another car entered the lane beside her, obscuring

her sight of the black car's driver, but as the seconds ticked by and the four-by-four didn't move, her suspicion grew.

After twenty seconds, another car came up behind it. Annabel crossed her fingers and hoped that the new driver was an impatient one; sure enough, it hadn't even been there for the count of ten when the horn started to blare.

The four-by-four drove on, sluggish. Annabel waited, watching it get ahead.

A blast of horn came from behind her, snapping her out of it. She glanced in the rear-view mirror, hand up in apology, but waiting just a little longer. Then she paid and went on her way, keeping an eye on the black car, now well ahead of her. She kept her speed low but the black car matched it, every other vehicle going just that bit faster than either of them.

Annabel considered her options. She couldn't think of any way they could have found her, but that was moot right now. If she was imagining all this (and she hoped to God she was), there was little to lose by giving the black car the slip all the same.

She saw an exit up ahead and moved into the left-most lane, timing it until she was almost past before pulling sharply across the other lanes and taking the exit, feeling a surge of triumph when she saw the black car forced to continue on ahead.

The triumph faded when she realized she had no idea where she was going, but she could deal with that in a moment. She looked around her. Still in the outskirts of the city, there wasn't much around: bare scrubland and run-down industry. She took the next right, the long straight road empty of vehicles. The surroundings were desolate, too: on one side of the road was an electricity substation, and on the other, what looked like an old industrial park, a series of beaten-up concrete buildings with no signs of life. Even though it was so early on a Sunday, she suspected that the life signs here were never exactly *healthy*.

Nobody around. The sudden privacy of where she was hit her as a wave of relief. A huge sigh escaped her lungs.

Then she glanced in her mirror.

'No,' she said. A black four-by-four, taking the same right turn she'd just taken. *Impossible*, she thought, then she looked again. It wasn't black. Dark blue. Not the same car, but that was hardly a comfort. The sense of threat was there. If both cars had been following her . . .

'Crazy, paranoid, sleep deprived, scared,' she told herself, keeping her speed steady and watching behind. 'Nothing more.'

This road was deserted; the buildings were deserted. A moment ago she'd been taking comfort in that. Now all it did was make her feel completely exposed.

The car behind seemed to lunge forward, and she knew the empty road had proved too tempting an opportunity for them. She could see it eat up the distance, and when she tried to pick up speed, her ancient Toyota did little more than shrug, the engine pitch rising with no significant change to the power it was actually putting out.

She looked in her mirror. It was coming. Unable to outpace them, and armed only with the canister she'd taken at the hotel, all she had left was surprise.

Do something drastic.

Something crazy.

The dark blue car caught up with her and drifted over to the oncoming lane. Annabel figured they planned on pushing her off the road into the wide scrubland that ran along by the substation fence.

Suddenly, she thought of something suitably drastic.

She shifted down a gear and veered hard right, towards the scrub, foot to the floor. Her car's engine was screaming in the lower gear, but it was enough to give her that boost of speed as she swung back again, almost perpendicular, and smashed into the rear of their vehicle.

She lost control, continuing all the way across the road, trying to keep track of what was happening to the other car, seeing it turn, slide, then roll before she herself hit a utility pole off-centre at the roadside. Airbags sprang into action, but she felt the hard thump of her head against the door window, much harder than she'd expected, hearing herself shout out in panic as she felt her awareness slip: grey, grey, and then black.

* .

She opened her eyes with a gasp, looking around to find the other car. It was motionless in the centre of the road. Her car's engine had stopped. She turned the key, hoping against hope, but there was nothing at all. The engine was a fatality.

She opened her door and went to the front of the car, ruefully impressed by the damage she'd managed to inflict on it. She looked across at the other car, which had come to rest upside down maybe sixty yards away. She knew she had to move. Given how rapidly she'd seen it roll, there was a good chance they'd been left unconscious, but . . .

There was movement from inside. An arm, flailing out of one open window, then moving with a little more purpose.

Annabel tore her eyes from the sight, trying to assess where to run. One ankle hurt like hell. Her foot had been hard on the brake when she'd impacted the utility pole, so maybe *run* was a little optimistic. The rows of small concrete units were the only cover she could reach.

She walked alongside the building as fast as her ankle allowed. Some of the doors had padlocks that looked as though they were in working order, suggesting they were still in use, but there were no markings or signs to identify if any businesses were being run from here. Certainly, there was nobody around this time on a Sunday morning. Little more than a set of garages, perhaps, stor-age with cheap rent and no facilities. She wondered if it was associated with the substation, perhaps – spares, maybe, or tools.

Tools. *Weapons.*

She reached the end of the row and saw that it continued along at right angles, maybe another twenty small doorways interspersed with a few roll shutters large enough for a vehicle. At the corner she took one last glance back at the other car and got a shock: both the men inside were working their way out, looking around them and towards her car, but she had some cover from foliage and they didn't seem to have noticed her. She took herself fully out of sight around the corner and worked her way up, testing doors.

Feeling a drop of sweat slide down the side of her face, she wiped at it. Her hand came away red. She was keenly aware of how much trouble her ankle was giving her, but what was really scaring her was a severe weariness, a sense that she didn't have long before she would simply fall.

A row of vegetation at the far end of the building was sparse enough for her to see the movement of traffic behind it, but reaching it would have proved difficult enough even without the men coming for her. She had to find somewhere to hide, fast.

She tried each of the unpadlocked doors in turn, but none gave. Then, five along, one door was badly dented and rusting more than the rest. She pushed at it, wincing at the shriek of rusty hinge and sending a look back to the end of the building, expecting to see the men lumbering around the corner.

She stopped pushing and put her head through the gap she'd made. Inside was a bare concrete room, perhaps twenty feet square, dirt and dry leaves and old cabling. She hoped for a bolt on the other side of the door, but there was nothing, so she decided to move on.

The next door seemed in better condition and to her relief it opened silently. Inside was a longer room, an L-shape that seemed to cut back around the end of the one she'd just been in, but it was clearly unused, the same kind of dirt and debris lying around. There was another door in the far wall, though, which might mean she would have another exit.

Her dizziness was increasing moment by moment. She shut the door behind her, disappointed but not surprised that there was no way to lock it. On the floor a few feet away was a square wooden post, around five feet long. She bent to pick it up, reeling for a second before regaining her balance, then carefully she braced the post against the door. The concrete floor of the room was sufficiently uneven to give the post some purchase, but she wasn't so naïve as to expect it to hold out against much. She just hoped it wouldn't have to.

She heard voices, deep muttering and harsh angry barks that couldn't be far away. Annabel allowed herself a little satisfaction that she'd managed to spoil their day thus far.

She backed away towards the other door, gripping the handle and turning. It wouldn't open. Perhaps a little more force would do it, but the last thing she wanted was to risk revealing her position. Instead, she moved around the end of the L-shape, out of sight. It was the best she could do.

She heard a thump a little way down; what she presumed was foot-on-door.

'No,' she heard one man say. 'Try that one.'

The familiar shriek of hinge came from the dented door in the neighbouring room, painfully loud. The sounds of shuffling footsteps were interspersed with complaints of injury – whoever it was on the other side of the wall, they were battered, just like her.

'Nobody,' came the voice, just a few feet away.

She noticed something on the floor near her, a two-foot metal rod. When she heard the shrieking hinges of the closing door, she crouched down and retrieved it, standing again. Solid, a good heft. If the wooden post she'd braced against the door didn't hold, she might get a lucky hit, maybe two. They were injured, after all.

She should have been ready for the solid *thump* on her own door, but it took her by surprise, the rod nearly slipping from her grasp.

A pause. She was waiting for them to say 'no' again, to move along. Annabel felt another drip run down the side of her head. Leaning back on the wall she wiped at the drip with her left hand.

Noticing just how much blood was on her fingers, an image hit her, along with a surge of weariness, and darkness at the edge of vision. The image in her mind was of the door she had come through as she came into this room. Old, off-white and dirty, yes, but not *so* dirty.

Not so dirty as to hide the smear of blood she must have left on it as she'd pushed it open.

Shit.

Another kick.

Another pause.

To get their strength, she thought. *No rush. Not now they know where I am.*

She knew she was beaten, knew it was done. She could feel tears running down her cheek, intermingling with the blood, but they were tears of frustration as much as anything. Frustration that she could be so easily cornered.

Another kick. The post slipped a fraction. Annabel gripped the metal rod in both hands.

Her tears were still coming but now she realized there was grief in there too. She was allowing herself to admit at last that Jonah and Never were likely just as dead as the cop who had been with them, Bob Crenner. Just as dead as she would soon be.

Another kick. A cry of pain, and some swearing. *Good*, she thought, *hurt yourself*.

'Keep going, she's in there,' said one voice.

'My fucking knee's gone, you finish it.'

Kick.

The post shifted again. Annabel raised her weapon, bracing.

Kick.

The post fell, the endless clatter as it bounced against the floor the loudest thing Annabel had ever heard, reverberating around the bare walls. The sound of her last hope dying.

Under cover of the noise she hurried towards the door, standing to the side of it against the wall. She would rather be right there when it opened, and have the chance to take as many swings at them as she could. Rather that, than cower with the child-like hope that if they couldn't see her immediately, perhaps they would leave.

Her teeth were gritted. Her tears were all anger now. The door swung open, its movement so gradual it seemed almost mocking. She held her breath, gripping the metal rod. Then she stepped away from the wall and faced the open doorway, ready to fight with what little she had.

It took her a moment to register that nobody was there.

Her eyes moved down to the gravel outside. Two feet, legs, the rest of the man out of sight.

She edged forward. Maybe they wanted to avoid being jumped. Maybe this was just a trick to get her out of cover. She stepped left to get a better view of what was at the other end of those feet.

The man was lying on his side, facing away from her. She could see blood in his hair. He wasn't moving.

Hell, she thought, *if it's a trick, I'll take my chance.* With one man on the ground, maybe one swing was all she'd need. It was certainly all she had in her, perhaps only a dozen more seconds before her strength would fail and leave her unconscious.

She raised the metal rod and strode out, looking left and seeing nothing, then turning right to face the other man. And there he was. On the ground. Blood still pumping from a small hole in his temple.

A woman was standing over him, arms folded. The slight girl from the hotel, with two dead men at her feet and a mischievous smile.

'A simple thank-you would be fine,' said the woman.

'Thank you,' Annabel managed, before her legs buckled and she fell.

*

The woman helped Annabel to sit up against the outside of the building.

Annabel watched her drag the bodies of the men inside, one by one, then pull the door closed. Stepping back from it, the woman looked thoughtful, before taking a handkerchief from her pocket, leaning over, and wiping away the bloody smear Annabel had left on the door.

'There,' said the woman. 'We have to get moving, but by the look of you, I'd better run and bring my vehicle here. Sit tight. Once we're far enough away I'll take a look at your injuries.'

The woman ran back towards the far corner of the building and disappeared.

Now that she wasn't standing, Annabel's weariness was under control, letting her think with a little clarity about what had just happened. Whoever this woman was, she had just saved Annabel's life. Without a better idea of what was going on, Annabel would have to be wary, but she was in no condition to try and run.

After a minute the woman returned, driving a sporty red Nissan that brought a smile to Annabel's lips. The car yelled *speed*, and right now speed was good. When they were both inside the car, the woman didn't hang about. She flipped it around and sped off back to the road, heading away from the crashed vehicles. Annabel could see another car there, someone standing beside it.

'He's only just shown up,' the woman said to her. 'I told him I'd found one person and was taking them to hospital. Said I reckoned the other driver must have caused it and run off.'

The road they were on was narrow and twisty, the woman pushing every corner hard but making it look as casual as sin. Soon enough the road opened out and straightened, joining another road with a little more traffic.

'What's your name?' Annabel asked, aware of how weak her voice was.

The woman smiled. 'You mean, "who the fuck are you"?'

'That's what I mean,' said Annabel, finding herself smiling back, in spite of her determination to be wary.

'You can call me Sly.'

'Well, thanks for saving my life, Sly.'

'Don't speak too soon, girl. We're not out of this yet.' Sly glanced at Annabel's head wound. 'I'd thought they were under orders not to hurt you. They weren't doing such a good job, huh? Oh, hang on . . .'

She brought the car to a sudden halt. They were on a bridge over the highway. Sly leaned back and grabbed something from the rear seat that Annabel took a second to recognize.

'You got my bag from the car?' she said.

'We're better not leaving anything behind,' said Sly, rummaging around inside until she produced Annabel's phone. 'Voilà!' she said. She stepped out of the car and stood watching the oncoming traffic below for a moment. She hurled the phone expertly towards a truck, getting it to land safely in a dip in the blue tarpaulin tied over the truck's load.

When Sly got back in, Annabel was looking bemused.

'Your, uh, "security expert" in London was compromised some time ago,' said Sly, shrugging. 'The moment you used the systems he'd set you up with, they could start to locate you.'

'Ah,' said Annabel. The damn phone.

'Yep. Fortunately, I was keeping tabs on *them*, so I knew your location too. And I was closer.'

Annabel noted the slight bruising on the woman's forehead, right where she'd hit her with the iron. She pointed. 'Uh, sorry about that,' she said.

Sly put her hand to the bruise. 'Yeah. Don't do that again. I needed to get you out fast and quiet, and I knew damn well you wouldn't trust a word I said. In, spray, and get you the fuck out of there; that was the plan. I wasn't expecting the iron.'

'It kinda took me by surprise too,' said Annabel.

Sly rummaged a little more in Annabel's bag. 'Yay!' she said, grinning. She pulled out the white canister Annabel had taken from the hotel. 'Did you get rid of the gun?'

'Yes.'

Her smile turned into a frown. 'Shame. Nice weapon. Pricey.'

'Sorry.'

'Yeah, well. You're rich. If we both live through this I'll bill you. Oh, something you should know. Your friends, Miller and Geary? They're fine, last I heard.'

Sly gunned the car, and Annabel was glad of the noise.

48

Wet and shivering, Jonah and Never had emerged from that cramped tunnel into the night, following Kendrick's instructions with the kind of numb shock they'd both seen many times in the grieving relatives of dead subjects. Jonah thought of Katherine Leith, of the expression he'd seen on her face as he'd talked to her about bringing her dead son back for a final goodbye; he thought of himself, lying in the mud as a fourteen-year-old boy, his mother dead in the nearby car.

Kendrick insisted they put an hour of driving in before even allowing them to change out of their sodden clothes. He was prepared, as always: there was a bag of spare clothing in the trunk. Dry at last, they each took three-hour shifts at the wheel. Jonah found that the routine of driving helped his state of mind. The shock settled, and the distance they covered over the next two days was as much mental as physical.

When they reached the new safe house, a one-storey end-of-street place in the north of Reno, it was early morning. They slumped onto the soft seating there, Never taking the couch, and within moments Jonah found himself tumbling into the deepest sleep he'd ever known, barely coming round when Kendrick shook him to tell him the news. 'Annabel's safe,' he said. 'She's on her way here.'

Jonah woke four hours later to find Kendrick and Never still sleeping. He was certain Kendrick's words had been in a dream;

tears pricked his eyes at the thought of how cruel that kind of dream was, where reality was a painful thing to wake up to.

Then the thrum of Kendrick's phone woke the man; he took the call and looked over at Jonah with bloodshot eyes. 'They'll be here in less than an hour,' Kendrick said.

'They?' said Jonah.

'Annabel and a friend of mine,' said Kendrick. 'I told you, didn't I?' He seemed genuinely uncertain. 'You should grab yourself a shower.'

Fifty minutes later she walked in, smiling, another woman coming in with her. One of Kendrick's people, he assumed, although she looked decidedly less lethal than he'd been expecting Kendrick's inner circle to be. His own age, he thought; slight, short.

Annabel's expression was a giveaway when she saw Jonah's face – a shock she failed to hide, one he understood. He'd seen his own face in the mirror when he'd showered, cuts and bruises underscored by haunted exhaustion.

Annabel, too, had been through it. She was wearing a beanie and took it off carefully, pulling a cotton pad away from the side of her head that was brown with dried blood.

'Be careful,' said the woman. 'You don't want to open it up again.'

Annabel put a tentative hand to the injury and took it away, clean. 'Busy few days,' she said, and Jonah could hear her voice breaking as she spoke. They took a step towards each other and embraced, saying nothing. Just holding on, breathing. All they could do. All they needed to do.

'This is Sly,' said Kendrick after a discreet moment. 'She's tougher than I look.' He smiled, and Sly smiled back.

'I'll vouch for that,' said Annabel, breaking off the embrace but not letting go of Jonah's hand.

'Sly,' said Kendrick, 'this is Jonah Miller, and Never Geary.'

They gave each other a nod.

Jonah caught the expression on Never's face as he looked at Sly, and felt himself wince a little inside; auburn hair and a great smile had often been Never's weakness.

'Aren't you, uh, a little short to be a stormtrooper?' said Never, his grin horribly nervous.

Sly's eyebrow arched high. She looked at Kendrick, her thumb jabbing back to Never. 'Keep this one away from me,' she said. 'And tell me we have beer.'

She went to the kitchen, Never following her, looking like a kicked puppy.

*

Kendrick left the safe house without explanation, emphasizing that Jonah, Annabel and Never were confined indoors. He left Sly there to watch them; she sulked at being a babysitter but kept herself to herself, while Never avoided looking anywhere near her when she was around. They spent much of their time resting. Jonah and Annabel slept spooned in one of the beds, the simple pleasures of contact and sleep feeling like the greatest of luxuries. They told each other everything that had happened since Bob Crenner's car was ambushed, but neither mentioned the biggest thing on each of their minds: what the hell they were going to do next. When Kendrick finally came back late evening, they put the question to him.

'Me and Sly will be gone for a few days,' he told them. 'In the meantime, you'll be here, alone. Stay indoors. You have plenty of food. We're arranging for the three of you to meet up with an acquaintance of mine who'll take you somewhere safe.'

'What about Andreas?' said Jonah.

'It's not your fight any more,' said Kendrick.

There was silence for a moment, as they took this in.

'And you?' said Annabel. 'What are you going to do?'

Kendrick smiled. 'Take care of things. More than that, you don't get to know.'

*

A welcome two days of *nothing* followed.

They were all still numb. Jonah kept his eye on news about the research at Winnerden Flats; all the revivers who had been accepted were at the site now, and in the most recent interview with Stephanie Graves she revealed that updates would be monthly.

'Just let us get on with it,' she told the interviewer, smiling.

For most of the time, they avoided talk of what came next. Whenever the topic did get raised, it was usually Never who started it.

'We can't go back,' said Never. 'Our old lives are gone and I don't even know *what* to feel about that. If Kendrick fails, we'll need new identities for the rest of our lives.'

'If Kendrick fails,' said Annabel, 'the rest of our lives is likely to be pretty short.' Jonah scowled at her, and she smiled back. 'But in good company,' she said.

After three days, Jonah was sitting with Annabel and Never eating through a mountain of junk food and watching terrible movies. He had almost started to feel human again. Whatever happened next, he would be with Annabel. There were worse ways to face the end of the world.

Just after 5 p.m., Kendrick and Sly came back. Kendrick stepped over to the television and switched it off. He set the black holdall he was carrying down on the floor, with a heavy metallic thunk. Sly had one as well, and when she set it down it made the same kind of sound.

'Time for answers,' Kendrick said.

*

'My plan was always to kill Andreas,' Kendrick began. 'One way or another. Tess didn't know for certain if killing him would really *end* this, and any attempt on his life would always be a one-off. One chance, so it would have to count. Even before Tess told us *when* we could make it count, we already had a means in place to get a team inside Winnerden Flats, armed to the teeth. When I found out what Andreas really was, I set about making sure people loyal to me got themselves into positions that could be important. Two of them are already in Winnerden Flats, in Baseline security. We have a good idea what's happening on the Baseline side, but very little about the restricted areas. We know Tess and Andreas are both there. But things have accelerated. We're out of time. We'd hoped to find out about the final component Andreas needed for his machine, and try and stop its construction, but we've just learned that we're too late. The last component has been delivered. Whatever the process of Andreas's rise is, it begins in the next day or two. We have no choice but to act now.' He laid out a few sheets of paper, a four-page mosaic of the site plan. 'Winnerden Flats,' he said. The complex was, overall, a rectangle. Two sets of tall wire fencing were marked, the innermost flagged as electrified. The main gate was at the long, lower end of the rectangle. 'This area in the middle is open, a courtyard with hard surfaces for recreation. Living quarters for the Baseline staff are here.' His hand swept across the L-shaped building at the left. 'Sleeping area here. Indoor recreation area, canteen. Kitchen. Gym and swimming pool at the top. There are a hundred revivers working at the facility, a further hundred research and support staff. Over here –' his hand moved to the lower right of the rectangle – 'this is Lab One, for Baseline research. Used only by day, this is our way in.' Then Kendrick pointed to the top right of the rectangle, at the heart of which was the large dotted circle labelled MCH. 'This area is called Lab Two. Officially the cryogenics lab. Off-limits to Baseline staff, and that includes the main security team. It has its own security, is self-contained, and even has supplementary power generation. Most of the complex is four storeys, concrete floor at ground level. Here, though, two levels are underground. The circular construct that houses their *machine* covers both levels. We know that those close to Andreas live in this area. They don't leave it. They don't mix with the research staff.'

'Of course they don't,' said Jonah. 'If the revivers caught sight of them, they might be able to see the shadows crouching on their shoulders.'

'Almost certainly,' said Kendrick. 'There are only twelve security staff for the main facility, but we don't know how many in Lab Two. Maybe another dozen.' He laid out another sheet of paper, the schematic of a cryogenic chamber he'd already shown Jonah and Never.

'We think this is the centre of the machine, where Andreas will be as he undergoes whatever process they have in mind. The plan I originally devised had an eight-strong team. That team included four of my associates, long-trusted colleagues willing to do whatever it takes. Together with myself and Sly, we would gain covert access to Winnerden Flats. The two insiders from on-site security would complete the team. They would meet us, and take us to a secure storage room. We would hide there until the time was right, which, thanks to Tess, we now know means once the rise has actually begun. Two of the team would then evacuate Tess, get her out of there. The information she has access to could prove critical, even if the rest of the mission fails. The other six team members would gain access to Lab Two and blow the internal generator, then move in to kill Andreas.'

'A nuclear weapon would be useful,' said Never. 'Given how good Andreas has been at *not* dying.'

'Wouldn't it just,' said Kendrick, irritated. 'Not *quite* that easy to get hold of.'

'So how do you plan to make sure he's dead?'

'Do you know what the perfect murder is, Never?'

'When there isn't a corpse to find,' he said with a shrug.

Kendrick nodded. 'Precisely.' He reached into the holdall at his feet and produced an unlabelled black cylinder. 'When I'm done, I'll know Andreas can't recover. Because there'll be nothing *left* of him.'

Everyone looked at the cylinder. Jonah wondered what it contained, but he could see the top of the holdall, and a compact gas mask sitting there. 'Good luck,' he said, but the look on Annabel's face was odd. He wondered if she'd taken it as sarcasm. 'I mean it.'

'I know,' said Annabel. She looked agitated; scared, almost.

'What's wrong?' asked Jonah.

Annabel shook her head, looking at Jonah and Never. 'Jesus, you two are slow sometimes.' She got blank looks. 'He just told us his plan. Don't you get it?'

'No,' said Jonah.

She turned to Kendrick. 'The associates you'd been counting on . . . They're not coming, are they?'

Kendrick shook his head. 'They were the team that took Lucas Silva, so no. We were trying to arrange alternatives when the news came in that the machine is ready. We're out of time and we're short-handed. Me, Sly and the two insiders can handle the assault. It's a smaller team than I'd like, but it's enough. Problem is, we can't spare anyone to get Tess to safety.'

Bemused, Jonah looked at Annabel, then at Never; he could see the penny drop on Never's face just as it dropped with him.

'In theory,' said Sly, 'all you have to do is take one of the patrol vehicles and drive away.'

There was silence for a few seconds as the news sank in. Finally, Never spoke up. 'You said this wasn't our fight,' he said.

'Things change,' said Kendrick. 'We leave tonight. Welcome aboard.'

49

Jonah lay in the dark on a hard cold surface. He was completely enclosed, save for a small gap left at the top of the zip for ventilation. It wasn't anyone's idea of comfort.

But then, body bags weren't made for comfort.

'There is one road,' Kendrick had explained. 'There are no approaches that offer cover. At the facility, the fencing is enough to keep out anything less hardy than a tank. When it was first announced, they had a few sightseers to ward off, but the coverage of the project and the remote location means that nobody's interested in coming to see it with their own eyes now. A patrol vehicle checks the perimeter every two hours. The question you should be asking is this: how do we get inside?'

With over a hundred revivers now at the facility, research teams were getting through at least ten revivals a day. The new Baseline had widespread support even from many of those who had vehemently opposed it before, and supply of volunteered corpses wasn't proving a problem.

'Our window is tonight,' said Sly. 'There's a scheduled delivery of revival subjects. Thirty-five bodies in a chilled container unit, being collected from Reno in three hours. A four-hour drive to Winnerden Flats, and the unit is delivered ready for subject preparations to begin in the morning. Five of those bodies will not be dead.' She smiled. 'Dress warm.'

They'd been met an hour later at the back of a faceless building, by a huge, slow-moving man. He shook Kendrick's hand, nodded at Sly, then cast a suspicious eye over Never, Jonah and Annabel.

'Last of the bodies came in not long ago,' said the man, sounding anxious. 'We need to take five of them out.'

They all took a hand helping remove the five corpses, taking them out of their body bags and putting them in the back of a van, a look of knowing disgrace on the faces of the living.

Annabel had been the one to voice it. 'What are you going to . . . ?' she started, then just gestured at the naked corpses.

The man sighed. 'Got a meat storage locker I'll use. What happens then, well, they'll turn up one way or another; the families will get them back. I don't feel right about it, but it has to be done.'

The five live replacements entered the shipping unit, with thirty corpses in black body bags and the morgue smell of chilled unease. There were three racks of metal beds in a single transport assembly, each rack layer with space for four bodies head to toe, three layers high. Their own beds were waiting, all five now-empty bags on the lowest shelves. Sly and Kendrick both had their holdalls with them. Sly took hers and put it in the foot of one bag, then lay down inside, zipping it up halfway.

'Pick your quarters,' Kendrick told the others. 'You'll want to zip yourselves in to retain heat, but give yourself enough ventilation. When this door seals, we don't talk again unless absolutely necessary, and even then only in whispers. The drivers are not my people. They have no idea we're here. If they catch the corpses chatting, you can be damn sure they'll cause us trouble.'

With everyone in, Kendrick pulled out a flashlight and went to the door, where the big man was waiting outside.

They shook hands again. 'I don't like it,' said the man, ready to close the cooled unit and shut them in.

Kendrick nodded. 'There's nothing to like.'

And with that, the door was closed.

*

After three hours the ground started to get uneven, the ride becoming a series of lurches and rolls as they reached the final stretch of the road to Winnerden Flats.

They slowed, then came to a halt. From outside they could hear muffled exchanges. The end of the container opened. Metal clanked, followed by a rattle and a shuddering thunk as mechanisms latched onto the rack assembly.

'All good,' said a voice. Jonah felt movement again, the assembly being removed from the container to a secondary transport. His body bag was ruffled by a breeze for a moment before they came to a halt again.

Some small talk followed, as the paperwork was signed. The drivers wished the security guards goodnight and drove away; after a few more seconds, the rack of bodies began to move, the effortful whine of an electric motor audible in a more restricted space now, the sense of breeze vanishing.

They were in the building.

After a minute or so they stopped. There was the sound of a large door closing, then total silence and a creeping sense of cold. Delivery complete.

Wordless, Kendrick came to each of them, unzipping their body bags, signalling them to get out quietly.

They were in a large chilled storage area, dimly lit and over twice as wide as the rack assembly was long. There was a floor-to-ceiling gate in the far wall with a smaller inset door. Three other rack assemblies were beside theirs, all filled with body bags.

'They're well stocked,' Jonah whispered to Never, nodding at the other racks.

'OK,' said Kendrick. 'Me and Sly will wait by the door for Rico, one of our insiders. He should be here within thirty minutes. He'll take us to a storage room where we can hide out until the time comes, which may be thirty hours or more. As soon as Andreas begins, Rico can get Tess to us. Then, our attack on Lab Two is also your cover. You'll take a patrol vehicle and drive.' He pulled a sheet of paper from his pocket and gave it to Annabel. 'Here. Details of where you'll be able to change vehicles and get further instructions. Clear?'

Annabel nodded.

'You three wait here,' Kendrick said, handing his holdall to Jonah. 'When we signal, follow with the bags, and stay quiet.'

'Make yourself useful,' said Sly, handing her bag to Never.

'Christ,' he whispered, feeling the weight. 'What's *in* here?'

'Plenty,' said Sly. She and Kendrick both held handguns; they checked their weapons before crossing to the far wall.

They waited in silence. After a minute, Never knelt down and slowly opened the zip on Sly's bag. He peeked inside. 'Christ,' he whispered. 'There's some meaty stuff in here.' He stood, holding a small black rectangular card and something that looked like a hockey puck.

'What are they?' said Jonah; Never handed him the puck and held up the black card for him to get a better view. It looked like a security card, but a cable ran from it to a small black square device an inch or so across, which had several other short cables running off it.

'Oooh,' said Never. 'Very nice. Security hacking kit, I'd guess.' He looked up at Jonah with a completely earnest face. 'I wonder if Sly would let me keep one of these?'

'And what about this?' said Jonah, looking at the hockey puck.

'Not sure,' said Never. 'Probably explosives.'

Jonah's eyes widened. He knelt by Never's bag and gently replaced the puck, catching sight of some of the rest of the contents. As he looked up to Never, he realized Sly was staring right at him. She started walking towards them. Jonah hurriedly zipped the bag up and stood, guilt on his face.

'Don't fuck about with this stuff, understand?' she whispered. Jonah mumbled a 'yes'; Sly went back to Kendrick.

It was another twenty minutes before there was a gentle knock. Kendrick opened the small inset door; he and Sly went out, leaving

Jonah, Annabel and Never alone. The seconds crawled by, Jonah feeling the cold seep ever deeper into him. Then the door opened again, Sly indicating for them to come. They hurried over, Jonah and Never carrying the weapons holdalls. They stepped out into a bright wide corridor. Sly closed the door then led the way.

Along the corridor in both directions were doorways, red lights on small wall units beside them suggesting they were locked. The corridor itself was clearly in a maintenance area – a step ladder lay on its side nearby, and just ahead was a cleaner's trolley next to a pile of garbage sacks.

Kendrick and his contact weren't visible, but there was a right turn just ahead, by the cleaner's trolley; Sly took the turn first, Annabel behind, Never and Jonah at the rear. 'Well,' whispered Never as they rounded the corner. 'So far so good.'

At the end of the corridor, maybe fifty feet ahead, was a large black door. Kendrick was already halfway there, another man beside him in a blue security uniform. Jonah presumed he was the contact, Rico.

Jonah felt his stomach lurch; he shouted out Kendrick's name, *screamed* it out, as he pointed.

Pointed at the thing on Rico's shoulder.

50

The moment Jonah shouted, Rico turned. He looked shocked, clearly not expecting to have been compromised. His hand reached for a weapon as he shoved Kendrick to the floor; Sly's gun was already rising, and it fired with a dull suppressed *thump*. The shot hit the shoulder of Rico's gun arm, exactly where Sly must have intended. Kendrick took him to the floor with a sweep of a leg and was on top of the man in an instant, punching the wound as Rico cried out in pain. Jonah saw the shadow glisten on the man's shoulder, writhing along to Rico's own agony.

Rico grit his teeth. '*Fuck*,' he said, his voice shaky. 'You brought that fucking *reviver* with you . . .'

'How long, Rico?' shouted Kendrick. '*How long?*'

'Long enough,' spat Rico.

Kendrick hit the wound again. 'Where's Templeton?' he said, but Rico didn't reply, just grinned through the agony.

Sly ran ahead to join him. The others stood where they were, starting to understand just how much trouble they were in, just how broken their plans had become in so short a time.

'Oh shit,' said Never. Jonah followed his gaze back along the corridor past the cold-storage area to the secure door at the end, the lights on the lock changing to green. The doors opened, blue-uniformed security guards hurtling through, yelling at them to get their hands up.

Jonah stared for a moment, shadows on all of them. He was

suddenly very conscious of the holdall he was carrying. He held it out from himself, setting it on the ground and taking a step back, his arms raised. He looked at Never, confused for a moment, Never's hands already empty and in the air, but no bag in sight. Then Never's eyes flicked to the cleaner's trolley beside them, and the garbage bags lying against it. Jonah caught sight of one holdall strap protruding.

The guards were on top of them in seconds. Annabel, Never and Jonah were urged on, arms twisted behind them, then forced to the floor.

Sly and Kendrick were both standing with their guns raised, Rico prone at their feet, the armed guards facing them down. One guard stepped forwards.

'Throw your guns down and get on the floor, hands on head. *Now.*'

'Do as he says,' Kendrick told Sly.

Sly didn't move.

Kendrick turned to her, put out his hand and pressed down on her gun to lower it. 'Do it,' he said.

Sly scowled at him, then complied, her weapon skittering along the floor. She stepped forwards, planting a solid kick in the groin of the prone Rico. She turned and walked to where Annabel lay, getting on the floor herself. She threw a look back to Kendrick, who was still standing, gun raised.

'Throw your gun down,' said the guard. 'Final warning.'

Jonah could see the rage in Kendrick's face, but his gun started to lower.

As it did, the security door at the end of the corridor behind Kendrick clunked and opened. Out came two men, dressed in identical black clothing that seemed almost military. Both were carrying large shadows. Jonah stared. The shadows were even larger than the one he'd seen on the FBI agent, Heggarty. Sinuous, writhing masses.

The men took a step forward, then one to the side, taking up positions by the door.

Michael Andreas emerged behind them.

'Gun down please, Larry,' said Andreas.

Kendrick didn't move, but even from this distance Jonah could see his gun lower slightly then rise again. And Jonah could see exactly where that uncertainty had come from.

Andreas had changed.

It wasn't just the sense of *bulk* Jonah noticed, a curious feeling that Andreas had grown larger than his body. It was the way that this bulk seemed barely contained, ready to break out. His face appeared oddly fractured, like a broken mirror glued roughly back together, dark lines across it that seemed in flux.

Kendrick fired eight rapid shots. Andreas didn't move; even though the guards were armed, they simply watched. Kendrick lowered his gun, staring at the holes in Andreas's forehead, tendrils of black smoke emerging from them, evaporating.

Andreas smiled.

'Come,' he said, beckoning to them. 'We're just about to begin.'

51

The moment Never Geary saw Andreas he knew they didn't stand a chance.

Kendrick's ineffective volley was the icing on the cake. The would-be saviours of the world were directed through the door Andreas had emerged from, into what transpired to be a security station, a mosaic of CCTV monitors showing external night views of the facility's surroundings.

The two dark-clothed men followed Andreas inside; the fallen Rico was brought to his feet by a guard, in clear pain but awed by the presence of his leader, and the door was locked again.

'Sit, please,' said Andreas. They complied, Never noting that neither Sly nor Kendrick were taking their eyes from Rico, clearly wanting to spend a little quality time with their betrayer.

The wounds in Andreas's forehead were healing, Never could see – but then he corrected himself. The holes simply became thinner, merging with the lines that, from this close, he could see criss-crossing Andreas's face; lines which yawned open and closed again several times. The impression Never had was of a series of mouths, yearning to be fed.

'You were wondering,' sneered Andreas, 'when Rico succumbed to me. Well, Rico?'

Rico's face was glistening with sweat and blood. One of his hands was trembling. The shock of his injury, Never presumed.

'Two months ago,' said Rico. He smiled.

'Two months,' said Andreas, commiserating. 'So close.' He took a step nearer Kendrick, who couldn't keep the distaste from his expression. 'Your friend Templeton had no idea Rico had been compromised, by the way. Up until Rico killed her. I'm impressed that they avoided attracting suspicion for so long, but when they did I gave them both a choice. Rico made the right decision. He's been on my personal security staff ever since, a detail he presumably omitted from any communication he sent you.' Andreas shrugged. 'And now he's brought you all here.' He turned his gaze to Annabel. 'Miss Harker. Mr Geary. I wasn't expecting you. Or you, Jonah. I'm particularly pleased to have *you* with us.' He said it with a leer.

There was a sound from behind him and another guard stepped inside. 'They had this,' he said, passing through Jonah's holdall. Jonah saw Kendrick glance at both him and Never, registering that only one bag had been found. Andreas took it, ignoring the zip, instead pushing the fingers of his right hand *through* the bag's material, a hiss and a wisp of acrid white smoke rising from the plastic as it melted. He ran his fingers along the length of the bag and looked at the faces around him, pleased with the effect. Then he peered inside. 'You brought toys,' he said, smiling. He started to take some items out – automatic weapons, ammunition clips. 'Imagine what fun you would have had with all this!' Andreas pulled out a sub-machine gun, turned it over in his hands, then set it back and shook his head, his smile becoming an exaggerated frown. 'No use to you now.'

He held the bag out for the guard to reclaim, then turned back to his audience.

'We don't have a prison cell as such, but the room behind you can be used as a holding area.' He nodded to another guard, who stepped past them to a door at the rear wall then swiped a security card and opened it. The guard went inside the small narrow room to check it; it looked to Never like a storage room, cardboard boxes stacked against the end wall. He thought back to the David Leith revival, and how rooms that aren't in constant use inevitably become a dumping ground.

The guard supporting Rico started to guide the wounded man towards the door. Rico cried out in pain as he took a step.

Andreas looked at him. 'I think I know how you can serve me best, Rico,' he said. 'Your time is almost here.' Andreas turned to Jonah. 'I've been honouring those most loyal to me,' he said. 'The sustenance they provide gives me the strength I'll need to become what I will become.' Rico broke into a smile that was almost one of ecstasy.

The guard who had gone into the holding room emerged. 'All clear, sir,' he said.

Andreas nodded. 'Get them inside. You and Wright stay here. Keep an eye on them and monitor the perimeter. The rest of us will go to Lab Two. We're not to be disturbed, understand?' The guard nodded, and Andreas turned his gaze back to Jonah. 'I'll take my leave, if you don't mind. Enjoy the show.'

The guard called to his colleague; they took Kendrick first, patting him down carefully and taking the building schematic printouts and another handgun before pushing him hard into the room. Kendrick stood at the back, glaring. Then it was Sly; the guard found another gun and an ankle knife, before taking off a pouch strapped around her waist. He handed it all to Andreas, who opened up the pouch to reveal a field medical kit. He looked at it and smiled at Sly. 'Interesting,' he said. 'You actually thought you might survive long enough to treat your wounded.'

Sly just looked back at him impassively, and was pushed in to join Kendrick. Then it was Annabel's turn to be searched, then Jonah.

Being last had given Never enough time to realize something uncomfortable. When Sly had caught him and Jonah going through her weapons bag, Never's instinct had been to shove the security card he'd been holding into his pocket. The moment he had seen the guards coming down the corridor he had hidden the weapons bag, but he'd also moved the card from his pocket to the front of his pants.

The pat-downs they were being given were thorough, and the guard was certain to find it. They needed that card if they were to have any chance at all. He had to create some kind of distraction.

Rico was being led out of the room, and Andreas turned to follow. As the guard finished with Jonah and started to pat down Never's arms, he knew he had to try.

'Don't we get popcorn?' he said, his voice loaded with as much sarcasm as he could manage.

Andreas didn't even slow down.

'Hey, you ugly *fucker*,' he said. 'Surely the end of the world needs snack food? You can't think much of your little show if you won't lay on something to eat.' Andreas didn't react. In the holding room, he could see the faces of the others, all giving him a wide-eyed warning. 'You're a shit host, anyone tell you that?'

Finally Andreas swung around, glaring at him. 'As I recall, you weren't exactly invited.'

'I can certainly think of places I'd rather be,' said Never. Andreas walked towards him, and Never felt his terror rise. Something about the man's eyes made Never want to scream. They seemed like a lazy approximation of human.

Andreas motioned to the guard patting him down. 'A moment,' he said, and the guard paused, standing beside Never but with one hand on his shoulder, ready to resume. Andreas smiled again, a smile that was pure malice, and from this close Never could see every fine crack, every dark *mouth*, pulsate in ripples across his face. 'You really are an incredibly annoying man. That mouth of yours might get you into *trouble*. I suggest you don't talk to me like that again.'

'I guess at your age,' said Never, the tremble in his voice impossible to suppress now, 'most things start to get annoying.' He forced a grin. If he stopped antagonizing Andreas now, he thought, the guard would just start the search again. A little more of a nudge and Andreas would hurl him into the holding room with his own hands.

'At my *age*?' There was pure anger in those eyes now. 'You have no idea what *age* means to a *god*.' The rippling lines on Andreas's face were growing more agitated.

'No offence, but you're not looking too good on it,' Never said. 'For a god. Can't even magic up a fucking *face* that works.'

Andreas glared, the anger seeming to overwhelm him. It occurred to Never that he'd pushed enough, that he should stop now, but Andreas looked at the guard and tilted his head. The guard moved away. Andreas came close and put his hand on Never's shoulder. Inches away from him, Never was suddenly aware of the *stench* coming from those rippling lines in his face.

He felt the grip on his shoulder tighten. Andreas leaned even closer, the rank smell growing, the thin black lines quivering, thickening, flashes of something *sharp* within. Never could feel heat on his shoulder where Andreas was touching his shirt; he was aware of a charred odour, too, and hoped it was just left over from the stunt Andreas had pulled with the weapons bag.

Andreas looked Never in the eye. 'Look at you, such a faithful little pet. Only here to watch after your friend. So loyal, but what has it earned you? Without Jonah, right now you would be at home, asleep. Safe and oblivious to what's coming. Instead, you're here to die. And look at *him*. He always gets the girl, doesn't he?' A quick glance at Annabel. 'Almost greedy of him, wouldn't you say? Don't you deserve a share? But you're right. I'm not a god, not yet. If I was a god, I could do anything, couldn't I? Do you know what the Christian Bible says was God's first act of violence against man?'

All Never's bluster had deserted him. He could only shake his head.

'Oh come on, you remember! Think of Adam. And think of Eve. God's first act of violence against man was the creation of *woman*. You must know how He did it, yes? All He needed was

Adam's rib, torn from the poor man's chest. Such a quaint little story. I can't help but imagine the *care* that a god would have to take. It's major surgery, after all: slicing through the skin, cutting under the bone without rupturing the thoracic wall, then severing the rib without puncturing the pleura. Not to forget cauterizing the wound, to prevent poor Adam bleeding to death. All done with the hand of a *god*.' Andreas raised his own hand and flexed his fingers, his smile widening, almost rupturing his face, and Never couldn't look away from the rippling black lines, a thousand hungry mouths opening and closing.

Andreas's smile faded. He turned to the guards by the storage-room door. 'Lock those four in,' he said. 'We don't want them getting in the way.' As the door started to swing closed, Never could see the look of dread on Jonah's face, on Annabel's. And while Kendrick was impassive, even Sly was looking at him with something that might have been dismay. Looking at the condemned man. The lock went red, and Jonah came to the door's window, desperation in his eyes.

'Now then,' Andreas said to Never. 'What say we give it a shot?'

He turned to his black-clothed escorts and nodded to the table along one wall of the control room. 'Clear it,' he said, and they swept monitors and keyboards from the surface. The escorts and two guards pushed Never down onto the table and held him as he struggled. Andreas looked gleeful, his eyes locked to Never's, the darkness in them infinite. His hand slid underneath Never's shirt.

It was only when Never felt the pain in his chest that he cried out, the touch of Andreas's fingers at his sternum, the heat growing, *growing*, as the touch became a push that became a terrible agony and he smelled the stench of his own flesh burning. He was aware of Jonah's muffled shouts, then the sound of his flesh cook, and crackle, the crunch of bone, all underneath the noise of his own screaming. He was desperate for the escape of oblivion, but the pain had too tight a grip of his mind.

With a slow, deliberate motion Andreas slid his fingers across and under the rib, pushing hard against Never with his free hand to keep him still, while the other hand tracked around to Never's side.

There was a final wrench, a final crack, as Andreas pulled the rib free. He held it up for Never to see, a piece of himself, *burned* out of his body: steaming gently, dripping charred blood.

Andreas held Never's shirt out of the way and examined his work, nodding with satisfaction. 'Good,' he said. 'Breathing seems viable, so the pleura's undamaged. Bleeding kept to a minimum. A job well done! You'll be glad to know you'll live, for a while yet. And you're finally quiet! Lesson learned! What now, I wonder? Have I got what it takes to turn this into a woman?' He held the rib up high, studying it, then shrugged, waving the wet, blackened bone. 'Another time maybe. It's not quite marriage material, I'll grant you. A shame, but then I'm not a god, am I? Not *yet*.'

As he dropped the rib to the floor, Never's consciousness finally slipped away.

52

With the holding-room door locked, all Jonah had been able to do was watch his friend suffer.

Andreas walked across and looked at him through the small window in the door, looking self-satisfied. He nodded to the guards; two of them lifted Never's limp body and moved towards the door, which a third guard opened. Guns trained on them, Sly and Kendrick stepped back slowly, Jonah and Annabel following their lead. The guards laid Never down and backed out again. On the floor, Never's eyes were closed, but his mouth was moving in silence. Blood from the wound had saturated his shirt and jeans.

Andreas smiled. He nodded to the guard holding Sly's field medical kit; the guard handed it to him, and Andreas threw it into the room. 'There. You have the option to put him out of his misery, but I doubt you have the courage. Soon enough you'll pray for death, but I'll keep you alive. I want to *feel* the despair within you.'

The door was locked again.

Sly knelt beside Never, and Jonah joined her. She examined the wound. 'Jesus, it's a mess,' she said, shaking her head. 'There's still some bleeding, but it's mostly cauterized.'

'Is he going to . . . ?' said Jonah.

Sly looked up at him. 'As Andreas said, his breathing is sound. That makes it unlikely the pleura's damaged. He's lost blood, and he'll lose more. We need to pad and strap the wound, and there's morphine in the kit to help with the pain. Right now that's all we can do.' She looked at the boxes that were piled at the back wall. 'Go and see what they've locked us in with, OK? See if there's anything I can use as padding.'

'Andreas is leaving,' said Kendrick, who was standing by the door, watching through the window.

Jonah stood. Annabel was moving over to the boxes but he found himself joining Kendrick, wanting to look at Andreas as he led his group out of the security control room and into the corridor, leaving two guards behind. One of those guards came to the holding-room door and flipped a cover down over the window, blocking their view.

Across the room Annabel had opened some of the boxes. 'Nothing much yet,' she said. 'Some have blank ID cards, some stationary. But there's a box of these.' She held up a white T-shirt with the 'B2' Baseline logo Jonah had seen used in media reports, and 'Revival Baseline Research Group' on the back.

'Bring me a few of those and give me a hand,' said Sly. Jonah stepped towards her, but she shook her head. 'Just Annabel, please.' Jonah looked at Never's unconscious face and knew she was right. He'd be no use to her.

'Keep looking through the rest of the boxes,' Kendrick told him. 'We might get lucky.'

'You think they might have left some *guns* by mistake?' said Jonah, but he shook his head, immediately sorry. Kendrick said nothing.

The window cover was opened again. Jonah saw Kendrick tense for an instant, but then the man's eyes narrowed with interest. 'Mm,' he said.

'What is it?' said Sly. Jonah looked down; Sly had raised Never's shirt and pressed a folded T-shirt on top of the wound. She was holding a gauze bandage in one hand, and Annabel was kneeling with her hands on Never's hips. They looked like they were on the cusp of something critical, but the tone of Kendrick's utterance had taken precedence. Jonah looked back through the door window.

As well as the window cover being raised, the main door of the security room had been opened. Jonah and Kendrick could see all the way down to the end of the corridor, to where Andreas and his entourage now stood, fifty feet away. The two dark-suited men were by Andreas's side, with Rico standing in front.

'What are they doing?' said Jonah. 'That's where Never ditched the other holdall. You think they've spotted it?' He waited, tense, but nobody moved to where the bag had been hidden.

'Whatever it is,' mulled Kendrick, 'it's something he wants us to see.'

Andreas held out his hand towards Rico. Jonah could just make out the shadow Rico carried, as it began to shift: agitated, perhaps even excited. Rico stepped to Andreas and allowed his master to take his hand then he fell to his knees, an expression of absolute joy on his face. He closed his eyes, as if in prayer. Andreas stood over him and took Rico's head in his hands. He started to bend down over him, then opened his mouth. The mouth touched the top of Rico's head and continued to open, wider, wider. Jonah watched as every part of the skin across Andreas's face opened too, each opening like a mouth, and all the mouths disgorged a wet, living darkness over the kneeling victim, flowing over the head, reaching the shoulders before Rico's legs began to kick out in useless desperation, the deep black tar flowing onward as the body thrashed against it.

Jonah watched, unable to look away, as the kicking of the legs gradually slowed, then stopped, and the dark engulfed them.

At last, the black was retracted into the mouths. One by one, they began to close. Andreas stood upright, facing the door Jonah watched through. It was a show, as Kendrick had said; Andreas had decided to let them see how he fed.

The last of the mouths was closing now: dark holes where his eyes should have been, his face returning to an approximation of itself, enough to allow it to smile at Jonah and Kendrick before

Andreas turned and walked on, leaving a blackened mound of gore and bone steaming on the floor.

Jonah turned to Kendrick. 'And you think we could kill *that*?' Jonah said.

'Yes,' said Kendrick. He sounded almost distracted, and Jonah said nothing, wondering if the hopelessness of their situation was more than Kendrick could accept. After all, what choice did they have? Embrace their fate and look on as shadow stole over the world and took everything? Even if all reason was against them, they had to believe. They had to believe in *something*.

At the sound of Never moaning in pain, Jonah turned to see Sly wrapping the bandage around his torso, Annabel lifting him enough for her to get under his body.

Two more passes with the bandage and Sly looked up. 'He's still unconscious,' she said, her eyes firmly on Jonah. 'He'll come round soon, though. The pain won't let him stay under much longer. A wound like that, the body treats as a continuing attack. It can override everything. I've seen people sprint with their intestines trailing behind them. We need him to stay calm and keep still.' On cue Never groaned, his legs shifting, an arm raising to his face. Sly went to her kit and took out a hypodermic syringe. 'Everyone hold him down while I—'

With a yell, Never's eyes opened and he tried to move. Immediately, Kendrick and Jonah crouched beside him. It took all four of them to pin him down.

'You're going to be OK,' said Jonah, tears falling. 'You're going to be OK.'

For a few long seconds, Never fought them. At last he stopped struggling but his body was still tense. 'No,' he said, his voice horribly weak, taking very short breaths. 'Wait . . . I . . .' His face screwed up in agony for a moment.

'Jonah,' Sly said, 'you hold down this arm. I need to prep the morphine.'

Kendrick restrained both Never's legs as Jonah shuffled to

beside Sly. He gripped Never's right arm as Sly took a vial from her kit.

'It's time you rested, Never,' Jonah said.

'Don't . . .' Never managed. He turned his head towards Sly. 'Don't you . . . fucking dare knock me out.'

'It'll ease the pain, Never,' she said, 'but it won't knock you out.' The syringe was filled and ready.

'Promise me.'

'I promise.'

With a nod from Never, Sly gave him the morphine. After a few seconds they could feel the tension leave him. Sly gestured for them to let go.

A smile worked its way onto Never Geary's face.

'I gave him plenty,' said Sly. 'He'll be a little high for a while.'

'I know something you don't know,' said Never, in a sing-song voice. Everyone was silent, and Never's ghost-white face smiled. 'I have a present for you,' whispered Never, looking at Sly. His right hand came up, and went down the front of his jeans.

Jonah saw Sly's eyes widen, but the look of vague disgust that crossed her face wasn't there long. It was replaced by something approaching awe, as Never pulled his blood-smeared hand out and held up the security card, grinning.

'Happy birthday,' he said.

53

Sly and Kendrick stood with their ears to the door for several minutes, the room in silence except for the occasional mutter from Never about how he actually felt pretty *good*.

He didn't *look* good, of course. To Jonah, he looked about as bad as was possible, his skin ghostly pale, smeared in blood; his eyes unfocused but still with an edge of desperation.

Finally, Sly and Kendrick exchanged a look and stepped away from the door.

'Just the two guards in the room,' whispered Sly. 'Andreas said the rest were heading for Lab Two.'

'Can that card get us past this door?' asked Kendrick. 'There's no reader.' He pointed to the side of the door; there was only a panel with a single blank button.

'That's a door release,' she said. 'For normal use they need one in here, but it's disabled.' She pressed it; nothing happened. 'See? Now watch this.' She took the still-bloody security card out of her back pocket and held it up so the tiny black square device and cables attached to it were visible. 'This isn't just a card,' she said. 'Observe.' She checked the base of the door panel, and connected one of the cables. 'Diagnostic port. That's all it takes.' On the black square, a green light flashed twice. 'The door-release button is now active.'

'Simple as that, huh?' mumbled Never. He grinned.

Sly nodded at him and smiled. 'Simple as that.' She looked at Kendrick. 'If we're going to do this, we do it now. Agreed?'

'Agreed,' said Kendrick. 'Jonah, do the guards out there carry shadows? Last thing I want to do is get into a fistfight with one of those things.'

Jonah nodded. 'I think all of them did,' he said. 'Small ones, except for the two men dressed in black.'

Kendrick sighed and looked at Sly. 'We need them unconscious as fast as possible.'

'Alive?' said Sly.

Kendrick shrugged. 'They could be useful, but see how it goes.'

Sly made Jonah and Annabel drag the still-amused Never right to the back of the holding room, where she checked his wound again. She seemed satisfied that the padding was enough to stem the bleeding.

'You three stay here,' she told them. 'Whatever happens, just keep out of the way.' She went to the door, then took five slow steps backwards.

'What are you doing?' said Never, looking dazed.

'Watch and learn,' said Sly. She nodded to Kendrick and took the stance of someone preparing to run.

Kendrick raised his fist and started to hit the door repeatedly. 'Anybody hear me?' he shouted. He kept shouting until the window cover slid down and an irritated face appeared.

'What?' said the guard.

'I need to piss.' Jonah saw Kendrick's hand, poised on the door release.

'I don't care,' said the guard, and pulled the cover closed.

'Suit yourselves,' said Kendrick. 'But if you don't at least get us a bucket, we'll make sure it leaks out under the door. You're the ones who'll have to stay here in a room that stinks of piss.'

There was silence for a moment. Jonah could see Sly tensing in front of him. The window cover slid back down.

'The next time I open this fucking door,' said the guard, 'it'll be to shut your fucking mouth for good, understand?' The guard held Kendrick's eye for a few seconds, then started to shut the window cover. As he did, he turned his head, speaking to his colleague. 'Can you believe the—'

That was as far as he got.

Kendrick pushed the door release; in the same motion he raised his leg and kicked at the door with an almost explosive force, stepping immediately to the side as Sly hurled past him and launched at the other guard; the man was wide-eyed with shock, Sly already in the air, her boot connecting hard with the side of his head. Jonah felt his own hand come up to his mouth at the sound of the impact. He was sure he'd heard something crack.

Kendrick followed her through the door, out of sight to where the first guard must have fallen. Jonah heard the sound of another impact; then Kendrick and Sly were both back in the storage room, perfectly calm, armed with the guns they'd taken from the guards.

It had lasted all of four seconds.

'I think I love you,' said Never, gazing at Sly. 'Can we have dinner? If we both live?'

Sly raised an eyebrow. 'If we both live, I'll *buy* you dinner.'

'Right,' said Never, eyes narrowing. 'But will you be there when I eat it?'

'One step at a time, Geary,' said Sly. 'One step at a time.'

*

Sly and Kendrick brought Never out of the holding room along with a box of T-shirts. She removed some and arranged them on the floor, lying Never on top. Meanwhile, Kendrick moved the guards into the holding room. They didn't look like they'd be regaining consciousness any time soon, but Sly disabled the door release again anyway.

Then Sly sat in front of one of the computers on the table in the middle of the room. 'We have camera access,' she said, after a little typing. 'And building schematics, including for Lab Two.

They look incomplete, but more up to date than the ones we had before.'

'Good,' said Kendrick. 'We go back to the original plan: get to the generator in Lab Two and disable it. If Tess is right, we have to be sure Andreas has started the process before we interrupt the power. Jonah, you're coming with me. If we cross paths with anyone, I want a heads-up on who has those fucking *leeches* on their shoulder.'

Jonah nodded, and looked across to Annabel. He'd been half expecting Kendrick to drag him along. The look on Annabel's face told him she'd thought so too; scared, but resigned.

'What about Tess?' said Jonah.

'We worry about her later.' Kendrick raised radios he'd taken from the guards. 'We'll pick an unused channel and communicate with these. Sly, you stay with Annabel and Never.'

Sly scowled. 'Like hell I will.'

He handed Sly a radio. 'I need you here to manage surveillance and security, OK? Guide me.'

Sly turned to Annabel. 'You capable of typing and talking?'

Annabel nodded. Sly looked back at Kendrick. 'Nice try,' she said, 'but I'm coming with you.'

*

'That'll do,' mumbled Never. He was covered in a foil blanket Jonah had found in the security room's first aid kit, and had pleaded for Jonah to place one of the PC monitors on the floor beside him, showing the schematics, in case he could be useful.

Sly was sitting in front of one of the other PCs.

'Bring up some security camera feeds,' said Kendrick.

The monitor wall still showed the feed from the outside cameras, well lit. Several of the camera shots changed to indoor corridors, some dark.

'Seems like there are some lost signals in the recreation and habitation areas,' said Sly. 'But as far as I can see, there's nobody around.'

'Everyone's asleep on that side,' said Kendrick. 'The route to the Lab Two entrance is all we need. What about the cameras within Lab Two? I want to see what Andreas is doing.'

Sly tried, then shook her head. 'I think it's a separate system. We should be OK, though, the way down to the generator is right inside the entrance.'

Kendrick took the last radio from the charging rack. He set the channels and threw it to Annabel. 'Time to go,' he said.

'Stop him overexerting,' Sly told Annabel, nodding towards Never. 'I've left another shot of morphine ready for later. He can have it in forty minutes minimum, an hour would be safer, but he'll start complaining long before then.' She handed Annabel the guard's gun, Annabel taking it with trepidation. 'With luck nobody will come,' said Sly. 'But keep an eye out. If things go bad, take a patrol vehicle and get yourself to the rendezvous.'

Annabel nodded, but Never stayed quiet. 'Good luck,' said Annabel.

'You too,' said Sly. 'And hang in there, Geary.'

'Plan to,' said Never.

54

'You ready?' said Kendrick.

Jonah nodded. He looked at Never, his friend's face death-white save for the smears of his own blood; he looked at Annabel, who smiled at him. Surely she felt it as well as he did: there was a finality here. Managing to stop Andreas would be difficult enough; getting away alive was surely more than they could hope for.

'Just stay behind me,' Kendrick told Jonah. 'Be silent. Keep close.' He pulled open the door, stepping out, looking around. Jonah followed, Sly taking the rear.

The door closed behind them. The lock went red.

The smell in the corridor was different to the one they'd left behind. The reek of burning from Never's injuries was one thing, but out here there was something even worse: something with an acrid, almost rotting edge to it. Jonah could see the remains of Rico at the far end of the corridor, steaming slightly. It was right beside the cleaner's trolley and the garbage sacks where Never had hidden the holdall. As they approached, the stench grew ever stronger.

'There,' said Jonah.

By the mound of gore was a thick, spreading residue. It had reached the garbage sacks, where one strap from the holdall was barely visible.

'Gold dust,' said Sly. She reached over what was left of Rico and lifted the bag. It came away with an unpleasant sucking noise, trails of clotted molasses-like residue clinging to it.

Jonah couldn't help but look at Rico's remains, unable to identify what it was he saw. Some of it had taken on an almost
translucent quality, like chunks of rotting jellyfish, as if the flesh
had been drained of far more than its blood. Andreas had fed on
Rico's shadow, perhaps on Rico's *soul*.

'Here,' said Kendrick, snapping him out of it. 'Copy what we
do.' He passed Jonah a black harness; Jonah watched as Kendrick
and Sly put theirs on. Kendrick dipped into the bag and produced
one of the small discs that looked like ice-hockey pucks, along with
what could have been a small cell phone. 'Remote charge and trigger,' said Kendrick. 'This is how we'll blow the generator, guarantee
they can't just switch it back on. We'll split them up between us;
that way, if any of us gets through, we'll be in a position to do
something. To pair the trigger with the charge, hold the two close
to each other with the pairing button depressed. You'll get a green
light on both the charge and trigger. You can unpair by repeating
it, and the light will flash red. You can pair the trigger with as
many charges as you want. They pack a punch, so be in cover when
you detonate.'

Kendrick showed him where to fix them to his harness, then
shared out what charges they had – four each for him and Sly,
three for Jonah. There were two flashlights, which went to Kendrick and Sly. Next, the satisfaction clear on his face, Kendrick took
out the black cylinder, together with a compact gas mask, both of
which he fixed to the front of his own harness.

Finally, he took a gun for himself, gave one to Sly, and offered
Jonah another.

Jonah declined. 'I'm more likely to shoot you,' he said, then
added: 'Not on purpose.'

Kendrick kept the gun held out. 'As I recall, you're the one who
jumps into the line of fire. Take it.'

Reluctantly, Jonah took it.

'That's the safety,' said Kendrick, pointing to the side of the gun. 'No need to show you how to reload. The rest of the ammunition was with the bigger weapons, in the other bag.'

They made their way under Annabel's guidance by radio, heading for the Lab Two entrance. The security cameras showed deserted corridors ahead of them, the path clear. When finally they reached the door into Lab Two, Sly brought out the security card kit and plugged it into the lock.

Nothing happened.

'Annabel,' she said. 'Can you see the Lab Two entrance displayed on your screen?'

'Ah . . . yes, got it.'

'Does it say anything about the status?'

'Nothing.'

Sly tried the security kit again. 'What about now?'

'It flashed up EXT DEADLOCK.'

'Fuck,' said Sly. 'It's deadlocked from the other side. That overrides the locking mechanism.'

'So no way in?' said Jonah.

'If we have to, we'll blow the door,' Kendrick said. 'We lose all surprise but maybe we reach the generator before them.'

Sly winced. 'With respect, boss, we're up against a small army of people who just stole our automatic weapons and can kill us with *shadows*. Surprise is everything. We need another route.' She spoke into her radio. 'Annabel, the schematics showed a maintenance entrance to Lab Two at the other side of the building. It's from a plant room that adjoins the gym area of the residential block. Can you confirm that's there?'

It was thirty seconds before Annabel replied. 'OK, Never says he sees it.'

Sly looked at Kendrick. 'That's our way in,' she said.

Kendrick smiled. 'She always does her homework,' he said to Jonah, then turned back to Sly. 'Options?' he said.

'We could cross the central courtyard directly to the gym,' said Sly. 'But that leaves us exposed to anyone looking out of a Lab Two window. Or, we go all the way through the residential block and canteen. There's a side exit from this building that's just ten metres away from an entrance to the residential section. It's the long way but we'd be far less exposed. As long as all the researchers are asleep it'll be a breeze.'

Kendrick nodded. 'Annabel, did you hear that?'

'Yes.'

'Check the cameras, see if the path to the residential block is clear.'

Another pause.

'There's nobody around,' she said.

'So,' said Kendrick. 'The long way it is.'

'One *tiny* problem,' said Sly, with a grimace. 'The central section in Lab Two would then lie directly between us and the generator. We'd have to get past Andreas's people unseen.'

Kendrick looked at her for a few seconds. 'Well,' he said, 'as long as it's nothing *dangerous*.'

*

They made their way to the Lab One exit. Sly hooked up the security card kit, and this time there were no problems. The door unlocked. Outside, Kendrick took a quick look around him. To their left was the main compound entrance, a wire-fence gateway two metres high, closed but brightly lit. To their right, they could see an outdoor recreation area, a large playing surface with basketball hoops either end, none of the lighting on at this late hour. Indeed, only the lights on the gateway and perimeter fence seemed active. Very few of the windows ahead of them showed any illumination, and even those were dim.

Ahead they could see the entrance to the residential block, the light on the lock red. Sly went first, moving without a sound, and took care of the lock. The moment it went green Kendrick ran across the exposed space in the same near-silent manner. Jonah tried his best, aware that his own scuffling run was far from quiet. They stopped at the other door.

'Look at Lab Two,' Kendrick said, pointing diagonally across the courtyard. 'Everything's dark.' Not a single light in any window. The levels below ground, Jonah thought, had to be where Andreas was.

Sly led the way indoors, the corridor much dimmer than those in Lab One had been, just low-level lighting in the ceiling. 'Annabel, I need you to check the route I'm about to give you,' said Sly. 'Check I've got it right, and see which cameras we have feeds from.'

'OK,' said Annabel.

'We go twenty metres, then right,' said Sly. 'Takes us to the rec room, then the canteen. Past the canteen, right turn takes you through to the gym and swimming pool. We need the plant room, connected to the swimming pool maintenance area. You get all that?'

'Got it,' said Annabel, then, after a few seconds, she spoke again. 'We have cameras up to the canteen entrance, all clear. Wait a second, though . . .' They could hear indistinct mumbling as Never and Annabel conversed. 'OK, none of the cameras from the recreation area and canteen are active – and nothing from the gym either.'

Kendrick and Sly gave each other a wide-eyed look, but Kendrick shook his head. 'Probably nothing to worry about,' he said, clearly for the benefit of Annabel and Never. His expression made it obvious he didn't like it, not one bit; Sly was the same.

'Hold on, Never has something,' said Annabel.

'How are you doing, Never?' asked Jonah.

'Bit fucked, if I'm honest,' he said. He sounded frighteningly tired, the voice on the radio weak and distant. He took a slow breath before continuing. 'Look, I spotted something – on the cabling in the schematics.' He paused again, for another breath; Jonah had a horrible realization of how similar it was to a revival, short statements with gaps for breath between, as if Never was already dead. 'The lower floor of that circular area, sublevel two, doesn't have access to the generator, but there's what looks like a power hub there. You could take out all the power by hitting that. It might mean not having to go through the middle of everyone to reach the generator.'

'Where is it?' said Kendrick.

'With the southern door at twelve, it's at three o'clock,' said Never. He paused for a few seconds before he continued, the effort clear in his voice. 'Probably a big wall-mounted box, shitload of cables leading to it.'

'We'll bear it in mind, Never,' said Kendrick. Suddenly, the already-dim lights in the corridor dipped low, leaving them in near-darkness for a moment before coming back up. Jonah and Sly shared a look, then Kendrick went back on the radio. 'You get that, Annabel?'

'Power drain?' she said. 'Yes, we got it. Systems are still up, though.'

The drain happened again after ten seconds or so, a slow cycle that kept going; Kendrick looked at Sly and Jonah, and they were all thinking the same thing. Whatever Andreas was doing, it had started.

They continued along the dim corridor, Sly a few metres ahead. Jonah felt tense; whatever the hour, there was always a risk of somebody opening a door at any time, and Jonah didn't want to think about what Sly or Kendrick might do to them as a reflex, innocent or not.

To their left, they could see numbered doors, presumably individual living quarters for each of the revival and research staff. Sly stopped, holding her hand up and waiting for Kendrick and Jonah to reach her. She took a flashlight from her belt and switched it on, pointing it at the floor ahead.

'Glass,' she said, running her flashlight beam along a thin trail of smeared blood. They walked slowly to where the broken glass lay, outside the door marked 17. The shattered fragments looked like the remains of a drinking glass. Kendrick frowned, then turned to the door. He reached out and tried the handle, taking his own flashlight out.

Inside was a small room, a single bed, desk, television, PC. Dark and empty. Kendrick turned to the smear of blood again, which continued in a trail. 'That's a cut to a foot,' he said. 'Dragged along. Presumably unconscious. The blood's dry, so it happened hours ago, maybe longer.' He looked back the way they'd come, then to the far end of the corridor. His flashlight picked up something else on the floor at the far end – a coffee pot, upended. Slowly, he cast his light on each door, before pulling his gun and walking purposefully back to room 16.

Sly came over to Jonah, and pulled her gun too.

'What is it?' whispered Jonah.

Kendrick reached for the door handle. It opened. He looked inside, then shook his head.

'Empty,' explained Sly. 'Whatever happened in 17, it had to be noisy. There's been time for someone to clean this up, but nobody did.' She shook her head, then caught Kendrick's eye as he reached room 15. She tipped her head further along the corridor, and Kendrick nodded. 'Stay here,' she told Jonah.

Jonah stood and watched as Kendrick and Sly covered both ends of the corridor, getting faster as they went. It didn't take long before every room had been checked. They returned to where Jonah was standing.

'Nobody,' said Kendrick. 'Two of the rooms had signs of struggle.'

'Nobody in mine either,' said Sly. 'What are you thinking, maybe kolokol? I can't smell anything obvious.'

Kendrick shook his head. 'Doesn't need to be a mass agent. They could do it one room at a time.'

'Do what?' said Jonah. 'Where is everyone?'

'Whatever happened here,' said Sly, 'few of these people

resisted. Andreas's men used something to incapacitate them.' She looked up to the ceiling; Kendrick and Jonah looked up too.

'What, everyone?' asked Jonah. 'You think all the other rooms are empty?'

'We don't have time to look,' said Kendrick. 'Come on.'

The trail of blood outside room 17 was going the same way they were. They followed it, taking a right turn into another corridor and soon reaching a set of closed double doors. A sign above them declared the recreation area to be on the other side. Kendrick put his hand on the door but hesitated. He shook his head and frowned. 'I smell blood,' he said. He glanced down at the trail by their feet. 'A lot more than *that.*'

Sly nodded. 'Something happened,' she said. 'Something big.'

'Before we even got here,' said Kendrick. 'Long before.' They both switched off their flashlights and checked their guns.

Jonah was getting a bad feeling, a very specific one: a sensation of *imminence* that was curiously familiar, something that had begun soon after that first fading of the power, something he'd not yet been able to place.

The lights around them continued to dip and rise, a slow pulse of energy drain, and with each pulse he could swear the sensation was growing.

Then he had it, and it wasn't comforting. The nearest thing he could relate it to was a point in a revival just before the surge, as the reviver was hunting, waiting for the subject to come into their grasp.

The last moments of quiet before a plunge into the dark.

55

'Annabel?' said Kendrick.

'Go ahead.'

'We're outside the rec area. Aren't there *any* cameras inside?'

Pause.

'No,' said Annabel.

In the background Never's weak voice chimed in. 'They're supposed to be there, but there's no feed from them,' he said. 'Could just be unplugged.' He coughed and cried out; Jonah felt physical pain in his own chest, his old wound taking a bow. 'Sly, can I have more drugs yet?' pleaded Never.

'Not if you want to continue to live,' she said.

Kendrick and Sly shared a look. 'We have to keep going,' said Kendrick; Sly nodded. 'On three.' The count was silent, but Jonah felt the tension grow all the same. Sly and Kendrick pushed open the double doors and they entered.

The recreation area was a large open space. It was fully dark; Kendrick and Sly pulled their flashlights, quickly scanning the room, one half each, picking out the telling details in rapid succession: security cameras high on the walls, torn from their mounts; all the lights smashed; large black circular tables heaped in a haphazard pile at one end of the room, intermingled with plastic chairs, the centre of the room entirely clear of obstacles.

It was the blood that stood out the most, though – vivid against the mainly white flooring and walls. Jonah tensed, expecting the flashlights to pick out corpses at any moment, but none were visible.

Kendrick and Sly started to move further into the room, keeping their voices low. Sly aimed her flashlight beam at something among the pile of furniture and Jonah realized it was an overturned pool table. Then she pointed the beam up to the ceiling. Blood spatter was easy to make out, lines showing sweeps of arterial spray. *Many* lines.

'When, do you reckon?' she said.

'Has to be at least twelve hours,' said Kendrick. 'But I'd guess longer. They would probably have taken people from their rooms early yesterday morning, when they were asleep and at their most vulnerable.' His flashlight beam lingered on another line of blood spray, more vividly red than the rest. 'Although that looks very recent.'

They were speaking with a level of detachment born of experience; Jonah also found himself clinically assessing what he was looking at, as if it was a crime scene. The detachment was a mercy.

The blood on the floor was substantial, and in places the white surface was completely covered. Sly's flashlight picked out what had to be drag patterning in the blood, leading out of the recreation area.

'Where are they?' asked Jonah, stunned by what he was seeing. In a few short minutes his sense of the facility had been turned on its head. When he'd arrived, the assumption had been that it was a working research base, the inhabitants oblivious as Andreas carried out his clandestine plans in a separate part of the facility. 'There were over two hundred people here, half of them revivers. Where are the *bodies*?'

Kendrick walked towards the opposite wall, taking care not to slide where the blood was still wet. He turned, his light pointing at something on the floor. It was a mound surrounded by the same oddly gelatinous substance they'd seen with Rico's remains, this time recognizable as the lower half of a ribcage. It was coated in a thick near-translucent layer that had once been flesh, deep in a clotted black pool. 'He's been a hungry boy,' said Kendrick.

'Over here,' said Sly, moving to where the tables were piled, the beam of her flashlight picking out something under a table at the edge of the heap.

A man, maybe late twenties. The left half of his face was gone, as was the front left of his chest, and nothing remained below the waist. All the wounds bore the cauterized hallmarks of Mary Connart's injuries.

'My God,' said Sly, crouching, peering at the look of horror fixed into what remained of the man's face. 'What happened here? What was this? Some kind of sacrifice? Is that why Andreas went to all the trouble of starting a new Baseline? A ready supply of victims?'

'Maybe,' said Kendrick, sounding weary.

'I recognize that tone,' said Sly. 'Out with it, boss. What's on your mind?'

Kendrick shook his head. 'Two decades back a handful of kidnappers took the CEO of a small oil operation hostage. We were standing by, ready to take them out, but over the next ten hours the negotiations went well. Money changed hands, the CEO was released, the kidnappers fled. When we went in afterwards, we found fifteen staff slaughtered in a basement. Nobody had even realized that they were there. We finally tracked the ringleader down, and he told us that ten hours was a long time. He said he was just letting his guys have a little fun.'

'What are you saying?' said Jonah. He looked around the room, unable to stop picturing what must have gone on here.

'Andreas had no need for these people any more,' said Kendrick, his eyes fixed on the dead man's contorted face. 'Maybe he and his acolytes just wanted to let off some steam. Have a little fun.' He looked up at Sly and Jonah. 'A little fun in the recreation room.'

*

They crossed to the far double doors, the ones that led to the canteen. The drag patterning led that way, too. Through the doors was a short corridor, another double door at the end; the lighting hadn't been damaged along here, but it was dim, pulsing more rapidly than it had been before.

The canteen was curiously untouched, save for the wide red trail that passed through it. They moved steadily, Kendrick and Sly keeping flashlight and gun held up ahead, not pausing until they reached the other canteen exit. Kendrick went through it with purpose, expectant; Sly motioned for Jonah to get a move on.

They were now in a large area filled with comfortable seating. There was a bar on one side, and Jonah had a real yearning for a drink of something strong.

'Nice set-up they had here,' said Sly; ahead, Kendrick was following the blood trail on the carpet, his pace steady. The next doors were signed for the gym. They went straight through, ignoring the doors to changing rooms either side. The blood on the tiled floor led to the doors at the end.

'Swimming pool,' said Jonah. He could smell the chlorine. It wasn't all he could smell.

The dark phase of the pulsing light deepened; even at peak, the fluorescent tubes barely had time to kick on before failing again, punctuating the black with disconcerting flashes that hurt Jonah's head.

Kendrick opened up the doors. They stood, staring. The trail of blood ended here.

They'd found the bodies.

At first it seemed to Jonah that the water had simply been drained and the pool filled with the dead, many half consumed, the way the young man in the rec room had been, others with their throats torn out, limbs wrenched off, blood and bone and brain on show. Closest to them were the uniformed bodies of a dozen dead security guards.

'The Baseline security team,' said Sly. 'Probably the first to be killed.'

More corpses lay in heaps around the edge of the far wall. For a moment, Jonah thought one of those bodies was dressed in the black uniform of Andreas's inner circle, one of his acolytes; he wondered if the victims had managed to claim one of their attacker's lives, at least. A small victory, he thought, but impressive, given what they'd been up against. Then the lighting grew enough for them to see by, briefly, and he realized he'd been wrong. Even that small victory had been an illusion.

They walked in. Kendrick knelt by the side of the pool. He reached out and tugged at the arm of the nearest body, then used his foot to carefully push it away. Underneath, the swirling bloody water was black in the torchlight.

'How many?' said Sly, casting her light over the surface, the bodies bobbing gently now that Kendrick had disturbed them.

Kendrick stayed silent, walking over to the far side of the pool.

'There,' said Jonah, pointing at one of the floating bodies, feeling his legs weaken. He'd seen her in the brief flashes from the pulsing lights and, for a moment, wasn't sure, but Sly aimed her flashlight and he knew. 'Stephanie Graves,' he said. Her face was bloody and blank. He felt tears pricking. 'She was a friend,' he said.

'The head of research,' said Sly, and Jonah nodded.

Kendrick came over. 'I'd guess we're looking at a hundred corpses,' he said, thoughtful. 'Jonah, do you recognize any revivers?'

Jonah felt cold. 'Why?'

Kendrick indicated the bodies. 'Half the people are still missing, that's all. So tell me if you recognize any revivers.'

Jonah held his hand out to Sly and she gave him her flashlight. He steeled himself and started to look at the faces, but no others were familiar. 'They wouldn't be . . . they wouldn't be *part* of this.'

'I'd known Rico for fifteen years,' said Kendrick. 'I trusted him with my life. I wouldn't be surprised *what* Andreas could convince people of. They killed off everyone they didn't need. If that didn't include the revivers, then we can be sure they're helping him.'

Jonah said nothing.

'We need to keep going,' said Sly. She and Kendrick started walking along the side of the pool, heading for the plant room.

Jonah managed to follow, but only slowly; unease was swamping him, and he was unable to hold back from shining the flashlight on each face, looking for people he knew, looking for Stacy Oakdale and for Jason Shepperton, looking for faces he'd recognize from national and international conferences. Feeling more and more apprehensive, he wondered if what Kendrick had said might be true.

The pulse and flicker of the weak lighting in the darkness was oppressive now; alongside it was the continuing sensation that had first struck him just before they entered the rec room. Then, he had thought it felt like a revival just before the surge; now, it felt more like a doorway opening up, and a massing of power of some kind, beginning to slip out of the gap. He was sensing the process Andreas had started, he thought – the rise, Andreas reclaiming his lost strength.

But the unease he felt was more than this, more than *all* of this, and he suddenly recognized that what loomed most of all in his mind was the sense of—

He stopped.

The sense of something there, with them. The sense of being *watched.*

'Kendrick . . .' he whispered, trying to move towards them but finding himself frozen. His whisper was too quiet, his throat tight as he realized just how strong the sense of *presence* was.

'*Kendrick,*' he said again, louder, more urgently. '*Sly.*'

They stopped walking and turned, Kendrick's flashlight beam dazzling him. 'What?' said Kendrick.

'Something's in here.'

'What do you—?' Kendrick began, but then his expression changed, and his eye line shifted higher. Looking right above Jonah's head.

56

Jonah turned his head slowly. He saw it – just a few feet behind, towering above him, the darkness glistening in the torchlight. As he looked, the regular pulsing of the power supply peaked again, fluorescent flashes marking the creature's silhouette and revealing its size: larger even than those that had come for Tess.

Shots came and Jonah could see the bullets pass through: ineffective, but enough to take the creature's attention away from him. He dived to the side and, as he did, he saw Sly charging towards it, her run stalling as she saw that her gun was useless.

The shadow strode ahead and reached for her. More gunfire ripped through its flesh, from Kendrick this time; little more than a mosquito bite to it, but the creature turned to him now, hurling Sly hard into the wall beside Jonah. She fell to the floor, out cold.

The shadow took purposeful steps in Kendrick's direction. Jonah could see that it was enjoying its game. *It wants you to run, Kendrick*, thought Jonah. *It wants to take its time.*

Kendrick was backing away, still holding his flashlight, pointing it at the creature that was coming for him, gun raised but holding fire. A gun could get the creature's attention, but nothing more. With the sunlight they'd created in the safe house they'd stood a chance, delaying the creatures, causing them pain, and perhaps – if the sight of the creature that had taken Tess was anything to go by – perhaps, given enough time, they could kill them.

But not here, in the dark.

Kendrick turned to run and the creature lunged; its dark claw wrapped around his neck, and it lifted him until they were face to face. It let out a hiss and threw him across the floor, back towards the pool entrance.

Jonah thought of the explosive charges he carried, the simple priming action, the easy remote trigger. Given the effect of the inferno Kendrick had engineered before, it was possible that the explosion could hurt this creature, but it would be sure to kill Kendrick. These creatures might be vulnerable to *sunshine,* but everything Jonah had was more likely to hurt the living.

The living.

As the thought came, the lighting flashed and he saw, at the far end of the pool, a man in dark clothes crouching almost out of sight behind stacked plastic chairs, watching the creature as it closed in on Kendrick again; his face was gleeful and blood-soaked, and Jonah instantly thought of the corpse in black he thought he'd seen lying among the bodies. The one that had gone by the time the lights flashed again.

Not a corpse.

Anger filled Jonah's veins. As darkness enfolded him again he started to run, leaving the flashlight on the floor. He only had a few seconds of cover before the lighting would pulse again and betray him, but he knew what he had to do.

He couldn't hurt the creature, but by God he could hurt its host.

He ran along the side of the pool in almost total darkness but he didn't have the luxury of caution. His hand went to the gun Kendrick had given him. He released the safety and started to raise it as the power surged again. The lighting flickered and his eyes sought his target, but there was nobody there; the man had moved, and that meant he'd seen Jonah coming. Unless something *else* had seen him . . .

Jonah stopped and turned his head to see the huge silhouette at the far side of the pool turn to look at him. He sensed movement nearby and spun as the man came at him from the corner of the room, too fast, too close, bearing down with a look of *rage* on his face, and a look of *entitlement*, of sheer outrage at the gall of someone trying to put an end to his entertainment. The shock almost made Jonah drop the gun even as he brought it up and pulled the trigger and saw the man's forehead blossom red. All in an instant, yet still enough time for Jonah to grasp how necessary and simple the action was, one that would surely haunt him always: killing someone, face to face.

And enough time to realize how much momentum the man was bringing with him.

He collided with Jonah and clung to him as he fell, on the point of death. Jonah fell back with the weight of the dying man on him, and he knew what he was falling into.

The pool.

He landed on a lifeless wet body, the lights fading again. For an instant Jonah didn't move, overwhelmed by the proximity of the man he'd just shot, the man still clinging to him, warm blood gushing from his forehead onto Jonah's chest.

The hands of the man spasmed, then released. Jonah pushed him off, trembling.

Then he could feel the body under him giving way to one side, in a slow betrayal. He was suddenly aware of how heavy the belt of ordnance felt, how heavy his boots and clothing were.

The lights pulsed on again, momentarily; just enough for him to see that the side of the pool was well beyond his reach. Just enough for him to see what it was he was slipping into. 'No,' he said aloud, reaching out and trying to grip hold of the dead surrounding him, but he felt the bloody water soak through his clothes, the gap he was slipping into widening until the inevitable happened.

He went under.

57

His descent was rapid. With the tainted water and the bodies covering the surface, no light could reach him. He was in absolute darkness. He had a momentary image of the bottom of the pool vanishing, an unlimited fall into the vast depths of a blood-drowned hell.

Then his feet touched the bottom. There was still a part of his mind able to think, and it told him to step towards the side, arms outstretched, hoping his disorientation wasn't leaving him striding out into the centre of the pool. The moment his fingers touched tile he crouched and kicked hard, sending himself back up; his arms collided with one of the corpses above him and stole most of his impetus. He managed to push it aside and scrabble for the edge of the pool, but his weight took him back down without his head emerging for even one desperate breath.

His lungs were agony. He waited for the bottom again, for another chance, and as he sank he looked up. He saw the blood-dimmed beam of a flashlight on the surface and kicked hard again, seeing the gap to aim for and bursting from the water, getting a firm hold on the side this time, taking air into his lungs. Hands were pulling at him, helping him out of the water until he was lying at the side, coughing, the bright beam of a flashlight in his face.

It was Sly, groggy and out of breath. 'The thing just vanished,' she said. 'It just *vanished*. Where's Kendrick?'

Jonah sat up. 'Across there,' he managed, indicating the other side of the pool area. Sly swept the light along, but there was no sign of him. They shared a look. She shone the light over the corpses on the surface of the pool as they slowly bobbed in the disturbed water.

'I don't think he went in,' said Jonah, but Sly was running along the pool edge. Jonah followed.

'*No*,' said Sly, trying to see where Kendrick might have fallen in, just in case there was . . .

Jonah heard a groan from nearby, behind the rolled-up pool cover. 'He's over there,' he said. Sly hurried across, kneeling beside the fallen man. 'Boss?' Sly said. 'Come on! Wake up!' She slapped Kendrick's cheek with her palm. 'Hey!'

Kendrick moaned. 'Quit hitting me,' he said, dazed.

'Damn,' said Sly. 'Don't scare me like that.'

Jonah heard a noise from across the pool, and flinched before he realized what it was. 'One of the radios,' he said.

The lights flickered into brief life again and Jonah got his bearings. 'I see it,' he said. 'And Kendrick's flashlight. I'll fetch them.' He started walking.

'Watch your step,' said Sly.

The dropped flashlight was on the way to where he'd seen the radio; he picked up the light, and as he walked he took in the full scene of butchery. He thought of the man who'd unleashed his shadow on them and wondered if he'd been left as a guard here. It didn't seem likely; there was supposedly nothing to guard against. Maybe the man had simply been asleep here when they'd entered. *And who could blame him?* thought Jonah. He'd had a busy day, after all.

He reached the radio and started to head back to Sly. '*For Christ's sake*, somebody tell us what's happening,' said Annabel. There was considerable interference to the signal, but he could still make her out.

'We were attacked,' said Jonah. 'One of Andreas's people. We, uh, dealt with him.' In the light of the torch he was holding, Jonah saw that the water dripping from him was leaving a red stream draining back into the pool. He knew that some of that blood could have come from the head of the man he'd just killed.

'You all OK?' asked Annabel.

'Yes,' said Jonah. 'Sly and Kendrick – you two are virtually indestructible, right?' He shone the flashlight across the pool. Sly was working on what seemed like a deep cut on Kendrick's forearm, but Kendrick was opening and closing the fingers of his hand to test function.

'Cracked my skull some when it threw me that last time,' Kendrick said. 'But I think I'll be fine.'

'We're OK here, Annabel,' said Jonah. He paused before adding: 'What about you two?'

'Peachy,' croaked Never's voice. There was a distance to it, though. One that was more than just physical.

'Yeah,' said Annabel, far from convincing. 'We're good.'

'I'll get back to you in a minute or so, OK?' said Jonah. 'We need to regroup a little.'

'OK.'

As Jonah approached them, Kendrick began to stand, helped by Sly. 'So, Jonah,' Kendrick said. 'While we got distracted, you saved us all. Just how the hell did you pull that one off?'

Jonah shrugged, trying to be casual about it, trying not to think of the muzzle-flash lighting up the face of the man he shot; the lights around the pool flashed bright for a moment, as if to mock him. 'The creatures need a host. Take away the host, and—' He stopped, staring; Kendrick's face took on a look of utter horror, reflecting the one that was written all over his own.

Sly looked from Jonah to Kendrick and back again. '*What, Jonah?*' she said. '*Jesus Christ, what is it?*'

Kendrick had every right to be scared, because it was his shoulder that Jonah was staring at. His shoulder, and the dark glistening shape clinging to it.

58

It needs a host, Jonah thought, *and it used the nearest person.*

'It's impossible,' said Kendrick, pale and terrified, looking at his own shoulder but seeing nothing. 'When the host dies, *they* die.'

Sly was holding the flashlight for him, the bright flickering from the lights in the pool area still coming every ten seconds or so.

On Kendrick's shoulder the shadow was writhing. One of its fingers seemed to have gained purchase, and the others were testing the flesh. As Jonah watched, a second seemed to seek out a vulnerable place and sink down.

'You're sure it's there?' Sly said to Jonah, unable to see it for herself.

'Trust me,' said Jonah. 'It's there.'

'Tell me what it's doing,' said Kendrick.

It's managed to attach, thought Jonah. *And now it's working its way in.* 'I don't know,' he said.

'How can we get it off him?' said Sly.

'I don't *know.*' He moved his hand a little closer to it and observed the creature back away slightly. It was wary of him, just as all the shadows he'd encountered had been. He couldn't bring himself to move his hand much closer, though, the vision of glinting teeth clear in his mind.

Then he recalled what Kendrick had said. 'When the host dies, *they* die? What made you think that? You'd seen it vanish when the host fell unconscious, but if . . .'

Jonah stopped. Kendrick said nothing. Jonah saw an ill mix of evasion and defiance written on his sweat-slicked face. 'Jesus,' said Jonah. 'Silva. Your team killed Silva.'

'We had to know,' said Kendrick, but he didn't meet Jonah's eyes.

'You *ordered* them to kill him.' It fell into place in Jonah's mind. 'You lied to me.'

'Of *course* I lied,' sneered Kendrick. 'We had to *know*. We couldn't risk keeping him much longer, and nothing they did to him was making him talk.'

'They killed him, and thought it had died?'

'Every time it came loose from Silva it was visible,' said Kendrick. 'So they expected to see it once Silva was dead, and see what happened to it. It didn't appear. They assumed it had died with the host.'

'But it hadn't,' said Jonah.

'Oh God,' said Sly. 'Was that how they were traced? Did it take one of the team?'

Kendrick glared at her, stunned. 'I don't believe that. Every one of them was committed, *fearless*. They'd *die* before that.'

The implications were ominous. 'Don't you get it?' said Jonah. 'That was how they found *us*. It wasn't Tess's presence that gave away the safe house. Silva's shadow took one of your team. It took one as a new host. Resistance to torture didn't matter a damn because there was no need to torture the information out of them. They *volunteered* it.'

From the fear on Sly's face Jonah thought she knew where this was going. She nodded, and picked up the line of reasoning. 'Sure, whichever one of them it was, they knew the decoy addresses they could give if they were under pressure, but instead they gave the real locations they knew. Andreas's people just worked through them until they found us.'

'No,' said Kendrick. '*No.*' He sounded even more desperate. He looked at Sly, pleading. The shadow writhed; the second finger to have gained a foothold suddenly flicked out, whipping around before returning to Kendrick's flesh and probing again. The man's demeanour scared Jonah. Here was someone who had stood face to face with the devil and chosen to fight, a man whose sense of outrage at Andreas's betrayal had allowed him to suffer through torture without capitulating. And now he'd been reduced to a shivering husk at the thought of this external taint, this *contaminant*.

'And it can't have taken long,' said Sly. She looked at Kendrick, distraught. 'Between Silva's death and the team being compromised was what, five hours?'

'Four and a half,' said Kendrick. 'But Tess said the host had to be complicit, they had to *want* it . . .'

Jonah didn't comment. It had always just been a guess, an appealing idea. Less threatening. He thought about the shadows he'd seen on Silva's wife and child, and his instinct that they hadn't even known about what was attached to them.

Sly looked at Jonah. 'You think they can just take anyone, given long enough? Maybe keep them out of sight until the process is complete?'

Jonah didn't know how to answer, but Kendrick spoke instead. 'Would it die, Jonah? Without a host? Without anyone nearby it could attach to?'

'Maybe,' he said. 'It was desperate enough to use whoever was nearest, so perhaps it didn't have much time.'

'Well, then,' said Kendrick to Sly. 'You know what to do. Incapacitate me, leave me here.'

'No,' said Sly.

'Do it. We have no way of knowing how quickly this could happen. You can't kill me outright or it'd just try and take one of you instead. Make sure I'm unconscious, too. They can't detach if the host is unconscious. But I don't want it to take me, understand? It needs to be slow, but the wound has to be fatal.'

Sly was shaking her head, eyes wet. 'With respect, boss, there's no fucking way I'm . . .'

'Please,' he said. He put his hand on hers. 'Sly, please.'

She closed her eyes for a moment; then, resolved, she opened them again. She pulled a thin knife from her harness. 'Tell me how.'

Kendrick nodded and was immediately less agitated. Jonah saw the creature writhe again, its long dark fingers shifting, another of them finding a way in, digging deeper.

Jonah stared at it, knowing he was missing something crucial. He shook his head. 'Wait. For Christ's sake, wait. There has to be more. If it was that easy, there'd be no reason for Andreas to be cautious. This one had no choice, and it's struggling. I can *see* it, it gets in deeper, then it loses ground . . .' And it was getting in deeper again, but what had changed? He could see another finger fix in place and start to worm its way in already.

'Jonah,' said Kendrick, 'it's too late. You have to go; you and Sly have to do what you can. I'm ready, just don't let me—'

Jonah clicked his fingers. '*Exactly*,' he said. 'The only complicity the host needs to have is *giving up*; let someone reassure them, believe everything will work out. Panic, terror – that repels it.' He looked at Kendrick, knowing the man had resigned himself to his fate purely to give *them* a chance. 'Listen to me. Whoever it was in your team that Silva's shadow took, I think it got lucky. I think they have to be damn careful who they pick, because most will fight it tooth and nail. The only reason you're not fighting it now is because you think it'll save me and Sly.'

Kendrick looked at him, desperate to believe.

'Then get it *off* him,' said Sly. 'For God's sake.'

Jonah looked at the creature. It was weak, but holding on; he needed Kendrick's fear to ramp up again. 'Can you feel it?' Jonah asked. 'Can you feel it burrowing into you?' The hostile look Sly gave him was withering, but he looked back at her, hoping she would understand what he was trying to do. 'It'll worm its way inside, get its fingers deep into your flesh, into your *soul*, and you'll accept it soon enough. It will *have* you.' As he spoke Kendrick looked at him in disbelief. Jonah's hand was moving towards the creature, every part of him wanting to avoid touching it, but somehow knowing that this would be the only way. 'It will have you, and there'll be *nothing* you can do about it. Then you'll be glad. You'll *welcome* it, and do whatever it tells you to do.'

As Kendrick's fear increased the creature suffered, squirming and writhing, a gap in its flesh opening like a mouth in pain, its dark fingers shifting. Jonah moved his hand ever closer, the creature writhing in distress. The thought of actually taking *hold* of the thing filled him with revulsion, but he had to try.

He had to try *now*.

Jonah thrust his hand towards it and clutched, horrified by what he was doing. He half expected to feel only air, for his fingers to pass through it, but he felt it within his grasp, wet and squirming. He pulled and it started to come away from Kendrick, still giving resistance that surprised him, but the dark fingers were coming loose, the two that had got deepest were surfacing now. With a jerk it was free of Kendrick's flesh. Jonah gripped tightly as it struggled, those long, dark fingers flailing, whipping in the air.

And as they flailed, he could feel them strike the flesh of his arms. He sensed the ragged holes being burrowed, the creature trying to root in him. The pain was intense, but the tendrils kept pulling out and withering.

That's why you're scared of me, he thought. *I'm poison to you.*

He kept hold and stood, keeping his arm stretched out far from himself and the others. Just as he was starting to wonder what the hell he was going to do with the damn thing he sensed a change within it, a sudden escalation in its desperate struggle. Then its movement slowed. The whip-like fingers stilled. The surface of the creature's shadow-flesh altered, and it began to putrefy, falling apart and dripping through his clenched fingers, the drips becoming like the smoke that had been shed by the larger creatures under sunlight. There was a strong stench of decay, with an acidic tang that made him gag.

As he watched, it boiled away to nothing. He opened his hand suddenly. Kendrick and Sly both flinched at the movement and looked at him, hopeful but wary.

'Is it dead?' asked Sly.

Jonah nodded. And in spite of the carnage surrounding them, he found himself smiling. Because whatever happened next, here and now he'd dug out a victory.

Even if it was the only one they'd get.

59

When the radio next burst into life Annabel crossed to the corner of the security room, to get out of earshot of Never.

He looked terrible.

She put the volume down as low as she could before she pressed the talk button. 'I'm here,' she said, keeping her voice down.

'We're ready to go,' said Sly. 'Been a little busy. I want to run through the route we're planning to take, see what the schematics say. Are your computers having any problems with the power fluctuating? It's severe at our end.'

'It's not so serious here,' said Annabel. 'The lights keep dimming, but the computers are staying up.' A minute before, Never had voiced concerns about the systems being affected. But it wasn't the computers that Annabel was worrying about. 'Sly, Never's not doing so well. He says he's too hot but he's cold to the touch. And I'm pretty sure his wound's opened up.'

'The dressing's wet?' asked Sly.

'Yes.'

'Is he conscious?'

'Just about.'

'Is he still asking about the morphine?'

'No,' said Annabel. The radio went silent for longer than she was comfortable with.

'OK,' said Sly. 'Warm him up, whatever he tells you. Get him some water to sip or something sugary, if you can find it. Do it now.' She paused. 'Two minutes, OK? Get back to me when you're set.'

Annabel signed off and walked back to Never. He looked up at her, and even that seemed like a struggle.

'Hey,' he said, with a smile as weak as his voice. 'I'm not deaf; I heard you muttering to Sly about me. What did she say? Am I a goner?'

'Not if I can help it,' said Annabel. She looked away for a second before meeting his gaze again. 'Try not to die, Never Geary.'

He coughed, the pain obvious in his face. 'Sly promised me free food,' he managed. 'All the incentive I need.' He smiled again.

Annabel made herself smile back; then she offered up a prayer to anyone who was listening.

*

Kendrick, Sly and Jonah made their way down a maintenance hatch at the rear of the pool area, into the plant room that connected with Lab Two.

It was low-ceilinged and hot, with the air-conditioning units and heating for the pool, the equipment sounding strained each time the electricity feeding it dipped in power. They crossed to the door leading to Lab Two, and Sly immediately tried unlocking it. All three let out a relieved sigh when the lock went green.

They sat waiting for Annabel to radio them again, Jonah certain that the rate the lights were pulsing at had increased. When the radio came on, the interference was even worse than before.

'All done,' said Annabel. 'I found a spare jacket in one of the cupboards, and a bottle of cola. He's had some, I'll keep giving it to him.'

'Good,' said Sly. 'I'm going to run you through the route we're taking. Check with the detailed schematics, OK?' The interference flared, and there was something about it that unnerved Jonah. He glanced at Kendrick.

'Building infrastructure,' murmured Kendrick, but Jonah didn't think he was as certain as he sounded.

'Go ahead,' said Annabel.

'We're in the plant room by the pool,' said Sly. 'When we go out into Lab Two, we'll be on sublevel one. Corridor straight to the end, then we have two options. If we go right, it'll take us towards the circular area, where we think Andreas's machine is. It's possible all his people are inside that structure and we can just use the corridor. But the levels above ground were all in darkness when we were outside, presumably empty. I'd prefer to go up a level and along, then back down to the generator. In the site plan I studied there were offices along the north wall, and a stairwell that's the only way up to ground level at this end of the building. What do your schematics show?'

The interference grew, a loud hiss of static that made it impossible to make out Annabel's voice. Jonah still couldn't get a handle on what it was about the sound that was making him feel so uneasy.

It settled at last. 'We lost you there,' said Sly. 'Say again.'

'It looks the same on this map,' said Annabel. 'Out of the plant room, turn left at the end of the corridor, five small offices then a doorway that leads to the stairwell. Yes?'

'That's it,' said Sly. 'After this, don't try and contact us unless we contact you first, OK? Last thing we need is a radio barking out our position.'

Jonah reached for the radio. 'And if the shit hits the fan,' he said, 'you run, understand? Take a patrol car and drive.' She said nothing. 'Promise me, Annabel.'

'Yes, all right,' she said. 'I'll get Never to the car and go.'

Sly took back the radio. 'You won't have *time* to take him,' she said. 'And if you ask him, he'll tell you the same thing. You hear me?'

'I hear you,' said Annabel. 'Good luck.'

The radio went silent. Sly smiled at Jonah. 'Something tells me she'll ignore both of us.'

'Let's go,' said Kendrick. He listened at the door for a few seconds, then led them out into the corridor.

60

Although the lights here were also pulsing, the corridor was bright; this whole side of the facility had the benefit of power from both generators, it seemed. Sly closed the door behind them and the noise from the plant room faded. Jonah could hear a different sound, of straining machinery, coming from further on in the building.

Kendrick strode ahead, gun ready. At the end of the corridor he slowed and took a quick look before continuing. Sly and Jonah caught up, but Kendrick was standing still. 'Doesn't look right,' he muttered. 'Not the way I expected, at any rate.'

Jonah could see what he meant. The corridor here was very wide, with a linoleum floor. More like a hospital than an office area, that was certain.

'The layout is nothing like the schematics,' said Sly.

There were only three doors, all double. Kendrick shook his head and went to the first set of doors. He opened one a fraction, took his flashlight and shone the beam inside, then opened the door fully.

The dark interior looked like an operating theatre, Jonah thought – one immediately after surgery. Blood-soaked pads sat on a metal tray by an examination table, used scalpels and other utensils beside them. 'Maybe this area was used to prep subjects for the revival research?' he said.

Kendrick raised an eyebrow. 'Whatever this is,' he said, 'it isn't

Baseline. Stay here, I'll be back in a moment.' He returned to the corridor.

Sly investigated the contents of the glass-fronted cupboards by the wall, which held a variety of medical gear. As Kendrick entered the room again, she opened one cupboard and took out a bag of saline. 'This is for the living,' she said. 'Not the dead. It could be where they prepped Andreas.'

'The other two rooms are exactly the same as this one,' said Kendrick. 'Blood and all. This wasn't about prepping Andreas. But we have something more urgent to worry about. There's another difference to the schematics: there's no stairwell. We need to take another route.'

Sly had taken a clean clinical waste refuse bag and was filling it with items from the cupboards. 'Raise Annabel,' she said. 'If there's another way up, we should try it.'

She caught Jonah looking at the bag she held. He could see what she was putting inside it – saline, cannulas, vials of medicine. She shrugged, tying the bag to her harness. 'In case we live. Just what Never needs.'

Kendrick tried the radio and only got a loud blast of interference. 'Shit,' he said. He turned the volume down a little and tried again, waiting for it to subside as it had before.

Jonah listened to the sounds and realized what it was that disturbed him. The hiss didn't sound like typical interference. Instead, it sounded like a hall full of whispering people, rapid and incoherent speech.

The feeling he'd had before, of a doorway opening, was continuing to strengthen. He wondered if this was the power flowing to Andreas, and if it was the source of interference.

It didn't subside. Kendrick turned off the radio. 'Your call, Sly. I know you. You wanted Annabel to confirm, but you had a close look at the updated schematics before we left the security room, yes?'

'Yes. But *these* rooms aren't even on the official schematics,' she said. 'If we can't trust them—'

'We don't have the luxury to worry about that,' said Kendrick. 'Tell me what you remember.'

'I focused on the area around the circular construct,' said Sly. 'We could stumble around looking for another way upstairs, or pray everyone's inside the construct and try using the main corridor. It runs around whatever the construct is, leading to the generator.'

'There's another way,' said Jonah. 'The power hub on sublevel two that Never suggested.'

'If it *is* a power hub,' said Kendrick. He looked at Sly.

'I don't like it,' she said. 'It's guesswork based on details in a schematic we already know is inaccurate.'

The pulsing lights grew noticeably darker, the pulse more rapid; the noise of straining machinery increased in volume. Jonah still had that sense of an opening door, and a *flow* of some kind. Whatever was keeping the door open was draining more and more power. It was an appealing thought, that interrupting the power could interrupt that flow, but time was surely running out.

'Those are the only options we have,' said Kendrick. 'If Andreas's people have been obliging enough to leave the corridor clear, fine, but otherwise . . .' He looked at Sly until she gave a reluctant nod. 'Come on, then,' he said. 'Keep close, Jonah.' He led the way double-time back along the corridor they'd come down, stopping just before the turn. 'The construct is at the end of this next corridor, yes?' he said. Sly nodded. He took a quick look around the corner.

'Well?' said Sly. 'Is it clear?'

Kendrick winced. 'Not exactly.' He turned to Jonah. 'Take a look.'

Jonah nodded, but the nervousness on Kendrick's face was unsettling. Kendrick moved back from the corner, allowing Jonah to stand there. Jonah took a deep breath, gave himself a count of three, and put his head around to look.

The corridor was wide, empty and long, maybe a hundred yards or more. At the far end was another wall, with an obvious curvature. It had to be the circular outer wall of the construct, and the area around it wasn't empty. Not at all.

There were six that Jonah could see, all in the same dark clothes Andreas's acolytes had been wearing before. They faced the circular wall, hands linked, heads bowed, parts of a chain that presumably went all the way around. Jonah guessed that, given how little of the circular corridor was visible to him, it meant that there were at least thirty or forty acolytes in all.

And behind each acolyte a shadow knelt on the floor, every one of them as big as the shadow they'd faced by the pool. Jonah was fixated by the sight, the posture of the shadows making him think of supplication, the creatures prostrate before their god.

Midway along the corridor Jonah could see the gap in the wall where the stairwell to the lower sublevel must be. A long way, without cover.

Kendrick's hand came out and pulled him back. 'A *quick* look,' said Kendrick, scowling.

Sly took her turn to glimpse up the corridor, coming back eyes wide. 'That's quite an army they have there,' she said. 'Even if we manage to take out Andreas, we'll have one hell of a fight on our hands.'

The mechanical whine was a scream, now; the pulsing of the lights even faster than before. The tug on Jonah's stomach, too, had increased. *Something is torn, somewhere,* he thought. The flow of power felt like darkness flooding through a rip.

'Time is short,' said Kendrick. 'After you, Sly,' he said, gesturing to the corridor.

*

With the mechanical whine growing Jonah wasn't worried about being heard as they sped along the exposed corridor, Sly leading, Kendrick at the rear. Being *sensed*, though, was another fear entirely. His eyes were fixed on the dark forms, shifting and pulsing to the rhythm of the light. Halfway to the stairwell the whine increased again, the lighting dimming ever more at each pulse. The hands of the acolytes started to lift into the air. The shadows began to stand, their height immense.

Sly reached the stairwell but as Jonah followed he caught a glimpse of movement of the head of one of the shadows, and a corresponding movement from its host. He kept going, but had a clear feeling that the head had been turning because it *had* sensed them.

Then he realized that Kendrick wasn't following them down the stairs.

'They see me,' hissed Kendrick, being careful not to turn towards Jonah and Sly. 'Keep going. As long as they didn't see you I can draw them off.'

Kendrick raised his gun and fired two short bursts before turning and running.

Sly was already at the base of the stairs but she held a hand up for Jonah to stay still. He felt it, then – a single shadow, moving past behind him, giving chase to Kendrick. Nothing else came. Jonah wondered if they needed to keep the circle unbroken, or if it was just another sign of the arrogance Andreas and his people possessed.

Sly and Jonah ran, reaching the floor below as they heard Kendrick's gunfire recede down the corridor; there was a cry of pain, Sly looking back for an instant, torn but not stopping.

The walls were bare concrete; fifty yards along, the wall to the left took on a curvature just as the corridor came to an end at a metal door. Jonah presumed it led to the lower part of the circular area. The mechanical whine was so loud now it had to be coming from there. *The machine*, Jonah thought.

'That has to be it,' said Sly, approaching a box on the wall: five feet across, thick cabling leading to it as Never had suggested. She took a charge from her belt and paired it to the trigger, waiting until the light went green, then removing a layer of plastic from the back, revealing an adhesive strip. She placed the charge against the box. 'Here,' she said, handing her trigger to Jonah. 'Faster, if you pair them and I place.'

She took the remaining charges from her harness and set them on the floor. Jonah started the pairing process, quickly getting through all of Sly's charges and starting on those of his own. The rapid pulsing of the dim lights was overwhelming now. Jonah kept half an eye on the base of the stairs they'd come down, knowing that whatever had happened to Kendrick, there had to be a good chance of that shadow, or another, deciding to investigate.

'That'll do,' said Sly. 'Check that door while I place these.' She nodded to the metal door thirty feet from where they stood. 'We'll need to take cover when we trigger this.'

Jonah pocketed the trigger and ran to the door. It wasn't locked, but it was obviously strong; the frame was metal too, and it looked like the door could form an airtight seal if need be. Inside was an empty narrow room, a row of four monitors on a table along the wall showing grids of slowly changing digits that meant nothing to him. The only other door led inwards, presumably towards the circular area. Within the room, the mechanical whine was extremely loud. Almost a scream.

He emerged from the doorway, and Sly looked towards him. He nodded – the door seemed sturdy enough to provide the cover they required. As Sly turned back to place the final charges, Jonah caught movement high on the stairs forty yards behind her.

A shadow was descending.

'Sly,' he called. 'Get over here. *Now.*'

Her head flicked to the side for an instant, then back to the task in hand. 'I see it,' she said. 'Just one more to place.'

It was already at the base of the stairs, coming slowly, walking with a casual, arrogant hostility.

'Come *on*,' yelled Jonah. He took position at the other side of the door, leaning out with one hand ready to pull the door shut. As

Sly stuck the last charge to the hub, she looked at the creature, and just as she did, it picked up speed.

Sly ran towards Jonah. Behind her he could see the shadow striding towards them, faster now, rapidly closing the gap on Sly. He took the trigger from his pocket and tensed, keeping the doorway as clear as he could, ready to close the door behind her. He thought of the screams of the shadows in the inferno Kendrick had engineered at the safe house, and desperately wondered if the charges Sly had laid would have any effect on this creature.

'Run, Sly,' he called. 'Don't look back, just *run* . . .'

Five more strides and she leapt for the doorway, the shadow almost on her. Jonah pulled the door closed as quickly as he could, seeing Sly falling and the shadow's claw coming around the door to take her.

He pushed the button.

61

Jonah opened his eyes to total darkness, so disoriented that, for a terrible moment, he thought he was back with his torturer, Hopkins. Only for a moment, thank God. He could hear nothing but the high-pitched ringing in his ears caused by the explosion. The pain in his left shoulder and wrist was severe.

'Sly?' he said, hardly able to hear his own voice. He waited for a few seconds, until his hearing recovered a little. The mechanical roar of the machine – impossibly loud when he'd opened the door – had changed to a stuttering wail, rapidly decreasing in volume and pitch. 'Sly?'

'Right here,' she called, very close by. He looked in the direction of her voice, and as he did, red emergency lighting flickered on in the ceiling. She smiled at him. 'Cutting it fine, wasn't I?' She looked at the door, suddenly wary.

Jonah stood, and as he did so he moved his left arm to test his shoulder. It hurt like hell, but it was still in working order. The pain in his wrist was settling, and he could flex it. He thought of the explosion: feeling his arm forced back along with the door as it slammed hard shut, the instant after he'd seen Sly falling. And the claw, the dark claw coming into sight . . .

He faced the door, feeling like it could be torn from the frame at any moment. It looked somehow *off*, and it took him a second to see why. At the top it had been forced inside the frame by at least an inch; in the middle of the door the tip of a shard of metal shrapnel protruded. Yes, it had been strong enough to shield them from the blast, but only just.

He realized something else.

'I can't feel it,' he said. 'The shadow. I'm sure I could feel it before, feel that it was there.' He moved his hand towards the door handle, certain that under the noise of the explosion he'd heard a truncated shriek from the shadow outside.

'*No,*' said Sly. 'No. Just leave it. If it's gone, great, but I'd rather we found another way out.'

Jonah looked at the door again; buckled slightly and wedged in the frame, he suspected it wouldn't open even if they wanted it to. 'OK. Can you walk?'

Sly winced. 'My foot was caught badly by the door. I can feel the bones grinding in my ankle. You'll need to scout ahead, OK?' She looked at the other door in the room, the one that led into the circular area.

The pitch of the mechanical whine was lowering as they spoke. There was a sudden deep thump and the sound stopped completely.

What replaced it was silence. They both strained to listen. For a few seconds there was nothing, then another sound began: a scream growing from beyond their only other exit, a deep, inhuman cry that filled Jonah's head and made him crouch for protection for the long seconds before it ceased. It was a cry similar to one he'd heard before, in his visions of the Beast striding over the dark landscape, but now there was an edge of pain to it. An element of despair.

'Oh Christ,' said Sly, looking at the door. 'Was that what I think it was?'

'Andreas,' said Jonah, weary. 'Has to be.'

'Hurt, right? It sounds hurt.'

Jonah nodded but said nothing. They needed it to be more than just *hurt.*

'Shit,' said Sly. 'The radio.' She fumbled at her side then

brought it to her mouth. 'Boss? Annabel?' Just the eerie interference they'd heard before, Jonah getting the same unsettling feeling that he could hear whispers in the noise.

'Turn it off,' he said, not wanting to hear it. She did, and he could see the anguish in her expression. 'He might have made it, Sly. If anyone could . . .'

She nodded.

'You and Kendrick must have a hell of a history.'

'Complicated,' said Sly. 'Long story. Family. Kind of.'

Jonah nodded, thinking of Never. Family, kind of. It wasn't that long a story, and it was one Jonah knew well.

Sly sat up, gritting her teeth against the pain. She untied the bag of medical kit she'd scavenged and looked inside. 'All intact,' she said. 'It fared better than me.' Then she offered her pistol and flashlight to Jonah. 'His people will still be there, wondering what the hell just happened. Disoriented, with luck. This might be your only chance.' Another cry came from beyond the door, drawing her glance, and Jonah's too. 'Finish him, if you can,' she said. 'Ignore the others.'

Jonah took the gun as though it was poison. He could still *feel* the warm blood pour from the man in the pool, *flooding* over him, the guilt and revulsion following close behind. He still had one charge left in his harness. He gathered the trigger from where it had fallen, then walked to the other door, towards the circular structure. With a last nod to Sly he went through, closing the door behind him and keeping low.

Within was a large chamber; small panels with LED indicators were the only lighting in here, but it was enough to give him a sense of the space he had walked into – a wide circular room at least a hundred feet across, the panels attached to large objects spaced around the circle in concentric rings. There had to be dozens of them, he thought. Towards the centre of the circle was something different, but the room was too dark to make it out.

It was cold, his breath clouding in front of him.

He went to put on the flashlight but another sound came, from above him. A long, low moan this time, mournful and angry, accompanied by a strangely wet thumping, like a large fish floundering on the deck of a boat. Thinking darkness might be safer, he lowered the flashlight and started to make his way around the wall of the chamber, looking for another exit.

He heard a noise, a rustling within the room. Instinctively, he took cover between two of the objects around the perimeter. The noise had come from the centre of the circle, but just as he was about to move closer he recognized the object he was crouching beside.

The cryogenic unit, the one Annabel had uncovered plans of a lifetime ago. Kendrick had identified it as the first missing component in Andreas's plans, and had assumed it was a one-off intended for Andreas himself.

But the room was full of them. Jonah stood. He decided to risk the flashlight and switched it on, seeing now the large torus suspended above the circle's centre, a white ring perhaps three feet in height and thirty wide. Something about it made him think of MRI scanners, the look of large, clean plastic hiding something deeply sophisticated within. He moved the light around the chamber, tallying the units. They were about eight feet long, five wide, the windows on them obscured with condensation. Arranged in four concentric rings, a quick count gave him an estimate of twenty or more per quarter-circle. At least eighty. Maybe a hundred.

He knew he was delaying it. Delaying the moment when he looked inside the unit next to him. There were pieces of a puzzle asking to be fitted together in his reluctant mind. The missing revivers. The aftermath of surgical procedures that they'd chanced on, the blood on the cotton swabs too *red* – he'd known it even then – for it to be the result of preparing corpses for revival. Too fresh.

Everything around him was part of the machine Andreas had built. He knew it instinctively. Kendrick had guessed that the cryogenic unit had been the machine's first missing element, but his guess had been wrong.

The first missing element had been what went *inside*.

Jonah turned to the unit beside him, flashlight pointing at the glass. The condensation was on the outside, and he wiped it away. He had to know.

Inside he could see a face. Still alive, he realized. Kept on that line between life and death. He couldn't tell if the eyelids had been removed or merely stitched open, but he could see there were no eyes in the now-empty sockets. The mouth was wide, held in a frozen scream. Above the ear, a three-inch-long part of the skull had been removed, exposing an area of brain. Thin needles protruded from it, garish wiring on the end of the metal.

The very sight of it was the first shock. The second shock came because the lips were moving. Barely, but undeniably, they were twitching. Jonah stared, wondering if he could sense the rhythm of speech, as if the victim was locked in a scream of prayer. He thought of the whispers he'd heard in the static, and wondered if he'd found the source.

He turned to the unit behind him and cleared the condensation; another eyeless face, but as with the first, one he didn't know. He went from unit to unit, wiping the glass, seeing the pain underneath. Faster and faster he went, bracing himself for what had to come.

What function they served Jonah couldn't even begin to guess, but one thing seemed clear. The true purpose of the new Baseline hadn't been about getting revivers out of circulation. It was a pretext to gather them together, ready for the living death Andreas had arranged for them: a key component in his arcane machine.

And then he found one he knew. Jason Shepperton. One of the two Richmond FRS revivers invited to Winnerden Flats, one of those Never had hoped to warn off. In a unit two away from Jason he found the other Richmond reviver. Stacy Oakdale's mutilated face was locked in the same silent scream as the others, but it hit him harder than any; he remembered the day she'd joined the FRS, when she'd come back at a typical slice of Never's wit with something far more barbed and far wittier.

And he thought of Never. He wondered if his friend was still alive. He thought of Stephanie Graves, floating in the pool. Throughout the chamber he stood in, there had to be other revivers Jonah knew from conferences and training. He was surrounded by dead friends.

It felt like the cold air had penetrated down to his soul.

He closed his eyes. In the stillness he heard the rustling sound again and made his way to the centre of the circle, towards the white torus. It sat mounted on four-foot steel poles, obscuring his view of what was inside. Only when he was past the innermost circle of cryogenic units did he crouch down to see.

It looked like a table.

No, he thought. *An altar.*

His mind made the unwelcome leap from *altar* to *sacrifice*.

There was someone lying on it. And there was blood.

Please, he thought. *No more dead friends.*

It was Tess.

62

He stepped closer. The blood on her face had streamed from her nose, her mouth, her eyes. Those eyes were closed now. He wondered if there was anything behind the lids.

Then she moved, her feet and legs pulling against the restraints that held her in position, making the same rustling sound that had drawn him to the centre.

'Tess?' he said, barely above a whisper. He unfastened the strap holding her left arm, and as he went to work on the other, her eyelids flickered open, the eyes unharmed. She looked around wildly until she focused on his face, then brought her free hand up to his cheek, staring at him with disbelief.

From above their heads came more sounds, a wet thrashing and a scrabbling of claw on floor, the noise horribly close to them. The sounds stopped. Jonah looked at Tess and put his finger to his lips, then undid the remaining straps.

She sat upright, dazed and weak. He gave her the flashlight to hold, and helped her off the table. Slowly they made their way out of the circle, under the torus. They threaded their way between the cryogenic units, passing some of those Jonah had wiped the condensation from. Tess stared at what was inside.

They reached the outer wall and sat. 'You'd not seen them until now?' said Jonah, his voice low.

She shook her head. 'But I'd heard. I'd heard Andreas talk about what went into their machine. The revivers. All of them needed to tear open the door, and let Andreas's power return to him.'

'And you. You were the final missing element, weren't you?' She nodded. He reached to her face and wiped some of the blood from her cheek. 'When I saw you I thought you'd been a sacrifice.'

'No,' she said. She looked up at him, eyes tearing, desolate. 'It was the Elder inside me that was the sacrifice. They needed it to find the door, before the revivers opened it. The Elder is gone, now. They hollowed me out, Jonah. Hollowed me out.'

The noises from the floor above came again. Jonah looked up, knowing he had to face whatever it was. When he looked back at Tess her eyes were on him. 'You thought it could be killed,' he said. 'We blew the power. It's *hurt*. I can feel it.'

'Jonah . . .' she said, dismay in her voice. She looked at the ceiling again. Each sound that came from above made her flinch. 'I felt its power, running through me. I was drowning in it. Then I felt it shift somehow, out of control. A surge. An overload.'

'When the machine failed.'

'Yes. It felt *destructive*, so maybe . . .' She sounded almost hopeful, but then shook her head. 'Yes, the power surge hurt it, but I don't know how badly.'

'I can kill it,' he said. 'I know I can. Somehow.' He looked at her, needing her to agree, because the reality was cold and simple: he had to *try*, whether there was any genuine hope or not.

Tess nodded at him, but she didn't seem able to speak. She gave him back the flashlight.

'Stay here,' he said. He walked to the far side of the chamber: a metal stairway, a sign on the wall reading 'Control/Obs', with an upward arrow. He took out Sly's pistol and started to climb the stairs.

63

Two tiers of metal stairway led to an open door. A figure was sprawled across the threshold, motionless. The woman was dressed in the black that Andreas's people had been wearing. Her face was covered in blood, and Jonah could smell a strong odour of decay and bile, the same acidic stench he'd encountered in the pool when the shadow had finally perished in his hands.

He crouched beside the woman. She had no pulse.

He shone the flashlight beam inside the door. It looked like an observation area, large windows opening onto what must be the focus of the circular arena. The windows were dark but the observation area had dim emergency lighting. There were simple metal benches on two levels, enough for a few dozen to watch what was happening inside, and the benches had been full. Now, though, the observers were on the floor, haphazard and still, just like the one across the doorway.

He entered carefully, the acid stench enough to make him gag.

An arm of one of the black-clothed figures on the floor moved, slowly, back and forth. Jonah readied the gun, but what could he do? He had no doubt what Sly would say, but there were no shadows here that he could see, not any more. These people were all either dead or badly injured. He watched as the arm gradually stopped.

Whatever catastrophic failure had been caused by the blowing of the power hub and interrupting the function of their machine, it hadn't just been Andreas to suffer. Every shadow – here, at least – had been caught in the aftermath of the uncontrolled surge Tess had felt. Caught and destroyed . . . the hosts, as all these people must have been, dead or injured as a result.

Then he heard the same sounds of scrabbling movement he'd been hearing from below. He went to the observation window. The emergency lighting within was weak, but it was enough to see by.

Jonah stared at what Andreas had become.

The glass seemed thick. He was glad.

The Great Shadow, Jonah thought. He felt cold, watching it: seeing the sheer power on display, even given its ravaged state.

The ruin of a stillborn god filled the chamber; smoke hung in the air within, but he could make out dark, wet flesh partly covering obsidian bone, amputated stumps flailing now, lashing out against the wall or floor then becoming still again.

Jonah tried to make sense of it, of its anatomy. It was centred on a shape at the heart of the circle. Wanting to see – *needing* to see – he brought up the flashlight and shone it inside. It was hard to make out in the black smoke, but there was enough for Jonah to see a suggestion of wing, and a distorted mass in place of a head. Pieces of it emanated from there, but in a chaotic form, as if it had erupted from inside, uncontrolled, unready. Unfinished.

Something raw and claw-like thudded hard against the other side of the glass, leaving a dark smear. He quickly stepped back.

Then a voice from behind him made him spin round. 'My God . . .' said Tess, staring at it.

'Nobody's god,' said Jonah. 'Not now.'

She came to stand beside him, then approached the glass. 'Look at it. It can't have been far from succeeding.'

'I wouldn't get so close,' said Jonah. The ragged claw hit the glass again, harder this time, leaving a small, visible crack.

Tess moved away. She ran her eyes over the bodies on the floor. 'Do you think all Andreas's people are like this?'

'We saw others standing outside in a circle.' He nodded

towards a secure door at the far side of the observation room, which he guessed led to the corridor where the rest of the acolytes had been standing. 'I think if they weren't dead or incapacitated, they'd be in here by now.' There was every chance that distance could make all the difference, he knew – that if there were others in the facility, further from the arena, they could have survived. He'd been lucky so far, but whatever he was going to do, he had to do it soon.

And for that, he needed a way inside the chamber. As well as the door they'd entered by, and the one he thought led to the corridor, there was a third. He went across and opened it, the acrid stench stronger in the more confined space: the control room, half the size of the observation area, eight bodies on the floor. Panel indicator lights showed there was some power. Here, too, there was a large viewing window into the chamber, but there was also an entryway. The lock panel showed a single red light.

Tess joined him. 'What can you do?' she said, anxious. She nodded to the chamber. 'Against *that*?'

He reached down to his weapon harness, and took out the trigger and the single charge he had left. He paired them and held up the charge. 'These pack a punch,' he said, whispering in case the sound from the room could reach the chamber. 'Maybe enough to kill the damn thing. Up close. All I'd have to do is get inside, get clear and press the button.'

Tess turned to the chamber, tears in her eyes. 'Do you think he's still there?' Jonah looked blank. '*Michael*,' she said. 'Not the creature that took his body. Michael himself. Do you think he's free of it now, or still trapped inside?'

'I don't know,' said Jonah, lying. He thought there was very little chance of him being free, and he thought Tess felt the same way.

He went to the chamber entry door and tried it, but it wouldn't open. Quickly he searched the bodies in the room. The last one he checked was the furthest, against the wall, out of sight of the observation window. It had a security card on a thin chain around the neck. Jonah set the charge and trigger on a low desk next to the body to give him a free hand. He looped the chain over the corpse's head then returned to the door and swiped. The lock went green. Jonah felt cheated, somehow. It should have been harder to get in; it should have taken longer, put this *moment* off for longer.

He reached for the charge and trigger, but Tess stayed his hand with her own. 'There has to be another way,' she said. 'Look at it. It wouldn't let you near.'

He looked. Some of the pieces of dark flesh seemed to be dissipating into swirls of steaming black smoke. For a moment he thought it might be in the throes of death, but instead the central bulk seemed to be drawing itself back in, abandoning the extremities to their fate. He could see Tess's point, though. In what remained, there was strength. There was tooth, and claw.

'I can get close enough,' he said, but he knew it would be difficult.

Tess looked at him. 'Even if you did, you wouldn't be able to get enough distance from the blast.'

He looked away from her scrutiny. Getting far enough wasn't a necessity, of course. His plan was to get close to the creature's malformed head, shove the charge down the damn thing's throat, if he could, and trigger it at once. 'I have options,' he said, picking up the charge. 'I can stick it to any surface.' He peeled the backing from the adhesive. 'If I have to, I'll throw it.' He was lying, of course; he knew he had to make sure of doing the maximum damage. Point blank was the only way. Any less could mean a wasted chance.

He set the charge back down carefully and put his hands on her shoulders. 'There's a woman on the floor below us,' he said. 'Her name's Sly. She's injured, but she'll get you out of here. Whatever happens.'

Tess moved forward and embraced him. 'There has to be another *way*,' she said again, but they both knew there wasn't.

They separated. Jonah smiled at her, tears in his eyes.

And then the creature spoke.

64

'*Jonah . . .*' it said.

Jonah could see no detail in the dark bulk in the middle of the chamber, but he knew that was the source of the voice. He looked at Tess.

'What?' she said.

'Didn't you hear it?'

Tess shook her head. The voice was only for him. Through the observation window he saw the dark shape moving, shifting, half hidden in the smoke that persisted from the dissolution of the rest of it. He had a sense of it being *crouched*, waiting. Ready for him, and angry.

'*You did this to me?*' it said. '*I'm impressed. I'll show you just how much, when I finally take you. Last, of course. You'll watch the world burn before I let you die.*'

'Look at you,' Jonah said, his voice raised. 'So this is what a dead god looks like.'

'*You catch me at a bad time,*' it replied, and laughed, like clattering bones. '*But not for long. The door is open now, Jonah. It will not shut. The power flows slower now, but it still flows. And I'm patient. Don't doubt me. Don't doubt that you'll watch all your friends perish, one by one.*'

'You think so, dead god?' said Jonah. 'Look at yourself.'

It laughed its dry-bone laugh again. '*Come, Jonah. Come inside and show me how weak I am.*' Something unfurled from the darkness, a long dark arm, and at the tip a powerful hand that made Jonah think of *teeth* as much as *claw*.

The creature was right, Jonah knew. With it disoriented and flailing he'd stood a chance. Now? He'd be powerless the moment he stepped through the door. He and Tess looked at each other. He shook his head, frustrated and despairing.

Tess turned to the window again. 'Michael . . .' she said.

Jonah felt the creature smile. He heard a long, satisfied sigh in his mind. '*Ah . . . Tess! She's still alive! And I can still USE her. You should kill her, Jonah. If only you weren't so weak.*'

From inside the chamber, the dark shape physically spoke, a tortured cry. The look on Tess's face was one of utter horror.

'Tess,' said the creature aloud. 'Help me, Tess. *Please.*'

She put her hand to the glass. 'Michael?'

'It's weak . . . it's dying . . . I've pulled free of it! Help me!'

Jonah put his hand on her shoulder. 'It's lying to you.' There was doubt in her face, though.

'I can *feel* that it's dying,' said the creature. 'It's going back to the void. I need you, Tess. I need your help or it'll take me with it. Your presence is the only thing that can help me.'

She looked at Jonah, torn; then she looked at the creature. 'What can I do?'

'*So easy!*' said the creature to Jonah.

'It's *lying* to you,' said Jonah. 'Don't listen to it!'

The creature wailed, as if in terrible pain. 'Tess . . . you feel so far away. I need you to be near. I'm so cold. So lost! Come to me!'

Tess cried out, and Jonah heard the voice in his mind again, mocking: '*Prepare yourself, Jonah. If you want to slow my rise, you'll have to kill her. If you want to SAVE her, you'll have to kill her.*'

The creature was enjoying this, taunting and goading.

Tess looked at Jonah; he saw something in her expression change, grow somehow cold, determined. She looked back into the chamber. 'Prove it. Prove you're Michael.'

There was silence from the creature, then a ripple of movement was visible. The dark shapes began to dissipate, separating, becoming shadow-smoke. Jonah looked hard, wondering if it was his imagination, but no: a human form was becoming clear in the swirl of darkness.

Tess watched, transfixed.

The darkness faded.

Standing in the chamber was Andreas, whole and unblemished, clothed immaculately in suit and leather jacket. Smiling.

'*Such simple lies, Jonah,*' came the voice. '*People give themselves no choice but to believe. No choice but to hope.*'

Jonah knew Andreas was right: he had no choice. No choice but to enter the chamber and walk, calm and slow, hoping Andreas wouldn't simply finish him before he came close.

He stepped away from the door and walked towards the desk where he'd left the charge and trigger, out of sight of the chamber.

'Don't, Jonah.' It was Tess, behind him.

'I have to,' he said.

She was watching Andreas with an expression of curious joy, her eyes wet. 'Michael,' she said.

As Jonah turned back to fetch the charge he sensed movement from behind. Something hit his head. He fell, his vision dark for a moment, and then he saw Tess go through the chamber door, taking the security card in her hand, the door locking again behind her.

Jonah ran to the observation window and hit the glass. '*Tess, please!*' he shouted, trying to break Andreas's hold over her. On the card reader by the door he saw an intercom switch. He pressed it, the sounds from the chamber coming through clearly now. He spoke again. 'Tess . . .'

'Don't worry, Jonah,' she said.

'*See how much she loves her Michael?*' said the creature in his mind. '*She's mine, now.*' Andreas's smile turned to a rictus grin, looking directly at Jonah.

Tess walked to the centre of the chamber.

'Good girl,' said Andreas as she reached him.

'Hold me,' said Tess. 'Hold me, Michael. I missed you so much. I'm frightened.'

Andreas smiled. 'Of course. My *love*.'

He turned to the side and held out his arms, triumphant, making sure Jonah had a clear view as he allowed Tess to embrace him.

She drew close, wrapping her left arm around Andreas, keeping her right arm behind her back. Andreas placed his mouth on hers and they kissed, deep, long. Jonah could see the back of Andreas's head shift and ripple. The shape was difficult for him to hold, Jonah thought. They separated, and Andreas smiled at her.

'I dreamed of freeing you, Michael,' she said, tears falling. 'From the day it happened. I love you. I always knew I wasn't worthy of you, but I love you.' She took a step back, looking him up and down, smiling. 'And here you are.'

'Here I am,' said Andreas. *'And all the while Michael is inside me,'* it said to Jonah. *'Struggling. Suffering. She'll join him when I'm done with her.'*

'I love you, Michael.' She was still stepping back, six feet, ten feet, twelve, Andreas too busy goading to notice the change in her tone when it came: 'I love you. I always will. I dreamed of freeing you. If you're really in there, I hope you can hear me.'

Jonah saw what was in her hand; his eyes went to the desk where he'd set down the trigger and charge. Nothing there now.

At last, the creature realized what she'd said. Its expression changed, the smile vanishing. Jonah could see the charge stuck to its back, just below the collar of the jacket it wore. Lines of mouths were opening across its face once again. It lunged towards Tess as she raised the trigger.

65

Jonah reflexively dived to the floor. He heard shrapnel break through glass and fly past him as he fell. He stayed down for three long breaths before standing again.

The glass in the doorway and in the observation window was shattered but holding steady in the frames. Jonah took a chair from behind him and swung it again and again at the door until the laminate fell away. He climbed through.

The first thing to hit him was the smell, of hot blood and rancid meat underscored by the same acidic odour the shadows had made. The stench was appalling. The dim red light of the chamber seemed even darker than it had been, and he paused – there was a layer of black mist close to the floor, and under the mist a shape was just visible where Andreas had stood. He watched it for a moment, but it was still.

He turned and saw Tess. He ran to her.

She was trying to sit up. Blood was pouring from a shrapnel wound in her side. He clamped his hands over it but the torrent of red couldn't be stemmed, gushing past his fingers. Tess looked up again, and he saw reluctant acceptance there. They both knew what was about to happen.

'I had to do it,' she said. 'He wouldn't have let you get close.'

'You have to hold on,' he said, crying. 'We need you, Tess.'

She shook her head, and smiled. 'No tears,' she said. Then the smile faded. 'Do you think . . . do you think Michael heard me?'

'I know he heard you,' said Jonah. 'You didn't think you were worthy of him, Tess, but you were. You always were.'

He took her right hand. It was already cold. He whispered her name. Her breathing grew rapid and shallow, her eyes unfocused.

'Jonah,' she said. Fading, almost inaudible. He leaned close and listened. Six words, the last things she would ever say. The weight of those words settled on him as her breathing grew even more rapid. Then, suddenly, it slowed and stopped.

He closed his eyes against the tears, her cold hand still in his.

Then he heard it behind him.

A choking, wet sound, a movement. He opened his eyes, not wanting to turn, but he had to.

The head was the worst. Ripped open and much of it missing, the remainder was somehow managing to cling together, scalp torn from bone. There was an expression of *defeat* in the sole remaining eye. The right arm was gone, too; the upper torso had been devastated. It was trying to pull itself along using the left arm, rising a little with each attempt.

There seemed little doubt that the creature wasn't able to simply re-form, that it was in genuine difficulty. Taken by surprise, Jonah thought. It had returned to a human form before it was ready, used too much of what strength it had left in its effort to torment Jonah.

Even so, he could see that it was trying to knit itself back, and while it was failing now, Jonah knew it would succeed eventually. *Time* was all it required.

Jonah felt drained. He imagined himself condemned to stay in this chamber, repeatedly destroying the flesh of this damned creature. Beating it to a pulp with his bare hands, if that was what was needed. He began to stand.

Then he caught movement from the control room. Through the spider-webbed glass of the observation window he saw a black-dressed figure enter. It came to the doorway, a silhouette, the face misshapen, inhuman. One of Andreas's acolytes had survived, he thought. It was over.

The figure ducked through the hole and stood tall. It looked first at Jonah, and then turned to the shape that was pulling itself along, desperate to survive.

It was only when the figure spoke that Jonah realized the face was covered in a mask. A gas mask.

'Let's finish this,' said Kendrick. He was a mess, left arm soaked in blood and strapped to his chest.

What was left of Andreas took another wet breath, shifting where it lay. Kendrick stepped over and brought a boot down on the open skull. He took the black cylinder from his belt.

'Out,' said Kendrick, and Jonah lifted Tess's body and carried her through the door. Behind him Kendrick began to deploy the contents of the cylinder. Jonah looked back to see white smoke billowing up, the bulk of Andreas trembling and twitching as the flesh dissolved. He kept watching until the movement stopped.

Jonah could feel his eyes sting, and knew he had to get out of the reach of the fumes before they became debilitating. The door to the upper corridor was open; he carried Tess's body out and set it down on the floor. The bodies of the other acolytes were on the ground, all as dead as those Jonah had come across in the control room.

It was a few minutes before Kendrick emerged and took off the gas mask. He had a long cut down one cheek, his left eye vividly red. He looked at Tess for a moment, then at Jonah. 'Andreas is no more,' he said. 'For what it's worth.' Kendrick seemed to steel himself before speaking again. 'Sly?' he asked. Jonah could almost hear the prayer in his voice.

'She's injured,' he said. 'She can't walk. Downstairs, across the circle, in—'

Kendrick was already moving.

Jonah waited in silence. Eventually Kendrick and Sly were

there, Sly leaning on Kendrick for support, taking each step as a hop on her good foot.

'We would've been faster,' said Kendrick, 'if she'd let me carry her.'

'*Nobody* carries me,' said Sly. She saw Tess's body and was silent for a moment. Then: 'Has anyone tried the radio again?'

'I lost mine a while back,' said Kendrick.

Sly handed hers to Jonah. Wary, he pressed the button. The static had decreased significantly, but it was still there, still with the eerie almost-intelligible background noises.

'Annabel,' he said. He waited.

'We're here,' said Annabel, relief in her voice. 'What happened?'

'We're on our way out,' said Jonah. 'Andreas and his people are dead.'

'Tess?' said Annabel.

'She didn't make it.' Jonah paused. 'Is Never—'

There was silence, and Jonah felt hope drain away. 'You need to hurry,' she said.

They took the direct route to the security room, the deadlocked Lab Two door opening from inside without a hitch. Lying on the floor, Never was unconscious. Annabel took Jonah to the side as Kendrick helped Sly over to Never, along with the medical essentials and saline taken from the surgical room. Kendrick started hunting for something in the cupboards.

'Hold this,' Sly told Jonah, handing him a bag of saline she'd hooked up a line to. She quickly put a cannula into Never's arm.

'Got it,' said Kendrick, brandishing a set of keys for a security patrol jeep. 'We need to leave.'

Sly looked at him and shook her head. 'We need to wait.'

Kendrick opened his mouth, then closed it again.

After ten minutes and one full bag of saline, Never's eyes flickered open. He looked at Sly, barely conscious.

'Hey,' said Sly.

'Hey,' said Never.

She looked at him, appraising. She smiled, a genuine one.

Kendrick took Jonah and Annabel, retracing the path they'd used when they'd entered the facility. In the corpse storage unit they found two gurneys and returned to the security room, carefully lifting Never onto one of them. Jonah used the other for Tess's body, and they made their way out to the patrol jeep.

The air outside was bone dry, but fresh. Jonah breathed it in. Once Never and Sly were safely in the back seat of the jeep, Kendrick threw Annabel the keys. 'You and Jonah will have to share the driving,' he said, nodding to his strapped arm. Annabel nodded and got inside.

Jonah insisted on putting Tess's body in the back of the jeep himself. He closed the tailgate and turned to look at the building they'd just left. Peaceful, now; impossible to think of how much death lay inside.

'What about the revivers?' said Jonah. 'You saw them, didn't you? They were part of the machine . . .'

Kendrick nodded. 'There's nothing you can do for them.'

'But we could find a way to switch off the cryogenic chambers, and put them out of their . . .' He stopped, seeing the expression on Kendrick's face: grim, and earnest.

'I already did.' They stood in silence for a moment before Kendrick spoke again. 'Do you think all the shadows died? Even those who weren't here?'

Jonah shook his head.

'Me neither,' said Kendrick. 'We need to go. I don't doubt for a second that they know something went wrong. They're on their way here, right now.'

Kendrick got into the jeep, but Jonah paused, looking again at the building. He thought of what Andreas had said in the chamber: *The door is open now, Jonah. It will not shut.*

He had felt it then, and could feel it now: their mission had not been the success they had hoped for. The flow of power had not been halted, not completely.

Andreas was gone, but it wasn't enough, because Andreas had only ever been a vessel. Whether that *specific* vessel could ever come back or not wasn't the important thing, not really, because there were others out there ready to take its place. Jonah thought of them, all those who carried shards of what had been within Andreas. Heggarty. Silva's family in Bethlehem. He didn't want to think about *how* many there could be, let alone how many were in positions of power.

Shadows were everywhere. The door was open.

Tess's final words came to him, then.

Killing Andreas had bought time to find an answer. He had no idea how long. Maybe months. Maybe years. Where would they even begin?

But they would try, however long they had. Because there was no other choice.

The Beast is coming, Tess had said.

Be ready.

ACKNOWLEDGMENTS

Thanks as always to my editor Julie Crisp, and my agent Luigi Bonomi. When I want to remind myself of how lucky I've been since starting down the writer's road, I don't have to think further than them.

Also, to my wife and kids for all the glorious chaos.

Finally, I want to thank the writers whose work I grew up with. The things that scare you as a child are often so much richer because the hard walls of reality have yet to solidify around your imagination. These are the formative fears, the ones that burn themselves into you wholesale and return to haunt you again and again: sometimes treasured, sometimes dreaded.

Those old ghosts have inspired parts of *Lost Souls*; terrors and images looming up after decades of mutation in the murk. Nigel Kneale, Alan Garner, Stephen King, Clive Barker, Alan Moore and others planted the seeds, as did the authors who contributed to the many ghost and horror anthologies I devoured as a child – in particular Ronald Chetwynd-Hayes, whose gleefully dark tales I always relished.